AF087703

D. F. BAILEY

SECOND LIFE

BOOKS

By D. F. Bailey

Will Finch Mystery Thriller Series

Five Knives (Prequel)
Bone Maker
Stone Eater
Lone Hunter
Second Life
Open Chains
Run Time
White Sphere
Burnt Embers

Vinci Books

vinci-books.com

Published by Vinci Books Ltd in 2025

1

Copyright © D. F. Bailey 2017

The author has asserted their moral right to be identified as the author of this work in accordance with the Copyright, Designs and Patents Act 1988. This work is a work of fiction. Names, characters, places and incidents are the product of the author's imagination or are used fictitiously. Any resemblance to actual persons, living or dead, places and incidents is entirely coincidental.

All rights reserved. No part of this publication may be copied, reproduced, distributed, stored in any retrieval system, or transmitted in any form or by any means, including photocopying, recording, or other electronic or mechanical methods, nor used as a source for any form of machine learning including AI datasets, without the prior written permission of the publisher.

The publisher and the author have made every effort to obtain permissions for any third party material used in this book and to comply with copyright law. Any queries in this respect should be brought to the attention of the publisher and any omissions will be corrected in future editions.

A CIP catalogue record for this book is available from the British Library.

Paperback ISBN: 9781036703356

Printed and bound in Great Britain by Clays Ltd, Elcograf S.p.A.

1978, Jonestown.
909 dead—two children survive.
Where are they now?

Inspired by true events

*We have two lives, and the second begins
when we realize we only have one.*

— *Confucius*

Chapter One

JONESTOWN, GUYANA

18 November, 1978

"Are there any snakes here?" Ruth Watts tried to steady her voice. She hated snakes and she'd seen far too many of them over the past two weeks. Nonetheless, she felt determined to press onward. She brushed the sweat from her eyes and stepped tentatively past an uprooted banana tree as she followed Danny Pass into the jungle.

Danny ignored the question. "Just ten more minutes in here and we'll circle around the gate and be out on the road."

"Front Road?" she asked, and realized how silly the question must seem, even coming from a seven-year-old. Everyone called it Front Road, but from the day she arrived in Jonestown, Ruth realized that it could just as well have been named Only Road.

"Yeah. And there's no snakes on Front Road." Danny thought about that and then made a minor correction: "A least no snakes that can *surprise* you."

Ruth decided to ignore this and took his hand. Danny was older than her—twelve—and the only friend she'd made since she'd arrived at the Peoples Temple Agricultural Project. Or simply Jonestown, as everybody called it. That was the name painted on the heavy wooden board suspended from a pole above the gate leading into the compound. Ruth didn't know why people here didn't just call things what they were. Two weeks ago, without any notice, her parents had taken her out of second grade in Brookfield Elementary School in Oakland, California and they'd flown in a rickety plane that landed on the dusty strip of dirt in the middle of the jungle. When Danny said he'd be her big brother, she felt special for the first time in months. Maybe for the first time ever.

Twenty minutes earlier Danny had appeared beside Ruth in the Flavor Aid line-up. Her mother had released Ruth's hand as she turned to her husband to whisper something into his ear. The distraction provided just enough diversion for Danny to guide Ruth by the elbow past one of the dozens of one-room cabins that stood in the central square of the camp.

"They're doing another White Night test," he told her.

"What's a White Night?"

"A loyalty test. Everyone has to do it. But this time it's for real." He'd continued to coax her across the field until they reached the edge of the campground. For the first time since she'd arrived in Jonestown, the guards seemed to have disappeared from the perimeter. Hand-in-hand Danny and Ruth stepped over the trip wire and into the jungle. The alarm failed to sound. They'd made it over the first hurdle.

"What does *for real* mean?" she asked and paused to look back at the camp.

He set his hands on her shoulders and peered into her eyes. Behind them they could hear the screams of children coming from the compound. The children went first, then the adults. They both took a deep breath as a wave of panic washed through them.

"It's over for them. For our parents, too," he said to alert her to the pending disaster.

"What?"

"Death!" His voice held a rising urgency intended to impel her forward. "It means they're all going to die."

But when he tugged on her hand to continue their escape, she pulled away. The thought of leaving her parents didn't bother her so much as the idea that they'd been leading her to some horrible place. A place called Death. The weariness of the people in Jonestown, their uneasy talk, the heavy weight of foreboding that had pervaded almost every conversation she'd heard in the past week, the irregular announcements blasted over the compound PA system —all of it now submerged under the rich chaos of chirping birds and the bugs and flies that whizzed incessantly around her face, eyes and ears. Which was worse? Her parents' deceptions or this horrid wilderness?

They're all going to die. Ruth repeated the words to herself and for the first time she understood. She gasped and braced herself against a tree.

When the shock of realization subsided, she knew that only Danny could take her away from the growing terror of the camp. Maybe he would save her. She jumped over a pool of murky water and followed him across a series of connected logs that crossed the fly-buzzing bog. On the far side of the swamp Danny found a trail that slipped into the shadows. The damp jungle swallowed them and the waning cries and screams from Jonestown faded as they plunged onward.

"Where's the road, Danny?"

"Not far." He held a pointed finger to his lips and turned to her. "Sssshhh."

They looked up through the canopy of the trees. Through the tiny window formed by a break in the leaves, they could see a small aircraft circle as it spiraled lower and lower in a tight turn above them.

"The landing strip," Danny said. "That's it! We'll go to the landing strip and hide in the bushes until the plane lands."

Jane Smythe sat in a wooden chair beside the unarmed officer in the Houston International Airport security observation room. Although she'd arrived two hours earlier, Jane had been told that she couldn't visit with her niece. No embraces, no hugs, no chance to offer the love Ruth needed. Not yet.

But through the one-way glass window she could see Ruth talking with two social workers in the next room. The social workers, both women in their early thirties, had their hair rolled into buns held in place with plastic hair claws. One perched a clipboard on her left forearm and from time to time made a note on a page clamped under the steel tongue on her board. While Jane couldn't hear what they said, she was surprised by her niece's calm demeanor, her upright posture, the easy way that she rested her hands in her lap, the lifeless smile that appeared on her lips when she spoke. It was as if the disaster in Jonestown had never happened.

A single knock on the observation room door was followed by the appearance of a tall, lean man wearing a business suit and a narrow blue tie. Just below his right eye sat a round mole the color of a ripe raspberry. His hair was cropped in a brush-cut that reminded Jane of the early 1950s. An Eisenhower man. Some people had completely jumped past the 60s, she thought, and this is one of them.

"Hello, Mrs. Smythe. I'm Gerald Gordon."

He shook her hand and sat next to the security officer. Gordon set his briefcase on the floor, briefly struggled to snap open the twin latches, then laid a file on the table.

"I've been appointed to work with you and your niece by California's Division of Youth Services. And you've come down here from Pennsylvania. Do I have that right?"

"Malvern. It's just outside of Philly."

He nodded. "You've met Officer Ray, I assume?"

"Yes. Together we've been watching my niece Ruth and the social workers"—she pointed to the one-way glass as if it held a mirage—"for the past twenty minutes. When can I actually talk to her?"

"Soon. As soon as you and I agree on the details." Gordon nodded obliquely and rubbed his nose with the front of his hand. "First, let me say how sorry I am for your loss. Were you close to your sister?" He opened the file folder as if he might find the answer in one of the back pages. "Sara Watts, isn't it?'

"We were. At least when we were young. After our teen years we drifted apart. I guess most kids do, don't they? Especially with her in the Bay Area and me and my husband in Malvern. Then when she joined the Peoples Temple, we ... lost touch." She pressed a tissue to her eyes and looked away from his stare.

"And Randy Watts. That was her husband?"

She nodded. "It's hard to believe. They're both gone."

"I'm sorry." Gordon looked away. Apparently he couldn't believe it either.

Jane Smythe locked her hands together and studied their emptiness. Yesterday, as she flew down from Philadelphia, she'd read everything she could about the Jonestown slaughter in two newspapers. Over nine hundred people dead. The biggest civilian mass killing in American history. And every one of them lined up to drink grape Flavor Aid poisoned with some God-awful concoction. To think they'd all *volunteered!* One of the four survivors called it "revolutionary suicide." More like revolutionary madness, she thought.

"Well, now the only thing that matters to us is your niece, Mrs. Smythe." Gordon tried to fix a smile to his mouth. "Have you ever heard of the witness protection programs?"

"Yes." She held two fingers to her mouth. "But aren't they for—"

He waved a hand to dismiss her objection. "Not entirely. And your niece will be one of the exceptions. The last thing she'll want is to relive this tragedy for the rest of her life. We want to give her a new name. With a new identity. And"—he held a palm up as if it contained an invisible gift—"a new life."

Jane paused to consider this. She'd already agreed to take the girl into her home. Her husband Bert insisted on it. Besides, they'd been unable to conceive a child of their own. A child they'd prayed for until their prayers turned into agnostic despair. Maybe the tragedy had "a silver lining," Bert had said when he saw her off at the airport. Then he'd added, "Bring home our little girl."

"Now we already have a name she can take on." Gordon tilted his head to one side and whisked the palm of his right hand over his brush cut.

"Well, she can have our surname. Smythe. It's a good name."

Gordon smiled as if everything was now on track, but with a slight adjustment required. "That would be nice, wouldn't it? But I'm afraid it doesn't quite work that way. We choose the names from children of the same age and gender. Deceased children. Just so we have all the documents already in place. Birth certificates and so on."

She smiled as though she'd made a small error that no one could fault her for. Of course the child didn't *have* to take her last name.

"So the name she'll use is Isobel Oehmke." His voice carried a note of hope.

She blinked. She'd always hated the name her sister had given to the girl. Ruth. Dredged up from the Old Testament, of course. It meant "friend." Could they not have found something more inspired? Anyway, now they were about to change that. To Isobel. A good-ole-fashioned American name.

"All right." She felt her face pull into a tight grimace as the reality of her niece's loss struck her once more. "That sounds fine."

"Good. Good. I've got the paperwork right here for you to sign. And I'll coordinate everything with Children's Services in Pennsylvania," Gordon said with a stiff nod. "For now, you and your husband will be her legal foster parents. A formal adoption could be arranged if and when you and your husband are ready for it. That can be sooner or later. Or not at all. Do you understand?"

"Yes. When can I take her home?"

"Soon. Maybe as early as tomorrow."

"Tomorrow?" Finally a genuine smile broke over her face. "That would be perfect. Just perfect."

"But if all this is going to work the way we hope, you can never publicly reveal that Isobel Oehmke was rescued from Jonestown. It could just be too damaging for her—especially in her teen years. And many years beyond for that matter. Do you understand?"

Jane nodded. It could be their secret, something private they would never reveal outside the family. At least for now. And in that moment she determined that she and her husband and Isobel would hide their terrible loss from the outside world. As if Jonestown were a private tragedy. Theirs alone to forget.

She hated the name. *Isobel Oehmke* sounded like a stuck-up donkey. An idiot child from Malvern, Pennsylvania, of all places. Where exactly was that?

"I hate it!" she protested to Danny during their final meeting. She looked along the corridor to the departures gates in the airport. They'd spent two whole days here and at the Houston Airport Holiday Inn. While the hotel provided a pleasant enough change from the jungle compound in Jonestown, all the arrangements her Aunt Jane had made felt like a second disaster designed to ruin her life.

"Well, at least I'll know how to find you," Danny said with a look of certainty. "There can't be many Isobel Oehmkes in Pennsylvania."

She rolled her lips into an angry pout. The fact that

she'd be the only Isobel Oehmke, possibly the only one in the entire world, offered little consolation. She tried to put it out of her mind. Maybe if she concentrated on Danny. *Or Jason.* They'd changed his name, too. He'd suddenly become Jason Wishart and he was being sent to live with his grandparents in Boston. Half a world away.

"So you'll try to find me?"

He nodded. "Don't worry. When we're older. Then we can do what we want."

"We can?"

"Yeah, of course. So just keep that name until I find you, Isobel Oehmke." His smile suggested that the new name might be pretty good after all.

"All right."

"And there's something else."

She waited.

"Save yourself for me, okay."

A blank look crossed her face. "What does that mean?"

"It's what people do when they pledge themselves to one another. Can you pledge yourself to me?"

She wondered if she could. "Do you?"

"Yes."

"Okay. Then I pledge, too."

An old man leaning on a black hickory cane waved his free hand at them.

"Jason. Time to go." Jason's grandfather called to the boy from the Eastern Air Lines check-in counter.

Jason leaned forward, gazed into her eyes and kissed Isobel's forehead.

"Good-bye, Isobel."

"Don't forget me," she called, and just as a baggage cart rumbled between her and Jason, she waved a hand in the air, a gesture he didn't see—and one that he did not return.

As she watched him leave, she thought that their pledge was a good thing. Maybe the best thing she could possibly hold onto right now. She would save herself by pledging to Jason Wishart and begin her life all over again. This time as Isobel Oehmke.

Chapter Two

"we're all just one step away from the angels!"

The audience erupted with laughter, shouts, jeers, and volleys of clapping. No one was holding back. Half the crowd prodded Kali Rood on, the other half couldn't contain their disbelief. Another chorus of boos interrupted her train of thought and she briefly stumbled.

At first Will Finch wondered if she could recover her momentum. He turned his attention from Kali Rood to her opponent, Dr. Martin Fast. He lifted his arms aloft in an effort to rally the crowd to his cause. New shouts of support rose in the chamber.

For the past twenty minutes, the two debaters had been vying for acclamation under the dome of San Francisco's City Hall. As part of their commitment to "freedom of speech and open discussion," the city had sponsored a series of monthly lunch-hour debates in the gala hall under the City Hall dome. The previous three debates had been polite, almost tedious. But today's topic, "Engineering a Solution to Climate Change," drew a standing-room-only crowd. A thousand or more citizens pressed together and expressed their agreement and dissent in chants and overt screams. When the last round of applause filled the air, Finch could see the security staff begin to fret. They were under-staffed and the crowd was over-excited.

Kali Rood held her hand up, a gesture for calm. She stood at her dais on the circular platform positioned in the broad staircase that descended to the main hall from the second floor balcony. Standing at his podium, ten feet away, Martin Fast studied her with a look that asked, good lord, what will she come up with now?

She stepped up to the microphone, her hand a little higher now. The gesture worked. A brief hush fell over the mob.

"I mean it," she said in a whispered voice that managed to echo through the auditorium. Then in a much louder voice she cried, "We're just one step away from the angels!"

Another roar sounded from her supporters. Martin Fast shook his head in disbelief as he took a step toward his mic.

"One step away from the angels? Sorry. We're not," he retorted. "If anything, we're one step away from the chimps and bonobos."

A new burst of laughter and heckles erupted from the crowd. Next the jostling began. Then the chants started in earnest. "Get her out! Get her out!"

Finch shook his head and wondered how long the anger could simmer without boiling into outright violence. Both debaters had veered off topic and into personal attacks. Somehow the discourse had dissolved into a fracas that resembled a European football match complete with jeering hooligans. Finally the moderator interrupted the proceedings by thanking the participants and the city for their support, then he brought the duel to an end. The audience released a collective sigh; a measure of both relief and disappointment. After a brief physical skirmish to the right of the staircase the crowd rolled out of the cavernous space onto the outdoor plazas surrounding the hall, trading taunts and insults as they went.

By the time the room emptied, two people had been injured after trading blows. Another had fainted. Finch made a note to add the toll of injuries to the conclusion of the story he'd submit to the *eXpress*. It was one more episode of civil unrest that he'd covered in a summer that was becoming more rancorous with every passing week.

What could be next, he wondered as he crossed Polk Street. Where would it all end?

―――――

As the traffic crept forward, Finch laughed to himself when he considered the debate between Kali Rood and Dr. Martin Fast, the eminent geo-science engineer at Stanford University. What began as a civilized discussion about climate change had quickly descended into an argument about God and free choice. Rood, the renowned evangelist and climate fatalist, had tried to shut down the atheist views of Fast with that single knock-out blow.

We're just one step away from the angels!

The words echoed in Will Finch's mind as he drove his Toyota RAV4 from the City Hall parkade through the Tenderloin District along Turk Street. Kali Rood was a true believer, no doubt about it. But there was something hopeful about her message, the idea that salvation was at hand. However, the message came with a kind of condemnation. If we needed salvation so badly, it implied that humans were failing to survive on their own. It was a well-worn trope that went back thousands of years: The End Is Nigh.

It was the one point Martin Fast agreed with. In the past twenty years he'd shifted his career focus from green science research to geo-science engineering. He'd been party to an international committee awarded a Nobel Prize in the 1990s. Later he decided that only climate engineering could save the human race from pending catastrophe. Five years ago, in an effort to adjust salt water pH balance, he helped engineer a project that poured hundreds of tonnes of iron sulphate into the Pacific Ocean off the coast of Canada. The enterprise earned him both praise and condemnation, and nearly cost him his tenured professorship.

BEEP-BEEP!

The driver trailing Finch leaned on his horn and gave Finch a second prolonged blast. Will glared in his rearview mirror at two young men perched in the cab of a black Dodge RAM. A web of tattoos crawled over their shoulders and up their necks. Chimps and bonobos, he mused as he inched forward in the snarled traffic.

He didn't much like this neighborhood—who in his right mind did?—but a series of traffic diversions and construction projects funneled the mid-afternoon traffic from the City Hall parking lot into this urban gauntlet of desperation, homelessness and crime.

Finch took a few deep breaths to release his anxiety along with the lingering malaise of the debate. But just as he felt a moment of liberation, the traffic on Turk Street ground to a full stop. He popped the transmission into park and gazed across the street. Should he cut the engine, or let it idle?

As he pondered this question, he saw a huge man hunched on a guardrail next to a row of empty playground swings. He wore a tattered chauffeur cap and a Seattle Seahawks hoodie whose dirty cuffs stopped a good four inches above his wrists. The fleece was obviously stolen, borrowed or begged. When the man turned his head Finch recognized something familiar. The bear-like snout, the sneer, the desolate stare.

It was Toby Squire.

A block down the road Finch found a space to park. As he walked back to the corner of Turk and Hyde Streets he tried to suppress his anxiety and collect his thoughts. When he approached the playground he studied the figure leaning against the metal railing. Could it really be Toby Squire? The madman who last year had drowned Giana Whitelaw below the Golden Gate Bridge and then crushed her corpse under his feet. The same man who had hammered Eve Noon into a coma with a steel golf club. The monster who, after a six-hour brain surgery, had managed to escape custody from the San Francisco General Hospital. And then simply disappeared.

Finch stopped at the playground fence and drew his cell phone from his pocket. With the camera set to video, he called out in a voice meant to wake the dead: "Toby Squire. Is that you?"

The big man startled. His shoulders tensed as he turned and considered Finch. A suit jacket lay folded across his left forearm. He withdrew his hand from the jacket pocket and took a moment to consider Finch's voice as he set the jacket on the middle of the iron railing. The stunned appearance on his face suggested that he might be hearing an inner voice, a confused utterance instructing him how to respond.

"Are you Toby Squire?"

The giant rose from the railing and walked toward the park gate on Hyde Street. As he ambled forward, Finch noticed Squire's right leg hitching to the side with every step. The distinctive gait reminded him of the night when Finch chased Squire across the lawn of the Whitelaw estate in Sausalito. Yes, this was Squire. Make no mistake.

After a brief hesitation Squire hobbled out of the playground and made his way along the sidewalk. Determined to follow him, Finch stopped the video and called Detective Jill DeRosa at the San Francisco Police Department. He'd become acquainted with DeRosa during two interviews in the weeks following Toby Squire's escape from the hospital last year. She answered on the third ring.

"DeRosa."

"Detective DeRosa, it's Will Finch."

He heard her draw a breath. "What do you need, Finch? And please, no BS about climate crimes."

"It's Toby Squire. I found him in the Turk-Hyde Mini Park. He's walking on Turk Street just past Hyde. Heading west on the north side."

"Toby Squire? You sure?"

"Yeah. I'm looking at him right now." On the green light Finch crossed the intersection. He could see the worn chauffeur cap on Squire's head bobbing above the crowd half a block ahead. "It's him. I called out to him. Believe me, it's him."

"Incredible."

Will could imagine DeRosa standing at her desk, waving her partner over to the phone. "Okay, Finch. I'll have a team on this in five minutes."

"Five minutes?" Finch picked up his pace. When was

the last time the SFDP had responded to an emergency in five minutes?

"Haussmann and me'll be there. And Finch"—her voice rose with an insistent tone—"you stand down on this. You understand?"

Finch ended the call. When he saw Squire cross to the south side of Turk, Will continued on the north side and slowed his pace so that he lagged Squire by twenty or thirty feet. Just outside the Vincent Hotel, one of the many flophouses lining the street, he watched Squire hesitate and glance about as if he were lost. He rubbed a hand over the front of his sweatshirt, across the hooked beak of the Seahawks crest.

Maybe this is the moment, Finch thought as he closed on his prey. He could cross the street, draw the belt from his pants, loop it around the giant's throat and drag him down to the sidewalk.

After another pause Squire turned around and hobbled another fifty feet back to Dodge Place, a dead-end alley littered with newspapers scattered by the windstorm that had blown over the peninsula last night. Finch followed him, crossed the road and stood at the T-junction of Turk and Dodge. He looked down the lane, then glanced back along Turk. In the distance he could see the silent flashing of two squad cars racing up the road toward him. He turned back to observe Squire as he wandered half way down the alley and stop just beyond a parked Toyota. His right hand struggled to pull something from his pocket.

"Toby Squire!" Finch yelled. "Don't take another step!"

He began to record a second video as Toby squinted at Finch. He stood as if he were suspended in time, a moment when he tried to decipher where he was and what might become of him. Finch realized that whatever remained of

Squire's intelligence had been diminished by the blow to his head last year in Sausalito. Or perhaps the surgery intended to save his life had left little more than an empty shell.

Finch heard the doors of the police cars slamming shut.

"Toby, the police are here," he said as he continued to run the video camera. "They want to take you into custody."

Squire blinked and drew his hand from his pocket. In his fist he held a small pistol.

"Toby, you want to put that away. The cops will not mess with you if you put that gun down."

Finch felt his arm pushed to the side as Jill DeRosa slipped beside him. "Finch, outta here," she said in a harsh whisper and stepped past him with Haussmann at her side.

Two more uniformed policemen followed. When they saw Toby Squire angling the gun in DeRosa's direction, all four cops drew their weapons.

"Toby Squire, you need to drop your pistol now. Do you hear me?" Haussmann's voice boomed with authority.

Squire shook his head. Not with a look of denial or refusal, but with an air of confusion, as if he were saying, I don't know what we're doing here. *And why are we all holding guns?* Then an expression of recognition crossed his face. Ah, yes. So. He turned the pistol in his hand and for a moment Finch assumed he was about to to drop it on the asphalt. Then his appearance shifted again, this time as if he'd discovered a solution that would satisfy everyone. He held the pistol to his right temple. A thin smile drew his lips across his gray, weary face.

"No, no, no!" DeRosa yelled and lowered her weapon. "Mr. Squire, we will not harm you. Drop your gun. I promise you. We will not hurt you!"

For two or three seconds it seemed as if Squire would

accept the terms of surrender. His wary smile vanished. He pulled the gun away from the side of his head. Haussmann took a step forward. DeRosa was about to holster her pistol. Then Haussmann started to sprint forward. And in that instant, the microsecond between forethought and afterthought, Squire pressed the muzzle of his gun to his ear and pulled the trigger. His body twisted to the left as if the bullet had snapped a steel coil somewhere inside his head. He fell backwards with a faint groan and his cap rolled on its brim a short distance then flipped upside down on the broken asphalt.

Finch studied Detective Jill DeRosa as she closed her notebook and clicked her ballpoint pen. He'd given her his statement, ten or twelve lines about how he'd recognized Squire as he drove by and then followed him into the dead-end lane.

He knew her well enough to know that she'd risen by individual merit through the ranks of one of the toughest police departments in the country. She had an hispanic background, good education and she was smart. The day that she and Will had met she mentioned that she knew Eve Noon—or rather, she knew what Eve had done for women in the force. That familiarity generated some respect for Finch, too.

"What about Haussmann?" he asked as they stood next to the ribbon of crime scene tape. Finch knew it was his turn to ask a few questions. "Did he find anything on Squire?"

"Not much. No wallet, no credit cards." She shrugged as if she needed to decide how much information to pass on to the reporter. "Some cash. A room key at the Vincent."

"The flophouse down the road?" Finch tipped his head to the hotel. "What room was he in?"

She frowned as if he was asking for too much information.

"Come on, detective. I'm the one who called this in." His voice carried a note of annoyance, as if he had to remind her of an unspoken quid pro quo.

"All right," she whispered. "Two-oh-three. But don't show up until we've swept it. Like at least a day."

"You going to canvass the neighborhood?"

"I'll check out his room in the Vincent. Anything more depends on what the lieutenant wants."

"How much cash was he carrying?"

"More than enough." She looked away with an expression that said, you've heard all I've got to say.

Finch knew he'd reached his limit. Still, he decided to press for a little more. "What about the revolver? Looked like a .38 Special. Was it a Colt?"

She sneered with a measure of disdain. Even for a seasoned cop she bore a hard look. She wore her hair pulled tight behind her head, and from time to time her fingers brushed the side of her neck to tend to a heavy bruise.

They exchanged a look, something Finch didn't quite understand. Something that inspired DeRosa to continue. Maybe she recalled the trauma that Squire had inflicted on Eve.

"As you know, we've been on the lookout for him for over a year. Ever since he escaped custody following the brain surgery." Her lips curled in a cynical frown. "No surprise he'd turn up somewhere down here."

"Yeah." Finch shrugged as they sauntered the short

distance back to the sidewalk on Turk Street. He could see his car parked a block up the road, the most godforsaken strip of real estate in northern California.

"The guy was a demented killer. Course, you know that." She'd been toying with her pen for the last five minutes, twirling it from finger to finger. Now she finally slipped it into her jacket pocket. "Maybe it's best to let you sift through the ashes. Could make the last chapter to your book."

Finch smiled at the thought. His publisher had released *Who Shot the Sheriff?* three months ago. After hitting the top ten on the *New York Times* best-seller list, the title had settled into the mid-thirties and held there. The book had already earned out his advance of two hundred and fifty thousand dollars. Two film options from Hollywood were under consideration. Now Netflix was whispering to his agent. The dream factory inflating the bubble of fame and fortune.

"Toby Squire wasn't really part of that story."

"No? Well, maybe you should write another."

She offered a hearty smile. A grin so deep and generous that it surprised him and for an instant he glimpsed some tenderness beneath her hardened veneer. In the right circumstances she could be engaging. Almost friendly.

"Maybe."

"All right. Let's let the forensics team do their job," she said and joined Haussmann at the curb.

"So that's it?"

"Yeah. That closes the file, Finch."

Will watched the ambulance depart with Toby Squire's corpse as the crime scene team completed their assessment. Moments later the two squad cars that had raced through the snarled traffic with such urgency an hour earlier, eased into the traffic and disappeared.

As Finch crossed the street and walked toward his car a new thought struck him. *The suit jacket in the playground.* Toby Squire had been pawing through it, his hand in one pocket when he'd turned to face Finch. He'd looked distracted, almost despondent. What was he up to?

Will returned to the Turk-Hyde Mini Park. Two hispanic kids were running up and down the slide while their mothers stood near the Hyde Street gate smoking cigarettes. On the green railing opposite the women lay the suit jacket. No one had touched it. As he unlatched the south gate one woman stepped in front of the slide. Before he could reach the rail, she lifted the jacket, tested the weight in one hand as if she were considering what might lie in the pockets.

"Uh, sorry!" Finch clutched the sleeve in his fist and gave it a light tug. "Someone I know left this here an hour ago. I just remembered it now." He smiled and pointed down the road to Dodge Place where Squire had shot himself.

"This yours?" Her face bore a look of disbelief. "You already got a coat."

She nodded at his windbreaker, turned her head to one side and looked at the inside label of the suit jacket. As she turned the fabric in her hand, Finch noticed two of her fingers had been sheared away above the second joints.

"What's the brand, mister?"

"Armani." He smiled without releasing the sleeve.

She studied the inside pocket tag and pieced together

the sequence of letters two at a time. "Ar-ma-ni," she said with a frown.

"Right. That's what I said." He offered a reassuring look.

She seemed to consider his claim more seriously but still clutched the lapel with her good fingers. "You're lucky to get this back. Know that? In this neighborhood nothing sits around here loose for five minutes. You're lucky I was here keepin' an eye on it."

"Guess I am," he said and fished a five-dollar bill from his pocket. "Maybe this'll cover your trouble."

"Well, now." Her mood brightened. "Maybe it will. But another one of those would disappear my troubles altogether."

He smiled at that. "What's your name?"

She paused with a reluctant frown on her lips. "Alice," she said.

"Alice. I'm Will." He produced another bill. "Final offer."

She released the jacket and slipped the money into a back pocket of her jeans.

"Makes a fair trade," Alice said and smiled a broad grin that revealed rows of nicotine-stained teeth.

"Maybe." Finch doubted it, but he felt committed to the deal.

He wrapped the jacket over his arm and walked through the Turk Street gate, along the sidewalk toward his car. Then he spread the jacket on the trunk, carefully straightened the lapels and arms, slipped the middle button into place and took a picture of the jacket with his phone. Something about the jacket made him want to preserve it just the way he'd found it. A feeling, not an idea. He didn't know what it meant.

Chapter Three

Finch unlocked the door to the Alta Street cottage and set his courier bag on the bench next to the antique umbrella stand that Eve had picked up from Heritage Auctions. When he heard the sound of metal clinking in the kitchen sink, he called down the hallway.

Eve appeared with two fresh-cut roses in her hand. "Look. I found these on the side of Napier Lane. There's dozens of them."

"Looks like you just finished your run." He noticed the perspiration stains welling around the armpits of her track suit. Since they'd moved into the cottage she'd made a project of exploring the jogging trails and lanes in the neighborhood. The area was famous for its wild parrots. And now, apparently, wild roses.

The previous owners had renovated the original 1929 cottage and transformed it from an urban hide-away into a twenty-two hundred square foot, two-story dream home with a secluded rooftop deck. Eve loved the location—tucked out of sight just below Coit Tower on the southeast slope of Telegraph Hill—and Will couldn't get enough of the view that looked past the Financial District onto the bay from the upper deck. The fact that their house was just blocks away from North Beach didn't hurt. "Our home in the zone," Eve had said after they signed the purchase agreement. "A match made in heaven. Just like us."

She studied him for a moment and smiled.

"So. How was the debate between Dr. Fast and the notorious Kali Rood?"

"Civilized chaos." He slipped off his shoes and padded toward her with the Armani jacket draped over an arm. When he kissed her she pulled him closer and embraced him tenderly despite the awkwardness of the roses and jacket riding between them.

"That feels promising," he whispered.

"You never know. Might want to try your luck later." She pulled away and tugged at his arm. "New jacket?"

"Not really." He gave her a dark look. "You won't believe what happened today."

They sat at the kitchen table overlooking the herb garden that Eve had recently coaxed back to life. Despite the winter rains, the on-going drought had returned in March. Every day Eve sprinkled the herbs with a watering can that she kept under the sink. She said the garden made her feel like an earth goddess.

But the feeling of domestic bliss faded when Finch mentioned Toby Squire. After he told her the story of Squire's suicide he realized that the drama would be difficult to eradicate from his memory. And tonight he knew he'd be sitting at his computer in the upstairs library writing an eyewitness report for the *eXpress*. Wally Gimbel, his editor, would be outraged if he discovered that Will sat on the story for more than a few hours. Detective DeRosa was right: Squire's death marked the final chapter in the tragedy that destroyed the Whitelaw dynasty. Wally would pin the story to the top of the web page and leave it there for a month.

"What about that jacket? It looks way too small for Squire."

"It's a 38-tall. I doubt Squire could fit his hands through the sleeves."

Will's fingers burrowed through the outside pockets once again. Nothing. Likely Squire had stolen anything of value before he abandoned it on the railing.

"DeRosa said she found a lot of cash on his body."

"How much?"

"Wouldn't say." Finch shook his head. "There was no wallet, no credit cards. I guess he kept the cash he found and dumped the rest."

"Let's see." Eve ran her hand over the material with a look of distaste. She examined the designer's label. "Jeez ... Armani. Looks brand new." Her fingers brushed over the outside pockets. "It's creepy just knowing he touched it," she whispered and glanced away.

"Think I should hand it over to DeRosa?"

Eve gave him a skeptical look. "What about the pistol?"

"From a distance it looked like your .38 Special, but when I asked, she wouldn't disclose any details. Except for the room key they found on Squire. Hotel Vincent, room 203."

"I'm surprised she'd tell you that."

"Personal charm, I guess."

"Of course. How could I forget?" She draped the jacket over the back of an empty chair. "Part of me wants to burn this thing. It's like anything that monster ever touched should be banished from the face of the earth."

"Should I get rid of it?"

"I don't know." She shook her head with a bleak frown. "Just hang it in the storage room for now, okay. I can't bear to sit here and have to look at it."

Finch walked down the hallway to the windowless storage locker and hung the jacket on a hook attached to the inner wall.

"For now I just want to forget about him," she said when he returned to the table. "It's like an old shark coming around for another bite. And how do you ever forget that?"

On the ground floor the renovated Alta Street cottage had a living room, dining room, kitchen, and a guest room next to the entry that Eve had transformed into her home office. An open-step plank staircase with glass siding and a steel bannister led to the three rooms on the second story that included the master bedroom, a two hundred-square foot bathroom, and an open corner space that Finch had converted to a library and his writing room.

At the far corner of the library, between the window that overlooked the street and another staircase that climbed to the roof deck, he'd installed a wide desk where his computer sat surrounded by the litter of correspondence from his agent and publisher. On the floor next to the desk stood the stacks of four-hundred-page drafts he'd written to produce *Who Shot the Sheriff?* It was a tidy mess organized by a system that only Finch understood.

Above the desk a pendant lamp hung from the ceiling to a position about a foot above his head where he hunched over the computer and tapped at the keyboard. The heat from the lamp warmed the top of his head. He'd meant to raise the lamp another foot or two, but never got around to it. Instead, he tugged on a Giants baseball cap which blocked the heat and shaded the intense lamp light from his eyes. He opened the window and a faint breeze drifted over his face, yet another modification to the heat-and-light configuration of his work space. The mewling of a cat crying in the darkened lane broke his concentration. When he heard Eve's footsteps in the hallway behind him he turned his head.

She stood at the doorway with an iPad in her hand. "Have you been following the newsfeed from the *eXpress?*"

"No." He continued typing, knowing that if he stopped in mid-sentence he could lose his entire train of thought. "I try and blank it out when I'm working," he mumbled and typed another two words.

"Then you should look at this." She stood beside him.

Completely distracted now, he looked at her with a frown.

"You saw Martin Fast at the debate this morning, right?"

"Yes. I told you that."

"He's dead." She passed the iPad to him and tipped her head to one side as if to say, drop the attitude—this is important.

"What?"

"Looks like he got caught in some kind of dime-store stick-up that went bad."

Finch read the headline: "Esteemed Climate Scientist Shot In Market Street Melee." The story was written by Fiona Page, Finch's colleague at the *eXpress*. He scoured the first few paragraphs and learned that just before one PM, Martin Fast had entered Triple-8, a convenience store on Market Street near Ninth. According to the cashier, a masked gunman dashed into the store, stole the cash from the till, mugged Fast for his wallet and shot him in the chest and through the head.

"I just saw him"—he turned to check the time on his computer—"less than ten hours ago." He shook his head in disbelief. "He had that crazy debate with Kali Rood. Then he must have gone for lunch."

"Which is when he was shot." Eve sat beside him. She set a hand on his forearm. "I'm sorry. I know it's been an awful day."

"My God. I just interviewed him last week."

He recalled Fast's crisp demeanor, the brisk way he had of stitching together the facts of his arguments, his mastery of data, the inescapable conclusions that he'd published in every credible climate journal in the world. Simply stated, his message offered little solace: due to the ineluctable forces of climate change, within one hundred years civilization as we know it will end. Therefore, the most important responsibility of government is to ensure the survival of as many citizens as possible. Will remembered the emphasis Fast had placed on the words "ineluctable forces" as if they were succulent desserts at a posh buffet. He took a certain pride in forecasting the doom and gloom that awaited humanity at the end of our gluttonous feast. It was an attitude that earned him a lot of scorn from Wall Street and politicians —whom he described as "blind, inept, and in bondage to one another."

As he recovered from the shock, Will tried to sequence the events of the early afternoon. Immediately after the debate, he'd climbed the stairs to the top floor of the public library, settled into one of the carrels in a quiet zone, and knocked off five paragraphs about the war of words and ensuing disarray. Then he'd emailed the story to Jeanine Fix at the *eXpress*, strolled up Polk Street to Brenda's French Soul Food and ordered the Croque Monsieur. After his meal, he'd walked back to the parkade, picked up his car and drove through the detour along Turk Street where he spied Toby Squire—the random coincidence that set in play the events leading to his suicide. By then it was almost four o'clock. Just two or three hours earlier, and less than five blocks away, Martin Fast had been gunned down on Market Street.

Chapter Four

During Will Finch's six-month leave of absence from work —the time he'd taken to write his book, *Who Shot The Sheriff?*—his managing editor, Wally Gimbel had tried to make some changes at the *eXpress*.

Since the collapse of their parent company, *The San Francisco Post*, the online readership of the *eXpress* had grown by eight hundred percent. On the other hand, advertising revenues had shrunk by a factor of twelve. Before this mix of good and bad news had been taken into account, Willie Parson, one of two brothers who owned the *eXpress*, had promised Wally he could hire two new journalists to bulk up the paid staff. But the financial realities of the looming catastrophe made Parson hesitate.

"Sure, we grew the readership by a huge margin," Parson said as he paced the floor in front of Wally's desk. "An historic margin." He paused and tipped his chin to one side. "But these readers don't buy a fucking thing! They're like ghosts. With a thirty-three percent negative cash flow we simply can't continue."

"What are you saying?" Wally felt his neck stiffen as he prepared himself.

"I'm saying the board reached a decision last night." He stopped his nervous pacing and settled his eyes on Wally. He shrugged as if he were a doctor delivering news of a terminal illness. "If you don't break even this quarter, we're cutting our losses."

They both took a moment to weigh the consequences.

"And then?" Wally hoped his boss might offer another angle to explore. Sell the *eXpress* to someone who actually knew how to run an internet news organization. Find a benefactor. Launch some kind of kick-start campaign.

"And then Parson Media will simply concentrate on building our profitable divisions."

Wally raised his eyebrows with a look of exasperation. The profitable divisions included internet gaming, dating sites, travel advertising, digital-coupon sales. Over the past ten years he'd watched Parson Media morph from a chain of respectable print publications (books, magazines, daily and weekly papers) to become a digital menagerie. And he knew there was no place for him in this zoo of phantoms and ghosts. If he wasn't careful, one of these beasts might eat him alive.

"So that's it?"

Parson's voice took on a sympathetic tone. "Wally, you know there'll be a place for you somewhere in Parson Media. But let's not even think about that yet. As I said, we'll look at it again next quarter."

"All right." Wally stood as Parson wheeled about to the door.

"And give my love to your wife."

"Yeah. Thanks."

Second Life

Finch settled into his chair at the far end of the row of desks the reporters called the bog. When he logged onto his computer and brought up the *eXpress* homepage, he scanned his story on Toby Squire's suicide knowing it was the final chapter in the Whitelaw saga. The epilogue. Good riddance, he thought and turned his mind to the murder of Martin Fast.

Since Will had covered yesterday's rancorous debate between Fast and Kali Rood, and Fiona Page had picked up the story of Fast's murder, somebody needed to draw the roadmap on how to move forward, especially if her story developed momentum. He picked up his desk phone and buzzed Wally Gimbel.

"Gimbel." Wally's voice was flat, dismissive.

"How do you want to handle the follow-up on Martin Fast's murder?" He paused. "I can tag-team with Fiona if you want, but I haven't seen her today."

"She's here with me in the boardroom. Come on over and we'll sort it out now."

When Finch joined Wally and Fiona, he saw three or four file folders open on the big oak desk. The editor and reporter stood at the edge of the table sorting through the papers, comparing them with the information on their computer tablets. Wally had his shirt sleeves rolled up to his elbows. Fiona glanced up and smiled at Finch. Over the past year she'd let her hair grow out and return to its natural color, a strawberry blonde that she wore in a pony tail bound together with a decorative scrunchy.

Finch could tell they'd just begun the process of piecing together the facts. Comparing Martin Fast's illustrious CV to the one-page fact sheet the SFPD had provided about his murder created a dissonance the media was scrambling to bring into balance. The question at the front of everyone's mind: how could a man of such storied accomplishments be snuffed out in a two-minute mugging?

"Just digging in?" Finch asked.

Wally drew an audible breath. "Yeah. I told Jeanine to pull up the *Post's* archive on Fast. But I didn't expect this." He pointed to the files. "I guess you knew he was part of a Nobel prize-winning committee."

Finch nodded.

"All right," he waved a hand. "Let's get Finkleman to make sense of this. For now we've got to tackle the breaking news."

Wally sat and waved a hand to two adjacent chairs. Finch sat opposite Fiona with a look of anticipation. They were about to tackle a story that could become either a short wind sprint or an agonizing double marathon. No one knew what lay ahead.

"I heard you were there with Squire," Fiona said and drew her lips into a frown. "Last chapter, huh?"

He smiled, amused to hear the same words Detective DeRosa used to describe the suicide.

"All right, let's get down to it." Wally closed the cover on his tablet. "Fiona, bring Will up to speed."

"This morning's police report says the .38 Toby Squire used to off himself fired three rounds."

"Three?" Finch leaned forward and set his arms on the table.

"And since two rounds were fired into Martin Fast, the ballistics and forensics team did a blast-and-match and discovered the same gun was used in both shootings."

Finch blinked. Squire must have pulled the stick-up just after noon, killed Fast, and then shot himself when Will cornered him. Was it possible?

"That might account for the money," he said.

"What money?" Fiona tilted her head.

"DeRosa told me they found some money on Squire."

"How much?"

"Wouldn't say." He tried to recall her exact words. "She said it was 'more than enough.' Given the fact I called her after I spotted Squire, she was pretty abstemious with the details."

"Abstemious?" Wally raised an eyebrow. "You still on the wagon?"

Finch smiled. "It's a way of life, Wally."

"Yeah, so is celibacy." He let out a friendly laugh as if he was referring to his own form of abstinence.

"All right. Here's how we pitch the next inning," he continued. "Fiona, you cover Fast's murder and the ballistics report linking the .38 to Squire's suicide. Will, you write the big-picture profile of Martin Fast's career. Try to get Kali Rood's take on him. After their debate yesterday, the Virgin Queen ought to bring a different perspective to his accomplishments."

They all smiled at this. Kali Rood and her foundation had acquired the aura of a cult after Jayne Waterston, a journalist at *The Village Voice*, dubbed her the Virgin Queen in a feature article last fall.

"I could do a full profile piece on her. After the story I did on Fast last week it would provide some balance, I guess." Even as he said this, Finch felt a sort of loathing. *Balance* was not a word he would normally associate with Kali Rood.

Wally nodded, an acknowledgement that it was the right road to take. "I hate to see her get the last word on him, but as they say in Hollywood"—he crooked a thumb in the direction of LA — "timing is everything. Anything else?"

"Not from me." Fiona picked up her tablet.

"I'd like to take a last look at Squire's world," Finch said as he stood up. "DeRosa told me where he was living in the Tenderloin."

Wally shrugged as if this side of the story lacked merit. "Only if you have time. But really, Squire's obit doesn't need an epilogue. Keep the focus on Fast. Sad to say, but by next week the death of Dr. Martin Fast will be old news. Nothing more than 'fish wrap' as we used to say."

Wally shook his head with a look of regret, and for the first time since he'd returned to his desk at the *eXpress*, Finch noticed the weariness etched into Wally's face. Something's wrong with the boss, he told himself, but he knew this was the wrong time and place to ask. Maybe later.

When it came to checking Squire's apartment, Finch decided not to wait. After his meeting with Wally and Fiona he grabbed his jacket and courier bag and made his way to the front desk. As he approached the receptionist Dixie Lindstrom, he asked her to make an appointment with Kali Rood for any time that afternoon or the next morning. She lived in New York and he knew she planned to return there within the next twenty-four hours.

"Text me when you have a place and a time when she'll meet me for an interview. Tell her I only need thirty minutes, okay?"

"You got it, Will." Dixie smiled. Her phone rang and she picked it up on the second ring.

She's probably the busiest person in the *eXpress*, Finch figured, but she always has a smile for everyone. He never understood how she managed to maintain her equanimity in the face of so many competing demands. One day he'd ask for her secret formula and advise her to bottle it.

As he drove back to the Tenderloin District he tried to calculate the odds of beating the cops to Squire's room. Yesterday DeRosa had suggested that sweeping his place was not a priority. But that was before Squire had been linked to Martin Fast's killer. There'd be enormous pressure to open the case to a public inquiry by the "political climatocracy"—a term Kali Rood had coined in her debate with Al Gore last summer.

There'd be equal pressure from the police chief to close down the investigation ASAP. After all, nailing Squire for Fast's murder ensured the SFPD would score a rare triple-bagger: Squire had murdered Gianna Whitelaw and now Fast. Maybe. After he shot himself the cops could score three runs on a bunt. Any option that opened the case to further investigation would never be considered.

When he entered the lobby to the Vincent Hotel, Finch took a moment to let his eyes adjust to the shadows that extended from the reception desk down the narrow corridors. Behind the wire grill that separated the front desk from the residents, a twelve-inch black-and-white TV silently displayed Anderson Cooper at the helm of a CNN panel discussing Donald Trump's wild race for the Republican presidential nomination. It was, as the Romans used to say, a circus maximus.

"Anybody home?" Finch rapped his knuckles on the lip of the counter that protruded under the grill.

"Wha'da ya need?" a voice called from the underside of the counter. The head of a man in his mid-forties emerged from below. His hair lay in a damp fold-over across the top of his head. A bead of sweat stood above his brow.

"You the manager?"

"I dunno. You the audio repair guy for the TV?" He stood and wiped his forehead with his sleeve. In his fingers he held a multitool.

"Not my specialty," Will conceded and wondered how to approach the problem at hand. Straight on. "Listen, I'm a reporter from the *eXpress*. Yesterday, one of your residents died in the lane down the block." He pointed to Dodge Place. "The SFPD told me he lived here. Room 203. They said I could check his room."

The manager slid a pair of wire-framed glasses over his nose and ears and studied Finch a moment.

"Just to finish off the personal angle to the story," Finch added.

"You mean Lenny Earl?"

"Lenny?"

"Yeah. The Brit guy with the lame leg."

Finch nodded. "That's him."

"You want into his room?"

"Yeah. He's not coming back."

He waited as the manager studied him again. He paused as if he were trying to snap a puzzle piece into place, shifting his weight from one leg to the other as he considered the options.

"You're the reporter, aren't you." He tipped his head to the silent TV screen.

"Who's that?"

"On CNN." He nodded to the TV. "The reporter who

covered that poor guy eaten by a bear in Oregon last year. And then the one who shot the sheriff."

"That's me." He smiled. Rarely did anyone link him to his reporting. "Will Finch."

"You were over in Baghdad, huh? In Abu Ghraib."

"Yeah." His sense of surprise now bordered on disbelief. "You seem to have pretty reliable sources."

The manager smiled as if the depth of his resources would amaze anyone who cared to probe his inner world. He set the multitool on the counter, opened the security gate behind the desk and approached Finch with an open hand.

"Frank McGill," he said and quickly added, "but everyone calls me Gilly. Yeah, I was with the 377th Military Police Company back in oh-five. That's when I caught this. Only ten days in. Who'd've guessed?"

As they shook hands Will realized that his new fan had an amputated left arm. The sleeve, knotted below the elbow, drooped like a torn flag where it fell to a spot above his belt. A wounded vet from the three-seven-seven. The numbers resonated like the whispers of a ghost. Finch decided to ignore the possibility that Gilly might have crossed his path back in Abu Ghraib. Better to disavow anything that he'd done in Iraq.

Will glanced at the staircase that rose to the second floor. From somewhere above he could hear a heavy coughing followed by a low moan.

"So is 203 upstairs?"

"Yeah."

"You have a key?"

Gilly needed to consider this. "I'm not supposed to—"

"I just want to look. Not touch."

Gilly narrowed his eyes as he pondered the proposition.

Then he stepped back through the gate, leaned over the counter and drew a key from a hidden drawer. He locked the gate to his cage, and when he saw Will hesitate, he wagged his good arm in the air, mumbled "all right, come on," and led the way up the dilapidated staircase.

When they entered 203 Finch pulled on his latex gloves. At first he was struck by the spare, tidy space that Squire had built around his broken life. A three-drawer dresser stood beside a small closet. Two straight-back metal chairs were tucked beside an arborite table stationed next to the window overlooking Turk Street. Along the wall a narrow cot had been made up with a sheet and blanket tucked under a flat, stained pillow. A low coffee table abutted the end of the bed, a makeshift extension to accommodate Squire's seven-foot frame.

"He was a tall one," Gilly said and let out a sigh.

"Yeah." Finch walked to the window and pulled aside the sheer curtain. The double-sash frame was locked. He could see his car parked up the road. A homeless couple stirred under their blankets in the doorway across the street.

He walked to the dresser and studied the few knick-knacks adorning the top shelf. A glass jar full of polished pebbles. A collection of teacups, a sugar bowl and creamer. A lace doily in a glass frame. A flashlight standing upright on the lens. And leaning against the flashlight, a three-inch square polaroid photograph of Squire and a friend sitting together on a park bench. The background looked familiar, but Will couldn't quite place the area.

"Looks like he lived a simple life," he said.

"Yeah. Not a lot of friends, you know?"

"I bet." Once again Will felt the remorse he associated with the city's homeless men and women. While he was insulated from their destitution, he suspected he was never more than two or three steps from the street himself. An irrational dread he could never quite shake. He turned his attention back to the room.

"No bathroom?"

"End of the hall." Gilly pointed his stump toward the corridor. "Ten rooms share one shower, sink and toilet."

"Ten?" Finch suddenly became aware of the murmurs in the surrounding rooms. The coughs, the whispers. A door opened and closed, followed by the sound of bare feet plodding along the hallway. Then, above the low undertone of despair sounded a loud shriek that collapsed into a drawn-out whimper.

Finch tried to ignore it and stepped over to the closet. Next to the door a row of five coat pegs had been screwed to the wall. A pair of pants hung from one hook, shirts and a jacket from two others. Two of the pegs held identical, but well-worn chauffeur caps.

"Hmmph." Gilly let out a gust of air. "He always wore one of those caps. Never thought he kept an actual collection of the things."

Finch opened the closet door. A pungent odor of urine wafted into the room.

"Jeez, what *is* that?" Gilly leaned over Finch's arm to peer into the darkness.

Finch clicked the switch beside the door and the closet was flooded with light from an overhead bulb. On the floor stood a two-foot high wire cage filled with shredded newspaper and garbage. The pen shook with a brief, near-invisible shudder.

"What the hell was that?" Gilly took a step backwards.

After he recovered his bearings, Finch leaned in and kicked the cage with his toe. A massive rat surfaced from the shredded paper and then burrowed back to the bottom.

"Sorry, Gilly, but you're going to have to call Animal Control to get rid of this." Finch turned his head away. As he did he heard more people plodding up the stairs and along the hallway toward them. Two, three people? He couldn't be sure.

"Animal Control? What for?"

But before Finch could explain Toby Squire's obsession with rats, Detectives DeRosa and Hausmann appeared at the door. A look of surprise crossed her face and then broke into a broad frown.

"All right Finch, time to leave." She bunched her fists on the tops of her generous hips. "I thought I told you to give us a day."

"You did," he said and stepped next to the dresser. "That was yesterday. This is today. That's a day, right?"

He smiled but a look of distaste swept over her face.

"Good God, what is that smell?" she said.

"Be my guest." Finch swept his hand toward the door. DeRosa and Hausmann stepped past him toward the closet with Gilly at their heels. During the diversion Finch plucked the polaroid picture from the top of the dresser and slipped it into his pocket.

"What are they?" Hausmann asked.

"Rats." Finch smiled again. The victory of beating DeRosa to the scene provided a boost, especially now that he had the picture of Squire's friend in his pocket.

"All right." DeRosa let out a bleak gasp of exasperation. "You, clear out." She waved a hand at Finch. "You the building supe?" She eyed Gilly as if she were about to clamp her cuffs on his wrists.

He nodded.

"Okay, *you* I talk to. Finch, like I said, *outta here.*"

"All right." Finch couldn't suppress his cheery glow. "I look forward to hearing the SFPD report on this."

He pulled the latex gloves from his hands, walked to the door and down the staircase to the street. The look on DeRosa's and Hausmann's faces told him that he'd scored a point. Maybe two. He could feel the rush in his blood. The game was on.

Chapter Five

Kali Rood stood at the railing of the penthouse balcony on top of the Fairmont Hotel and gazed in the direction of Stanford University at the south end of San Francisco Bay. As she studied the gray band of fog that stood above the water and cloaked the distant hills, she considered what had happened here—the birthplace of all that she had become.

It began when Reverend Jim Jones moved the Peoples Temple Christian Church Full Gospel from Indiana to California's Redwood Valley in 1964. By the the late 1960s the Peoples Temple had expanded to the Bay Area where it flourished. His social programs caught the eye of local politicians and for a few years everyone wanted to be seen with the charismatic visionary. San Francisco's Mayor George Moscone, California's Lieutenant Governor Mervyn Dymally, even *The Chronicle's* city editor served as a cheerleader. Then things slowly began to drift. The cheering became a chorus of boos, the accolades became threats. In the mid-1970s Jones moved the Temple to the jungle wilderness in Guyana where he tried to relaunch his revolutionary church. Then came the drugs. The mass slaughter. And the Reverend's suicide by a gunshot to his head.

In some ways it was not an unusual story. The Bay Area specialized in failed cults. The most recent being Dr. Martin Fast and his clan of true believers. While she'd never had a personal relationship with Fast, Kali knew that he'd lived in Palo Alto and made a life for himself at Stanford. His career flourished and over the past ten years he'd taken on the mantle of a modern-day hero. A dragon-slayer of some kind—who knew how he imagined himself?—a modern Saint George who could kill the curse of capitalism and restore the world to an atheist Eden. Well, he was gone now, and with him all his illusions of righteousness had vanished.

"The media say that he died quite absurdly," she said in a near whisper.

"Yes, ma'am." Jacob Bell stood behind her, his hands clasped behind his back. "The police claim he was shot by someone who escaped custody over a year ago."

Kali considered this. "Perhaps it was unwise for Dr. Fast to be wandering along Market Street. Even in broad daylight."

"Unwise?" he scoffed. "To say the least."

Moreover Fast was a fool, Kali thought. A Nobel-prize winning fool, which is probably the worst kind of all. A man cut from the same cloth as Edward Teller, one of the scientific Merlins behind the bombing of Hiroshima and Nagasaki. And for the next twenty-four thousand years, the children of God will endure the ticking half-life of plutonium decay until the mutation into iron atoms is complete. Was this wisdom or folly? She knew the answer, of course. Knew it by chapter and verse. Revelation 8:11. *The third part of the waters became wormwood; and many men died of the waters because they were made bitter.*

The pain came back into her stomach and then rolled through her chest. She shuddered and drew a deep breath. Sometimes that worked, just breathing through it. She blinked when she felt the leaden discomfort lighten and fade away. If it came back, she'd take another pill. Thank God for the small relief they gave.

When a breeze drifted past her head she held the corner of her hat in one hand. Funny how it is out here, she thought. San Francisco was physically beautiful but she could never embrace the local obsession with lifestyle and street culture. It was a form of collective narcissism she decided, and so much self-love could only lead to a state of moral decay. Indeed, it already had. That was the message she needed to deliver to Will Finch if she was going to make him understand the predicament they all faced.

"Jacob, is everything set for my meeting with the reporter?"

"Yes, ma'am.

"And you're sure it's Will Finch?"

"It is."

"Good." She made a final assessment of the view. "Call and tell him I'm running ten minutes late. Then arrange to have a taxi meet me outside the lobby."

The B Restaurant—a decent enough eatery despite its second-class name—had an outdoor patio nestled above the Yerba Buena Gardens just a few blocks away from the *eXpress* office. Dixie had texted Will that Kali Rood would meet him on the patio at two-thirty. A second message said that she'd be ten minutes late. By three o'clock he'd finished his first espresso and began to doubt that she'd appear at all.

Then he saw her emerge from the far side of the deck and heard her heels clicking on the paving stones as she marched toward him. She wore a dark, wide-brimmed hat and an ivory chiffon dress that cascaded from her shoulders to her knees. A decorative belt matched her shoes and hat. An inch-long gold cross hung from a chain that dipped below her neck. The cross had a loop at the top and Finch recognized it as an ankh, the Egyptian symbol of life. At close range he realized that she was quite beautiful, almost stunning. Her look conveyed a sort of 1950s New York City chic. As she strode toward him she raised her right hand. An image of Audrey Hepburn flashed before his eyes.

"Will Finch? Sorry I'm late." She extended her fingertips for him to touch and studied the surrounding tables. "This is my assistant, Jacob Bell."

The long, lean subordinate tipped his head to Finch and discretely stood aside without a word. Something about his fawning manner caught Finch's attention. He presented an obsequious sneer that suggested a sort of superiority. Odd.

"Let's sit over there. Do you mind? The further away, the more privacy we'll have. Besides, I like to stay out of the sun."

She let out a laugh and led the way to the furthest table and sat in the far chair where she could observe everyone coming and going.

"This okay?" she asked brightly. She sat without waiting for his reply.

"Fine." Will took the chair beside her and opened his bag and took out a notepad and pen. He always wrote down key phrases and usable quotes during interviews, but like everyone else in the business he recorded all interviews on his phone. Whenever threats of libel came his way, it helped to have a verbatim transcript on record.

A waiter came to the table and they ordered Americanos.

"You mind if I record our talk?" he asked and launched the recording app before she could answer.

"Of course."

"Then we're underway." He planted a smile on his lips and studied her a moment. Some people, especially those with oversized egos, would jump into an interview without prompting. He waited.

"Your secretary said you wanted my perspective on Martin Fast's murder."

He nodded.

"It goes without saying that we're all shocked, of course."

"We?"

"The foundation. I talked to my executive committee last night in New York." She adjusted her hat to block the sunlight from her neck. "As you know, Dr. Fast and I hold—*held*—contrary views on a lot of issues. To be honest, I suspect you support his perspective, too."

"Why would you say that?"

"I've read some of your articles. Green science, climate change. Whatever you like to call it. And that profile you wrote on Martin Fast last week. Basically endorsing his politics. He's a geo-engineer who encouraged dumping over one hundred tons of iron sulphate into the Pacific Ocean in Canada. Supposedly to fertilize the dying sea-bed. Do you support that sort of meddling with nature?"

"I wouldn't say I support him," he offered. "I'm here to provide readers with a balanced view. I featured Dr. Fast last week. Now it's your turn."

The waiter returned with their coffees. When he stepped away, Kali added cream and sugar and stirred them into her cup. The procedure bore all the signs of a meticulous ritual. He wondered if she took such elaborate care with every beverage that she drank.

"Well, these days balance is hard to find," she continued as if there'd been no interruption. "But tell me something. You used to be a crime reporter. Why the new focus on climate change?"

Occasionally an interview turned inside-out and the subject would start to interrogate him. He usually allowed a few questions, and in this case he sensed they were necessary to ensure Kali Rood would open up. He wanted her to reveal more than she'd ever disclosed before. To let readers know exactly where she was leading her thousands of followers.

He took a second sip from his cup. "You want the truth?"

"Mr. Finch," she said with a smile, "one thing you can report about me is that I always want the truth."

"Burn out." He shrugged. "I'd spent months reporting the Whitelaw story. Then I took a six-month leave from the *eXpress* to write a book about it."

"Who Shot The Sheriff?"

"Yes." He glanced away a moment. She'd done her homework. Or one of her handlers had. "After that I knew I needed a change. Despite the urgency, reporting climate change has faded from the media agenda. I decided to pitch it to my editor. And here we are." He waved a hand between them to suggest a bond of sorts.

"What if it's all a crock?"

"What is?"

Her hand rose to the pendant at her throat and she caressed it between her thumb and forefinger.

"The notion of man-made climate change."

"You think it is?"

"Worse than that." She sipped her coffee. "It's a conspiracy taken up by the leftists who lost their cause after the failure of communism in Russia and China."

He scratched a word on his pad. *Conspiracy*. He knew she had more to say. It was simply a question of how to open the breach.

"And?"

She stared into the distance to think. "And to fill their secular void. They embrace every word from the mouths of people like Al Gore and Martin Fast."

"What about the science? The Intergovernmental Panel on Climate Change claims that climate change is real and it's man-made."

"But is it really man-made? If you think that our natural destiny is to thrive and grow, then climate change can only be seen as natural destiny, too. Rest assured, Mr. Finch, there's a plan for all of this"—she waved a hand across the patio, as if to indicate the entire world and the universe surrounding it—"and for each and every one of us, too."

"So, let me see if I understand this." Finch tilted his chin to one side. "Man-made climate change is in fact a natural phenomenon. Simply because humans are a force of nature."

"Essentially. Yes." She smiled again, with a look that revealed her famous charisma. "And to interfere with climate, food production, gender"—she swept a hand above the table to indicate an unmitigated disaster—"everything that Martin Fast championed is deviant. To use your word, it's man-made depravity."

"Depravity," he said, echoing her tone. He decided to prod her a little more. "At the risk of getting too arcane for our readers, let me ask this. How do you define nature?"

She smiled as if she were preparing a clever trap. "Nature, Mr. Finch, is God's custodian of the universe."

As he listened, Finch discerned the depth of Kali Rood's beliefs. Here was a true believer, someone who had constructed a system governed by her own convictions and theories.

"But what about the science?" he asked again. "The Intergovernmental Panel on Climate Change."

She shrugged as if she was about to dismiss the question as an irrelevancy. Then she decided to respond.

"As I've said before—and you heard me at the debate with Martin Fast—the IPCC is the epitome of political climatocracy. Martin Fast is in the same boat as those who support genetically modified food and transgender surgery. Just because it's technically possible to alter our God-given world, doesn't make it right. And just because scientists take a vote on a change in the weather, doesn't make it true. If that were the case, they could simply vote God out of existence, couldn't they?"

He chuckled at that. So many transgressions rolled into one. She acknowledged climate change and all the challenges it presented—but because it was man-made, it was fundamentally a force of nature. And any attempt to change "the change" was itself perverse. Climate science was a sort of voodoo—and climate engineers like Martin Fast, the devil incarnate. When he wrote a profile of her, it would take some finesse to clarify all this.

"Some of them already have," she continued.

"Have what?"

"Voted God out of existence." Then she leaned forward and continued.

"You know Mr. Finch, our situation is much more serious than most people think. I know I sound alarmist to people like you. And to some of your readers I may seem like a joke. But I do embrace science. Credible science. The fact that our planet, Earth, can adequately sustain only two billion people. That freshwater resources are diminishing. The oceans are acidifying. The forests are vanishing. All that and more."

She paused to sip her Americano.

"As a result, in our lifetime five billion people will be displaced. *Five billion, dead.* Think of it. The process is already underway in the Middle East, Africa and Asia."

"And you plan to save the survivors?" An odd turn of phrase, he realized, but the words fit. "And who gets to select them? Who gets to herd them onto the ark?"

"Well, someone has to."

"You?"

She narrowed her eyes and glanced away as if these questions were offensive.

"Sounds like Armageddon," he added, dangling this word before her.

"Ah, yes. The prophecies of John. The thing about Armageddon is that everyone has to prepare for his own reckoning, Mr. Finch. It's not as though we'll be collectively vaporized. Armageddon is a very personal thing. The pain is real." She turned her head slightly as if she were granting him an insight into his own fate. "You need to ask yourself, are *you*—William Finch—prepared?"

Finch put his pen down and finished his coffee. He scanned the gardens behind their table. Lush, verdant, clipped and pruned. A man-made paradise, the genesis of climate change.

"I'll tell you what I am prepared for. I'm prepared to write this story as I understand it. I'm prepared to research the facts. I'm prepared to profile the people involved. People like you. And your followers."

She adjusted her hat slightly. "And just what *do* you think of me?"

"Honestly?"

"Of course."

He leaned forward in his chair and picked up his pen again. "There's something false about you."

"False?" Her voice lifted with a note of disbelief, as if no one had suggested this to her before. "In what way?"

"Your pendant, for example. It's not a cross, it's an ankh. Some Christians would see it as offensive. An object of heresy."

"I'm surprised you don't already know this, Mr. Finch. I've publicly declared that I'm not a Christian. Like all people, I am a child of God. Christ is our brother, not our Lord," she explained wearily, as if she'd had to make this distinction far too often.

Of course Finch did know about her public declarations and the fine distinctions that she'd made to her followers and those who derided her as an apostate. But the probe was simply a lead in, a jab to warm her up.

"I see. So you're a plain vanilla theist."

She didn't respond.

"And what else about me do you find so false?"

He knew he was at the heart of the interview now. Her inner world. Just how far could he take this? He pressed on.

"Your name." He studied her face for signs of hesitation or anxiety.

She held his eyes, but took a shallow breath. "To those who know me, the facts are known well enough. When I was sixteen and living in Pennsylvania, my guardians"—her hand rose an inch or two above the table—"were … *called.*"

She arched an eyebrow to suggest a not-so-easy departure from Earth. "Then when I was twenty-one, when I was in my final year at university, I had a conversion experience. That's when I took the name Kali Rood."

"Who provided the name?"

"I did." The self-assured look returned to her face. "Rood is an old English term that means living near the cross. In Greek, Kali means good woman. It may sound a little self-serving, but my name gives me something to live up to."

Finch considered this. "Isn't Kali also a Hindu goddess? The goddess of destruction, as I remember it."

Her head turned to one side. "You're half right. But you got the wrong half. She was the destroyer of demons and evil forces. That would put her on the side of the good, don't you think?"

"Maybe."

On his pad Finch made a note to check the name derivations. "What about the Virgin Queen? Do you embrace that name, too?"

She let out a gasp of surprise that suggested she was both shocked and delighted. *"That* came from Jayne Waterston's profile of me in *The Village Voice* last fall."

"I understand you filed a lawsuit against her and then dropped it."

"It's just one more problem in America, Mr. Finch. Once the media discover they can use you to sell their papers, magazines and broadcasts, then people like me become little more than a news commodity. My lawyers advised me once that happens my legal protections against slander and liable vanish."

Although he'd never spoken to Jayne Waterston, Finch knew the story. He made another note—*call Waterston*—to see if she'd experienced any fallout from her article and the retracted lawsuit.

She picked up her purse and set it in her lap.

"Acknowledge the facts, Mr. Finch. Get over your righteous journalistic idealism. The only reason we're talking right now is so the *eXpress* can sell more ads."

He tipped his head to one side with a look of doubt. "Then why did you accept the interview? Any interview?" He paused to let her respond. When she looked away, he pressed her. "I think it's because you know the publicity draws people to you. A beautiful, articulate woman who holds out the promise of personal salvation. Who wouldn't be curious, at the very least? Let alone pay millions of dollars each year to attach themselves to you."

"Good questions. I urge you to speak to members of the foundation to get their answers. But what about you, Mr. Finch. There's something false about you, too, is there not?"

A look of surprise crossed his face. "Me?"

"No, not false," she corrected herself, "but you are hiding something. A pain you refuse to acknowledge."

"Am I?" He tried to laugh off the accusation but when her gaze would not release him, he had to look away.

"Yes. A loss of some kind. Something has been stolen from you and the pain of loss continues to rob your life." She paused as if she wanted him to absorb this insight. "If you're not careful, it will destroy your ability to love again."

He felt a rush of confusion, as if she'd been able to see inside him. The feeling was both frightening and thrilling. In that instant, he understood how she'd been able to recruit the thousands of followers who subscribed to her foundation. Kali Rood felt the pain, the fear that haunted so many people. She could lift the veil and touch the festering wounds of human suffering. Was it really possible?

"I don't think so," he said. He felt an urge to push away the danger that she might be right. "That might work on others, but not me."

"Well. Then I think that ends our conversation."

She glanced away, then opened her purse and took a moment to search for something. Apparently unable to find whatever she needed, she let out a sigh of exasperation. She stood and waved at Jacob Bell who waited patiently under an awning near the cashier. Then she turned back to Will.

"Mr. Finch, I urge you, before it's too late. Look into your heart, listen to the unanswered questions. Not about me. Not about Martin Fast or climate change. Ask about yourself. Then answer the questions in your soul."

Chapter Six

Eve clicked off her phone and wandered from her office into the living room. She sat down on the love seat and gazed out the window to think a moment.

That was a strange conversation, she concluded. She studied the call list on her phone as if she needed to verify the last call. Yes, there it was. Sam Parson, one of the Parson brothers, owners of Parson Media—and more important, Will's employer at the *eXpress*. He'd called to set up a meeting for one o'clock that afternoon. Said he couldn't tell her anything beyond the fact that he had a business opportunity to discuss.

He wasn't the first. Over the past six months, as word leaked out about her recent windfall, at least fifty people had invited her to consider various options and schemes. Everything from international finance investments to pizza franchises. She'd declined them all. Not that she wasn't interested in starting a new business life. Quite the contrary. She'd grown weary of running her PI agency on her own as a sole proprietor. She wanted to work with new talent on something bigger. Something that she could nurture and grow. But none of the previous suitors offered anything of substance.

When she asked Sam Parson if Will knew about the proposal, Sam had said, "No, but after our meeting I'd be happy if you bring him up to speed." That made her suspect something, but she didn't know what. Nonetheless, she agreed to meet Sam at Scala's Bistro for lunch.

Gazing out the window, she heard a few drops of rain tap against the glass. Three or four winter storms had provided some relief to the ongoing drought and once every few weeks a summer shower would surprise her. As she prepared for the lunch meeting with Sam she decided to dig through the storage room for her umbrella. She pulled aside the still unpacked boxes from the recent move and in the back corner she found the umbrella standing next to her leather boots. As her hand brushed against her raincoat she saw Toby Squire's Armani jacket.

"Oh my God." She took a step backward. She hadn't forgotten the coat, but she'd managed to reduce it to a vague shadow state in the back of her mind. She touched the sleeve with her fingers, then stepped forward and lifted the jacket off the hook.

"So. Definitely time for *you* to go."

She carried the jacket into the kitchen with the intention of tossing it into the cardboard box of old clothing that she planned to give to the Salvation Army. But before she threw it into the box, she ran her fingers over the pockets and along one sleeve. She studied the fabric a moment, pressing the material between her thumb and fingers. Very high-end. Cashmere, she guessed. She opened the jacket flap and studied the rectangular black label with "Giorgio Armani" written in white letters. She knew enough about men's fashion to know that of the three Armani lines, black label was the top brand, designed by Giorgio himself. The complete suit probably sold for three grand, she figured.

She sat at the kitchen table and draped the jacket over her knees. "So strange," she whispered. Why did Toby Squire have a jacket that didn't fit him? One that he certainly could never afford. Ah well, just throw it away and be done with it, she told herself and as she folded the jacket over her arm, she felt something pucker under the left breast pocket. She rubbed her hand against the cashmere. Her head turned to one side as her fingers traced a subtle pattern in the lining. What's this?

She opened the jacket flap again and began a careful search of the inner pocket. Nothing there—yet she was certain now that something lay between the inner lining and the inside pocket. Then a fingernail caught the edge of a tiny plastic zipper that ran about four inches along a seam. She pulled the zip tab down and opened a secret pocket. How clever, she thought. Giorgi Armani, master of deception.

Her fingers probed the pocket and she drew a narrow strip of paper from the jacket. It reminded her of a Chinese fortune telling that had been folded in half and tucked into a cookie. It contained a one-word message: @r3v3lationnow.

She studied it a moment, unsure what it could mean. Then she recalled that all Twitter handles began with an atmark: @. She walked back to the kitchen, opened her laptop and clicked on her Twitter feed. In the search bar she entered @r3v3lationnow and was taken to a Twitter page containing only one sentence: "@r3v3lationnow hasn't tweeted yet."

The name attached to the account was I.M. Unknown.

Strange, she thought. Was this a teen prank to ensnare Twitter in an identity scam? Then she noticed one more bit of text, an unpronounceable combination of letters and numbers that formed an internet link.

She clicked the link and was taken from Twitter to a single web page. There, typed in a sans serif font was a list of names and addresses. She counted them. Twenty-three. As she read through the list she recognized a name, the scientist Will had interviewed and written about in the *eXpress* last week. Martin Fast, who'd been murdered two or three hours before Toby Squire had shot himself.

When she heard Finch close the front door, Eve wandered from the kitchen into the hall. She wasn't quite sure how to break the news and decided to test his mood before she began.

"How was your day?"

"Good." He slung his courier bag onto the love seat in the living room. "Best thing about this job is that every day's different. Today I got an irate email from Kali Rood claiming I'd misrepresented her in the interview. Wally loved it, of course, so he posted her reply just below my feature on her."

He studied her a moment, tried to decode the drawn expression on her face. "How 'bout you? Anything new with dungeons and dragons?"

Dungeons and dragons: his term for her PI agency business. Which in the last six months had deteriorated into little more than inquiries into the illicit affairs of rich husbands by scorned wives. More than once he'd suggested that she move on to something more aspirational, a business where she could make a dent in the world. She knew it was a vote of confidence in her, not a dismissal of the livelihood she'd eked out since her departure from the SFPD three years ago.

"Nope. Neither dungeon nor dragon today, I'm afraid." She leaned against his chest and they kissed. "But I do have some news."

"News? Tell all."

They walked back into the kitchen. Finch got busy brewing two espressos while Eve sat at the table overlooking the garden in their small but private back yard.

"All right. Two pieces of news, actually. You choose. The good news or the bad?"

"Good." He set two espresso cups under the machine drip spouts and pressed the BREW button.

"I had lunch today with Sam Parson."

"Parson?" He turned his attention away from the machine while it hissed. "That is news. What's he want?"

"Money." She shrugged. "He wants me as a partner to help finance new growth at the *eXpress.*"

"Really?" He paused to consider this. "Wally told me they're having cash flow problems. I don't know how bad, but...." Finch gave her a look that said such matters ranked above his pay grade. He finished the coffee preparations, set the two cups on the table and sat opposite her. "And your role would be what?"

She hitched her shoulders and let out a slight sigh. "To be determined. It's just preliminary. I have to give it some thought. Get my accountant and lawyer involved. You know, the idea appeals to me, but the fact that you work there—"

"Implies nothing," he interrupted and then drew back a moment. "I mean it shouldn't *dissuade* you. And frankly, working at the right level, you could add a lot to what we do."

"Really?" She smiled.

"Of course." He waited another moment. "Okay, so with that kind of good news—which is like nine-point-oh out of ten—I'm guessing the bad news could be *really* bad." He waved a finger in a loop as if he'd been circling the air waiting to land.

She picked up her coffee but didn't take a drink. "It might be."

He lowered his gaze. "What is it?"

"The jacket."

His eyebrows knit together and a puzzled look crossed his face.

"It's so strange. And I don't know what it's about. Maybe nothing," she added. She set her coffee cup down on the table and passed him the slip of paper. "I found this in Toby Squire's jacket."

"In the jacket? We both searched that thing. Where?"

"In a concealed pocket zipped into the lining."

As she walked to the hallway closet to retrieve the Armani jacket, he examined the scrap of paper and studied the mix of text and numbers: @r3v3lationnow.

"What *is* this?"

"I'm not sure."

She drew open the jacket lapel and showed him the hidden pocket. Then she unzipped it so it gaped open.

He gazed at the jacket without touching it. "I must have searched that a dozen times. Never saw the pocket." He turned his attention back to the paper. "So you found this in there?"

She nodded.

"What do you think it means?"

"So it begins with an atmark, the first sign in every Twitter handle," she said as she opened her laptop and clicked onto her Twitter feed. "Have a look."

She clicked on the sole link on the page belonging to I.M. Unknown. The list of names and addresses appeared in a single column from the top of the page. All of it neatly aligned in apparently random order. They studied the list a moment and then Eve let out a gasp.

"It's changed." She covered her mouth with her hand. "My God, Will. I swear it wasn't there this afternoon."

A silence weighed on them as they read the last entry and address. William Marc Finch, 114 Alta St, San Francisco, CA 94133.

"What the hell?" His stomach tightened and he exhaled a low moan.

They both leaned closer to the computer screen. He now wanted to examine this very carefully. Apart from his name and Martin Fast's, he recognized two others: Eleanor Pilarz, an outspoken glaciologist at the University of Calgary, and Jayne Waterston, the journalist from *The Village Voice* who'd dubbed Kali Rood the Virgin Queen.

"So. All right," Eve said, her voice confident, "let's just figure this out."

"Yeah. We better." He shook his head and leaned back in his chair to try to fathom the situation. Was this a prank? A coincidence? Something one of the writers at the *eXpress* had put together as a joke?

Over the next hour they sat opposite one another at the kitchen table with their laptops open, cups of coffee at their sides, searching the internet to determine the identities of the twenty-four people named in Toby Squire's list. It didn't take long for them to determine that most of the list members were either academics, scientists or media personalities and reporters. As they concluded the process of googling the names their sense of curiosity took a serious turn. Besides Martin Fast, a second member on the list had died in the past three weeks.

"Phillip Hirsch. London, England," Eve announced in a flat undertone. "Killed last month in some sort of early evening home invasion."

"That's one outside the country and one here in the States." Will considered the implications.

"Two out of twenty-four dead. And it's not like these are execution-style mob hits. They're more like botched stick-up jobs. Like when Martin Fast stumbled into that store two days ago." She waved a hand at the list on her screen and shrugged.

"I know." Finch leaned back in his chair after he checked the Wikipedia profile on the second-to-last name on his laptop. Phillip Edward Hirsch. A shiver rolled up his back.

"I can tell you one thing that's certain," he said after a long moment. "Toby Squire had nothing to do with this list."

"No?" Her voice held a note of skepticism, as if she knew Squire might be capable of anything. "Then where did he get it?"

Finch glanced through the window when a boom of thunder rumbled above them. They both gazed at the dark clouds packed above the roofline. Thunder and lightning storms were rare on the west coast. Especially in the summer. Likely this would fade and pass in the next ten minutes.

"I don't know. But look at this objectively. After his brain surgery and his coma the surgeon told us that Squire had the functional IQ of a ten-year-old. And when I saw him that day," he said and paused as the image of Toby Squire's suicide broke his thoughts, "I doubt he could barely *read* a list like this."

"So you're saying the list has nothing to do with Squire." She gave him a serious look. "But the list itself may be evidence of ... something."

Finch pondered this with a frown. "Maybe. And maybe."

She smiled. "Well, that's the sort of decisiveness that always gets my attention."

He returned her smile with a grim nod. "Tell you what, why don't you talk to your friend in the SFPD. What's her name?"

"Leanne Spratz."

"Right. See if there's anything the cops are holding back about the ballistics report on the .38 they found on Squire. Something that doesn't match up with Squire and Fast being killed by the same weapon. Meanwhile I'm going back to the Vincent Hotel and see if I can dig up anything more about Toby Squire. He had a friend. Maybe I can track him down."

Eve scanned the page on her screen once more. "What about the list?"

He tipped his head to one side and considered the possibilities. "Remember Gabe Finkleman? He's the research guy at the *eXpress*. I'll ask him if he can decode it."

Leanne Spratz wandered into the Caffe Trieste, nodded at the barista and waved a hand to Eve who sat at the small round table in the far corner. She set her purse on the chair next to Eve.

"Let me grab a latte," she said and made her way to the coffee bar.

Since they'd moved into the neighborhood, Caffe Trieste had become Eve's and Will's go-to coffee shop. It was illuminated by natural light that streamed through the floor-to-ceiling windows along two sides of the room. A hand-painted mural of a seaside Italian village adorned the far end of the bistro. The adjacent walls were decorated with scores of framed portraits of the proprietors' family and friends, passing celebrities and loyal habitués. In the evenings and weekends a trio or quartet might entertain the clientele with the sort of musical nostalgia that Eve imagined would be commonplace in the Mediterranean. The sign above Eve's shoulder read: "Petosa Accordians. Official instrument of Trieste Music." But today no musicians had ventured into the shop and apart from a few patrons' laughter and the two or three writers who quietly tapped at their laptops, the mood in the cafe was subdued.

"So. Thanks for coming." Eve smiled, happy to see her old friend when Leanne returned to the table.

"For you? Our glorious Saint Eve? Anything." As she sat at the little table, Leanne crossed a hand in the air, a gesture of mock blessing.

Saint Eve. The nickname bestowed upon her after she'd exposed the years of sexual harassment and intimidation against the women in the SFPD prior to her discharge. Her bitterness had been sweetened by a two million dollar out-of-court settlement. And the tacit admission of her employer's guilt. However, she still felt a mix of embarrassment and pride whenever one of her old colleagues addressed her as Saint Eve.

"But I'm on the clock," Leanne continued, "so I can't give you more than fifteen minutes or so."

"Okay. So the .38. I just need to check that the official statement about the Martin Fast murder isn't hiding anything."

Leanne shook her head.

"And it's the same pistol Toby Squire used to kill himself that afternoon?"

"It was." Leanne leaned forward and dropped her voice to a whisper. "I had a chance to examine the ballistics report. It's a match. There's no doubt."

"And everyone accepts that Squire killed Fast?"

"Makes for an easy two-fer. Two dead, one gun." She shrugged, a weary gesture to suggest there isn't a cop in the world who wouldn't put both cases to bed based on the ballistics evidence alone.

"Look, Eve. Listen to me," Leanne continued in a plaintive voice to draw Eve's attention. "Everyone knows you're probably still suffering from what Squire did to you." She paused as if she wondered how to continue, then decided to simply dive in. "Why do you think there has to be *more* to this?"

"I don't know. Will was there when it happened. He said Squire looked almost psychotic."

"And that's a reason to *doubt* he's the perp?" Leanne smirked with a cynical laugh. "You've been off the beat too long, girl."

"Maybe."

Perhaps Leanne was right. She'd been too wounded by Squire to think rationally about him. The case linking him to Martin Fast was cut and dried. Move on.

"Speaking of Will, I read his feature story on Kali Rood. Let me tell you, she's a piece of work."

"Really? How do you know that?"

"Her whole foundation. If anyone needs salvation, it's her."

"What? You think the Virgin Queen needs help?" Eve winked. They both laughed, both somewhat embarrassed to be gossiping this way.

"Right." Leanne pushed her empty coffee cup aside and leaned forward. "I have a cousin who has a friend who knew her in high school in Malvern, Pennsylvania. Her parents died in a some kind of house fire. Anyhow there was this tragedy and then she moved out of town. That's when the rumor mill began to churn."

Eve's head ticked to one side. "What rumors?"

"That she was somehow responsible. There'd been an arson inquiry but nothing was ever proved. The night of the fire, Kali was at a sleepover."

"With who?"

"Another girlfriend. All very convenient. Like, a little *too* convenient." Leanne glanced away as if she needed to back out of the conversation. They'd both seen the sort of trouble that could emerge from third-hand gossip.

Eve finished her coffee and gazed through the room with a troubled expression. She realized that over the past ten minutes the cafe had filled to capacity. The buzz of laughter and the wrangle of chatter and debate gained intensity.

Eve considered asking if she could call Leanne's cousin, but when she took her purse in her hand and stood up, Eve felt her curiosity fade. Besides, if she ever needed it, she knew she could come back to Leanne for another favor. That door was always open.

As they walked toward the exit, three musicians slipped past them toward the makeshift stage at the back of the room. Each carried their instruments above their chests to avoid bumping into the patrons who crowded around the coffee baristas. A guitar, a mandolin, and an antique accordion: a rustic trio.

"Thanks, Leanne. You're gold, you know."

"Oh, I know!"

They both laughed, then hugged one another.

"You want my advice?" Leanne said in a serious voice. "Let this thing go. Toby Squire and Kali Rood. They're both poison."

Chapter Seven

Finch leaned his head against the wire fence surrounding the reception counter at the Vincent Hotel and tried to get Frank McGill's attention. The hotel clerk's ears were covered by high-density headphones, the sort of equipment the writers back at the *eXpress* used to block the constant banter of phone calls surrounding them in the bog.

"Gilly!" he yelled. "Gilly, over here." He slapped his palm on the laminate counter. When that failed to break Gilly's trance, he reached through the grill of the protective cage, tore a sheet of paper from the desk blotter, balled it in his fist and tossed it at Gilly's neck.

"What?" The wounded vet turned in his swivel chair and pulled the right headphone from his ear with his good hand. "Oh, sorry." He stood up and laid the earphones next to a laptop. After a second thought, he closed the lid on the computer and applied a weak grin to his face. "Will Finch, right? What can I do for you?"

Will smiled, a look intended to put Gilly at ease. The last thing he needed was to offend the only lead he had.

"Look, I don't mean to bother you, but after the cops broke up our little open house visit the other day, I need to ask you some more questions."

"Yeah?" Gilly leaned on his side of the counter and studied Finch through the wire cage. "I can't get you back into Lenny's room again if that's what you're after. It's already let out to a new guy."

"No, it's not that."

"Then what do you need?"

"The name of this man. Looks latino to me. Maybe you've seen him." Finch pulled the polaroid picture from his pocket, the same picture he'd stolen from Squire's dresser when the cops were distracted by the rat cage. The photo showed Toby Squire and Mr. X sitting in an outdoor park somewhere. They weren't posed in an embrace, but they bore the look of mutual respect, the sort of deference that came from surviving in the same battle zone for months on end.

Gilly took the picture in hand and shook his head. "Don't know him. But that's definitely Lenny Earl with him."

Finch pointed to Toby. "His real name is Toby Squire."

"Toby Squire?"

"A murderer who escaped police custody last year. That's why the SFPD was so interested in casing his room upstairs."

Gilly tipped his head to one side. Finch wondered if the fact that a murderer had lived above Gilly's work station bothered him in some way.

"Nope," he said and returned the picture to Will. "But I can tell you *where* that pic was taken."

"You can?" Finch leaned in. "Where?"

"The Turk-Hyde Mini Park. Just a block down. The

kiddie park where Lenny used to hang out. I'd see him there from time to time." He adjusted the sleeve on his amputated arm and then rubbed his narrow chin with his hand. "Used to make me wonder, you know? Hanging around kids like that. Some of the men down here, they got real troubles."

"I guess." Finch didn't want to know any more about the troubles swimming through the surrounding streets. Over the years he'd seen enough of it. "All right, Gilly. I appreciate your help. It means a lot."

"Yeah?"

"Really." Finch hiked his courier bag strap over his shoulder and turned to leave.

"Mr. Finch? Look, I know you're a big name reporter. On CNN and PBS. All those things. But would you like to do a ten-minute spot on my podcast one day?"

Finch turned to him with a look of surprise. "You host a podcast?"

"Yessir. Once a week. *Gilly's Last Gasp.*" He pointed to the laptop where he'd been editing one of his broadcasts. "Been going almost five years now. Except for every Christmas, never missed a week. Got over twelve thousand fans."

Impressed, Finch's curiosity brought him back to the reception cage. "What's it about?"

He smiled and swept his arm in a broad arc. "The one thing I truly know. Life in the Tenderloin District."

Finch nodded and tried to imagine Gilly's inner world. A jungle of frightened strangers hiding in plain sight, all of them eking out an existence in the gutters and garbage bins.

"All right," he said. "Let's do it. Not this week, but soon." He passed him his business card.

"You mean it?" Gilly had a doubtful look in his eyes.

"Yeah. Seriously. I do." As Finch left the building he gained a sense of optimism, a hunch that if he worked with

Second Life

Gilly, something positive might emerge from this bleak, dark hovel. Something good and whole.

Finch left the Vincent Hotel, walked across the street and down a block to the Turk-Hyde Mini Park. In the corner two women sat on a small wood bench, eyeing the children who were clambering feet-first up the playground slide. The same bench where Alice sat a few days earlier and where he'd bought the Armani jacket for ten dollars.

As he stood at the park gate he held the polaroid picture at arm's length. Sure enough, Gilly had it right. The bench where the women now chatted idly marked the exact place where Toby Squire and Mr. X had settled while a third person took this picture, the image of two men sitting side-by-side. And who was Mr. Y, the photographer? And where had he ever found a Polaroid instant camera, let alone the film? Will was sure the camera and film had been obsolete for at least a decade. Nonetheless, the proof was in his hand: in Toby Squire's dull, almost lifeless face staring back at him.

Finch walked through the gate and angled towards the women, slowing his pace as he neared them.

"Excuse me." He smiled, knowing he had to win their trust.

A hush came over them and they turned their heads in unison. Even in their light jackets, they seemed overdressed for the weather. They possessed the same nut-brown eyes and auburn hair that fell in loose curls to their shoulders. He thought they might be sisters.

"I don't want to trouble you," he continued. "But I wonder if you have seen either of these men." Reluctant to give up the picture, he held up the three-by-three inch photograph in his fingers.

They shook their heads in silence. One of them flipped her hand at a mosquito buzzing near her ear.

"You've never seen them here?"

"No," one of them said.

"You sure?"

"No speak. No nothing," the other said in an insistent voice.

The few words they spoke sounded eastern European to him. Hungarian? Romanian? Only a guess; he'd never been close to either country.

"All right," he said and slipped the photograph into his shirt pocket and wandered back to his car. As he drove down to the *eXpress* office a dull feeling seeped through him, a kind of worry that he was chasing a phantom. A ghost just out of reach. Then he thought of his name at the bottom of the list on the web page. That was real. Wasn't it?

"Finkleman, I need your help," Finch said as he sat beside Gabe Finkleman at the window bar in the Starbucks on Fourth Street and Mission.

"You do?" Finkleman took a first sip of his mochaccino, then pinched his lips as if the drink was too hot.

"And this has got to be off-record for now. Wally doesn't know about this. Not yet anyway."

Finkleman hesitated and pushed his glasses along the bridge of his nose. "What is it?"

"I can't tell you unless you agree to keep it secret." Finch understood the blind jeopardy this created. Nonetheless, it was the only disclosure he could provide right now.

"I think that's called a Hobson's choice." Finkleman looked away, torn by his allegiance to his mentor or having to deny a favor.

Finch nodded. "I guess. You either take the option or walk away."

They both drank from their cups and after a long moment Finkleman let out a sigh. "All right. What are we talking about?"

Following his summer internship at the *eXpress*, Gabe Finkleman finished his grad degree in journalism at Berkeley. After a few weeks of negotiation with the Parson brothers, Wally was able to swing a deal to bring Finkleman onto the staff as a part-time researcher. To make his case for more money, Wally convinced "The Brethren," the staff nickname for the owners of Parson Media, that if the *eXpress* was going to turn a profit, it would have to pick a news niche and fully exploit it to the exclusion of all else.

After the successes that Will and Fiona had achieved in breaking open the murders and fraud in the Whitelaw case the previous year, Wally convinced The Brethren to steer the *eXpress's* media positioning toward crime and corruption —and simultaneously drop sports, lifestyle, food, the arts and every other classic news beat. They knew it was a gamble but Wally and the Parsons understood that to survive another year, the *eXpress* had to distinguish itself from every other internet news outlet. Specialization was the strategy. A laser focus on crime and corruption provided the tactics. To do that they would need to make two adjustments.

One, reassign the current reporters, stringers, freelancers and interns to the crime and corruption beat. Those who accepted the new assignments would be trained by Fiona. Those who did not, would be shown the door.

Two, beef up the research capacity of the *eXpress*. Uncovering organized crime, government corruption and corporate fraud required behind-the-scenes, in-depth investigative reporting. So when The Brethren agreed to the changes, Wally's first new hire was Gabe Finkleman.

Finch knew it was a smart move. Although Will wanted to quit crime reporting, he believed that the *eXpress* could make the shift. But they needed to move quickly. He hadn't told Wally or Eve that he'd had enough. The crime beat was too grim, too dangerous, and bad for his mental health. Privately, he'd decided to see the *eXpress* move through the transition and give them six months to settle into their new groove with his support. Then he'd take his agent's advice and try his hand at writing a second book.

Every time Finch came across Finkleman he had to smile. He liked the kid. Fresh-faced, toothy and whip-smart, he stood about six-four but couldn't weigh more than one-forty. Like an unanchored Tower of Pisa, he walked with a sway that suggested he might topple over at any moment. More important, Finch knew he could trust Finkleman's research skills. During his internship, he'd unearthed the corporate details about GIGcoin that allowed Finch and Fiona to break open the case against Senator Franklin Whitelaw. For that, Finch and Eve had rewarded Finkleman and his girlfriend (who was blessed with much more balanced proportions) to a five-course meal at the Ritz-Carlton.

Finch took another sip of his coffee and drew a copy of the list from his jacket pocket. "Twenty-four names on this list, see? I want to know who these people are right down to the color of their underwear. And I want to know what, if anything, they have in common."

Finkleman took the sheet of paper in his hand and studied it. "You want to give me any hints?"

"No. I don't want to bias you. And ignore the fact that my name is on the list. Research my connection just like everyone else."

"So when do you need this?" Finkleman's eyebrows notched into twin arcs. "You should know that I've got a lot on my plate. And I'm still just working mornings only."

"Yeah. I understand." Finch waved a hand. He'd lobbied Wally to give Finkleman a full-time position, but the managing editor couldn't convince The Brethren. "Everyone's carrying a double load. And until I can bring this to Wally, I know it can't be your priority. Still, I'd like to see what you've dug up by next week."

"What about Fiona. She know what this is about?"

He shook his head. "Just you, me and Eve."

"All right. I'll see what I can do." Finkleman smiled with the look of a man who's just been invited into an inner circle. One that he'd been hoping to join from the day he'd caught sight of it.

Later that afternoon Finch slipped on his sunglasses and tugged his sweatshirt hoodie over his head. When he felt suitably disguised, he returned to the Turk-Hyde Mini Park and sat on the green bench.

He had the park to himself and a moment to indulge in contemplation. The playground was barely larger than a standard backyard in suburban Hillsborough or Piedmont. Unlike those idyllic spaces, however, this was penned in on all four sides. It reminded him of the cage that surrounded Gilly at the Vincent Hotel.

Decades ago self-imprisonment had become a means of survival in the Tenderloin District, a forced choice in the dog-eat-dog world of the street creatures who inhabited the surrounding flophouses. The area frightened Finch, not with any imminent physical threat, but because of the shadows it cast against his future. As he watched a grizzled hobo pawing through the garbage bin across the street, he tried to imagine himself living here in twenty or thirty years. How do you survive in your fifties or sixties when all you have is a pair of cast-off shoes, a torn jacket from the local church, and maybe a pocket peppered with a few dimes and quarters? He didn't see how the life he now lived could lead to such destitution, but the prospect haunted him with recurring premonitions. A shudder rolled through his shoulders and he forced his mind back to the problems at hand.

Over the years his intuition had been sharpened by experience and he learned to rely on his instincts when pursuing a lead, especially at the moment when the heat of the chase jumped to a full gallop. Then he would just gut it out, charge over the top and wrestle the beast to the ground. On other occasions, when all the threads to a story drifted in the wind, he constructed a systematic approach to his job. He'd set up a plan of attack, stick to it like a military operation, sift through the ruins and track down every clue. He knew that his current situation called for the second approach. For logic, patience and persistence. He had to wait out Mr. X, let him show his face. And then pounce.

He nodded to himself with a sense of self-assurance. He decided to patrol the area once a day for a week. If he couldn't find anyone to identify Squire and Mr. X, then after seven days he'd give up the plan. Give up and wait for a new opening to appear.

As Finch studied the empty park from the interior of his car he began to doubt his instincts—and his plan. Every day over the past week he'd staked out the Hyde-Turk Mini Park, either from the interior of his RAV4 or from the wood bench inside the park. And each day he took ten or fifteen minutes to walk the sidewalks in the surrounding area. After a while he began to recognize a few of the locals, but whenever he approached them with the polaroid picture, no one would identify Toby or Mr. X.

Nonetheless he gained new sympathies for the citizens who sauntered past him or hunched on the street curbs or tried to stretch out in the narrow building doorways. Most seemed lost in a haze of booze or drugs, others inhabited a near-complete psychosis that left them babbling to themselves while others engaged in screaming matches with ghosts. At best he figured twenty percent of the people living in the Tenderloin District were in full possession of their faculties. Of those, the majority were immigrant women walking in twos and threes with a procession of children following them along the sidewalks. Only a few could respond to Will's questions in English.

As he calculated these percentages he noticed a familiar face walking along Hyde Street pushing a stroller with one hand. In the other she nudged along a toddler who stooped to pick up a series of pebbles and toss them into the road.

"Come on now," he heard her say. "Natty, those rocks ain't for playing."

He smiled. It was Alice Armani, the woman who'd

surrendered Toby Squire's jacket for ten dollars. She wore a white-on-black polkadot blouse and white shorts that bore a small coffee stain on the right leg. A pair of rose-tinted sunglasses covered her eyes. He watched her slip through the park gate and settle on the bench. When her son raced over to the slide, Finch approached her.

"Alice, good to see you again." He smiled, an effort to disarm her automatic shrug. "Remember me?"

"No forgetting you, Mr. Will," she said and adjusted the sunglasses on her face. "Made ten dollars for saving your jacket."

"That's right." He paused a moment, surprised that she remembered his name. Then, unable to think of how to ease into a conversation about the polaroid picture, he decided to just press on and pulled it from his shirt pocket.

"Look, I'm having a hell of time trying to find anyone who knows this guy." He presented the picture to her. "The one on the right."

Alice lifted the sunglasses onto her forehead, studied the image for a moment then lowered the glasses back into place. "Yeah. I know him."

"You do?" He sat at the far end of the bench and leaned toward her. "Do you know his name?"

"Sure I know his name. *Rat Bastard.*" Alice stared at Finch through the glasses and then turned to watch two boys enter the park with another woman. The children ran a loop around the perimeter before stopping at the slide to watch Natty heave off and drop to the ground.

"Natty you play with them nice now, understand?"

Finch tried to draw her attention with an earnest look. It was difficult trying to communicate with her while the shades covered her eyes. "Rat bastard? So who is this guy?"

"The one who hurt Fay so bad. And her little girl,

Teejay. One day the two of them just disappeared. I never seen them again. Not ever."

"Who's Fay?"

"Fay Flood. I used to know them when we all lived in Emeryville. Her and Teejay. Raymond would come round every few days to torment them."

"Raymond who?"

"Raymond Guzman." Alice rolled her lips into an angry sneer and jabbed a finger at the photograph. "Teejay's father. But Fay never did marry him. Said he was poison. Then they disappeared from Emeryville and two years later Natty and I had to move over here and wouldn't you know it? I start seeing him around Turk Street. Rat bastard."

"So you're saying this man is named Raymond Guzman."

"None other."

"Do you know where he lives?"

"In the sewer, I guess." She spat on the ground.

"What about the other man?" He pointed to Toby Squire. "You know his name?"

"No. But I seen him, too. Sometimes sitting right here."

He sensed she was growing weary of his questions and he didn't want her to brush him off before he learned all he could.

"You see them together a lot?"

"Half the time maybe. Look, why all these questions? What's he done now?"

"You remember that jacket?"

Finally she let out a half smile. Barely a grin. "All ten dollars' worth."

"Well, I'm trying to find him. I think he might know where that jacket came from."

She lowered her head and looked at him over the top of her glasses. "So that wasn't your friend's jacket after all."

"No," he confessed.

She shook her head and gave him a look of disgust. "Mister, ten dollars or not, you're just like all the rest."

He thought of asking what exactly she meant, then the implication dawned on him. He was just another liar trying to justify his means by his ends. And she'd known far too many double-talkers to give him another thought. Still, he had to press her.

"Alice, is there anything else you can tell me about Guzman?"

"I prob'ly told you too much already." She scoffed and looked away. When she spotted her son at the gate she called out to him. "All right, Natty, time to go."

Will watched her pull herself off the bench. "Thanks," he called out to her.

As she walked toward the gate she waved the back of her hand at him as if she were swatting away a pesky fly. It was then he noticed her missing fingers, the third and fourth fingers of her right hand severed at the second joints. He'd forgotten about the injury. He wondered what had happened—what trauma or accident had struck her? As she sauntered through the gate and out of his sight, he realized this was one more mystery he would never unravel.

Chapter Eight

When Finch returned to his desk in at the *eXpress* on Monday morning he found three voice messages waiting for him. One from his agent with a rambling apology that ended on an upbeat note: "Sorry Will, but Netflix has nixed my pitch to produce *Who Shot the Sheriff*. Let Nix-flix go, I say, 'cause guess what? HBO is ringing my phone off the hook. They want it. And they want it bad."

The second message came from Fiona Page asking if he'd give her ten minutes to help sort out the new "mandate shift."

The third message was from Gilly. "Mr. Finch, Gilly here. Just following up on the podcast idea. If you're honestly interested, then we can record a session tonight. The studio's in the basement of the Vincent. My shift at the reception desk finishes at 7.00. Meet me there at 7.30. In case you're wondering, the topic is always the same: living large in the T-loin. In your case we'll talk about how the media sees us. Call me if you want to green light this."

Before he could respond to Gilly, Fiona peered over the top of the office partition into his pod.

"You're here," she announced with a hint of surprise. She rounded the corner and crooked her thumb back to her desk. "I didn't notice you come in."

"No? I saw you talking to Wally." He arched a brow. "Looked important."

"Yeah. It is I guess."

She propped herself on his guest chair and ran a hand through her shoulder-length hair. Despite her continuing addiction to lipgloss everything about her look had become more natural over the past six months. No hair dye, no eyeshadow, pastel cotton blouses and twill pants, clear varnish on her nails. And her demeanor was more calm, more at peace with herself. Everyone in the office respected her for the way she'd emerged from her abduction by Justin Whitelaw last year. She appeared stronger, tougher, more compassionate. The new, improved Fiona.

"So what do you mean by 'mandate shift'?" Will tipped his chin to his phone. "I didn't quite understand your message."

"I don't know if you've heard, but the Parson brothers and Wally have been talking about a new approach." Her voice dropped to a whisper and she pointed to the other writers in the bog. "Moving the *eXpress* to focus exclusively on criminal and corporate corruption. No more sports, arts, food, lifestyle. No more celebrity dramas."

He smiled at this, their common disdain for the lives of the rich and famous. "Yeah. Eve told me something about this." In fact, he knew all about it, but he didn't let on.

"Eve's in on this?"

"Maybe. She's not sure yet." He felt constrained. He didn't want to reveal too much about The Brethren courting

Eve. "Anyway, you think we can do it and make payroll every month?"

She glanced away to consider this, the one question at the heart of every struggling newsroom in the world. "Maybe. Look what we did with the Whitelaw scandals. For the first time the *eXpress* broke a major story. You and I *did* that."

"We did." But he knew he never wanted to do anything like it again.

After a pause, Fiona continued. "Look, I don't know how to say this. I think you might be offended somehow."

"What?"

"That I'm jumping rank."

He shrugged. "What are you saying?"

"Wally talked to me about re-orienting the other writers. You know, turning them from sports writers and film critics into investigative journalists. I told him you should be the one to do it."

He laughed and waved a hand. "Nonsense. I'd be terrible, and we both know it. I'm a lone wolf, not a shepherd."

She laughed too. "True enough. You'd start gnawing on their shanks before they'd had a chance to sharpen their pencils."

He smiled, happy that they were comfortable enough to talk this way, trusting one another. He only had that with Wally and Eve. And maybe Finkleman. His inner circle.

"Do it," he concluded. "Once they realize they have to adapt or die, they'll adapt. Besides, they're all smart and they know how to dig a story out of the swampland. And every one of them can write three thousand words a day without breaking a sweat."

"All right," she said and stood up. "I'll do it. But I'm going to lean on you. You know that, right?"

His desk phone rang.

He ignored it. "What's that song?" He began to sing: *"All you have to do is call."*

"Carole King. You've Got A Friend."

The phone buzzed again.

"That's it. You've got a friend," he said to her and picked up the handset on the third ring.

As Fiona walked back to her pod, Gabe Finkleman whispered into his ear: "Okay, I've got it. But you're not going to be happy."

Once again, Finch met Finkleman in the Starbucks on the corner of Fourth and Mission. The cafe sat on the street level under the Yerba Buena Garage, a four-story concrete box, typical of the parkades that dotted the downtown core.

"Sorry." Finch apologized for his delay, sat on a stool at the bar seat overlooking the street and took a tentative sip from his Americano. "Been waiting long?"

"No." Finkleman thumbed his glasses to the top of his nose. "But I can't stay too long."

"Okay, in that case, I've got another job for you." He pulled the picture from his pocket. "I need you to dig up anything you can on this guy on the right." He tapped a fingernail under Guzman's throat.

Finkleman took the picture in his hand. "Who is he?"

"Raymond Guzman."

"Pretty common name. The latino equivalent of Jerry Brown." Finkleman chuckled with a look of amusement. Everyone in the office knew that Finkleman admired the aging state governor. He'd pinned a "Re-elect Brown" lapel button to the cork board beside his computer. "Okay. I'll do what I can."

"Thanks, Gabe. All right, what've you got for me on the list?"

"Probably more than you can use, but it's all here." Finkleman passed a him three-ring binder. "In a nutshell, of the twenty-four people on the list, fifteen are either researchers or academics, five—including you—work in various forms of media, and three are politicians. Nineteen are male, four female, one transgender."

As Finkleman spoke, Finch thumbed through hundreds of pages in the binder. Most of it information printed from web pages. A back section marked off by a stiff sheet of yellow paper contained detailed profiles of each list member.

"Oh, and one of them," Finkleman continued, "doesn't fit the pattern at all. Edmund Austen. He's a controversial minister from the Anglican Church in Canada."

"What's so controversial about him?"

"He's an atheist."

"An atheist minister?" Finch shrugged as if the contradiction simply added one more puzzle piece to the overall mystery. "Okay, so where are they from?"

"Thirteen in the US, two in Canada. There's four Brits, two Germans, and three Frenchies." He pointed to the three-ring binder. "If you want, I'll send you a link to all this stuff."

"Good. But send it to my private email address. You got it?"

He nodded.

Finch shoved the binder into his courier bag and took another drink from his mug. "So Gabe, you ever hear Wally talk about a WTF question?"

"Yup." He took a final sip of his Mochaccino and nudged the cup aside. "What the fuck."

"So WTF? What's so special about the list?" A look of exasperation crossed his face. "What's the part you said would make me unhappy."

"The demographics. All the people in the list are caucasian and between twenty-seven and forty-two. In the western world the death rate in that cohort is one hundred ninety-two per one hundred thousand. That's point zero-zero-one-nine-two percent. But in your list"—he pointed to Finch's bag—"the death rate is thirteen percent."

He paused for a moment, as if he expected Finch to compute the deviation in probability.

"And that's ... what?"

"Sixty-five times the normal rate for the demographic."

"*Sixty-five?*" Perplexed, Finch held up a hand. "No, no. The death rate is closer to *eight percent.* Two out of twenty-four. Martin Fast and the guy from England. Right?" His face betrayed a look of doubt, that he couldn't quite trust Finkleman's calculations.

"As of last Friday, yes." Finkleman hiked his shoulders as if he were trying to shrug off the bad news still to come. "But yesterday, Hans Schreiber, a post-doc researcher at MIT, was pulled out the water near the Charles River Yacht Club in Cambridge. He was number twelve on the list."

Unsure how to respond, Finch stared through the cafe window at the AMC movie theater across the street. The news sank in slowly, then all at once seemed to drown him. He had to draw a deep breath before he could reply.

"So now *three* of the twenty-four are dead?"

"Yeah. Numbers sixteen, three, and twelve."

A new thought occurred to Finch. "Do you think there's something in the order?"

"Not so far." Finkleman nodded with a solemn look on his face. "But since the first death four weeks ago, on average, the list is losing one member almost every nine days."

Finch felt his stomach churn.

"Look, I'm not sure how reliable any of this really is," Finkleman murmured in a tone meant to soften everything he'd just said. "I mean the sample size is very small. Too small to draw any conclusions."

Will studied him a moment. "There's more, though, isn't there."

"Well ... yes." His solemnity shifted to a look of despair, as if he couldn't bear to reveal the most important possibility he'd unearthed. He narrowed his eyes and continued. "I'm sorry, Will. But at this rate everyone still on the list will be dead within six months."

As Finch climbed down the staircase into the basement of the Vincent Hotel, he understood that the chances of surviving a mid-tier earthquake would be slim to none. Anything bigger than a six-point-oh shake could easily shatter the clay bricks and masonry blocks that formed the foundation of the hotel.

But when Gilly turned a corner and unlocked the twin deadbolts to the studio, Finch felt more assured. Or at least convincingly deluded. The small windowless space had been retrofitted with cross-bracing on three sides, steel X-bars that had telescopic hydraulics intended to absorb the death shocks from The Big One.

Or so Gilly explained after he sat down on the far side of a narrow desk that divided the room in two. On Gilly's side stood an array of electronic audio recording tools, sound baffles and twin microphones with pop shields. Opposite him sat an overstuffed guest chair with two worn pillows and a foot stool on the floor. Along the adjacent wall stood a neatly made army cot. Finch wondered if Gilly spent the odd night here when he couldn't stomach the hotel's stench wafting into his room in the manager's quarters.

A narrow shelf held five coffee mugs emblazoned with the words *Gilly's Last Gasp*.

"Everybody gets a free mug," Gilly said with mock pride. "You want a coffee?"

Finch glanced at the makeshift coffee bar behind Gilly's shoulder. A plug-in kettle, a can of Folgers, a jar of Coffee Mate powdered creamer, plastic swizzle sticks.

"No thanks." He glanced away. "Coffee after dinner and I don't sleep." In fact Finch now required five to seven cups of coffee a day and at least two every evening.

"Right. Give me a few minutes and we'll be set to go." He plugged a laptop into a set of cables and with his right hand he busied himself adjusting an array of meters and levels. Impressed by his dexterity, Finch simply absorbed the clever adaptations that Gilly had made to his studio. Most able-bodied indie podcasters would be envious.

"I've got a theme tune for the intro and outro, but I edit them in after the interviews. The podcast will air later tonight. I'll email the link to you. Let me do a level check and I'll be ready to roll," he said as he continued his preparations. "So how I like to run this, is to open with a brief introduction. Then I just let 'er rip."

"Suits me."

Gilly settled into his chair and pulled the desk mic towards him so that the pop shield stood about six inches from his chin. As they sat eye-to-eye across the table, Will made a similar adjustment to his mic and nodded to show that he was ready. Gilly held three fingers in the air and counted them down in a whisper: "Three, two, one." He pointed his index finger at Will and pressed his lips into a narrow smile.

"Welcome to Gilly's Last Gasp, the Tenderloin's voice of the people. Ladies and gentlefolk, lend me your ears. Tonight we have a very special guest with us. A journo who's been crawling our streets over the past week with his eyes peeled to what's up—and as always in the T-loin—what's down. Welcome with me Mr. Will Finch, the star reporter from the *SF eXpress*. You may remember his reports from Oregon last year when he uncovered the murder of Raymond Toeplitz. At first the mainstream press reported that Toeplitz had been devoured by a bear on a hilltop road in the northwest of the state. In fact, Toeplitz had been shot and left for dead *by the county sheriff.* Or you might remember Will Finch as the man falsely accused of murdering California Senator Franklin Whitelaw. Turns out *that* was a suicide by the terminally-ill legislator. Then again you may have seen Will Finch's face on CNN and PBS. But tonight you'll hear his voice on Gilly's Last Gasp as he tries to breathe new life into these bleak streets."

Finch felt his pulse quicken as he watched Gilly slip into his broadcast persona. Gone was the crippled war vet who lost the bottom half of his left arm on day ten of his tour in Iraq. Gone, the wisp of a wounded soul hiding in a locked cage at the reception desk of the Vincent Hotel. In his place sat a man in his element, with a voice strong and steady. A tenor who lifted the cadence of each sentence with a melody that rose into the air on wings. The hypnotic effect was so powerful, so contrary to everything Finch had assumed about the man, that when Gilly put his first question to Finch, he could barely shake himself from the trance.

"So tell us, Will, what brings you from the flight deck of CNN down here to the landing strip on Turk Street?"

Finch gazed into Gilly's face and shot his eyes to one side. The trance had broken. Now he felt a flash of panic. A form of stage fright that he hadn't anticipated.

"Hard to say," he murmured and silently cursed himself. He needed to recover and find a focus. Fast. "I'm trying to follow up on a story I covered last year."

Gilly's features revealed a sympathetic air, a need to bring his guest star up to scratch. "Are you talking about the murders up in Oregon, or about what happened with Senator Whitelaw's family?"

"All of it, really."

"You saw the inside story, chapter and verse. Gianna Whitelaw, Raymond Whitelaw, the senator and his son. Four dead in as many weeks. Can you bring us up to date?"

Impressive. Not only did Gilly produce and broadcast his own show, obviously he'd done his homework, too. Finch leveled his shoulders and eased forward. He began to tell the story of corruption and greed that had killed Sochi and almost destroyed him and Eve. Gilly prodded him gently, asked a few clarifying questions, but overall he let Finch tell the tale in his own words. After five or ten minutes—he soon lost track of the time—he felt a need to bring the story home.

"The only unanswered questions, Gilly, can be found right here in the Tenderloin District."

"You're talking about Lennie Earl."

Finch nodded and realized he should let Toby Squire's alias stand. "Yeah. That's how he was known on Turk Street."

"Until he died a week ago. I understand you eyewitnessed that."

"I did." Finch drew an inch closer to the mic. "I was there. With him and the police."

"Some say the cops set Earl up. You see it that way?"

"No." Will paused for effect. "No, it was suicide. I saw the whole thing. The police tried to stop him. They should be applauded for it." He wondered if DeRosa and Haussmann would ever hear the podcast. Wondered what they might think if they could hear him singing their praise.

Gilly shrugged doubtfully and continued. "What about the murder of Dr. Martin Fast? Three hours before his own death, the police say Lennie Earl killed him in a convenience store robbery. You buying that piece of candy?"

Finch chuckled at that.

"I wasn't there, so I can't say. But I understand the ballistics from the two shootings demonstrate that the same pistol was used in both cases."

"The SFPD claim the ballistics tests prove it's an open-and-shut case. Martin Fast and Lennie Earl. Earl, who'd also been tied to the death last year of Gianna Whitelaw, the senator's daughter."

A memory of Gianna ghosted through Finch's mind. The monster had raped and then drowned her. "Makes it look pretty tidy, doesn't it?" he said.

"Well." Gilly's voice climbed a note, as if he felt a nibble on the end of his line. "Sounds like you think it might be *too* tidy."

"Might be," he conceded.

"And that's why you've been prowling the streets for the last week. Trying to uncover the dirt swept under the rug. Am I right?"

For the first time Finch felt a need for caution. Could

Gilly be laying a trap? Some sort of on-air take-down? He let the question hang. When Gilly detected the hesitation, he pressed on.

"So maybe there's someone else involved?"

"Not so much involved, as ... informed."

"Really?" Gilly's voice dropped to a baritone whisper. *"Informed.* Who's that?"

Finch turned his head to one side. This was the one question he'd prepared for. He wanted to lay his answers out over a few beats. Maybe a listener would be caught up in the suspense. Someone who knew Raymond Guzman.

"A friend of Lennie Earl. They used to hang out at the Turk-Hyde Mini Park. They've been seen together. And I've got something to return to him."

"What's that?"

"Something that Lennie had just before he died. He left it in the park, then turned down Turk Street to Dodge Place. His last walk."

Gilly hesitated. He knew exactly where Lennie had shot himself. But he seemed unsure which question to ask next: about the suicide or the abandoned item. He made a choice and continued his interrogation. "So *what* is it you've found?"

"I can't disclose that." Finch shrugged to suggest the answer was off limits. "It falls within the domain of evidence."

A startled look crossed Gilly's face. "Why not? There's no police investigation. The SFPD closed the file last week. What kind of evidence are you talking about?"

Gilly had outed him. Finch had planted the notion of evidence and non-disclosure to catch the attention of anyone who knew Guzman.

"Again, I can't disclose that publicly. Let's just say it's something that Lennie's pal will want."

Gilly exhaled a sigh of exasperation. "All right. Then what's the name of Lennie Earl's friend? The man you want to meet."

Finally. Finch pointed two fingers at Gilly in a mock salute. "Raymond Guzman. He's a local resident. People have seen him and I know he'd want this item from Lennie Earl. Now can I ask *you* something, Gilly?"

"Of course."

"If any listeners know Raymond Guzman, can they call me?"

"Sure." Gilly's voice adopted a more pedestrian tone, as if the show was about to wrap up. "Why don't you give Last Gaspers your contact info. That might help, too."

In a slow, clearly articulated voice, Finch provided his email address and phone number at the *eXpress*. Then Gilly closed off the podcast with a standard signature piece and a brief pump for Will's book, *Who Shot the Sheriff?* After another moment, he clicked some icons on his computer, drew his hand under his throat and nodded with an affirmative dip of his head.

"That's it. Over and out, Will." He pointed at his laptop. "That was good."

"You think anyone will call in about Raymond Guzman?"

"Maybe. I get calls after every show." He shrugged. "Depends on who his friends are."

And whether they want to see him dead or alive, Finch thought. But he didn't let on about the roll of twenty-four names connected to Toby Squire's jacket, and the connection Guzman might have to three people on the list who were already dead.

Chapter Nine

They'd lived together for just over a year. In that time, Eve had found their renovated cottage in Telegraph Hill, Will had written his book, and together they'd established a domestic life that offered enough "personal space," as Eve called it, to suit their individual needs.

They'd also developed compatible routines. Unless one of them had an early meeting, they always took breakfast together. The ritual required Will to brew two espressos while Eve prepared bagels or toast or croissants. Most nights they cooked a light dinner and the first person home organized the meal.

Most important, in Eve's mind at least, was the small victory she'd won in coaxing Will to embrace her jogging regime. Three times a week he joined her as they jogged the tracks and trails through Lincoln Park or the Presidio. After three months, he'd found his wind and could handle five miles without breaking his stride. Inspired by his new-found fitness, he took out a membership in a gym two blocks from his office and began to lift weights two or three times a week. For the first time since his ten weeks' basic training in the Army his abs had developed a rippled definition. As Eve said, he was "nicely ripped."

Other habits evolved from their personal temperaments and eccentricities. Eve noticed that whenever they had time to share the events of their day, she usually began the conversation. Was it because of Will? The way he needed to brood over some inner problem before he could articulate it? Or was it because of me, she wondered. She knew that sometimes she could be a dumper. Leanne had told her that once. Over coffee, she'd dump out all her anger, frustrations, anxieties before anyone had a chance to ask for cream or sugar. The effect was most pronounced during her conflict with the SFPD that led to her dismissal from the force.

Above all, Eve required a confidante. She could always count at least a dozen friends, but she'd only allow one person at a time to enter her inner life. First Gianna Whitelaw. Then Leanne Spratz. And now, of course, Will Finch. She'd never met anyone like him. She could tell him anything and everything. He had an ear for her voice, could hear it when she expressed a note of worry, fear, affection. He provided tenderness when she needed it, and support when—despite her brash exterior and apparent confidence—she felt like an outright fraud.

After he returned from his interview with Gilly, she could detect a sense of reserve in Finch. The brisk way he kissed her cheek, his immediate need to eat. She knew she'd have to give him some time to completely arrive. Body first, then mind. Sometimes as much thirty minutes apart.

"So," Eve began as she settled on the sofa in the living room. She pulled her calves up onto the cushions and nestled in her cat pose. She took a sip from her coffee mug and studied him for a moment before continuing. "I had an interesting meeting with the Parson brothers today."

"Interesting?" Finch echoed the word with a half-hearted smile. "I'm famished. Completely starving."

"Dinner's on the counter." She thought he looked tired and a little angry. "The seafood sauce is in the fridge."

He returned from the kitchen, sat on the recliner, and set the plate of spinach salad and crab cakes on his lap. He checked the clock on the fireplace mantle: 9:38. He dipped a piece of crab cake in the pool of seafood sauce and devoured it. After the third bite, his hunger pangs began to subside.

"So I think I'm going to accept their offer," she continued as though there'd been no break in the conversation.

"Seriously. This is going to be real?" He paused in mid-chew. "You're going to buy into the *eXpress?*"

"I think so. Part of it, anyway. My lawyer and accountant think it's a legit business, although neither of them see any upside in online media outlets. They think the market's saturated. But if we refocus the *eXpress* on covering crime and corruption exclusively—well, that's been my life for the last eight years. You've got to admit, I know the turf."

She paused to assess his reaction. She knew this would be a big move, not just for her, but for them as a couple. At some level it would affect how they related to one another. The balance of power. The sexual dynamics. She didn't want to change any of that. Things were perfect as they were and this decision could upend their world.

He forked some salad into his mouth and set the plate aside. He chewed steadily with a look of contemplation. After he swallowed he wiped his mouth with a napkin and took a sip of coffee.

"What are they offering?"

"Ten percent for five million with an option to buy another forty-one percent after one year. The accountant says I should offer three and settle at four mill."

She watched him run though some mental calculations.

"Could be about right," he said. "We have thirteen people on payroll. There's the cost of paying freelancers, operations, rent—which by the way, goes to another Parson holding company. Four million will probably carry us through one more year. So you'd be buying time. Enough time to determine if you should invest in the option. During the first year you'd have to come up with new income streams. Wally told me last week that ad revenue is faltering even though readership is expanding. So be prepared. The internet has made an already crazy business go insane."

True enough, she thought. But she had an idea that might solve the revenue flow. An idea she'd keep to herself for now.

"Well, it's just money," she said with a wave of her hand.

He smiled at that. Their private joke. "You know I still can't believe it sometimes."

"Me too." She thought about her windfall. Millions of dollars, stocks, bonds—and bitcoin, of all things—had suddenly poured into her life. Unasked for. She'd donated twenty percent to a national foundation to support abused women. And millions more still sat in the bank. Money to coax this new dream to life.

"But I'm worried about something, Will." Her face took on a serious expression. "If I buy in, what happens to us?"

He looked at her and nodded, unsure how to respond.

"This deal can't stop what we have," she added and waved a hand around the room, a gesture to include everything surrounding them. The cottage. The life they'd built. "I won't do it if you don't think it's right."

He smiled. "Don't worry about that. It's safe, Eve. We're safe." He walked to the sofa and sat beside her. "This deal will be good for you—and us. Take it."

"You're sure?"

"Yes."

He wrapped an arm around her and they kissed. After a moment, he pulled away.

"But there's something I've got to tell you."

"What?"

"About the list. Finkleman found something new about the list."

"What?"

"A sort of statistical analysis." He looked away. "Let me brew another coffee. Then I'll tell you everything I know."

On his way into the newsroom the next morning, the severity of the threat facing Finch began to weigh on him. The previous evening he'd spent almost three hours dissecting his situation with Eve. She was unshakable in her belief that the SFPD would never reopen the file about Fast's murder. "No cop in his right mind," she'd argued, "would unzip a triple-bagger without outside pressure. Fast, Squire, Gianna. It ain't gonna happen."

Instead, she'd insisted that the FBI would have to pick up the investigation. With one death in San Francisco, one in London and now a third at MIT, they could tap into Interpol and tie all three murders from the list into an international murder-for-hire conspiracy. In the meantime, she wanted Will to start packing a gun. When he refused,

Second Life

she unlocked the bedroom vault and slipped her Colt Cobra .38 Special into the nightstand drawer beside her pillow. The same pistol he'd used to kill Alexei Malinin. Five slugs to his back and chest. The memory still haunted him.

By the time they'd rolled into bed, they agreed to wait another day to consider the options. To reopen the case, Eve and Will knew they needed proof that someone other than Toby Squire was behind Martin Fast's death. But where could they find concrete evidence? Maybe from the man in the photograph, Raymond Guzman. Who was he? What was his role?

When Will sat at his desk at the *eXpress*, he noticed the message light blinking on his landline phone. He tapped his password onto the keypad. The AT&T voice messenger calmly announced, "You have thirty-three new messages."

Of course. The tipsters and whistle-blowers in Gilly's podcast audience would be all over this. It took him over two hours to sort out the spam from the more likely leads. Whenever he hit upon a genuine possibility, he returned the call to determine if the informant possessed any valid information about Raymond Guzman.

It wasn't until he hit the nineteenth message that he felt a surge of optimism when a woman spoke into the voice mailbox in a near breathless whisper: *"I know him. The man you're looking for on your radio show. Guzman. He's done some time, but he ain't paid for his crime. Room 505, in the Mentone on Ellis. Don't try calling me. You never heard of me. And you never will."*

He knew the message was hot. Every other tip required a call-back. "Phone me for details." "For fifty bucks I'll show you his room." "Saw him last night at the Whiskey Thieves Bar. Meet you there at six." Message nineteen was different in every way.

As he played it a second time, Finch wrote down the

details. When he finished he saved the message, then turned to the map directory on his computer and found the address of the Hotel Mentone on Ellis Street. He grabbed his courier bag and phone and slipped past the other writers in the bog, all of them diligently ticking away at their keyboards.

On his way out the door, he paused at Finkleman's desk and caught his attention. "Gabe, have you got the picture of Toby Squire I gave you? I need it."

"Right here." Finkleman pulled the picture from his drawer. "I scanned it and I'm running it through some low-grade facial recognition software."

Finch paused. "The *eXpress* has facial recognition software?"

"Open source. Nothing special, and it takes forever so don't lose sleep waiting for it."

Once again surprised by Finkleman's resourcefulness, Finch gave the rookie a thumbs-up and took the picture in his hand.

"By the way, I got a lead on Raymond Guzman. Check through the state penal records. I think Guzman did some time in the can."

"You got it," Finkleman said.

Finch turned into the corridor and made his way to the staircase at the end of the hall.

The Mentone Hotel rose five storeys above a bar and pool hall called the Cinnabar on the corner of Ellis and Jones Streets. A brick-faced box, the hotel looked to be one of the many Depression-era projects constructed to restore the broken economy and draw a few more men back into the labor force.

Finch parked his car on Ellis and crossed through the unlocked security gate under an arched canopy. The lobby appeared to be empty, the front desk abandoned. A single hallway led to a staircase near the rear of the building. Finch took the stairs two at a time. At the first landing he had to climb over an old man with a gray, foot-long-beard spotted with what Finch assumed was day-old spaghetti sauce. The hobo's skin was so pale that Finch worried that he might be dead. He detected a faint pulse in the man's wrist and prodded his arm with a gentle nudge. After a moment the old-timer's eyelids fluttered open and shut.

"You all right, pal?"

"Ga fack off'n me," he mumbled.

Finch released his arm and continued his climb up the stairs.

As he ascended to the fifth floor, Finch absorbed the sounds of the building. The low groans and psychotic shouts of men shuttered behind the thin doors mixed with the wheeze and sighs of the building's creaking vents and broken floor boards. The stale air, laden with the odor of cigarette smoke, human spunk and excrement brought a new sense of despair to Finch's recurrent fears for the city's homeless. How could life sink to this depth? And one day, would it drown him, too?

On the fifth floor he ghosted past the row of six doors on the street-side hallway. 501, 503 — 507, 509. He returned to the unmarked door between 503 and 507 and knocked once. Nothing. He examined the keyhole, an old-fashioned eyelet designed for a standard lever-lock key. He dug through his courier bag and pulled out the wallet of lock-pick tools that he'd acquired during his training in military intelligence. The large pick and levering bar both slid into the keyhole without resistance. He jimmied the two together until he felt the longer blade hit the cylinder teeth. After a few seconds he found the resistance point, gave the pick a clockwise turn and entered Raymond Guzman's room.

A cot, a hot plate, a kettle, an empty can of Campbell's Tomato soup holding a collection of assorted cutlery. Two glass mugs, a can of Folger's coffee sealed with a cracked plastic lid, a chipped laminate desk, one plastic deck chair, a narrow closet covered by a torn curtain. On the desk: a worn Bible written in Spanish, sales flyers from local merchants, the front section from a two-day old edition of *El Tecolote*, the local Spanish newspaper. The closet contained a pair of worn work boots, three shirts hung on wire hangers, a lumberman's jacket and a pair of denim jeans double-parked on a hook. Next to the closet floor were two open cardboard boxes holding unsorted socks, underwear, t-shirts, a belt, an empty canvas duffle bag.

Within five minutes Finch had surveyed the room and its contents. Then he stood at the window and pulled the tattered drape to one side. From his vantage point, five storeys above the street, he could see the City Hall rotunda in the distance. Its grand appearance, with the gold accents on the domed peak, added one more insult to the misery on the sidewalks below.

On the longest wall, perhaps ten feet in length, a dozen Polaroid pictures of a woman and a young girl had been taped to the plaster in a rectangular arrangement. Perhaps these two were the mother and daughter that

Second Life

Alice had mentioned to Finch in the Hyde-Turk Mini Park.

Finch's phone pinged. He sat at the desk and read an email from Finkleman: *Bingo. Guzman did two stints in prison for assault. Chuckawalla and Ironwood. Arrested for the abduction of Fay Flood and her daughter, Teejay Flood, but released because the mother refused to testify. See the attached PDF for details. Not much else on this one. Good hunting, Gabe.*

Before he could open the PDF, he heard footsteps treading along the corridor towards 505. The door swung open. Guzman stepped inside and closed the door behind him before he realized that he had a guest. He hesitated and then slipped his denim jacket onto the cot. Finch guessed he was in his late thirties. He stood about five-foot-ten but he had a broad chest and probably weighed close to two hundred pounds. He dragged his fingers through his short, black hair and let out a tight snort through his nostrils as if he were a bull preparing to charge.

"Who the fuck are you?"

"Since Lenny Earl shot himself, I'm your new best friend." Finch smiled and gestured to the cot. "Have a seat, Raymond. We need to talk."

He hesitated, just long enough to assure Finch that he had the right man.

"Earl? I don't know any Earl." He shifted his weight on his feet. "I don't know who you're talking about."

"Then tell me who's the man in the photo with you." Finch pulled the polaroid from his pocket and held it a few inches from Guzman's face.

"Wha' the fu… Lemme see that."

With a quick snap of his wrist he tried to grab the photo. It fell to the floor and then Guzman shifted his weight and took a swing at Finch's nose with his left hand.

Finch side-stepped, let the fist glide past him then caught Guzman's extended arm and twisted it backwards and down. It was a two-step move that immobilized Guzman in an arm lock.

"Do that again," Finch whispered in his ear, "and I'll put you down." He tightened his grip on the forearm and notched it tight. One more inch and the ulna would snap.

Guzman's chest slumped forward in a show of resignation. After a moment Finch relaxed his grip and released him. Guzman expelled a long jet of air and sat on the edge of the cot. "Look, I don't talk about nothin' until you tell me who the fuck you are."

His English was almost accent-free. It resonated with a note of latino intonation, enough to suggest he was American-born but raised in an immigrant family.

"I'm not a cop, and I'm not going to turn you in. *If you help me, that is."* He picked up the photograph, slid it into his shirt pocket and fixed a smile on his lips.

Guzman's posture stiffened. "Turn me in? For what?"

"Take your pick." Finch pouted as if he were considering the options from a list of possibilities. "How about accessory to murder."

"What?" Guzman jumped up from the bed and glowered at Finch. "What the fuck are you talking about?"

Will waved a hand, a gesture to settle down. "Raymond, I know you've done time in Ironwood *and* Chuckawalla. One more strike, amigo, and you're going away for a very long time. So don't even think about it." He notched his head to one side to suggest that even if Guzman won a fight, he'd still end up in a pen.

Guzman clenched his jaw, walked toward the window and grabbed the curtain. As he scanned the street he seemed to consider the gravity of his situation.

"What murder are you talking about?"

"Last week. When Lenny Earl shot Martin Fast down on Market Street. Just a few hours before he did himself in."

Guzman turned to face Finch. "I heard about that. How's that touch me? *I did nothin'.*"

"You got him the gun."

"Gun? I don't know nuthin' about no gun." Guzman scoffed and walked back toward the cot.

"Lenny Earl had the mind of a child, Raymond. Did he tell you about his brain surgery? About the coma he was in? He wasn't capable of stealing a gun on his own."

"I told you, I don't know about any fuckin' gun."

Will could detect Guzman's weariness, his pending capitulation. For the first time Finch noticed a fading bruise on the side of Guzman's cheek below his right eye. Someone had given him a good shot and left his mark. He decided to press harder. "And then there's the Armani jacket you stole."

"What fuckin' jacket? I don't have no jacket!"

Finch swept his fingers over the screen on his phone and brought up the image he'd taken on the trunk of his car after he'd bartered for the jacket with Alice. When he saw the image, Guzman's face betrayed a look of surprise.

"What bothers me is what I *don't* know," Will said. "I don't know how and where you got the jacket and the pistol. But one way or another that .38 ended up in Lenny's hands. And you helped him. Then Lenny shot Martin Fast. Killed him. That makes you an accessory to Fast's murder."

Finch could see Guzman's throat tighten as he realized how the implications could doom him. His Adam's apple wobbled as he tried to speak and then choked back his words.

Finally he managed to speak coherently: "Who are you?"

"You don't need to know that. It's better for both of us. All I want to know is where—and how—you got the jacket and the gun."

Guzman sat on the cot again and dropped his head into his hands. He let out another sigh, lifted his head and studied Finch's face as if he had to make a choice before he could continue.

"Right now you have to make a very simple decision, Raymond. Do you talk to the cops—*or to me?* If you talk to me, after today you will never see me again. But if you talk to the cops ... well, that could be the last conversation you have as a free man."

This was the second time that he'd raised this prospect and now Finch decided to stop talking. He had nothing more to say, no better deal to offer. Years of experience had taught him that when he reached a precipice like this, he should simply shut up and let the weight of silence apply the necessary pressure.

"If I show you something," Guzman whispered, "if I show you *anything*—what do I get in return?"

Finch shrugged and softened his voice. "That's a good question." Now that Guzman had turned the conversation to the bargaining stage, Will knew he could draw out all the information he needed.

"First, one more day of freedom. Second, one hundred bucks. Enough to buy you a meal with a cold beer and a bus ticket to Tijuana." He paused to wave a hand around the room. "From there you move on, find another town and a new name. And your link to Lenny vanishes."

Finch snapped his fingers as if they were both watching a magic act where a rabbit disappears through a top hat. He waited until Raymond looked him in the eyes again. When he did, Finch arched his brows with a look of assurance.

Guzman nodded with a bleak expression. "You got this money on you?"

He opened his billfold to display a stack of twenties. Guzman made a move to pull it into his hand, but Finch pocketed the cash and stood up.

"After you show me where you got the jacket. And the .38."

Guzman and Finch strolled across the concourse under the City Hall rotunda. The cavernous space was surrounded by tiered galleries where visitors could peer down onto the walls and marble floors below. The centerpiece was a stepped-up podium at the foot of a grand staircase that descended from the second gallery. It reminded Finch of an ornate wedding cake with layer stacked upon layer — and at the top, a newly-wed couple posing arm in arm. Indeed, the podium often served as a venue for well-heeled locals to trade wedding vows. Or for public speakers to address corporate conferences and for politicians to make grand pronouncements.

It had also served as the site for the debate between Kali Rood and Martin Fast. The acoustics were far from perfect for a debate, but during the war of words the hall had been filled to the upper gallery and the sheer mass of people in attendance had absorbed the potential echo of the debaters' voices. It had been Martin Fast's last public appearance.

As he followed Guzman across the hall toward the men's bathroom, Finch recalled Fast's insightful words: "We're one step away from the chimps and bonobos."

And the madmen, Finch added to himself.

"Over here," Guzman said in a soft voice. He spoke as if he didn't want to be overheard by the passing groups of tourists and city employees as he returned to the scene of his thefts and muggings.

Finch followed him into the long, wide bathroom. Another ornate heritage space finished with polished marble tiles.

"So this is where you got the jacket?"

Guzman walked to the end of the row of stalls, checking under the doorways as he lumbered along. When he was confident they were alone, he crooked a thumb at the last stall. "In here," he said.

"What's in there?"

"Where Lenny hid hisself."

Finch walked past the line of urinals to the last stall and nudged the door ajar with an elbow. He took a moment to envision the scenario. Toby Squire had been a huge man, just under seven feet, broad and very heavy. A bear. Anyone who came across him would be intimidated.

"What was the play, Raymond? You'd follow a patsy inside and if the coast was clear you'd give Lenny a signal and the two of you would mug him?"

Guzman shrugged a bleak acknowledgement. Finch understood that he didn't want to say anything incriminating, especially here at the scene of a crime. He scanned the ceiling for CCTV cameras. Nothing.

"What about building security?"

"They clock in once an hour. You wait for them, they make their sweep, then we'd move in."

He pointed to the security lock on the wall next to the row of sinks opposite the stalls. Finch examined the mechanism, a timed key system, that required the guard to turn his key in the lock as he made his rounds. When the key rotated it generated an electronic time stamp and the guard moved on to the next station.

Finch turned around and stepped back to Guzman. "So then what?"

"Depends. It worked different every time."

"Tell me about the time with the Armani jacket. Did you know who he was?"

He shook his head. "No names. It's always best."

"You ever see him before?"

"Never."

"What about after?"

"I don't go looking."

"All right. Then what?"

"He came in"—Guzman glanced at the bathroom door again—"then me. He wore a hoodie. Took it off soon as he got in here. Underneath that he wore the jacket. Matched his pants, a full-on suit. Then he walks over to the sink"—Guzman leaned over the sink as if he were about to wash his hands and face—"takes off the jacket and lays it next to his hoodie right here." He pointed to the counter under the soap and towel dispenser.

"And then?"

"Then he starts to scrub up and I give the cough"—he let out a sharp, guttural cough—"Lenny sweeps out of the stall and makes the grift."

Again Will took a moment to imagine the scene as it must have unfolded. The bear appears as if from nowhere, leans on his victim and sweeps any valuables into his arms, then makes a run for the door.

"What about Mr. X. He didn't put up a fight?"

"Oh, he put up fight enough." Guzman pointed to the

bruise on his cheek. "Must have taken me five minutes to put him down."

"What? You killed him?"

Guzman scoffed at the idea. "I never done that to nobody. And don't be saying I did."

"What about Lenny?"

"Last I seen him. From what I hear, he was dead three hours later."

"I know. I was there." He shrugged as if the suicide still didn't make sense. "Why'd he do it?"

Guzman glanced away as if he were recalling something his friend had once confessed. "He told me he'd never go to prison. That he'd sooner be dead than locked in a cage with a bunch of monkeys."

Finch tried to fit the pieces together. "And where'd he get the gun?"

He hiked his shoulders. "I told you from the beginning. I never seen it. I don't know dick about any gun."

"Don't bullshit me, Raymond. There's no payoff until I know how he got the .38."

Guzman's face slumped into a worried sneer. "I'm not shittin' you. If he had a gun, it must of been in that jacket of yours."

Finch considered this. He decided to ask Eve to test the jacket pockets for gunshot residues. Maybe Guzman had it right. The hitter had shot Martin Fast, slipped the gun into the suit pocket under his hoodie, then made his way back to City Hall to change. If the timing was right, it made sense.

"So when did all this go down?"

He shrugged with a blank look.

"You said the guards roll through here once an hour. And you set up the hit just after they key-in and move on. So what time was it?"

Guzman stared across the room for a moment and then blinked as if the answer just struck him.

"It was always at fifteen minutes. It's on the half hour at the library. And exactly on the hour at the bus depot."

Finch shook his head in wonder. The two cons had a schedule of muggings timed to avoid the security rotations around town.

"So it would've been one-fifteen," he said.

Guzman's eyes brightened once more. "Yeah."

Finch checked his watch. Eleven-sixteen. And at that moment the door swung open and in walked a security guard wearing a bleached white shirt, black tie, pressed pants and a key attached to his belt by a retracting steel coil. He nodded to Finch and Guzman, walked to the security lock, keyed in and moved on. One minute late, give or take fifteen seconds.

"So that's how it works?" Finch asked.

"Yeah. That's it." Guzman glanced away.

Finch studied him a moment and detected a sense of shame. He was sure now that Guzman didn't have anything to do with Fast's murder. He was just another con man, a grifter who'd run his long stretch of good luck into the dirt.

Chapter Ten

The next morning Will and Eve drove down to the *eXpress* office together. They entered the board room and sat at the massive oak table across from Wally Gimbel. Fiona Page sat at his right, Gabe Finkleman on his left. Wally immediately took charge of the meeting.

"Gabe, Fiona," he began, "in case you haven't met her, this is Eve Noon. Eve's the new associate publisher and part owner of the *eXpress*, therefore technically your boss." He smiled and waited for the notion to sink in. "She'll be joining us for a lot of editorial meetings especially now that we're re-positioning the *eXpress* to cover crime and corruption—which, as an ex-member of our illustrious SFPD, happens to be her home turf.

"All right," he continued, "Will asked for this meeting because of a story that's breaking right now." He pointed his index finger at Will. "So, tell us what you've got."

Finch leaned down to the floor and pulled three objects from his bag and set them on the table: the photo of Toby Squire and Raymond Guzman, the list of twenty-four names, and the Armani jacket which he laid on the surface of the table.

"Okay, this goes back to the day when I spotted Toby Squire and followed him along Turk Street to a dead end lane where he shot himself." He paused to look at the others. "We now know that the pistol he used was the same .38 that killed Martin Fast earlier the same day. Eve has already verified the details with the SFPD. No question. It's the same gun."

"The ballistic forensics and gunpowder residues are all a match," she said. "There's no way to dispute the forensic report."

"Now following the suicide," Will continued, "on the way back to my car, I noticed this jacket lying over a railing in the park." He lifted a sleeve and rubbed the cuff between his thumb and index finger as if he were assessing the fabric quality. "When I saw him in the park, Squire had the jacket in his lap—but then left it behind when I confronted him. Something bothered me about that, I don't know what exactly, so I brought it home and showed it to Eve."

Eve held up a hand, a gesture for Will to pause a moment, and turned to Finkleman. "Gabe, you probably don't know this, but last year, Toby Squire attacked me—"

"Brutally attacked her," Fiona interjected.

"So when I saw the jacket," Eve nodded at Fiona and pressed on, "my nerves took over and we hid it in the storage locker where it sat for the next few days. When I took it out I discovered a slip of paper in a secret pocket." She passed the paper to Fiona.

"It looks like a Twitter handle," Fiona said. "But one that's really arcane."

She passed the paper to Wally. A puzzled look crossed his face.

"All right," he sighed. "Somebody please tell me what this means."

"So when you look up @r3v3lationnow on Twitter the user is identified as I.M. Unknown," Finch said.

"I'm unknown?" Wally frowned and glanced away with a look of disbelief.

"But the page contains a web link." Eve picked up the thread. "When you click the link it takes you to a list of names. Last week, the list had twenty-three names. Until Will's name was added to the bottom of the file. He became number twenty-four."

Finch passed print copies of the list to Fiona and Wally. Then he turned to Finkleman. "I'll let Gabe fill you in. He's already spent a few hours trying to make sense of it."

Finkleman coughed into his fist and leaned forward. "All right. It's complicated, but let me try to walk you through this."

He opened his research binder to the first page. Over the next ten minutes he revealed what he'd told Finch in the coffee shop. As he spoke his voice grew increasingly anxious. When he completed his summary and it became obvious to Wally and Fiona that Will was in danger, the mood in the room shifted. A dark chill descended on them and Wally looked from face to face.

"So what you're telling us, is that this is a hit list of academics, researchers and reporters who are being murdered one by one, every few weeks." He sounded as if he were accusing Finkleman of the crimes. "Do I have that right?"

"Every nine days. On average," Finkleman said and slumped into the back of his chair.

"And what's this?" Wally demanded as he pointed at the polaroid picture.

"A picture of Toby Squire and Raymond Guzman."

Finch passed the picture to Wally. "It took me a while, but I tracked Guzman down to a flophouse on Ellis Street. He told me how he and Squire had developed a mugging operation in City Hall, the library and bus station. More important, he confessed that he and Toby stole the jacket in one of the men's rooms in City Hall."

"When was this?"

"Less than an hour after Martin Fast was murdered on Market Street."

"What?" Wally snarled. "And who the hell owns that jacket?"

"John Doe." Finch hiked his shoulders, a gesture to acknowledge that the trail had gone cold. "I don't know. I couldn't see any CCTV cameras in the washroom. Weeks have gone by so ... I just don't know."

"You were there?" Fiona asked.

"Yeah. Yesterday Guzman walked me through the entire scam."

"Where's Guzman now?" Wally asked in a more even tone, as if he was just coming to grips with the gravity of the situation.

Finch shrugged again. "I don't know. He's worried. He's done time twice already. He knows on the third strike it could be for life. If he's smart he'll move to a country with no US extradition treaties. Venezuela. Maybe Ecuador."

Wally rolled his head from side to side with a doubtful look. "All right. Will, what's your theory on this?"

Finch placed his hands on the table. "It begins with the list. With what we know for sure. Three dead already. One of them is Martin Fast. Let's start with him."

He glanced at the ceiling and continued. "John Doe carries a .38 pistol in the pocket of an Armani suit"—he waved a hand at the jacket—"over the jacket he wears a sweatshirt with a hoodie so he can cover his face. Sometime after the debate with Kali Rood, he follows Martin Fast to the Triple-8 on Market Street. Before he enters the store he pulls the hood over his head, draws the gun into his hand, and does the robbery. He starts screaming to convince everyone he's out of his mind on drugs, grabs all the bills from the cash register, points the pistol at Fast and executes him: one shot to the chest, one to the head."

He paused as if the events were just now lining up in his mind and the sequence finally stood in proper order.

"Then he shoves the cash into one pocket in the Armani jacket, and the gun back into the other. Before anyone can catch their breath, he's out the door and walks the two blocks back to City Hall. He enters the bathroom, tugs off the sweatshirt and the jacket so he can wash up at the sink and remove any traces of gunshot residue.

"Then Raymond Guzman follows him into the bathroom where Toby Squire is hiding in the last stall. Apart from John Doe, Guzman sees the room is empty, gives the signal—a loud cough—and Squire appears. Together they make short work of the killer. Squire grabs the Armani jacket and hoodie and hobbles out of City Hall. Guzman stays behind to run interference, which turns into a brief sparring match with the gunman. As of yesterday, Guzman's still sporting a bruise from the punch he took under one eye."

He stopped so that everyone could absorb the story. Was it probable? More important, was there a better, more likely scenario? He couldn't think of one.

"And that's the last contact he had with Toby Squire?" Wally asked after no one offered any alternatives.

"Guzman says he never saw him again. I believe him. I saw Squire with the jacket in the park. After he shot himself,

Officer DeRosa said she found a wad of cash in his pocket. That means Squire had already taken the pistol and the cash from the jacket. After he'd emptied the pockets, he had no need for the jacket itself and left it behind. But he was wearing a hoodie sweatshirt when he was killed—probably the one used during the murder."

Then a new idea occurred to Finch. "What if we can get the cashier at the Triple-8 to identify the sweatshirt?"

"Wouldn't help your theory," Eve said. "It would only support the SFPD claim that Toby Squire killed Martin Fast. They've already locked this case in the morgue. Don't give them another reason to throw away the key."

"Right." Finch nodded when he realized the error. It was too easy to overthink a theory and lead yourself astray.

Everyone slipped into a moment of dazed silence. To Finch, the mood had shifted to a realization that they faced an insurmountable problem with little prospect of finding a solution. When he recovered his composure, Wally set his hands on the table and lowered his head. He reminded Finch of a pit bull preparing for a scrap.

"All right, this is what we do. Our guiding principle is this: we will chase this story down until the SFPD reopen the murder case of Martin Fast. Gabe, I want you to keep working that list. Keep digging for commonalities, diversions, idiosyncrasies. If ten of them all use Delsey Toilet Tissue, I want to know it."

Finkleman replied with a leaden nod of his head.

"Fiona, time to get the other writers in on this. I want you to assign Brian Stutz and Jenny Wengler to profile the two victims other than Martin Fast. Who were they again?" —he turned to Finkleman—"a Brit and a postdoc at MIT, right?"

"That's right."

"Okay then. Fiona, get them to profile these guys. First their career credentials, then their last days and hours leading up to their deaths. Tell them I said if there's any hint that they were murdered, they're to stick it in the lead paragraph."

Turning to Eve, he said, "Do you want to be part of this?"

"I already am. Next to Will, I've got more skin in this game than anyone."

"All right. I know the SFPD don't want to reopen this case but they'll be forced to if we break the story and provide some evidence. Find out what it will take and work with Fiona on that. Maybe that jacket still holds some secrets. Fingerprints. Gunshot residues. Whatever." He paused to consider any other angles. "Is there something else you think we should do to jack-hammer this thing open?"

Eve nodded. "If there's evidence of foul play in the death at MIT, that'll bring in the FBI. And murder of the Brit means Interpol gets pulled in."

Wally rolled his lips together. "Yeah. It's that big, isn't it."

Again, everyone paused to absorb the implications.

"And Will," Wally continued in a tone to suggest he was wrapping up the meeting, "I want you to write the story we've got so far. Squire, Guzman, John Doe, the jacket and gun."

"What about the list itself? Do we identify all twenty-four names?"

Fiona raised a finger in the air and leaned in. "In the last four months ISIS has published *nine* kill lists. The latest had eighty-three *hundred* names. So far no one's been harmed. But this"—she lifted the sheet of paper in her hand—"*this* is different."

Wally nodded to acknowledge her note of caution. "Okay, you can mention the list but don't identify anyone on it until I check with Lou Levine in Legal. All right, what else you got?"

Finch looked away, then turned back to Wally. "I'm going to call the four other reporters named on the list. Just feel them out, try to get their angle on this thing without letting them know our concerns. Not yet, anyway."

Wally pondered this and then nodded. "Be careful. I don't want anyone to break the story ahead of the *eXpress.*"

Finch winced at this. There was no changing Wally. The veteran newsman always put the story ahead of the people involved. Including Will himself.

"All right. I get it." Finch felt a wave of adrenaline surge through his chest. "But there is something else. Something I've got to talk to you about. Alone."

After the others left the room, Finch closed the boardroom door and sat beside Wally.

"Look, this isn't just another story," he said and rapped his knuckles on the desk top.

"Yeah, obviously." Wally waved a hand as if he wanted to dismiss his last comment about breaking the story. He closed his eyes and looked away. "I know. It's a direct threat."

"You ever get in a fight so desperate you knew from the start someone's going to die?"

Wally balled his right hand into a fist and gently covered

it with his left hand. "In Vietnam. We had more than a few days like that. Same as you in Iraq, I guess."

Finch nodded to acknowledge their common bond. "And then with Witowsky and Malinin."

"Yeah. Right." Wally's face softened as he recalled Finch and Eve's battle last year. "That's what this is like, isn't it."

Finch gazed through the interior window that looked from the boardroom onto the bog. Fiona stood with a hand perched on her hip as she talked to Brian Stutz and Jenny Wengler, likely coaching them on the stories Wally had assigned to them.

"This time I'm not going to wait for it, Wally." He kept his eyes on Fiona. She leaned over Stutz's desk and pointed to something on his computer. "I'm not going to let them bring this into my home. Not to Eve."

Wally uncurled his fist and set his hands flat on the table.

"Not after what Toby Squire did to her last year." Finch turned back to Wally and narrowed his eyes. "I'm not going to let anything like that happen again."

"No." Wally leaned forward, just enough to divert Finch's penetrating gaze. "So what are you thinking?"

Finch stood up and walked to the window, then turned back to Wally. "I'm going to run this fucking ball into their end zone. First, I'm going to write these stories to flush them out. Get the cops and FBI focussed on them. Let them feel some heat. Then after their next hit, if it comes"—he shifted his weight from one foot to the other and back again —*"when* it comes, I'm going after them."

"Mmm." Wally's voice had a note of resignation. Then he said, "What can I do?"

Finch walked back to the desk and leaned toward Wally. "You can keep Eve here. Do *not* let her follow me. Get her to do the background digging with Fiona and Finkleman. Get her to bridge into the SFPD and FBI. And Interpol if it comes to that."

Wally smiled with a look of forbearance. "You think anybody can hold her back? I tried to do that after you were accused of assassinating Senator Whitelaw." An expression of hopeless folly crossed his face as he recalled his efforts to keep Eve at bay. "And we should both thank God that she didn't listen to me."

"Not this time, Wally." He inched forward so that his boss couldn't mistake the expression on his face. "This time, I'm counting on you to keep her here."

It took Finch two hours to write the story that he hoped would break open the case. The key to everything was the list itself. After he named the first three victims he continued the article by describing the supporting elements. The suicide of Toby Squire, his involvement with Raymond Guzman and their method of surveying public washrooms and mugging unsuspecting loners between scheduled security checks. He identified the Armani jacket, the gun, the undisclosed sum of cash in Squire's possession. The missing link was the identity of John Doe, the mugging victim and quite possibly Martin Fast's murderer. A killer still at large.

As he sat at his desk in the bog reviewing his article, he could hear Fiona talking to Stutz and Wengler. They were working out the details about their sides of the story, the backgrounds on the two other victims. As he listened to them grappling with the journalistic fundamentals to the crimes—who, what, where, when, why and how—he realized the scope of reporting on the murder spree was expanding. But where was the center to it all?

The question brought him back to the morning of Martin Fast's murder. The string of events began at City Hall and his acrimonious debate with Kali Rood. The virgin queen. It was Jayne Waterston who'd come up with this moniker—and Jayne herself was on the hit list. Number eight. Could she provide some insight?

He checked his watch. Coming up to five—eight o'clock in New York City. He made a mental note to contact Waterston in the morning. By then Lou Levine would likely green-light the publication of the twenty-four names and Finch could begin to call all the people on the list—beginning with the identified journalists. He'd start with Waterston and see if she'd be willing to collaborate with him. If she felt vulnerable, she might even share her sources, especially if he could convince her to work together with him. Share the by-line, share the source. A common quid pro quo amongst writers of every stripe.

That evening Finch returned to the cottage on Alta Street before Eve. She had to settle the final legal issues with the Parson brothers that would complete her purchase of ten percent of the *eXpress*. While he waited, Will sautéed some prawns and scallops, stirred them into a fresh marinara sauce and brought a pot of water to a boil, then set it aside and grated two cups of parmesan cheese. Once Eve arrived he'd prepare the pasta and they could enjoy the meal on the rooftop deck. She loved shellfish and he wanted the dinner to be special. He knew it might be their last meal together for some time. For how long, no one could predict.

With the meal preparations completed, he climbed up to the second floor and unloaded his courier bag on his office desk. He removed all the non-essentials and carried the bag to the bedroom and began to rummage through his dresser and closet. He packed the bag with two clean shirts, a pair of pants, hiking shorts, three pairs of socks and underwear. He tossed his razor, toothbrush and toothpaste into an inner pouch. The basics. When he was satisfied he returned to the office and added the tools of the trade that he would normally carry on a road trip: his laptop, coiled notebook and pen, the charging cords for his phone and computer, latex gloves, two or three evidence sample bags, a multitool knife, his lock-pick wallet, micro-zoom binoculars, flashlight, Ray-Bans.

In an afterthought he took his passport from the strong box in the office closet, along with the forged identity and credit cards for Joel Griffin. He'd acquired the phony IDs last year after he and Eve had to travel incognito from Washington following Senator Whitelaw's suicide. At the time he determined he'd never be caught in the same predicament again. He now knew it was the right decision.

He double-checked the documents and ID cards then zipped them into the inner pocket of the courier bag. Then he walked down to the main floor and stowed the pack in the hallway closet. It was better that Eve didn't observe him making these preparations. The last thing he needed tonight was an emotional distraction.

A moment later he heard the key turn in the front door lock and Eve entered the hallway. She smiled. A look that said, *mission accomplished.*

"You get your ten percent of the *eXpress?*"

"Yes!"

She slipped her arm around his back and kissed him on

the cheek. He turned his head to one side so that their lips joined in a warm kiss.

"Then let's celebrate," he whispered in her ear. It would be a good night for both of them, he thought, and he kissed her again.

"Let me get dinner going first," she said and pulled free of his arms.

"Nope. Already done." He smiled again.

"Really? So, that's two reasons to celebrate."

They sat on the roof deck in the Adirondack deck chairs that Eve had purchased at FL!PP, a used furniture shop in Russian Hill, and ate the pasta dinners with the plates perched on their laps. The prospect overlooked the financial district. Beyond lay San Francisco Bay and in the distance—on a clear day, at least—they could see the hills rising over Berkeley. But this evening they could only imagine the panorama; a pack of heavy clouds had gathered above the basin and obscured the distant views.

As they ate Eve talked about the details of her purchase of the *eXpress*. Just ten percent, but a legitimate piece, she argued, of what one day might become a bigger slice of the pie. Especially if she could help Wally re-orient the paper to the new reporting mandate. They both knew the opportunities were limitless. However, corporate criminals were usually so devious, so smart, so well-funded that it would take an equally savvy and well-resourced investigation to bring the culprits to light. As she finished her meal, she began to focus on their current situation.

"So before I left the office," she said as she dabbed at her lips with a napkin, "Wally said your latest story is causing a stir. Trending somewhere in Twitter's top twenty. It also looks like Lou Levine will give the go-ahead to publish the names on the list."

"Good." Will set his plate on the deck and folded his hands together. "Maybe it'll be enough to flush these bastards out."

"Maybe." She shrugged with a hint of uncertainty. "One thing's for sure, you'll flush out the SFPD and FBI. Now that we've established criminal plausibility, they'll have to respond. They'll want the list, the jacket and an interview with you."

"Let Wally give them the list." He tried to smile. "And I'll talk their ears off if it'll help."

She looked away. "I'm not sure that it will."

"And your suggestion is?"

"That you get a gun."

"You know my answer to that."

"Don't be a fool."

He scoffed at that. Over the years he'd seen how weapons only increased the danger around him. As soon as someone pulls a gun other options tend to narrow. With two guns in play, the event horizon becomes one-dimensional. Someone either gets hurt or dies.

"Then at least you should hire some protection."

He glanced at her with a look of surprise. "You can't be serious."

She rolled her lips together and considered the alternatives. "So what are you thinking?"

As he studied her their eyes wove together.

"You're not going to like it."

"No?" Her face took on a worried expression.

"The next time there's a hit, I'm going after them." He waited a moment and then added, "Alone."

She let out a wary laugh. "No, you're not. It doesn't work that way."

"Yes, it does. I need you to handle everything here. The

SFPD, the FBI—whatever. I need someone to crack the research open on this. You and Finkleman. Your friend, Leanne. Look Eve, we have no idea where this is headed. But it's not going to be like before. With Toby Squire—hell, you almost died."

"So did you."

"Yeah, but this time I have no choice. *You do.*"

She stood up and walked to the rooftop railing, inhaled a long draught of the evening air, then turned back to face him. "You know it's crazy, don't you?"

"What's crazy?"

"Your idea that anyone you love has to die."

Finch walked across the deck and stood beside her. He put his arm around her shoulder and toyed with the collar on her blouse. "No one *has* to die," he said in a quiet voice. "It's just that too often, *they do*. So it's all about being safe. Making *you* safe," he added.

"Well, I suppose I should be flattered." She turned to one side so that his arm slipped away from her.

"Flattered?"

"Maybe. If this is your way of telling me you love me." She looked at him and waited. When he failed to reply, she continued. "Do you know that you've never told me that? That you love me."

He nodded with a look of regret. "Of course I do. You have to know it."

"Know what? That you love me. Or you can't admit it."

He smiled, an acknowledgement that she'd cornered him in her little web of words.

"That I love you," he said with a light gasp. Why had he held this back for so long? After all, it was true. In an instant he felt the foolishness of his on-going restraint, then the guilt for the pain he'd caused her.

"What?" She held a hand to her ear. "Sorry, I missed that."

He let out a chuckle. She was pulling this off with more class than he could muster. Time to capitulate, he decided. Wave the flag of surrender and marshal all the pomp and circumstance of a complete confession of love. He dropped to one knee, took her hand in his and gazed up at her.

"Eve Noon," he began, "I love you more than the day itself. I love you and I promise with my life to keep you safe."

She smiled. Her face flushed with a warm radiance, as if she'd finally won a prize that had been out of reach for far too long.

"Okay. That's enough." She pulled him up by the hand and into her arms. "But don't ask me to marry you. I won't have it. Not from anyone."

He nodded with a sense of empathy for her. No matter who she loved, or for how long, Eve would never surrender her freedom. And thank God for it.

"Isn't this when we're supposed to make our way to the bedroom and shut off the morning alarm?"

"It could be," she whispered and kissed the side of his throat. "But why no alarm?"

"Because I'm going to make love to you straight through the night. There'll be no sleep for anybody."

She laughed and pulled him toward the staircase that led down to their room. "Darling, you have only the smallest idea what it takes to love me all night long." She paused on the steps to kiss him again. "And you are about to learn a lesson you will never forget."

Chapter Eleven

The early morning rain-showers relieved some of the humidity and smog in midtown Manhattan. But it offered little redemption from the unrelenting heat that had gripped the Eastern Seaboard from Florida up to Boston over the past month.

Jayne Waterston sat at the desk next to her apartment window overlooking East Seventy-third Street and watched the raindrops drizzle against the windshields of the passing cars. She took another moment to study the bronze Cadillac parked across the street in front of the Bohemian National Hall. Most days parking was impossible on Seventy-third, but somehow the same Caddy had steered into the same parking slot the last three mornings in a row. Either coincidence or good luck. Or maybe a personal situation arranged by the manager of the Hall, Georg Svoboda, whom Jayne had interviewed when she was writing the feature article about Syrian refugees scrambling up the chain of east European countries last fall.

She shrugged off the thought and turned her attention

back to her laptop. Today she had to finish the story on Donald Trump's latest allegation of "Crooked Hillary's" email scandals. The FBI and Justice Department had concluded that no criminal charges were warranted against Clinton. Trump charged the system was rigged. And journalists everywhere eagerly reported the ongoing circus.

Jayne, however, couldn't be more exasperated. She'd hoped to challenge the candidates' positions on climate change policy and green science. But before she could pitch a string of article ideas to her freelance employers, the election had dissolved into a series of ad hominem attacks, rumors, libel and slander. A reality-TV election. If that's what the media wanted, that's what they would get. And contrary to her best intentions, Jayne was up to her nose in the slime.

When her phone rang she paused. It could be a welcome distraction, but the call display showed a 415 area code. San Francisco? Why would Robert be calling her now —after two years? She clicked on the third ring and waited to hear the voice on the other end of the line. If it was Robert, she'd tell him to go screw—

"Hello? Is Jayne Waterston there?"

She paused for a beat. "Sorry, yes. Who's calling?"

"This is Will Finch from the *San Francisco eXpress.*"

"Will Finch?" She switched the phone to her good ear and set her elbows on the table. "Hi, how can I help you?"

"I'm calling about a couple of things. Uh, listen, give me a sec, I just need to go somewhere more private."

"Sure."

Will Finch, she thought. Do I actually have *the* Will Finch on the phone? She glanced at the coffee table. She'd just bought his book at Barnes & Noble on Saturday. Hadn't started it yet, but—

"Sorry," Will said. "I'm just in the office and something's going on in the bog, so I had to grab my editor's office."

"The bog?"

"Our newsroom. Speaking of which I just heard you left *The Village Voice*. Their receptionist passed on your number."

"Yeah, since last fall. After three years it was time to move on. By the way, it's strange that you called me. I mean, last weekend I bought *Who Shot The Sheriff?* I haven't started it yet, but the reviews are through the roof."

"Right." He sounded distracted, she thought, as if he'd forgotten why he'd called. Then in a subdued voice he continued. "Look, something troubling has come up here."

"Oh?"

"Yeah. Earlier this month I covered what was supposed to be a climate change debate between Martin Fast and Kali Rood."

"Oh my God, I heard. And then he was shot, right?"

"Yeah. An hour later. On Market Street."

"Unbelievable."

"That's the thing. It *is* unbelievable. Anyway, just to get her perspective on the murder, I interviewed Kali Rood. And I know you did a huge feature on her last fall when you were still at *The Voice*—'The Virgin Queen.'"

"The one and only. She's a grade-A pretender, believe me. And I know she'd say the same thing about me. About most journalists, probably. You don't have to be special. She might even have words for you too, Will."

"Oh, she does." He paused a moment. "Listen, this is going to sound kind of strange, but I want to ask about your sources for the story."

"My sources?" She laughed with a nervous chuckle and glanced around the room. How could he ask for her sources? "You know I can't tell you that. Why are you even asking?"

"Because I don't have time to dig this up myself. Something's come up and I need to know who you talked to and what files you found."

Jayne felt a sudden urge to hang up—and she would have until she reminded herself who she was talking to. "Look, you need to explain this to me."

"Okay. I was working on the story about Rood and Martin Fast's debate. And few days later something came into my possession." He hesitated. "A list."

"What kind of list?"

"A list of names. Twenty-four names. My name is on it, and so is yours."

"Really?" She stood up and gazed at the bronze Caddy parked across the street. Was someone sitting behind the wheel? Hard to tell through the smoked glass windows of the car. "So, it's what? A list of journalists covering climate change?"

"Five of them are in the media. Three in politics. But most of the others are researchers and scientists."

"Some kind of honor roll thing?"

"No. We think it's a kill list."

"What?!" She sat in the chair again and propped her head against one hand. "What the fuck are you saying? And who's *we?*"

"My editorial team. Check the *eXpress* web site. We put the story up yesterday."

"Just a second." Jayne put her phone down and brought up the web page on her laptop. She scanned the article and then read the headline again. *Three Dead in Four Weeks.*

"So what does this mean?" she asked when she recovered her poise. "I've been threatened before, but I don't like the look of this."

"Neither do I. That's why I want you to share your sources with me."

She waited a moment to consider this. What exactly was his game?

"Tell you what, you email me this list of twenty-four names. I'll look at it and get back to you"

"You'll have it in a minute," he said.

"And if I open my sources to you—if, and that's a *huge* if, so don't count on it, okay—then we share the story credit for anything on this going forward. Agreed?" She heard a rustling on his end of the line. As she waited, she pressed the heel of her hand against her head until it hurt. *"I said, do you agree?"*

"Sorry, I was just sending the list to you."

She checked her email service. Nothing. She clicked the refresh button. Nothing.

"Look, this isn't just about the story," he said in a pleading tone. "This is more about survival, Jayne."

"Survival?" She let out a pish of air as his email appeared in her in-box. "Okay, I got your email. So if we're doing this together, you have to know something about me. I have conditions."

"All right. Name them."

"One: don't contact my sources without asking me first. Two: do not claim credit for the work that I've done. And three: do not fuck with me—and I mean that in every conceivable way. And that's no pun, either, okay." She raised her voice so that he'd make no mistake about her determination. She'd had enough of ballsy editors and so-called collaborators. "I mean it."

"Okay. I get it."

Second Life

He sounded contrite. A good sign. But could she trust the tone of his voice? Was that enough?

"All right, I'll get back to you after I've gone over this list. But just so you know, I'm not sure about any of this. I mean this is a fucking shock."

"Yeah. I know."

She clicked off the phone and printed a copy of the list. Then she stood at the edge of her window and examined the Cadillac parked in front of the Bohemian National Hall. She checked her watch. Time for a break. A little earlier than normal, but it seemed like a good idea to get out of her apartment and plant herself at a table in a cafe. Somewhere public, open, safe.

To prepare herself, she decided to apply some internal fortification. A wee toot for the road. She took the collapsible two-step stool from behind her bedroom door and propped it open beneath the kitchen cupboard. Standing tippy-toed on the top step she reached to the back of the highest shelf and clasped the baggie between two fingers. She carried it over to the table, slid the tip of a fingernail inside the plastic seal and drew it along the width of the bag. Then she opened the narrow drawer in the desk and fumbled a moment for the antique silver salt spoon that she'd purchased in the West Village.

"Ah, there you are, my friend," she whispered to herself and dipped the spoon into the finely granulated cocaine. She pressed a finger against the left side of her nose and held the spoon under her right nostril. Then with a quick snort she loaded the coke along her sinus membranes. She applied the same remedy to her left nostril, sniffled loudly and rubbed her fingers over her flared nostrils. Then she sat back and rolled her head in several back-and-forth rotations over her shoulders.

"Ohhhh," she moaned in a long, ecstatic sigh. "My-my-my. Just what the good doctor ordered."

Rain, snow, sleet or hail—Jayne Waterston had become the US Postal Service of freelance writers. Despite the obstacles, she delivered. Every day she nailed down two or three interviews before nine AM when most of her sources could spare five minutes to cough up some usable quotes. Then she'd write until noon, take a half-hour break, and cap off the morning with a sequence of yoga asanas. Over the lunch hour she'd call her list of editors and see where she stood on the five or six story ideas she'd pitched the previous week. After the calls, if she felt the juice, she could write for another hour. If not, then she'd pack up her laptop and notes and trek over to Klutch where she'd research and write uninterrupted for another two hours. Late afternoons were reserved for networking. Fortunately, New York City offered a plethora of lunches, mingles, and shake-n-takes where freelancers of every stripe shook hands and took their rivals' business cards. Evenings were reserved for her increasingly varied social life—which these days often included a freelance hook-up with benefits.

Although it was almost twenty blocks up Second Avenue from her apartment, Klutch had become Jayne Waterston's favorite working cafe. It offered a well-lit space, decent coffee and no distracting music. She fancied the rustic atmosphere, bare brick walls, the Queen Anne chairs. And after she left her job at *The Village Voice*, she realized she needed some form of exercise—a stress-buster—and the hike back and forth to the Yorkville area provided a daily

Second Life

regime that dragged her out of her apartment into the real world.

Sometimes the stress and whirlwind nature of her life left her feeling a little dizzy. She could see the possibility ahead of her, a mental landmark of sorts, where she might spin out of control and lose her bearings. It seemed quite possible that she could live four or five different lives all at the same time. The writer, the activist, the rebel, the mythic hero, the sex bomb. To complicate things, she suspected that each of these personas could dwell in various zones of what she called the psychic bubble, a sort of shared headspace populated by millions of New Yorkers.

So which part of the bubble do you inhabit today?

That was the question in Jayne Waterston's mind as she rattled down the three flights of stairs from her three-room walk-up and opened the front door onto Seventy-third Street. The paranoid part, the realistic part or the ostrich part? She liked to imagine that she resided in the left-of-center zone of realism, somewhere above the dumbed-down unionist block, and a little left of the LGBTQ partition (her favorite neighborhood by far). But she detested the ostriches of the world, though she admitted that she had spent a good deal of her early twenties with her head stuck in the desert of nineteenth century novels, devoutly ignoring the everyday trauma that surrounded her. And frankly, New York City had more than its fair share of public trauma.

But the paranoid sector, the place that seemed to discretely encroach on her upper east side apartment—that zone was amorphous, a cloud that could sweep into your life without notice. There were no street signs and curb markers to let you know when you exited realist normal and entered the labyrinth of paranoia. However, she had her suspicions as she stepped onto the curb. And she knew from experience that the best way to hack out of the jungle of paranoia was to confront the most obvious, most pressing anxiety that hit you.

And today the key source of anxiety was the bronze 2015 Cadillac SRX parked in front of the Bohemian National Hall. Still buzzing from the twin blasts of cocaine, she crossed the street and paused to study the license plate. Then she took a photo of it with her Samsung. Just in case.

She rubbed the back of her hand over her nostrils as she recalled her twin brother's admonition ten years ago when they walked hand-in-hand into the morgue in Buffalo. They'd just turned sixteen and as they rode the elevator down to the basement of the Mercy Hospital she felt her heart sink into her belly. She entered the windowless room where they had to identify the corpses of their parents. Then she felt her heart come to a stop when she saw their cool, still bodies lying side-by-side. They'd been killed that summer morning when a city bus blew out a tire, skidded across the median on South Park Avenue and crushed the Ford Taurus. Their parents were on the way to pick up Jayne and Simon following the junior mixed doubles tournament at the Amherst Audubon Golf Course. They'd shot two above par and moved into the final round.

"Be brave. Take a deep breath and be brave," Simon had said.

Jayne took a deep breath as she stood on the sidewalk opposite her apartment and examined the Cadillac. Not a scratch on it. Still unable to make out the presence of anyone sitting behind the smoked glass, she tapped a knuckle on the front passenger window. Nothing. She tapped a second time, louder. "Hey, anyone in there?" Definitely nothing.

She pressed a finger to the side of her right nostril and

sniffed the air—then repeated the process with her left nostril—and waited a long moment to see if she'd stirred up any ghosts in the world of paranoia-ville. Convinced that she could now safely depart this micro-vector of her delusions, she crossed behind the car and stepped onto the street. Yeah, get back to reality, she whispered to herself. Stop pretending you're so special that the world is conspiring against you. *You're not special and you should know it by now.* She picked up her pace, rounded the corner onto Second Avenue and began the hike up to Klutch.

But once she was out of sight of the Caddy, she couldn't see the door open or the tall man in the iron-gray leather jacket ease out of the car. She couldn't see his gaunt face, his weedy hair or his ice-blue eyes. Or the rough scar that zig-zagged from his right ear past his neck to his shoulder.

During her walk up Second Avenue, the misting rain morphed into a steady drizzle. Before Jayne entered the cafe she took a moment to shake out her curls and primp her hair. After she had her cappuccino in hand, she settled in an upholstered chair next to the long brick wall in Klutch and took a moment to organize her laptop, phone and notebook in a tidy arrangement on the table.

She spent five minutes examining the list of names that Finch had sent her. Because she'd been covering the environment in one way or another for the past ten years, she knew most of the people, if not personally, then by reputation alone. The common denominator was not their decisive research or publications (though they'd all won some acclaim) it was their outspoken behavior.

Over the past decade they'd screamed their warnings to

anyone who would listen. By 2100 the lights would go out. The waters would rise. The cities would be swamped. The bees would die and locusts would consume the surviving vegetation.

But the omens seemed so improbable, so remote from the latte lifestyle embraced by urban bohemians. Perhaps that was why so many of the science oracles became so shrill and unrelenting. And why they were now targeted for destruction.

However, of all the names on the list, Will Finch seemed out of place. He'd only taken up the cause in the past year. Granted, the feature story he'd written on Dr. Martin Fast was penetrating and incisive. Fast himself seemed unable to articulate the human consequences of permafrost melt in the common idiom. But Finch's exposition had been brilliant. For once, the pending catastrophe in the lower Arctic circle could be understood by anyone in the tenth grade. Thanks to Finch.

But ... no thanks, Finch. She decided to decline his offer to collaborate. Why bother? She didn't need him or his demands to see her sources. She had the hit list, she knew the science, and she could approach the listed names one-by-one and crank out a series of articles over the next week. The *Times* and *Post* would be outbidding one another to grab this. Maybe fifteen thousand dollars for an exclusive five-part series.

The crowd in Klutch now filled all the tables and chairs and Jayne was surrounded by people talking in groups or by the soloists like herself who worked on their laptops or ticked away on their tablets and phones. She checked her watch and realized that before anything else she had to complete the article for *Gawker*. Halfway through her second cappuccino, she'd almost finished the piece on Trump and

Clinton's green policies. Or lack thereof. At first the story seemed impossible to write. But when she finished the first draft, she felt relieved that she'd devised a piece of snappy satire likely to get a nod from the editor. At the top of the page she typed in a headline, a brazen rip-off of Eddie Cantor's 1922 hit tune: *PRESIDENTIAL CANDIDATES IN HARMONY ON EMPTY CLIMATE POLICY: "Yes! We Have No Bananas."*

After a quick read-through, she closed the lid on her laptop and glanced around. The man at the next table caught her eye. He wore a gray leather jacket and had a thatch of hair that had never seen a comb.

"Excuse me," she said in a low voice. "Can you watch my stuff while I take a break?" She tilted her chin toward her purse, computer and note pad.

He studied her a moment before answering. His fingers traced a knotted scar that dropped from his ear to his shirt collar. Jayne thought he might decline her request and the delay made her hesitate.

"Oh, forget it," she said before he replied. "I'll just take everything with me."

"No, it's fine." He forced a smile to his lips. "You can trust me."

Trust me. Amber alert. How often had she heard that? But now she felt a twinge of embarrassment. She'd asked him for help, he'd accepted, so now what? "You sure? I don't want to be a bother."

"Look, I'm good. But I've got to run soon. How long?"

She held up a hand, all digits pointing to the ceiling.

"Five minutes. Call of nature." She smiled to let him know she was capable of small intimacies with strangers.

"Fine." He nodded and turned his attention back to his newspaper.

Ten minutes later Jayne returned to the table with her phone clutched in her hand. She hadn't meant to take so long, but from the bathroom stall she'd ended up trading texts with Brittany. A moment of anxiety swept through her when she saw that the stranger she'd assigned to mind her laptop and purse had disappeared. She sat at the table and checked her bag, then opened the laptop. Nothing amiss. But no sign of the man or his newspaper or jacket.

She decided to proofread the green politics story once more before sending it to Maxwell at *Gawker*. She sipped at the half-cup of cappuccino, then drank it off in one shot when she realized it had turned borderline cold. She imagined that Maxwell would be impressed to see the story arrive in his in-box two hours before deadline. She had a hunch that he liked her and the prospect of more gigs with him seemed within reach. A monthly column with *Gawker?* Ka-ching.

The first sign of trouble came with the taut pain in the pit of her stomach. She blinked. What's that? She set her hands on the chair armrests and tried to think. Fuck, *what is that?* Then a bolt of pain shot from her stomach through the top of her head. She stood up as a wave of dizziness washed through her and she tried to cry out. A dash of vomit burst from her lips and in an instant of crystalline clarity Jayne Waterston realized that she would now die.

She had no opportunity to beg for reprieve. No chance to say goodbye, to express forgiveness or love. When her legs buckled under her and she toppled to the floor between two tables, all that she could see was the fading light. And then, nothing.

Chapter Twelve

A few hours after Finch's article appeared in the *eXpress*, the FBI demanded to know the names on the list. A few hours after that, they told him they needed to interview everyone involved with the story: researchers, writers, editors. Everyone including all the *eXpress* sources.

FBI Agents Lorna Munn and John Elphick began their interrogation of Finch a little after three-thirty. Following Finch, they planned to talk to Eve, Fiona, Finkleman and Wally. Wally agreed to allow the cops to use the *eXpress* boardroom for their interviews in exchange for permitting Lou Levine, the company lawyer, to sit in on each conversation. The alternative was to require everyone to troop down to the interrogation rooms at the Bureau's regional offices.

As Will walked into the boardroom he felt more confident now that the FBI had been assigned to the investigation. It meant that someone at the top had pushed the SFPD off the case and demonstrated the seriousness of the situation. Finally.

He draped the Armani jacket over the chair beside him

and then sat down beside Lou who was already engaged in conversation. Lou nervously tapped the edges of the agents' business cards against the wood surface of the table, a distraction that made Finch wonder what they might have discussed before he entered the boardroom.

The two agents introduced themselves, shook his hand and passed him their business cards. Lorna Munn held up a palm-size recorder so everyone could see that she was recording the interview.

"For the record, the tape is just to help us keep the facts straight. At this time no one here is under investigation. All right?"

She paused so Lou and Will could absorb the rules at play. When they nodded, she continued.

"Okay. Time is critical here, so I suggest we get down to it." Munn tipped her chin toward the chair beside Finch. "That's the jacket?"

"As requested." Finch smiled, an effort to show that he'd complied with the first item on their list of demands.

Munn tugged on a pair of gloves, crossed the room behind the table and lifted the jacket in her hands. She held it up to the light and examined it for a moment, then carried it back to Detective Elphick who gave it a cursory glance. She then slipped the jacket into a laundromat-sized evidence bag, draped it over the end of the table and removed her gloves.

As she handled the jacket and evidence bag, Elphick leaned forward.

"A lot of people like to think the more the merrier," he said, "but when it comes to evidence, less is always more. Especially with fingerprints and DNA. So ... who else has touched it?" He spoke with a flat midwestern accent. From his natty attire, Finch assumed he was from Chicago. Likely the North Side.

"A woman named Alice—last name unknown—who gave it to me in the Hyde-Turk Mini Park, then me and Eve Noon," Finch said. He decided to omit Toby Squire, at least for now. The conversation would swing around to him soon enough.

"Noon. Ex-SFPD?" Elphick asked with a frown.

Finch studied him a moment. Almost four years after her dismissal from the city police force Eve still bore the reputation of a saint—or pariah—depending on your point of view. Apparently her renown had spread to the FBI.

"Yes."

"Then we'll need both your prints," he said.

"I think you've got mine on file. And she's already registered with the locals." Finch put on an amused look. Obviously Elphick hadn't performed a background check before he took on this assignment.

"Yeah, we do." Munn shot Elphick a look. "From last year. Senator Whitelaw's suicide."

Elphick muttered something to himself and glanced away.

"So you found a list," Munn continued.

"Yes." Lou Levine pointed to the sheet of paper in front of him. "We sent it to you soon after it came to light."

"So who else knows about it?" she asked.

"The four of us plus some staff. Fiona Page, Wally Gimbel and Gabe Finkleman," Finch said as he pointed through the interior window to his colleagues working in the bog. "And Eve Noon."

"And that's it?"

Finch nodded. "By the way, I see the Twitter page has come down. Can we assume the Bureau pulled it?"

"Let's stay focused on one thing at a time." Agent Munn drew herself up in the chair, a movement to establish her dominance in the proceedings. "Now from the beginning, Mr. Finch. Take us down memory lane on this one." She fixed a thin smile on her lips and rotated a finger above the table surface, a gesture that said, get on with it.

Will had prepared for a grilling, and he led the investigators through the sequence of events as he knew them. When he revealed that Raymond Guzman served as Toby Squire's accomplice, he felt a pang of guilt. But he recalled that his only pledge to Guzman was to withhold his name for a single day. Perhaps by now Guzman had fled the country and taken up residence in a seaside village. A room with a view.

"Sounds like you mounted quite the investigative enterprise. You uncovered the identities of the twenty-four names. And you identified most of the players in the robbery." Agent Elphick nodded as if he himself couldn't have done much better.

"Except for John Doe." Will shook his head with a look of regret. "The man who owned the jacket. My guess is that he's the perp who murdered Dr. Martin Fast on Market Street."

"How do you figure that?" Munn asked.

"Squire used the same pistol to shoot himself. He stole the gun along with a wad of cash from John Doe's Armani suit jacket. But when Martin Fast was killed, Squire and Guzman were two blocks away in City Hall, setting up their next mugging." In fact, Finch couldn't be sure of the timing sequence at all. But by stating this with such certainty, he was making a play that he hoped would draw out some unknown details from his interrogators.

A moment of silence settled on the room as everyone considered the possibilities.

"Could be," Elphick mused. "When you look at the CCTV footage from City Hall gallery. You have the timing just about right."

Finch nodded his head in silence. He recalled scanning the ceiling of the men's room for cameras. While he'd seen nothing obvious, at the time it didn't occur to him that Squire's victim might have been recorded on a camera outside the door.

Munn coughed into her hand and continued. "Now I understand that you called a Ms. Jayne Waterston in New York City today."

Finch felt a ripple of surprise. Had the FBI tapped into his calls?

"Yeah, first thing this morning."

"Have you spoken to her before?"

"No. What's this about?"

"Let me ask the questions. It works better that way." Munn put on a faint smile. "How do you know her?"

"By reputation only. She's a colleague. Specializes in climate change journalism. Plus, she's on the list." Finch rolled his head toward the printed paper on the table in front of Lou. "Number eight."

"What did you discuss?"

Finch studied the wall for a moment. Where was this going?

"We talked about collaborating on a story. About Kali Rood."

"Who's she?" Munn asked.

"The head of a private foundation. Headquarters in New York City, with a training center in Ashland Oregon, outreach offices in the UK, Europe, Asia. It registers over fourteen thousand dues-paying members, each of them who hand over a thousand dollars a year for the privilege. Do the math. Every year she becomes a multimillionaire all over again." Finch shrugged knowing the information was readily at hand. "You can read my profile of her in the *eXpress*. Or Jayne Waterston's article in *The Village Voice*. That's where Kali Rood was dubbed the Virgin Queen."

"Waterston called her that?"

"Yeah."

Elphick leaned in again. "And did Waterston agree to collaborate with you?"

"Not yet. She wants a day to consider it."

"What else?" Elphick asked.

"What do you mean, *what else?*"

"Did you tell her she was on the list?"

"Yes."

"How did she react?"

"She said she'd been threatened before." Finch shrugged. "Look, what's this all about? Anyone working in this business longer than a year has been threatened."

"Does she know who else is on the list?" Munn asked.

"Yes."

She leaned forward. "You sent it to her?"

Finch paused to consider their line of interrogation. The questions were penning him into a box. He sensed that a trap lay just ahead.

"Previously you said the only people who'd seen the list worked for the *eXpress*. Now you're telling us Waterston has it," Elphick said. "Which is it?"

Lou raised a hand to take a moment to whisper into Will's ear. "Be careful. It's a criminal offense to lie to the FBI."

"Sorry," Will said. "Look, I'll be honest, I'm pretty shaken by all this. I simply forgot to mention her."

"And you sent the names to her. How?" Elphick's voice rose with a tone of disbelief. "By email?"

Finch nodded and realized he'd now made two mistakes. Forwarding an unencrypted message to Jayne Waterston was akin to sending a postcard through the mail. Anyone could read it as it passed from hand to hand. Nothing he could do about that now.

Elphick glanced at Munn, a look to encourage her to continue the interrogation.

"And are you planning to call the other names on this list?"

"Once Lou says so." Finch crooked a thumb to Lou Levine hoping to deflect their attention to the lawyer.

Lou smiled at Finch. "And effective right now, I'm giving that a green light."

"Good. Then I've got a job to do." Finch made a move to stand up, but Munn waved him back into his chair.

"Not so fast. We want to contact them first." She narrowed her eyes and stared at Lou.

"Sorry, we've got First Amendment rights," Lou said in a rising voice, "and a duty to inform the public of a present danger."

"We'd like you to give us one more day," Munn said. "Then it's your story."

Finch sensed an opportunity. Now he leaned toward Munn. "One day? In exchange for what?"

Again the agents traded a look. Elphick nodded to her, a gesture of approval. Finch guessed that they'd prepared an offer before the meeting got underway.

"Possibly in exchange for exclusive information." Munn

replied in an even, measured voice. "And I emphasize the word *possibly.*"

"What information?"

"About Jayne Waterston." Munn paused and then added, "Do we have a deal?"

"You know something about her that I can use to move this story forward?"

"Definitely. But you have to agree to not publish the list for twenty-four hours."

Finch glanced at Lou. He blinked, yes.

"All right, deal. So give."

Munn glanced at Elphick again.

"Jayne Waterston was murdered early this afternoon," he said.

"What?"

"Less than two hours ago." Elphick checked his watch. "A little after eleven o'clock our time."

"My God." Will struggled to respond. He'd spoken to her just this morning. Stick to the basics, he told himself. Focus. "How did she die?"

Munn shrugged and shook her head with a bleak expression that suggested the situation was more dire than anyone imagined.

"We're waiting on the ME report," she said. "But it looks like poison of some kind. She collapsed in a Manhattan coffee shop called Klutch. By the time an ambulance got her to a hospital, she was gone."

Will left the boardroom, walked through the bog to his cubicle and grabbed his courier bag from the footwell of his desk. On his way to the reception area he found Fiona and told her he had an urgent meeting and that he'd file a story on Jayne Waterston's murder before midnight.

"What?" she asked in a plaintive voice.

"Talk to Lou Levine."

He waved a hand back toward the boardroom and jogged along the hallway to the staircase exit. He clambered down the steps two at a time until he reached the building entrance on Mission Street. From there he strode up to the BART station on Market Street. Thirty minutes later he arrived at San Francisco International Airport. After a quick reconnaissance he discovered that United and Jet Blue still had unsold seats in their economy sections. He bought a window seat on Blue and made his way to their departure gate. While he waited to board he searched for breaking news about Waterston's murder on his laptop. A stroke of luck: so far no one had broken the story. Munn had given him an exclusive.

He opened a new file and began to type the first sentence that came to mind: *Jayne Waterston was pronounced dead on arrival after she was transported by ambulance to a local hospital from Klutch, a Manhattan cafe where authorities claim she may have been poisoned. The FBI is investigating her death in relation to a series of recent murders of climate change scientists and media advocates.*

Finch glanced at the time and realized he had twenty minutes before his plane would load. He knew he couldn't finish the story without any background research. Nonetheless, he plowed ahead and every time he needed to insert a fact or identify a source he wrote *X-check this-X*. Most of what he wrote was based on the conversation he'd had with Waterston that morning. Because of their interview, she knew about the list, and most of the players on it. He included a short bio of her and identified her as a leading reporter in the field of green science and politics. By the time the Jet Blue desk announced his boarding call, he'd written six paragraphs—just enough for the *eXpress* to claim a stake in breaking the story. He closed the file and emailed it to Fiona with a note: *Breaking fast. Get one of the team to lock in the facts wherever I've left a hole. Will check in from NYC.*

As he boarded the plane he called Eve. No answer. As he began to leave a message for her, his voice faltered. It was the first moment in the past two hours that he'd had a chance to reflect on what he was about to do.

"It's me. I'll call you from New York when I get a break. Check with Fiona, she knows what's going down. And look ... Eve." He paused, unsure how to continue. "That was really something last night. I just want you to know that it wasn't a joke. I meant what I said. You know ... that I love you."

As he buckled the seatbelt over his lap, he shook his head with disbelief at his own hesitation. His fecklessness. How could he fail to express his feelings for her for so damned long? She'd waited to hear his pledge for more than a year. There's something wrong about that, he told himself. Something wrong about *you.*

Chapter Thirteen

Simon Waterston stood in the living room of his sister's apartment and tried to make sense of Jayne's sudden death. He checked the clock. Five-thirty-two AM. The weariness accumulated from the long day dragged through his bones. He considered stretching out in Jayne's bed, but somehow the idea seemed invasive. Incestuous.

For a moment he stood next to the window overlooking Seventy-third Street and stared into the bleak night, then he sauntered over to the futon against the near wall and decided to try for some sleep before sunrise. He unlocked the frame hinge and folded the mattress out into a bed. He took off his shoes, shirt and pants and tucked one of the corduroy cushions under his head and closed his eyes. As he lay there, he replayed the scenes that had unravelled his world over the previous twelve hours.

From the moment FBI Agent John Vickers appeared at Simon's door in the DA's office he felt as if he'd been swept into a whirlwind. Vickers had been efficiently sympathetic—a chilling combination as it turned out—and escorted him to Lennox Hill Hospital to identify Jayne's corpse. The attending physician explained that while the cause of death appeared to be a very potent poison, the medical examiner's report would soon provide some certainty. "Likely within twenty-four hours," he'd said as he glanced at Jayne's medical chart. "Thirty-six at the latest."

After Simon absorbed the shock of her death and murmured a few parting words at her side, Vickers advised Simon that a crime scene team had confiscated her cell phone, laptop, notebook and purse from the table where she'd sat at Klutch.

"They'll process everything they find," Vickers had said. His voice was confident. Reassuring. "With any luck that should toss up some leads we can pursue."

After they left the hospital, Vickers escorted Simon to Jayne's apartment so that he could answer questions from the detective working with the forensics unit. Vickers introduced Simon to FBI Agent Calinda Cruz, a black woman in her early fifties with a face etched by worry lines that extended from her forehead to her chin. Her body was lean but sturdy and Simon knew she was a force to be reckoned with. The three of them sat at the small table that served as Jayne's home-office.

"First let me express my condolences, Mr. Waterston." A practiced expression of sorrow fell over Calinda Cruz's face. She paused as if she wanted to give him a moment to embrace her empathy. She saw his face soften and continued.

"I understand you work in the Manhattan DA's office."

He nodded. "The Cybercrime and Identity Theft Bureau. I've been there just under a year."

"Then you know how this goes. We've got a lot of questions—but not much time if we're going to find whoever killed your sister."

He blinked and glanced away.

"Did you see her often?"

"I guess." He shrugged as if he couldn't come up with an accurate answer. "We saw each other maybe once a month. Called a little more often, maybe once a week. Sometimes less."

"What about your parents? Other siblings?"

"They died ten years ago. No other sibs." His voice faltered. He drew a long breath and pressed on. "It was just the two of us. She was my twin."

"I'm sorry," Cruz paused to reflect on this. "What about you. Are you married? Have a partner?"

He shook his head.

Calinda Cruz glanced at Vickers and nodded. The glance suggested they'd seen this sort of loneliness before and understood the isolation that would soon overwhelm the man sitting next to them.

"Did Jayne have any enemies you know of?"

He considered the possibilities and shrugged. "No."

"Jealous boyfriends? Someone who might want revenge?"

"None of them seemed to last that long."

She arched an eyebrow. "Girlfriends?"

"Maybe." He tipped his head to acknowledge the possibility. He'd never liked her choice of romantic partners, so they— or rather, *he*—chose not discuss it.

"Mr. Waterston, the forensics team discovered some drugs above one of the kitchen cabinets." Cruz pointed a finger in the direction of the kitchen.

He frowned and looked away. No surprise. "All right. So what kind of drugs? Pot?"

"Some. And at least two ounces of cocaine."

"Two ounces?"

She studied his face. "Did you know she was using?"

"Coke? *No.*" Suddenly he felt betrayed, almost trapped.

"Did she mention any threat from dealers?"

"No. Nothing like that."

Then in a moment of clarity a new question occurred to him. "Tell me something. Why are you two—*the FBI*—on this?" He waved a hand toward them. "Where's the NYPD? Is there some kind of interstate crime involved?"

Vickers ignored the question, set his elbows on the table and leaned forward. "Mr. Waterston, this is important. Are you aware of any kind of list that your sister might have been working on?"

"List? What list?"

Agent Cruz opened her bag and showed him a copy of the list which the crime scene team had found in Jayne's purse at Klutch.

"This," she said and pushed it across the table toward him with the tip of her finger.

He studied it carefully, read each entry until he reached his sister's name. The pain of his loss was now turning to frustration with their plodding approach. "No. I don't know what it means. You tell me."

"We can't disclose that just yet. When we can, you'll be one of the first to know. "

She adjusted her weight in the chair. Simon looked at Vickers who tipped his head, a gesture that deferred to Agent Cruz. The exasperation building in Simon began to simmer.

"Then how am I supposed to help you? You refuse to explain what's behind your investigation. You won't tell me what this fucking list is about. So if you want my help, you need to let me in on this. I work for the District Attorney for God's sake. Tell me what's going on!"

Agent Cruz tucked the sheet of paper back in her bag.

"Let's talk about her neighbors," Vickers said as he inclined his head toward the front door. "Did she mention anyone who'd bothered her? Someone who might have paid her too much attention."

"No. Nothing!"

Simon clamped both hands over his ears and stood up. He walked in a tight circle, then turned his back on them and stared through the doorway to her bedroom. He could see that the forensics team had rifled her bureau drawers. Pulled the bed sheets and lifted the mattress.

"Mr. Waterston, please." Agent Cruz spoke in a near whisper, her voice filtered with an undertone of sympathy. "I know this is traumatic, but...."

Simon shut his eyes and managed to suppress his rage. He turned to face Cruz and Vickers and instantly saw them in a new light. They too were damaged by his sister's death. Damaged by legions of wounded and injured souls. How did they do it, day after day?

"Sorry," he said. "I just needed a moment."

He walked back to the table and sat in his chair. The interrogation continued for another hour, perhaps, two. He lost track of time. When they departed he took another hour to run an inventory of his sister's belongings. The wall of clothing in her bedroom closet. The portfolio of photographs she'd taken years ago when photojournalism seemed to be her calling. The palm-size boxes brimming with costume jewelry, bangles and bows. Her medications, the dozens of lipstick tubes. The hidden sex toys. Cardboard boxes filled with research materials from the stories she'd written for *The Village Voice*. Her bag of golf clubs parked next to the front door as if she were about to depart for Chelsea Piers to knock some balls into the nets. Hundreds of books. And a new title lying on the coffee table: *Who Shot the Sheriff?* The sales slip from B&N still tucked under the cover flap.

When his aimless search was complete, he washed up and settled down on the futon. He'd slept on it three or four times before, and knew not to roll onto the steel bar on the right side.

Then he thought about her computer and cell phone. Last Christmas they'd traded passwords. "Just in case," Jayne had said and jabbed his shoulder with an open fist. "One day you might need to access my millions."

Her millions. "You lived your whole life in a fantasy land," he said aloud as if she were here—still alive right now. He shifted onto his back and tried to find a comfortable spot on the mattress. "Well, today is that day, Jaynie. Show me your millions."

He decided that when he got back to his apartment he'd log into her account to see what he could discover. She kept everything in the cloud; he wouldn't need her confiscated laptop. If the FBI won't disclose what this case was about, he'd figure it out on his own.

He yawned and just as sleep was about to take him he heard the knock on the door. Three light taps. He ignored it. Then he heard the metallic click of steel-on-steel. Someone picking the lock.

Finch slipped the lock picks back into their leather wallet and tucked the kit into his courier bag. Then he stood and tested the tension in the handle. He felt it click, but before it moved an inch the door swung wide open and tugged him forward. The momentum carried him into Jayne Waterston's living room. Before him stood a half-dressed man with a golf club raised above his shoulder and ready to drive it into Finch's face.

"Who the fuck are you?!"

"Whoa." Finch raised his open hands and took a backward step.

"I said, *who are you?*"

A worried look crossed Simon's face, an expression that betrayed a lack of resolve. Finch felt no need for a fight, and he kept his hands up in a gesture of submission.

"I'm Will Finch. I'm trying to make contact with someone who knows Jayne Waterston. I thought this was her apartment. Who are you?"

"This *is* her apartment. But what the fuck are you doing picking her lock?" He kept the golf club ready to strike and glanced at the wall clock. "At six in the morning for God's sake."

Finch studied the club—a four iron, he figured—and the man holding it. His opponent stood about five-foot-seven and probably weighed less than one-fifty. Finch had at least six inches and forty pounds on him. He looked young, maybe in his mid-twenties, and probably had never seen the inside of a serious street fight. However, the edge of the club face could open a nasty cut. Or worse. Finch pressed his hands forward slightly, a signal to back off an inch.

"Look. I'm sorry if I frightened you. I just flew in from San Francisco. I thought Jayne's apartment would be empty."

"Yeah? Why's that?"

Finch hesitated. "Because of what happened."

"You know what happened?"

Now that he had a conversation going, Finch realized the danger of violence had diminished. At least for the moment. He cleared his throat.

"Maybe," he said. "I talked to Jayne yesterday morning. About a list. A list with her name on it. And mine. I'm a reporter at the *eXpress*. If you let me, I'll show you my card." He arched his eyebrows with a look that said, just give me a chance.

Simon nodded once and the tension in his jawline slackened a little. "All right."

Finch passed him his card. Simon considered it a moment and glanced at the coffee table.

"Same guy who wrote that book?"

Finch spotted his book on the table. "Yeah. She told me she just bought it last weekend. From B&N."

Simon narrowed his eyes and lowered the golf club. He'd already seen the bookstore receipt and the date of purchase. "All right. I'm Simon Waterston, Jayne's twin brother. Close the door and tell me what you know."

Within ten minutes Simon had dressed and prepared two cups of coffee. Meanwhile Will explained the little that he knew about the list and the growing number of victims. Simon listened in silence, a hand pressed to his lips as he assembled the facts into a coherent whole.

"So you sent this list to her yesterday morning?"

"By email. I only wish she'd taken the threat more seriously."

"What makes you think she didn't?"

Finch grimaced as if the answer was obvious. He decided to change course.

"Since we'd both been identified on the list and we're both journalists, I thought we could solve this thing together. But she wanted another day to consider it." Since all of this was now impossible, he shrugged with a look of futility. "The list should be on her computer."

Simon curled his lips with a hint of bitterness. "The FBI took her laptop at the cafe where she was killed. And her cellphone."

"They were here, too?"

He nodded. "Until just a few hours ago."

Finch glanced around the apartment. It looked to be about five hundred square feet. He could see a bedroom just past the kitchenette and an open door leading into a bathroom. A well-stocked bookcase lined one wall opposite a folded-down futon.

"Did they take anything else?"

"It's hard to say. I wasn't here at the time. They showed me a copy of the list and that's about all they were willing to reveal."

So she'd printed it out, Finch thought. That meant anyone else could have a copy, too. Not that it mattered since the *eXpress* was about to publish all the names.

"Tell me something, Simon. What do you do?"

"I'm a lawyer. Last year I joined the Manhattan DA's office. Cybercrime and Identity Theft Bureau."

CITB. It caught Finch's attention. Although the feds had picked up the serial murder spree, there might be some crossover with the Manhattan DA. Likely Simon could access the DA's database even if he had to do so covertly.

"And what about Jayne's computer files. Any chance you can get inside?"

Simon weighed the question with a look of caution. "Why?"

"Look, I'm on a mission to track these bastards down. I've got to get them before they get me—or anyone else on their kill sheet. And the fact is, while the FBI may be relentless, they are ten steps behind in this race."

He paused to consider his plans. "So here's what I offer. I'll give you everything I find if you do the same for me. And everything I've told you so far is the truth, straight up."

Simon pondered this and then shook his head. "I don't think so. I'm not crossing any lines set down by the FBI. I could lose my job. Or risk jail for criminal interference."

Finch glanced away knowing that in Simon's place he'd make the same decision. The safe choice. "All right. I get it. But let me ask you this. What have the FBI offered you so far? Have they told you ten percent of what I've told you in the last ten minutes?"

When Simon gave up a shrug Finch knew he'd hit a nerve.

"Have they even told you why they're handling Jayne's murder instead of the NYPD?"

He blinked and glanced away. "No."

"Well then?"

"Let me think about it."

"Okay. You've got my card, so call me if you need anything."

"Sure."

Finch waited a moment. "You got a card?"

Simon padded over to the coat tree where he'd hung his jacket, drew his wallet from a pocket and handed a card to Will.

Finch shrugged with a look of despondency. Perhaps this was the best he could do for now. But if he offered Simon something more alluring, information that no one else could access, then maybe they could strike an accord and he'd gain entry to the DA's database. Maybe.

He decided to leave the offer at that, give Simon a few hours to rest and call him after they'd both had time to consider their options.

"All right," he said and made his way to the front door. "Sorry I startled you. Get some sleep. I guess we could both use it."

Chapter Fourteen

A little after nine AM Will made his way over to the Hotel Pennsylvania on Seventh Avenue and checked into a twin-bed unit under the name Joel Griffin. Whenever he needed a pseudonym, Finch adopted that of one of his fallen comrades-in-arms during his tour in Iraq. Griffin and Finch were both in their early twenties when they'd met in the Baghdad Public Affairs Office assigned to handle the debacle of Abu Ghraib. They'd shared the same quarters, the same jokes, the same warm beers. Two important differences distinguished them. Griffin was an actual Public Affairs Specialist, while Finch had been assigned there as an undercover operative for Military Intelligence. The second difference was that Finch made it out of Iraq alive.

He tossed his courier bag onto the chair next to the window overlooking Seventh and studied the flow of traffic. The intensity of the morning rush hour had faded. He folded his jacket over the back of the chair and tested the bed closest to the window by pressing both hands against the mattress. He then ran a quick check of the bathroom and nodded his head in satisfaction; no sign of cockroaches, silverfish or bedbugs. He decided to put off a shower until he caught up on some sleep, and stripped off his clothes and settled into the bed. He pulled a pillow under his head and tried to imagine how he could convince Simon Waterston to collaborate with him. Soon his thoughts dissolved in the haze of his weariness and he fell into a dead sleep.

Just before noon his phone buzzed. As he scrambled to locate his Samsung, it took him a moment to realize where he was. He pulled the cell from his jacket pocket, saw Eve's name and swiped a finger across the glass face of the phone. The battery indicator showed a three percent reserve and he realized he'd forgotten to charge it.

"Hey."

"Hi. You awake?"

"Just," he said and wiped a hand over his face.

"Good. We've had a break with the John Doe mugging in City Hall."

"Really?" He stood up and walked to the window and pulled the curtain aside. Below, the traffic chugged south along Seventh Avenue. On the sidewalks he could see people dressed for another scorcher: the women in sundresses or sleeveless blouses, the men in shorts or cut-offs. Almost everyone wore sunglasses.

"With Jayne Waterston gone, the FBI has mounted a full-court press."

"Yeah, well with four down and twenty to go, that had to happen." Finch could barely hide the cynicism in his voice.

"Their first move was to review the CCTV tape outside the men's room in City Hall. I identified Toby Squire for them. Fortunately, he glanced directly into the camera. Even wearing the hoodie, you can't miss him."

Finch felt a dash of revival. For the first time, he sensed a way forward. He sat in the chair and studied the intricate patterns of swirls in the laminate surface of the table.

"What about Raymond Guzman?"

"Got him. After a few minutes, two other men followed Toby out of the bathroom. We used the polaroid picture to ID Guzman as the second man. The feds are trying to use facial recognition software to ID John Doe. So far, no luck."

Finch stretched his back along the length of the chair. "Eve, I've got to see this tape."

"I've already sent you the link. So in the scramble to break this open, the Bureau decided to go public. They've published the CCTV tape on the internet and are asking anyone who recognizes these guys to contact them. Wally pinned it to the top of the *eXpress* website this morning."

As she spoke Finch drew his laptop from his bag and launched his web browser. He watched the connection wheel spin, then an error message appeared: *No Internet Connection.*

"Damn it, I didn't get the Wi-Fi password when I checked in here. I'm going to have to get back to you on this."

She paused a moment. Finch imagined she felt his frustration, too. A couple more rookie moves like forgetting to charge his phone and neglecting the internet connection could hurt him. He heard his phone beep with a low power alert.

"Look, my phone's just about to crash. I'll call you when I'm up and running again. What else do I need to know?"

"The FBI wants to talk to you again."

"That's good. I guess. Means they're taking this seriously."

"Yeah. That's what worries me." She hesitated as if she

wished she could take her words back. "I told them you're in New York. I imagine they'll put their regional office onto you."

"Again, that's good, right?"

"I know. So one other thing." She paused. "I still love you."

"Yeah. I know." He smiled at this. "And I love you, too."

Finch plugged his phone into the charger and made his way to the bathroom. After a five minute shower, he brushed his teeth, shaved, and then put on his short sleeve shirt, hiking shorts and Ray-Bans. When he checked the cell battery level again he decided to leave it in the room and let it charge during his absence. He slipped his laptop into his bag and rode the elevator down to the lobby and walked through the exterior brass doors onto Seventh.

He immediately entered the swirl and mash of midtown Manhattan, an experience that always thrilled and surprised him—for about two minutes. After that he became just one more atom in the beast that churned incessantly beneath the concrete towers. When he found his bearings he crossed over to Madison Square Gardens and down to Penn Station. From there he entered the subway and made his way up to Klutch on Second Avenue.

To his surprise, the entrance to the cafe wasn't blocked with crime scene tape. The barista who prepared his latte explained that the police had closed the restaurant immediately after Jayne Waterston's collapse and that the FBI had completed their assessment yesterday evening.

"Everyone knows that crime's bad for business," she said as she passed him a coffee mug. "B-A-D," she added, spelling the word for emphasis. "You linger on it, that's no good for anybody."

Finch didn't doubt it, and after he asked where Waterston had been sitting, he walked over to her table and sat in the chair where she'd spent her last hour. He didn't expect to see any evidence that might point to her killer, and there was none to be found. If nothing else, the FBI was thorough.

He opened his laptop, logged into the wi-fi network and settled in for the task ahead. He opened the *eXpress* link to the CCTV video from the San Francisco City Hall and began to study the images on his screen. A minute into the video stream he saw Toby Squire emerge from the men's room. Just as Eve had described the action, Toby carried the suit jacket draped over one arm. The sweatshirt—at least two sizes too small—was tugged over his stout frame and arms. With the hoodie up, it barely covered his ears. Then just before he stepped out of the camera's field of vision, he glanced at the ceiling, directly into the eye of the camera lens.

In the corner of the video, a digital timer clicked through the passing seconds and minutes. Two minutes, ten seconds later, Raymond Guzman emerged from the washroom with a desperate look riveted to his face. He held a hand to his jaw, and Finch recalled the bruise under Guzman's right eye. Standing at the doorway, Guzman turned from side to side as if couldn't decide which way to run. After a beat he marched off in the direction opposite to Squire's retreat.

Another two minutes and forty-three seconds scrolled by and then John Doe appeared at the door. He stood at an angle, his tall, lean body teetering slightly to one side. His shirt was torn at the collar and he held a wad of paper towels to his left cheek. His right hand was pressed against his belly. After a moment he turned to the right, the same route Toby had taken. As he approached the camera Finch felt a moment of anticipation, then delight. Just as Toby had done, John Doe looked directly into the camera. His narrow, worried face held a cringing expression. Finch had seen him before—but where?

To jog his memory, Finch decided to take a long walk. He made his way south on Second Avenue and west on Ninety-second Street to Fifth Avenue. The heat and humidity felt almost unbearable. He decided to cross into Central Park and take cover under the shade of the trees. He walked along the east side of the lake and then ambled mindlessly through the labyrinth of paved pathways, essentially following his nose. He'd forgotten how the urban humidity could sap your energy and stamina and when he reached the Loeb Boathouse, he sat on a bench under the shade of a massive maple tree and watched the stream of tourists and day trippers slip past him.

He tried to fit the image of the face he'd seen on the CCTV clip onto the passing strangers. A few men had the same lean body of John Doe, but none resembled the man he'd seen. Where? After ten minutes, the scents emanating from the Boathouse grill stirred his appetite. He remembered a restaurant on the edge of Hell's Kitchen that he used to enjoy during his last year as a journalism undergrad at NYU—the year before he'd enlisted in the army.

His mother had died during his final term in high school. Four years later his father passed on. When the weight of his losses seemed most unbearable he'd made the decision to enlist on a whim, at a time when he knew his life needed a sharp course-correction. For better or for worse, he mused. He got both, as it turned out.

When the name of the restaurant came to him— Hummus Kitchen—he felt a measure of relief. At least he was able to dredge up one distinct memory, and buoyed with a hopeful feeling he left the park at Columbus Circle and strolled down Ninth Avenue to Fifty-second, keeping under the shelter of the store-front awnings whenever he could.

The restaurant was just as he remembered it. A long narrow space with a bare, red brick wall opposite an equally spare wall of bone-white plaster. The sturdy wooden tables and chairs that lined the long aisle were the same as they were in his student days. Nothing had been altered. Even the cutlery, beaten by decades of daily abuse in the dish-washer, retained their flat, iron patina. He sat at the far table next to the brick wall and faced the door—better to see anyone coming at him.

He studied the menu and realized that the selection remained unchanged. Perhaps he was now holding the actual menu that he'd used to choose his meals so many years before. The idea appealed to him, the thought of a physical connection that linked the past to the present. One life to another.

He ordered his old favorite, chicken shawarma, and a pot of mint tea. While he waited for the server—an older, mid-eastern gentleman with steel-gray hair and a cranky demeanor—to deliver his meal, he opened his laptop and re-played the CCTV video. Maybe he could jog his memory by watching the video another ten or twenty times. However long it took, he decided. Let the dull repetition simply pound the recollection from his subconscious mind into tangible reality.

When his meal arrived, he put the laptop away. He spent the next twenty minutes enjoying the food and the nostalgia that it offered. In 2001 he'd sat here maybe a half-dozen times with his girlfriend, Lydia Bronfman, a self-described Jewish princess whose mother had barred Finch from setting foot inside their Westchester mansion. What had become of Lydia? So many people, once intimate, had moved on to another place, another time. Grains of sand slipping through a bottomless hourglass. He shook his head, worried that this kind of thinking could lead to a bout of depression. If Eve were here with him now, any sort of despair would be impossible. He decided to call her—after he dredged up John Doe's name.

When the time came to collect his bill, he waved a hand at the waiter. The old man approached him with a scowl on his face. "No more work. I'm off," he snarled. He shot a hand at a lanky young man leaning on the banister next to the till. "Get the bill from my assistant."

Then it hit him. The round, polished pebble of a distant memory dropped into his open palm. Finch smiled at the old man's assistant and pulled his billfold into his hand. He had the name now. Jacob Bell. *Assistant.*

After he paid for his meal Will leaned across the front counter toward the cashier and asked if he could use the restaurant phone.

"You have no cell phone?" He curled his lips with a look of surprise.

Finch shook his head. "Forgot to charge it."

He glanced away as he worked through a moment of indecision. "Local call only?"

"Of course." Finch smiled. "You can watch me dial."

The man waved a hand dismissively and Finch reached into his pocket for Simon Waterston's business card. Waterston answered on the third ring.

"Simon, it's Will Finch here." When there was no response he added, "We met at your sister's apartment this morning."

"Yes." His voice was hesitant, wary. "How can I help you, Mr. Finch?"

Will knew he had to play this carefully, but he hadn't thought out the specifics. Experience told him to fall back on what had worked in the past. Straight ahead, fact-based truth-telling.

"Look, I know you have no reason to trust me. In fact, because of your sister's murder, you might think I'm part of what happened. But I promise you, I'm not. You saw the list I sent her. My name is one of twenty-three others who are either dead or are targeted by the same assassin who killed Jayne."

He paused to see if Simon would respond. When he didn't, Finch continued.

"I told you that if I found any information I would share it with you. That's why I'm calling you now."

He paused again. Finally Simon picked up the thread.

"So what do you have?"

"A name. Jacob Bell."

"Who's he?"

Finch took the time to describe the video of Bell emerging from the City Hall men's room. Then he described the circumstances surrounding his mugging, and the murder of Martin Fast, the first victim of Jayne's killer.

"So you're saying this Jacob Bell murdered Martin Fast and then Jayne?"

Finch knew it was a minor leap of faith, but one with compelling logic. "Maybe."

"And how did you know him?"

"He's the personal assistant to someone I interviewed after Martin Fast died. And someone Jayne profiled in *The Village Voice* last fall. Kali Rood."

"Kali Rood?" After a moment Simon continued, "I found a file on Kali Rood in Jayne's apartment when I tried to sort out her stuff. The file was sitting on the floor next to her desk. I guess the FBI didn't think it was worth taking. Now you're telling me it is?"

"Yes. Exactly." Finch felt his pulse quicken. "And Simon, that file could be very important." He paused. "Could I have a look at it? I don't need to take it. In fact, if I could meet with you for coffee somewhere—just let me look through her notes. It won't be out of your sight for a second."

When Simon failed to respond, Finch thought he might have overreached. "Look, I'm offering to work with you to solve this. But I need you to help me, too. I've given you the name of Martin Fast's killer. But—"

"Have you told the FBI?"

"Not yet. I told you that you'd be the first to know. And you are."

After another weighty pause, Simon agreed. "Meet me at three o'clock at Lenox Coffee shop on One-twenty-ninth near Malcolm X. And Finch, don't call my office again. If you need to reach me, call my cell." He passed on his cell phone number and hung up.

As Will ended the call another thought struck him. He sensed that he was making good progress for the first time since he'd landed in New York. Which meant that a surprise could lie ahead. He knew that whenever the way forward seemed clear and unobstructed, ghosts would often arise from the shadows. He smiled at the cashier.

"Can I make one more call?"

The man took a long breath and pointed to the phone. "Is for business."

"I'll pay you." He drew ten dollars from his billfold.

"All right. One call only."

"This one is long distance. San Francisco. Just two minutes."

The cashier shook his head with a look that revealed he'd been duped—and that he wanted further compensation. "Five dollar more."

Finch put a fiver on the counter.

"Go." He checked his watch. "Two minutes only."

Will dialed Eve's cell phone but he was greeted by her voice mail message. As he waited for it to play out, he tried to think of an unambiguous statement to pass on.

"Eve, I looked at the CCTV. John Doe is Jacob Bell. Kali Rood's personal assistant. Ask Finkleman to profile the guy and send me whatever he's got. I haven't talked to the FBI yet, but I will whenever they track me down."

He paused to consider the FBI's game plan and realized that they might be tapping her calls. And his. They probably had enough information to spin the murders into a terrorism theory and present their evidence to a federal judge to invoke the provisions of the Patriot Act. That would give them access to all the tools—including a roving wiretap—they needed to track Finch's and Eve's every move via their cellphones.

"Look, I can't say anything more right now. Just focus on Jacob Bell and get back to me ASAP. All right. Love you," he added and then wished he'd left that off. No need to let the feds in on anything personal. The FBI had a hundred ways to break your heart and throw away all the pieces.

The entrance to the Lenox Coffee shop was distinguished by a colonnade of four Greek columns. It provided a marked contrast to the tidy but pedestrian atmosphere of Harlem. The up-scale, genteel interior was furnished with puffed leather sofas and rows of tables and comfortable looking chairs. More important, an air conditioner with the control knob set to deep chill.

Finch picked up an iced coffee from the barista and found Simon sitting at a round table near the back of the room. Simon wore a suit and tie. Finch sat beside him and scanned the room. Had anyone followed him to the coffee shop?

"I've got no more than ten minutes," Simon said and pushed a legal-size folder across the table. "Here's the file."

"Thanks." Finch opened the file cover and skimmed the contents. Inside were some materials Jayne had photocopied from a public source, some printed email, and three pages of handwritten notes. Beneath these documents lay a series of corporate brochures—the headline on the topmost read, "Making Things Right."

"This is her handwriting?"

He nodded. "But there's nothing in there that I can see of any value. Obviously the FBI didn't either."

"No?" Finch took a few minutes to read Jayne's notes. At first glance they seemed to contain nothing extraordinary. On the other hand, he knew they deserved closer attention. He closed the folder and studied Simon for a moment. A look of resignation had settled on his face. Perhaps he was coming to terms with his sister's death.

"Can I borrow this for a while?"

Simon tilted his head from side to side, weighing the decision. "You asked to see it, not to take it."

Will decided to let the objection stand without argument. "Have you heard any more from the feds?"

He shook his head. "You?"

"No, but I expect to. They'll want me to go on record identifying Jacob Bell in the CCTV video."

Finch realized that he had an opportunity to strengthen his tenuous bond with Simon. He decided to bring him into his confidence. He took a sip from his coffee and leaned forward.

"As it turns out I'm the only person who can identify all three men in the washroom. Toby Squire, who killed himself within two hours of Martin Fast's murder, Raymond Guzman—Squire's partner—who told me how the two of them ran their mugging operation. And now, Jacob Bell."

"I don't see how all this ties into Jayne."

"I'm getting there. The list of names that Jayne had—the list with her name and mine—we found the link to it in the jacket that Squire stole from Jacob Bell."

"What jacket?"

Will spent the next ten minutes relating the story that had brought him to New York. From time to time Simon shook his head with an expression of disbelief, but as Finch carried on with the tale Simon appeared more convinced. When he finished, Will leaned back a moment to consider Simon's perspective.

As he took another moment to digest the story Simon

shifted his lower jaw from side to side. He seemed to be debating something new. "You know, there's more to this than you think."

"What do you mean?"

Simon's eyes shifted away. He seemed to be scrutinizing someone near the cashier. Finch turned to look at a couple talking discretely to the barista. Cops? They were big enough. Simon looked back at Finch and replied in a quiet voice.

"All right, look. I've checked you out. I know what you've done in the past, and I know that Jayne respected you. And I agree with your assessment. The FBI *is* too secretive. Jayne was my twin, for God sakes!" His voice rose with a burst of emotion. He took a breath then seemed to bring himself under control. "Besides, something else has come up."

Finch scanned his face as Simon continued.

"Jayne and I shared one another's computer passwords. It's a twin thing." He struggled to get these last words out, then managed to press on. "Anyhow after I left her apartment, I logged onto her Google account from my machine. She kept everything in the cloud. Files, email, work projects, proposals. Everything."

"And?"

"And her photos. She once had career opportunities as a photojournalist. Then let it go. I think she just lost interest. In the past two or three years, all she took was shots for her Facebook page. Except for her very last picture. Just two hours before her death."

Finch narrowed his eyes. "What's in the picture?"

"A license plate."

"From a car?" Play it slowly, he told himself. Reel this in very gently.

"Looks like a late model Cadillac. It was parked across the street from her apartment. You can tell the location because the door to the Bohemian National Hall is in the background."

"Can you read the plate number?"

Simon reached into his pocket and passed a folded slip of paper to Finch. He glanced at the note. The plate ID was typed in a generic font.

"New York?"

Simon nodded again.

"Can you send me the picture?"

"Look, I'm not doing that." He laughed with a cynical smirk. "You may think I'm helping you, but all this is deniable." He waved a hand to suggest everything they'd discussed so far was about the scorching temperature and more bad weather to come.

Finch put the paper in his pocket and leaned back in the chair again.

"Are you giving the plate number up to the feds?"

"Withholding evidence—are you kidding me?" Simon closed his eyes as if he were trying to shake off a bad dream. "I'm calling them right after I leave here."

Finch thought for a moment. "Look, this is dangerous for *both* of us. But I'm going to write a profile of Jayne. Of what happened to her," he added. "I don't need your permission. I just want you to know what I'm doing, so you don't think I'm blind-siding you when it's published." He pulled his courier bag onto his lap. "Are you okay with that?"

"Do what you like. You're right, I can't stop you." Simon paused to consider their situation. "As far as I'm concerned, we've just had a talk. If you want anything more from me, it's going to be one step at a time. I'm not giving you a blank check. In fact, I doubt there's anything more I can help you with."

"All right. But if I learn something I think you should know, I want to bring you in on it, Simon."

"I don't know." He turned his head away, then shifted his attention back to Will. The drawn look on his face suggested that he'd been thinking of his sister again. Finch could see that his ambivalence was tearing him apart one heartbeat at a time. "All right. But only if you think it's necessary."

Finch thought Simon looked as if he'd made a bargain with the devil. As if he knew some future torment awaited him. What it would be and when it might strike, no one knew. But for now, he would accept the risks. For his sister.

Chapter Fifteen

Before he returned to the Hotel Penn, Will offered the barista five dollars and called Eve from the desk phone of the Lenox Coffee Shop. Once again her line branched into her voice mailbox. He took a few seconds to compose himself and then recited the letters and numbers on the Cadillac's license plate and asked Eve to do what she could to tap into the New York State vehicle registry.

"If we can get the name of the owner and driver," he whispered into the phone, "maybe we can sew this thing up."

He took the subway down to Penn Station. As he crossed through the thousands of people funneling toward Madison Square Gardens he glanced up at the event banner: "Bad Boy Family Reunion Tour."

Might be nice to head out for a rap concert, he thought, and as he waited for the signal light to cross Seventh Avenue, he came close to turning about, buying a ticket from a scalper and entering the stadium. He could get lost in the crowd, spend the night splitting his head open on the raw sound of angry black men, all of them in a fury about the ongoing street murders by cops. Over the summer the national rage had reached a boiling-point, especially after five white cops were executed as "pay-back" in Dallas.

But the reality of his weariness—and his whiteness— kicked in and he crossed the street, entered the Penn, passed under the marketing banner ("5000 Fully Renovated Rooms"), made his way to the elevator bay and up to the seventeenth floor. As he sauntered along the corridor to his room he checked for signs of anyone following him. No one. He walked three doors past his quarters, turned and waited with a look that would suggest to any passing strangers that he'd forgotten his room number.

Convinced that no one had tracked him, he slipped into his suite and locked the door. Everything appeared to be as he'd left it. A dot of green light blinked in the corner of his cellphone screen. It was now fully charged.

Before he could retrieve his phone messages a heavy thumping beat at his door.

"Will Finch. FBI. Open up!"

His heart lurched in his chest. Where had they come from? As he approached the spy-hole on his door he tried to think what to do. Through the convex eye he could see two people in the corridor; a white male, mid-forties, gray hair and a black woman of the same height, maybe five years older.

"Let me see your ID," he said through the door.

The woman held her shield up to the eye. FBI.

"And your face again," he said.

She stood up to the door and spoke in a low voice. "Mr. Finch, we are not here to arrest you."

Finch decided to take no chances. "Let me see your partner's ID."

The male agent held his badge aloft and then stood up to the door. "We just have some questions for you," he said.

Finch wiped a hand over his face and opened the door. He took a step backward and the two cops slipped into his room.

"I'm John Vickers and this is Agent Calinda Cruz."

They nodded in unison and walked past him. Finch closed the door and stepped towards the first twin bed.

"We've been trying to reach you all day," Cruz said with a sigh of exasperation. "Don't you check your messages?"

"Out of juice."

Finch pointed to his phone and sat at the round table next to the window. He realized that the phone had served as a homing beacon. Obviously they'd been granted a roving wiretap. He pointed to two chairs and when his guests settled beside him he attempted to put on a convincing smile.

"All right, I'm all yours. What can I do for you?"

Agent Cruz set her phone on the table and indicated that she would be recording their conversation. Then she focussed her gaze on him and said, "Quite a lot, I suspect."

"So you're saying you've already seen the CCTV video?" Agent Vickers leaned forward and set his elbows on the table as he spoke.

"Uh-huh. My publisher sent me the link when the *eXpress* posted it on the company website this morning."

"And you can identify all three men in the camera?"

"Yeah." Finch looked from Vickers to Cruz. "I may be the only person to meet all three of them."

A brief silence passed between them.

"All right. Let's go through it together," she said. She had the CCTV video on her iPad screen ready to roll. She touched the play button.

Finch watched the video replay the same scene he'd watched at least ten times. As each of the men emerged from the washroom he identified them to the FBI agents. Toby Squire, Raymond Guzman, Jacob Bell. When they asked if he knew their background Finch provided all the details he could about Squire. But with Guzman he balked. Although he'd only spent a few hours with the man, he still felt an obligation to protect the one person who'd opened up to him. If Guzman had followed Finch's advice, he'd be long gone.

"What about Jacob Bell?"

"This is where it gets interesting." Finch planted his elbows on the table and leaned forward. "He killed Martin Fast, probably ten minutes before he got caught up in this clip." He pointed to the iPad. When they pressed him, he explained his theory that Bell had pulled the hoodie over his suit jacket then followed Martin Fast after his debate with Kali Rood in the City Hall rotunda. That he'd used the guise of a bungled Market Street robbery to cover his assassination of Fast. Then he'd doubled back to City Hall, peeled off the hoodie and suit jacket just in time for the mugging by Squire and Guzman.

"Really?" Vickers sounded skeptical. "The SFPD have Squire locked down on Fast's murder. According to the chief, the case is closed."

"Come on," Finch said evenly, careful not to jump at Vickers's tone. "You know the numbers game they play. It's all about tightening their close ratios. They closed three files when Squire died. Martin Fast, Squire himself and the woman he raped and murdered last year, Senator Whitelaw's daughter, Gianna."

The two agents paused to consider this. After a moment Vickers said, "You covered that, right? The Senator's suicide."

Finch nodded and looked away. He didn't want their attention to drift from the case in hand.

"All right." Agent Cruz shook her head with a doubtful look. "And you know this Jacob Bell—*how?*"

Again Finch leaned forward. "He's Kali Rood's assistant."

Vickers shook his head as if he'd now been introduced to one too many characters in a Russian novel. "And who's he?"

"She. The leader of Salvation Nation." Cruz gave him a subtle look that said, where have you been?

"Okay. And they are?" Vickers sounded sheepish, as if he knew he was playing catch-up.

"Salvation Nation is a right-wing, quasi-evangelical, head-in-the-sand cult with tens of millions of dollars and thousands of ardent believers." Finch recited this as if he were reading the profile Jayne Waterston had written of Kali Rood last fall. "If you're a true believer appalled by things like genetic engineering or transgender surgery— Kali Rood and the Salvation Nation have a place for you. Especially if you can cover the thousand dollar annual fees."

The two agents nodded in unison. Will seemed to provide enough meat to satisfy their appetite. Thinking that he could now show them to the door, Finch made a move to stand up. But Calinda Cruz waved a hand to settle him back into his chair, an easy but firm gesture.

"Let's talk about other things," she said.

"Like?"

"Like who is Joel Griffin?"

Finch glanced at the wall. This was exactly where he did not want the conversation to go. To focus on him. However, he knew he had to answer their questions truthfully, otherwise he could be tossed in jail.

"Joel Griffin was a hero of the second Iraq war. I met him during our stint in Baghdad in oh-four. He didn't make it home."

This statement had the impact he hoped for. A reverent pause.

"All right. So you checked into the hotel using his name. And why are you impersonating him?"

He took a moment to glance at his hands as if they held an answer that might satisfy them. "I'm not impersonating him. I'm here on assignment for my employer, the *eXpress*. I've been covering this story under my by-line from day one. In fact, I broke this story and I'm going to continue covering it until you people take these bastards down—whoever they are." He could feel his temper bubbling as he spoke. For a moment he thought he should check himself, then decided to level them with both barrels. "And until you do, I'm going to use every trick in the fucking book to work under the radar—including using my dead friend for cover—because as you might know—maybe, *just maybe*—that my name is on that Goddamned list, too!"

"All right, Finch. Cool your jets." Despite his warning, Vickers seemed to enjoy Finch's display of bravado. "Part of the reason we're here is to assign you protection."

"Protection?"

"One man. For the duration," Calinda Cruz said. Her look said that it was a non-negotiable offer. "Until, like you say, we take these bastards down."

Finch hadn't imagined this possibility. A bald, iron-pumping dick in a cheap suit with a wrist radio following twenty paces behind him through Manhattan.

"No thanks, I—"

Agent Cruz waved a hand to dismiss his objection before he could finish it. "You got no options, Finch. He'll be here within the hour." She checked her watch, then stopped the recording, slipped her phone and iPad into her bag and rose from the chair, tugging at a pant leg that had gathered around her crotch.

Vickers stood up and smiled. He seemed pleased with the result of their discussions. They'd identified everyone in the CCTV clip and drawn a fresh lead to Kali Rood. Furthermore, they were about to lock a clamp on Finch's investigations.

After they left, Finch stood at the door with his face pressed to the spy hole. He could see the two agents standing at the elevator bay talking, no doubt, about lining up an interview with Kali Rood. Was she at her headquarters here in New York or at one of the training centers in Oregon or Arizona? Soon it would be time for him to pay her a second visit, too. But not yet.

Once they disappeared from his view he eased open the door to ensure the corridor was clear. Then he packed his belongings into his courier bag and slipped his cell phone into his pocket. Suddenly a new thought occurred to him and he plugged the phone into its charger again and left it on the table. Best to leave that in place, he told himself, just to assure the FBI that I'm still a sitting duck. He locked the room and rode the elevator to the second floor. From there he walked along the hallway to the east side of the building then descended an interior staircase and exited the building onto Thirty-third Street. The heat and humidity were still cooking the city and an unbroken stream of pedestrians ambled along at a crawl, their faces aglow with perspiration. He strolled along the shaded side of the street to the Empire State Building and got into a cab heading downtown on Fifth Avenue.

"Where to, sir?" The cabbie had a whisky voice, raw with no soft edges.

Finch had to think a moment. "Down to the Village," he said. "Some place so noisy, it feels quiet."

He had no idea where to go next. Then he thought of the Village Vanguard, an iconic jazz hotspot started in 1935 and still under management by the founder's wife, Lorraine Gordon. The thought of a night digging jazz made Finch think of Chet Baker's tune "Let's Get Lost" and that led him to the notion of faking his own disappearance. It was one thing to wander off the FBI's radar. Quite another to escape the assassin stalking the next twenty victims on the kill list.

By the time the taxi dropped him on Seventh in front of the Vanguard, his hunger had caught up with him. He stood under the red awning at the club entrance and peered through the doorway. He briefly wondered why the room was empty until he felt the waves of heat steaming up from the concrete sidewalk. No air conditioning. Of course, everyone in the city was trying to beat the heat. He walked a half block along Seventh to Waverley where he rolled into Morandi, an Italian restaurant with a few sidewalk tables set under the shade of an awning. He wandered inside, sat at a table next to the wall, ordered a bottle of San Pellegrino on ice and what he imagined would have been Eve's choice for dinner, Cavatelli al prosciutto. The waiter provided him with a wi-fi password and as he waited for his meal he checked for incoming email on his laptop. Dozens of messages popped into his in-box. He checked the latest from Eve, the title in caps: WILL, THIS IS URGENT.

The text of the message said, *Call me.*

"Not so easy, my darling," he muttered to himself. He realized that she didn't want to commit a detailed message to email so he provided a brief reply: *I have no phone. Are you there?*

He received no response until five minutes after he finished his meal. Just as the waiter delivered an iced coffee to his table his computer blinked with an incoming email from Eve. *Go to Messenger. Should be secure.*

Of course. Last month Finkleman had convinced Wally that everyone at the *eXpress* should have a Messenger account so they could communicate through an encrypted channel when they needed heightened security. It wasn't perfect, especially against the tools the FBI could muster to crack open their lines, but Finch knew it would keep most predators at bay and probably put Agents Vickers and Cruz off his trail for another day or two. He clicked on the app and began a text dialogue with Eve.

Will: Did you get an ID on the license plate?

Eve: Not yet, Wally may have a connection that will help.

W: What about a profile on Jacob Bell?

E: Stutz will have that together by noon tomorrow. Where's your phone?

W: Left the phone as a lame duck decoy. BTW, not now—but tomorrow morning—get someone to call into Hotel Pennsylvania and check me out of room 1773. Put the charge on the eXpress *corporate tab. I don't want to leave financial footprints on Joel Griffin's VISA card. Then three or four hours later call back, and say I left my cell-*

phone behind. Ask the reception desk to hold it in their lost-and-found. Also—what's so urgent?

E: Breaking news. Edmond Austen, #13 on list, was attacked with a knife in Paris yesterday. He's in serious condition, but may survive.

Finch pondered this as he tried to recall Austen's background. He was the ordained minister from Toronto, notorious for announcing he'd become an atheist—but he refused to leave the church or stop preaching from the pulpit.

W: What's he doing in Paris?

E: Attending an ecumenical conference.

A new thought struck him. Austen had been attacked in Paris just after Jayne Waterston's murder in Manhattan. He tried to put the sequence of events in order and realized he needed more information.

W: What was the time of the attack?

A pause followed then Eve replied: *Two hours after Waterston's death.* Then she added, *Can't be the same perp.*

Exactly. For the first time Finch realized they were now caught up in an international murder conspiracy with at least two hitmen. The scope of the crimes had just changed by another degree of magnitude. A shudder ran through him as he considered the implications. Everything in his heart told him to flee, but everything he'd learned from experience told him the only way to survive was to move forward. He leaned over the keyboard and continued to type.

W: Can you get me the name and address of the hospital in Paris?

Another long pause followed and then Eve typed her final message.

E: Don't have it now, but will get it to you by the time you land. Be careful.

Finch nodded. She understood his thinking and what had to happen next. She didn't question it because she agreed with his assessment of the situation. Eve was perfect for him. With him. To him.

He typed his last message to her — *Don't worry. Caution is my new mantra*—then shut his laptop, paid his bill and flagged down a passing taxi on Waverly Place. Ninety minutes later he stood at a counter talking to an Air France agent in the JFK Departures concourse. The next flight to Paris was a red-eye.

While he waited for his flight, Will found an empty place on a bench seat in the far corner of the Air France boarding lounge. He opened his laptop and sent a brief message via Messenger to Wally and Fiona.

I'm on track with the case. Writing a profile of Jayne Waterston. Will email it to you ASAP. Understand Edmond Austen was attacked in Paris. Fiona, please provide bio on him. Clearly at least one other perp involved. Also, important to get name of owner / driver of NY state plate number sent to you earlier. Any way to break through on that? Finkleman maybe?

Will considered the perfunctory message, wondered how he could soften it somehow and make it seem more personable. Then he dismissed the notion and sent it on its way without a change.

The thought of Finkleman hacking into the New York State Department of Motor Vehicles database reminded him of Oscar Pocklington, known as Sochi to his friends and comrades. Sochi would assign Rasputin, his quantum computer app, to the task and within a few hours, he would deliver the name of the Cadillac's owner to Finch. Will could almost visualize it now: A light tap on his apartment door, then the greeting from the bearded, red-headed geek-Viking king. "Here it is," he'd say. "Rasputin cracked the database in six hours, eight minutes and forty-three seconds. A little longer than I guessed, but wa-a-a-ay short of the record longest hack on NASA. Doubt anything will ever beat that." He'd let out his horse laugh, the deep voice full of love for his own jokes. But Sochi was long gone, of course. Destroyed by his own folly.

Finch set his remorse aside and continued his internet research on Kali Rood. Her organization occupied the top two floors of the building on the corner of First Avenue and East Eighty-ninth Street in Manhattan. She owned the penthouse, her private residence, which few people had ever visited. Did she have friends, relatives, lovers? No one could provide a satisfactory answer. One floor below the penthouse, a twelve-thousand square-foot office complex housed the international headquarters for Salvation Nation. The foundation employed eleven staff. As if she wanted to confound the notion of her sexual ice, she'd made a point of hiring men only. If they were privy to any company secrets, none had been betrayed. A volunteer board of six men and six women served to provide guidance and direction as the foundation grew its base from local supporters to a national organization. Over the past few years they had established an international platform to espouse its extreme conservative values. Some called it fascism, but Finch knew the foundation was defining a new form of human cynicism. Where it might lead was anyone's guess.

After Jayne Waterston's profile in *The Village Voice*, the rumors of Kali's chaste, secluded lifestyle purled through the media in a kind of anti-gossip. No one could point to an ex-husband, a boyfriend, a male companion. The media couldn't find—and therefore, couldn't leak—any photos or videos of hidden indiscretions. She'd endured no scandals, no lawsuits, no misdemeanors. Jayne Waterston had nailed it on the head. Kali Rood's strange piety became her brand. She *was* the Virgin Queen.

When he finished his research he began to write the profile of Jayne Waterston. He decided to write a first-person, I-was-there piece. He began with the moment when he sat in her chair at her table in Klutch, less than a day after she'd been poisoned. Next he cut back to the telephone conversation he'd had with her. He suggested the possibility of collaborating on a story about Kali Rood. How she'd wanted a day—her last day, as it happened—to consider his offer to write as a team and share the by-line. He went on to describe her apartment on Seventy-third, the little table where she wrote overlooking the street where the bronze Cadillac stood parked at the curb in front of the Bohemian National Hall. Then he offered a glimpse into the moment that for some reason, as yet unknown, she'd photographed the Caddy's license plate. It was the last picture she'd taken before she walked up to Klutch for her last cup of cappuccino.

Finch wrote quickly, and as he worked he thought of Jayne's twin brother. He felt an urge to protect Simon and didn't mention him by name—or reveal that Jayne had any siblings or parents. The story was tightly focussed on her last day—and what must have transpired during her final hour. When he considered this, a title came to him, which he typed at the top of the page and set in uppercase: "WALK THE LAST HOUR IN HER SHOES."

Five minutes later the boarding announcement for the flight to Paris sounded. He decided to email the unedited draft to Jeanne Fix, the web master at the *eXpress*. He asked her to forward the copy to Fiona and added a note to Fiona: *Sorry, rough draft: fix any typos and fill any holes you find.*

With the job done, he let down his guard and felt a tug of exhaustion ebb through him. If he was lucky he could sleep through the flight. And if he couldn't sleep then he'd let himself slip into a long fantasy about Eve. A fantasy about loving her so long and hard that all her doubts about his love and affections would be forgotten.

Chapter Sixteen

From the moment she'd arrived in New York City Kali Rood knew that she wanted to establish her foundation here. In 1993, the year following her graduation from university, she'd taken the train up to New York. After it pulled beside the platform in Grand Central Station, she walked into the main concourse, marveling at the marble walls and tiled floors, the arched ceiling, the light illuminating the broad space through the rooftop half-circle glass windows. When she dragged her suitcase onto Forty-second Street she drank in the city in one gulp. Everything sprawled before her. Here was the intersection of ambition, wealth, homelessness, dread, sex, and a million other obsessions and prohibitions—all of them bartered and traded, sold, stolen or ransomed—for more of the same.

Or redeemed by the salvation she offered.

She knew that in New York she could turn the spiritual void into something Reverend Jim Jones had barely glimpsed. Had he even sensed it? Did he really understand the great power that death offered to those who got away—

and lived a *second* life? The door that death opened for survivors like her and Dorion.

How different she was from the masses. The fears that obsessed them. The unrelieved anxiety that squeezed the feeble and lame. The loneliness they endured. Yes, she understood all this and knew that inside the gates of this great satanic city she could build her empire.

For over twenty years she had done just that. From where she now sat in the corner office of her tower she occasionally looked down the avenue toward Grand Central Station and thought of the day of her arrival. She'd never been naïve. Never innocent. Perhaps that was the one childhood quality that Jim Jones had stolen from her. But it was a gift in disguise. She came to New York with nothing but righteous belief, intelligence and iron determination. And now she'd launched a new project. A program to remake the world based on the vision that came to her after her diagnosis. She understood that the natural order moved forward in exactly this way. From disease comes the cure. From death, salvation.

Someone had to make it happen and she decided that no one other than Kali Rood could achieve what had to be done. She called it Revelation Now.

When the agents appeared at her office door, Kali Rood betrayed no surprise. She glanced up from her laptop with a look of expectation. Jerome Bennes, her receptionist, held a hand to his chest, a docile gesture to excuse his abrupt interruption, and took a step through the doorway.

"Pardon me, Ms. Rood, these are FBI Agents John Vickers and Calinda Cruz. They insist on seeing you. I vetted them by calling the FBI regional office." He shrugged as if he couldn't do more to dissuade them. "It all seems legitimate, ma'am."

Cruz and Vickers stepped into the room and with a tip of her head Cruz dismissed Bennes from the room. When he departed, she closed the door. She stood next to Vickers and glanced at him. Kali recognized the look they shared, an air of scorn. As if on cue, they settled into the black leather chairs facing her.

"Please, make yourselves comfortable." Her voice prickled with irony. "However, I'm quite busy. If it's possible, I'd prefer it if you'd make an appointment for another time."

Agent Cruz gave her an icy stare. "We could do that. In which case, the appointment will be ten minutes from now in an FBI interview room down on Federal Plaza." She paused. "I hope that won't be necessary. But you decide."

A moment of silence passed between them. Kali knew the agents were used to getting their way. To obstruct them now could only strengthen their hand. She nodded, closed her laptop and pushed it to the side of her desk. Then she paused to tap two buttons on her desk phone and turned her attention to the two agents.

"All right. For the moment I'm prepared to do it your way."

"Good. I have to advise you that we are taping our conversation." Cruz waved her phone in the air, set it on the polished desk, clicked the record icon and announced the date, the time and the other legal protocols required for a formal interview.

"And what exactly do we need to discuss?"

"We need you to examine a video recording. We're trying to identify someone who is of interest to us."

Kali leaned forward without breaking eye contact with Cruz. "Of interest? Why do you assume that I know anyone of interest to the FBI?"

Cruz ignored the question and pulled her iPad from her bag and set it on the desk. She cued up the video and adjusted the tablet so that the three of them could see it clearly.

"Watch this," she said and tapped the screen with her index finger. The CCTV clip from the San Francisco City Hall began to play.

When the video ended Kali took a moment to consider how to respond. She looked at Vickers, then settled her attention on Cruz. "Sorry. I'm afraid I can't help you."

"No?" Vickers tipped his head with a look of doubt and leaned forward. "Have a second look, Ms. Rood. Focus on the third man."

Cruz tapped the iPad again and the video replayed the entire scene. When Jacob Bell emerged from the washroom, Vickers paused the clip, drew two fingers across frame until the expanded image of Bell's face staring up into the camera filled the screen. Vickers bore an expectant look. "Recognize him now?"

Kali smiled with a hint of contempt. Perhaps it was time to toss them a bone.

"Maybe." She paused. "Yes, now that you've enlarged the image. I think that's Jacob Bell."

"Jacob Bell." Cruz arched her eyebrows. "And how exactly do you know him?"

Kali sat back in the chair and set her arms on the armrest. Her lips dipped at the corners of her mouth and she glanced away with a dismissive shrug. "I hired him two or three weeks ago when I was in San Francisco on business."

"Does he still work for you or your foundation?"

"No. I fired him when he made some inappropriate comments."

Vickers leaned forward. "What kind of comments?"

"The kind that I will not tolerate." Kali narrowed her eyes. "Look, I think someone has misled you. I have no idea what you want or where this was recorded. Now please, I have work to do and—"

"Misled us? Who do you think misled us, Ms. Cruz?"

Kali let out a light chuckle. "Isn't that your job? It could be anyone who duped you into thinking that I'm responsible for whatever Jacob Bell has done. Anyone who believes the foundation is engaged in a misdirected cause. And believe me, there are thousands of them. It could be a political operative, a member of the press, some socialist sympathizer. You tell me."

Cruz nodded her head as if she grasped the possibilities —as if she herself had been duped a hundred times before —but in this case she had considerable assurance. "We have a respected authority who claims he saw this man working as your assistant in San Francisco during your visit to debate Martin Fast."

"As I said, he *was* working for me. Then I fired him. End of story." Kali rose from her chair with her hands up in a gesture of mock surrender. Then she turned away, walked over to the window and swung back to the two agents. "And who, exactly, is your so-called authority?"

Vickers cut in again. "Ms. Rood, are you aware that lying to an FBI officer is a federal offense?"

"I am." She shrugged off the accusation. "But I have to say I'm surprised you're bringing that up. And let me add that I'm pleased you're recording our conversation. Just as I am"—she pointed to the red light glowing on her desk phone— "because I'm also aware of the federal laws about police harassment and intimidation. Now, for third time, I am very busy. If you want to speak to me again, make an appointment through my lawyer, Raymond Busman. Now leave."

"All right. You can count on it." Cruz set her jaw and slipped the iPad into her bag. As she rose from her chair she clenched her phone in her fist and glanced at Vickers with a look that said, we're not done here.

After the agents left her office Kali realized that she would have to accelerate the pace of her program. Everything would have to go faster now. Move forward before her opponents could assess their predicament and realize how lost they already were.

She turned back to her desk and pressed a series of keys on her telephone to save and store the recording she had of the two FBI agents. Then she touched the intercom button on her phone. Jeremy Bennes responded within seconds.

"Yes, Ms. Rood?"

"Jeremy, use a secure channel to reach Jacob Bell in California."

"Do you want video or voice only?"

"Just his voice." She knew the sound of her voice alone would be more assuring than a video link. The human voice had none of the distractions that come with body language and facial expression. Nothing exceeded the intimacy of the spoken word to a solitary mind.

"Of course, ma'am. And your code?"

"Tell him Revelation eight, verse seven."

With the phone pressed to her ear, Kali swiveled her chair toward the windows overlooking the city. When she allowed herself to relax, the view provided a soothing, almost hypnotic effect. More than any other tower in midtown Manhattan, she admired the Chrysler Building, an art deco masterpiece designed by William Van Alen. With its pointed spire set atop seventy-seven stories it appeared to puncture the sky. If you loved the world, *this* world, then you loved Manhattan. And if you loved the next world, the one that would follow, then you learned to despise Manhattan. No matter how magnificent they might be, she knew that one day all the towers of man would fall. The only wisdom to be drawn from this inevitability was complete acceptance. As Nietzsche said, *Amor Fati.* Love your fate.

It was a test, she knew. To love the disease that held an unrelenting grip on her life. Last year she'd been diagnosed with multiple myeloma and told it was incurable. The oncologist prescribed a series of chemo treatments and after that, "Well," he'd said, "let's wait and see." She never saw him again. She would deal with her disease with healing prayer. That and a rising dosage of pain medication.

"Sorry for the holdup, but I have Jacob Bell on the line now, ma'am." As always Jeremey Bennes spoke in a contrite voice. She liked his calm, unruffled demeanor. Over the past two years he hadn't presented a moment of drama.

The delayed connection to Jacob Bell didn't surprise her. Over the last twenty-four hours Jacob would be shaken to the core as he absorbed the implications of the video that had been released for the world to see. His face, unmistakeable, staring into the overhead camera as he left the washroom of the City Hall. Simply stated, he'd made an error. Consequently, a price must be paid.

Despite the wait, she knew that he would take her call

and accept everything the she had arranged for him. Like all the members of her inner circle, she'd prepared the path that led Jacob forward. Once a month she spent an hour with each devotee, a private session that she called "personal revelations." Dozens of them opened their hearts to her, poured out their pain, confessed their failings and sins. No matter how depraved—or inane—their crimes, she embraced their suffering, cleansed their broken spirits and bound each one to her. They found redemption and she became their savior.

Kali shifted the phone to her right ear and when she heard Jacob's line connect, she swiveled around in her chair to face the office door. She wanted to ensure that it was closed. It was.

"Jacob. How are you feeling?"

"Shaken, Ms. Rood. I have to confess that. I had no idea that a camera was above the door in City Hall." He released an exasperated sigh. "Or that the men who mugged me would tie me to Martin Fast's death."

"Of course not. An innocent mistake," she said in a near whisper, as if saying these words under her breath could almost erase the harm Jacob had caused.

"But a mistake, nonetheless," he replied.

"Yes. You're right." When Kali heard this admission, she knew she had to seize the opportunity. It would be a huge error to relieve him of the guilt he now accepted as his own.

"And have you prepared yourself, Jacob?"

She could hear his breathing, and his voice emerged in a near whimper. "Yes, ma'am."

"Good. This is a time that requires strength. Strength from all of us. We all entered this pact knowing that one by one we would cross over. The only surprise is that you have been chosen to lead us as we take our final steps forward. Did you expect that?"

"No." A breathy chuckle escaped his mouth. "No, I didn't expect that at all."

"Well, you've been blessed with an extra honor now, haven't you?"

"I didn't think of that."

"Well you should. Now is the time to embrace it, Jacob. Let me hear you say it. Say, *I have the honor.*"

A silence filled the line and just as Kali was about to repeat herself, she heard Jacob's voice.

"I have ... I have the honor."

"And the honor is mine," she added. "Say it, Jacob."

"And the honor is mine." His voice held steady and carried a measure of certainty.

"Now do you have the code?" She waited a moment. "Revelation eight, verse seven."

"Yes."

"Repeat if for me."

" 'The first angel sounded,' " he recited, " 'and there followed hail and fire mingled with blood ... and they were cast upon the earth.' "

"And do you understand it? Understand that this promise will carry you to the other side."

"Yes, ma'am. I do," he whispered.

She imagined him sitting in his one-bedroom apartment with its bay window looking over the corner of Dolores and Fourteenth in San Francisco. She could see him staring into the floor, gazing at the grains of sand that had spilled across the worn linoleum, knowing that his time had run out.

"Then I will see you there." As she spoke a mild tremor rippled under her voice. She wondered if he'd heard it, this tremble of doubt. To cover her hesitation she pressed on.

"And Jacob, I know you will be there to greet me when I arrive."

"Yes. I know."

"Good-bye."

"Good-bye, ma'am."

She waited a moment, wondering if she should say more, tell him that he had been a dutiful and reliable soldier, but then she thought that more talk might dampen his resolve. She set the phone back in its cradle and pressed her aching forehead into her open palms. Jacob was the first to go, she thought. Just the first. Her turn would come soon enough.

Jacob Bell stared into the open page of his Bible. Page 963 of the Gideon Bible that he had stolen from the night table in his room at the Motel Six near the Interstate 80 in Reno after he'd flushed out the last of his stake in the Saltmill Casino on a rainy night in November. He'd bet his last hand on three of a kind—sevens—but lost the gamble to a full house.

The Gideon Bible was the one thing he'd salvaged from his final washout. It offered some kind of hope. Faith that something—who knew what it *really* was?—would follow the complete emptiness of his collapse. As it turned out, that something was Kali Rood and her foundation. A cause for soldiers of faith. A mission for those who'd lost their way. And beyond ... well, soon he would understand that, too.

After another moment he carefully tore the page from the Bible and set the book on the table next to his bed. He stared at the vellum paper and let the words enter his mind. Last year, when Kali Rood had told them of its importance, he'd highlighted the verse with a yellow marker to aid his memory. *The first angel sounded.* That was Kali Rood herself. *And then there followed hail and fire mingled with blood.* That was the shooting of Martin Fast. He himself—Jacob Bell—had done that: had delivered the hail of fire mingled with blood, as a human agent of the divine Book of Revelations. *And they were cast upon the earth.* This is the consequence that must now follow. The last step which would open the door to eternity. To *his* eternity.

He set his cellphone on the floor, raised his foot and crushed the plastic under the heel of his boot. The phone crunched into a dozen pieces and scattered across the linoleum flooring. He gathered them up, staggered over to the bathroom and dropped the broken fragments into the toilet bowl. He flushed the water and watched them disappear. Then he pulled the ID and credits cards from his wallet, cut each one in half with a pair of scissors, released them into the bowl and washed them away.

He drew a deep breath, walked over to the double-hung window looking onto Dolores Street and raised the lower section that led onto the fire escape. Although he had to climb only one story, he knew he had to steel himself for the ascent. He clutched the Biblical passage in his left hand and stepped onto the metal grate. As he stood there considering his situation, he pulled his watch from his wrist and threw it across the street towards the far sidewalk. He listened to the metallic rattle and clack as it hit the pavement, skipped over the curb and disappeared behind a garbage can.

He turned to the ladder, put a foot onto the first rung and then decided that he needed both hands free in order to clamber up to the flat roof of the apartment building. He folded the page from Revelations and tucked it into his shirt pocket. Then he grabbed the rung above his head, set his foot on the lowest bar and began to climb. As he pulled himself up to the roof he found himself silently repeating the line that foretold his death. *And they were cast upon the earth. And they were cast upon the earth. And they were cast upon the earth.*

The words had a hypnotic effect and when he stood on the precipice and peered down onto Delores Street his trance was complete. All the questions about life that had so perplexed him now evaporated. He no longer knew what they were. In fact, all thoughts dissolved into nothingness. All that existed was this single moment in time and his penetrating awareness of it. As he dove head-first toward the earth, he felt the wings of angels brushing the hair against the nape of his neck. There was that, and then nothing.

Chapter Seventeen

The light sprinkle began to intensify as Eve Noon turned from Montgomery Street onto Vallejo. She didn't mind the rain. Like everyone else in the Bay Area, she'd been hoping for a break in the four-year drought and she knew it would take more than a few days of scattered showers to ease the mounting anxiety everyone felt.

Today especially, the drizzle reinforced her mood, the dreary funk that she'd slipped into since Will had left town for New York, and now, Paris. She knew he had to leave, knew that his pursuit of the killers was his way of confronting the threat before it destroyed him.

"The best defense is a good offense," he'd chuckled on their last day together. An old cliché, but they'd both embraced its bleak wisdom. And despite the odds against him, she couldn't dispute the logic. She knew it was his way of trying to protect her from becoming collateral damage in the escalating terror. But his absence had already become painful. It was an ache that throbbed just below her heart, a weakness in her gut where part of her body had been cut out and discarded.

Since she'd come into her astonishing fortune Eve had tried to establish a new balance in her life. The twin inheritance from the estates of Gianna Whitelaw and her fiancé Raymond Toeplitz—including the millions in his bitcoin wallet—provided a blessing and a curse.

On one hand, the money bestowed an invisible safety net. Which she needed. As a single woman working independently as a private investigator with a female-only clientele, she knew her prospects were limited.

On the other hand, it had a not-so-subtle way of changing the course of her life. She wanted something better not only for her clients, but for herself, too. After months of indecision she finally broke through her ambivalence, sold her condo on Geary Boulevard and purchased the renovated cottage on Telegraph Hill. Meanwhile, Will had taken a leave of absence from his job to write his book. Since he had no monthly paycheck coming in, she invited him to move in with her. She told him he could use the little office on the second floor. There he could write his book, *Who Shot The Sheriff?* And share her bed.

She remembered the look on his face when she made this proposal. The bewildered laugh he gave in return. She knew that he loved her—or something very close to it—but he couldn't bring himself to say the words. His past got in the way. The unresolved relationships with his parents and their separate, solitary deaths. The tangled feelings about his previous wife's cancer. The personal tragedy he suffered when his son Buddy died while in the car with his drunk girlfriend. And then there was the unrevealed mystery of whatever had happened to him in Abu Ghraib during his three years with military intelligence in Iraq. All of it led to his irrational belief that whatever he loved would die.

The insane part of all this, or at least the part that drove her half crazy, was that the more he demurred, the more determined she was to love and nurture him. Besides, she told herself, their sex life was perfect. *Perfect*. So even though the scales weren't ideally balanced regarding her emotional life, just like the Tony Bennett song said, she still loved him body and soul.

The money also bought power. Since she'd purchased ten percent of the *eXpress*, she realized how true that old cliché was, too. Now she had an opportunity—*a responsibility*—to bring her cause into the broad public debate. There were only two conditions she'd set out with her purchase agreement. One, that the *eXpress* would shift its focus to expose criminal government and corporate corruption. Two, that within a year she had an option to increase her share of the company to fifty-one percent. Above all she wanted a purpose that she could call her own, an engine for social change.

As she considered all this the rain began to fall in sheets across the road and roll off the storefront awnings along Vallejo. Down the hill, two blocks ahead of her near Grant Street, Eve could see Leanne Spratz as she entered Caffe Trieste.

Eve pushed open the door to the Trieste and saw Leanne carrying a cup of espresso to the corner table set next to the back wall. Good, she thought to herself. We'll need the privacy to discuss Jacob Bell and why he'd landed face-first on Dolores Street.

Leanne bore a worried look. She held her open palms against the sides of her temples as if she was sheltering her head from an impending migraine. "The lockdown on this case is tighter than I've ever seen before. Hey, we've both seen how the feds like to grab the ball, close down the game and move to their own baseball diamond. But this thing with Jacob Bell has gone to a whole new level."

Eve nodded in sympathy. When she heard that Jacob Bell had been found dead following his dive onto the sidewalk below his apartment building, she assumed the FBI would snatch the file out of the hands of the SFPD while his body was still oozing. After all, the local police still maintained that Toby Squire had murdered Martin Fast. But once Will identified Jacob Bell in the video with Squire and Raymond Guzman, finding Bell became the new priority. And now that he'd surfaced—literally—the feds would do their best to uncover Bell's hidden world and the links to Fast, Waterston, and the other victims on the kill list.

"Can't say I'm surprised," Eve offered. "But there must be a few leads that slipped from the FBI into the SFPD's fingers."

"A few. Fortunately, Jill DeRosa was the first responder after Bell's face plant. The same cop who Finch called when he spotted Toby in the T-Loin."

Eve nodded. The T-Loin meant the Tenderloin district. "And?"

"And so I was talking to *her.*" She dipped her shoulder to suggest that DeRosa had let a detail or two slip out. "Jacob Bell had nothing on him. No watch, no rings, no wallet, no cellphone. Nothing. Or in his apartment. He was living like a ghost."

"So. He intentionally stripped himself of his own identity. Either that or he was killed for it. Could be murder or suicide."

"Fifty-fifty," she conceded and continued. "All that was left were his fingerprints."

Eve let the black humor pass without a smile. "So how many priors did he have?"

"Just one. Fraud, 2013."

"Yeah? Who was his victim?"

Leanne frowned, a look that revealed she'd seen it all too many times before. "His wife. Served two months, then got sprung on appeal."

"So he had the smarts to get a good lawyer."

"I guess."

Eve studied Leanne's face and waited. She knew more details would follow. Despite the FBI's information embargo, Leanne had more juice to squeeze out, and she always saved the last few drops for a guessing game to taunt Eve.

"It turns out that Bell was a card player. Loved the casinos in Reno. Specialized in classic five-card draw poker."

"No imagination, obviously."

Leanne laughed at this. "Gotta miss you, Eve. Anyway, after he's released on the fraud conviction he virtually disappears. On paper, that is. Until yesterday."

Eve grimaced and glanced away. "So that's all you've got?"

Leanne rolled her shoulders from side to side. "Well, there is one more thing."

"From DeRosa?"

She shook her head as if she didn't want to confirm the source. "A page from the Bible was found in his shirt pocket.

A page from Revelations. Someone had highlighted a verse with a yellow marker."

"Which one?"

"I don't know." She shrugged. "Top secret, apparently. The feds have it locked down. You know how they get."

Eve paused to consider this. The FBI loved enigmatic crimes. Passages from the Bible, Shakespeare, Homer—it didn't really matter what the source might be. Anything that resembled part of a puzzle was turned over to their teams of cryptologists, profilers and analysts. She guessed that Jacob Bell's death had been elevated from a probable suicide to part of a national murder conspiracy. Maybe they were right. In which case Will's theory that Bell was tied to Kali Rood made more sense.

Her fingers tapped at the side of her head. "Leanne, what if the feds have this right? That Bell is tied to something bigger."

"Like?"

"Like Kali Rood. Will saw him working for her when she was here in San Francisco."

"Okay, but like I said, the feds have officially moved all this into a different ball park. The trail is cold." She shrugged and held her hands up in a gesture of capitulation. "So what can you do?"

Eve set her elbows on the coffee table and leaned forward. "Last time we met, didn't you say you had a friend who went to the same high school as Kali Rood? In Philadelphia, right?"

"A friend of my cousin. In Malvern, just outside the city."

"Right." Eve pressed her lips together and focussed on Leanne with a steady gaze. "So. Now I need to speak to your cousin."

As Eve walked into the *eXpress* office, Wally caught her eye and flagged his left arm in the air. She'd known him for less than a year, but today he looked a decade older.

"Can I have ten minutes with you?" He smiled with a benign grin, a welcome look undermined by the burden of fatigue.

"Of course, Wally."

She entered his office and noticed Fiona sitting in one of the chairs in front of his desk. Eve sat beside her as Wally closed the door. The latch closed with a quiet click and he sat facing them.

"Something's come up, I'm afraid." He tapped two fingers against his lips as if he hoped to stop himself from saying more. "Eve, I was just bringing Fiona up to date, and you need to know this, too."

"All right." Eve glanced at Fiona and settled her hands onto the arm rests. "How can I help?"

"Thanks, but I doubt that you can. Let me just say this straight up. It's about my wife, Ginny." He tented his fingers over his mouth. "We got the diagnosis six months ago. She has pancreatic cancer. Now they're saying we've only got three to six weeks left."

Unsure how to respond, Eve looked away. She covered her mouth with a hand and then turned back to him. "Wally, I'm sorry. That's terrible news."

"Yeah." His lips sputtered slightly as he held back a sob. Then he drew himself up in his chair and leaned forward. "I've talked to the Parson brothers and they're giving me a part-time leave. I'll be in when I can, and available by phone when I'm needed. Anyway, things should continue on here without any hiccups. Fiona's been appointed

Interim Managing Editor and taking on my responsibilities until Ginny and I get through this." He paused as if he were imagining what that might mean. "I want you to know that the Parsons and I, and all the staff here, have complete confidence that Fiona will do a fantastic job"—he swept a hand toward her with a genuine smile—"especially as we sharpen our focus on criminal corruption."

"Thanks, Wally." Fiona nodded with a smile of appreciation and turned to Eve. "I just want to make sure you're comfortable with this."

"Of course." For a moment Eve felt as if she'd been ambushed. Even as a minority shareholder, shouldn't she have been included in any personnel decisions? She considered the situation and decided to take the high road. "Wally, as far as I'm concerned you should take as much time as you need. I can only imagine what this is like for you and Ginny. So. No question—go home and tend to your wife. And yourself."

She turned to Fiona. "And you've got my complete support. More than. We're all going to be leaning on you, especially Will. And I'm going to dig in on this, too. I've got some contacts in the SFPD I'm working with. This morning I spoke to a source about Jacob Bell."

"Did they confirm it's a suicide?"

"Could go either way, but as you know, the case has been picked up by the FBI. Which makes me certain that they've tied him to the other murders on Will's list. If that's the case, then they've found a conspiracy at play, which Will believes is tied to Kali Rood."

"I've been thinking the same," Wally said.

"I have a lead," Eve continued, "to someone who once knew her when she was in high school. I was just about to track it down."

"All right." Fiona glanced at Wally, then turned her chair to face Eve. "This is what I want you to do. Dig up whatever you can on her. If you need to get into online databases or internet research ask Gabe Finkleman to help you. He's our research ninja. Once you have enough info to profile her, pass it on to Brian Stutz in the bog. He'll write the story and I'll sign it off when I'm ready to break Rood's part of the story." She paused to consider something. "Are you in contact with Will?"

Eve nodded. "Only once so far. He's just gone to Paris to track down what happened to the latest victim. Looks like he's still alive."

"Edmund Austen."

"Right, the Anglican minister."

Fiona nodded. "Okay. Next time you're in touch, tell him to file a story whenever he can. We got his profile on Jayne Waterston but we need more. Once a day if possible."

Fiona turned to Wally with a look that revealed she'd now taken control of the newsroom. He smiled and gave her a nod of encouragement.

"You probably know this better than anyone," Fiona continued, "but the FBI will try to shut us down every step of the way. However, the longer we can keep the story on the front burner, the sooner the whole case is likely to break open. It's all about momentum. Once we start we don't let go until we win."

Eve felt the rush of the story building. *So this is what it's like.* The drug that drew Will into this intoxicating addiction. No wonder she couldn't stop him.

"All right. Anything else?" Fiona looked from Eve to Wally.

"Yeah, one more thing," Wally said with a sheepish look. "With all that's gone on at home, I neglected to tell you. That license plate that Will asked us to trace. I got something on it this morning from the New York Department of Motor Vehicles." He paused to search through his iPad. "The car is registered to someone named Dorion Salter. I'll forward the details to you."

"Dorion Salter." Fiona made a note on her pad and arched her eyebrows with a look of surprise. "So tell us. How *exactly* did you get into New York State DMV files?"

"Old dog, old tricks." Wally smiled his marvelous cheshire cat grin. For a moment he seemed to have forgotten his wife's cancer. "You know, I think you kids are going to miss having me here to boss you around."

Chapter Eighteen

Will Finch clambered up the stone steps to the Hôpital Hôtel-Dieu and found his way to the nursing station in the intensive care ward. The desk hummed with activity as several nurses and physicians clustered in groups of twos and threes, all of them speaking in rapid exchanges that Finch could barely grasp.

In his early teens Finch's French speaking skills had been passable. In the first year of the 1990s recession Will's maternal grandfather hired Will's dad as a sales manager in his jewelry store in Montreal. On short notice his mother, father and Will moved from New Jersey to the Montreal suburb of St. Laurent where they lived until his mother's death in 1997, the year he graduated from high school and returned with his father to New Jersey. In those five years Finch learned to speak French well enough to navigate most pedestrian conversations. But when it came to religion, politics—or a technical subject like emergency medicine—he fell out of his comfort zone. Not only did he fail to comprehend the specialized vocabulary, he couldn't grasp the colloquial jargon and acronyms.

"Pardonnez-moi," he said in a loud voice.

When no one responded, he slapped his hand on the countertop and tried again. He caught the eye of a nurse who had been studying a file on her computer.

"Excuse me," he said in French. "I'm looking for Edmund Austen. Can you help me?"

"And you are who?" The nurse spoke with a heavy accent. Her face was fixed with a stoic cast, as if she needed a stern demeanor to fend off the constant interruptions.

"You speak English. Thank you," Will began. "I'm here to see Edmund Austen. I understand he came into the hospital yesterday. A stabbing victim."

"Not very well." Her face softened with a look of compassion. "You are his frère? Or from his famille?"

With these questions in half-English, half-French, Finch realized that she was trying to help. If he could claim some relationship to Austen, Will might be able to visit him.

"Beau-frère," he said—brother-in-law—and quickly realized this was the correct ploy. He and Austen were roughly the same age, but as brothers-in-law they wouldn't share the same surname. He told her his name was Joel Griffin, leaned toward her over the countertop in a gesture of confidentiality and attempted to continue the conversation in French. "I just flew in when I heard what happened. Do you know where he is?"

The nurse nodded and checked the desk monitor.

"I'm afraid he needs another surgery," she said in slow, careful French. "Do you understand?"

He nodded.

"But his wife is here," she added. "At his room. Perhaps she's your sister?"

He smiled. "What room is he in?"

"Cinquante-six B." She shrugged to suggest she didn't know the English equivalent.

He glanced behind him and saw the corridors branching in four directions. "Where?"

"To the right," she said and waved with her hand past his shoulder.

He turned and entered the hallway and began his search for 56B. After a few moments he found Austen's room and tapped at the door.

Finch took a step into the dim light and wavered. The antiseptic smell of the ward mingled with a stale odor of feces. The single window was shut tight and a pale drape had been pulled halfway across the opening. Next to an empty hospital bed a woman sat in a wooden chair, a damp tissue balled in her hand. She dabbed at her eyes and studied the nurse who stood next to the wall.

"Can you say that again? How long will the surgery be?" she said with a knot of exasperation in her voice. Finch imagined that she'd posed this question several times and either hadn't received a satisfactory answer, or she'd been unable to communicate with the nurses and doctors attending her husband.

"Maybe two hours," the nurse said in French and pointed two fingers toward the clock, then shrugged and looked away in frustration. When she spotted Finch she took a step toward him.

"Can I help you?"

"She said, 'maybe two hours'." Will looked from the nurse to the bereaved woman and stepped forward. "I'm here to see Mrs. Austen."

"That's me. You speak English?" Her expression took on a look of relief.

"Yes. I'm Joel Griffin." He smiled and held his hand out to her.

She grasped his hand and attempted to stand up but then faltered, slumped back into the chair and released a heavy sigh.

"I'm sorry. I'm so exhausted," she said. "I couldn't sleep on the plane and I haven't slept since the moment I saw Ed." She paused a moment. "Do you know him?"

"In a manner of speaking."

She clasped her hands together and scanned his face. "Then maybe you can help me. I don't speak a word of French and I've only met one doctor who can even half-explain what's happened to Ed. Then the police came with all kinds of questions. I don't understand any of it. Then Ed suffered from some kind of cardiac crisis and just now the surgeon told me he has to operate on Ed immediately."

Finch held a hand up in an effort to slow her down. "What did the police tell you?"

"I don't know." She pressed the frayed tissue to her eyes. "He was brought here by ambulance. He'd been crossing the Seine on one of the bridges when he was attacked. *Someone stabbed him....*" She struggled for breath and then forced herself to continue. "Then the doctor sent them off, and I don't know, what—" She burst into tears and covered her eyes with both hands.

When he realized that she couldn't go on, he turned to the nurse and spoke to her in French. "I need to speak to Mrs. Austen privately. Can you give us a moment?"

The nurse glanced over his shoulder as if she'd seen something important taking place in the hallway. "Of course," she said and left the room.

Finch turned back to Mrs. Austen and sat on the edge of the empty bed next to her. This put him about three feet above her, and he had to lean down to place his hand on her shoulder. As soon as he touched her she shuddered with a light gasp, and then relaxed.

"Listen, I can't imagine what you've been through, but I do know it's been very traumatic. Can I take you out of here? I saw a small waiting room down the hall. Then we can sort this thing out, okay."

She nodded and turned her head from side to side as if she might be searching for her purse.

"Would that be all right?" he asked.

"I don't want to leave him. You say it's just close by?"

He offered her a sympathetic smile. "Just three doors down."

"Yes. All right." She managed to lift herself from the chair and took her purse in both hands.

When they reached the waiting room, Finch guided her to two chairs next to a window that overlooked an inner courtyard. The exterior walls were made of chiseled stone, and the yard was paved with uneven cobblestones that must have been three or four hundred years old. In any other circumstance, Finch reasoned, tourists would be marveling at the antique construction and architecture. But he knew Mrs. Austen barely understood where they were, let alone what might happen next. Once he settled her into a chair, however, she seemed to quickly assess her predicament.

"I'm not sure how you know Ed," she said. "How did you find us here?"

"It's complicated. But if you bear with me, I'll try to explain everything. I work for the *San Francisco eXpress* and I've been covering a series of murders that have taken place over the past few weeks."

A dark look crossed her face. "You mean this cursed list."

She pronounced it *curse-ed*. Finch imagined that she lived in another era. An earlier, more formal time and place. "He told you about it?"

"It's crazy. He was told the morning he left Toronto to fly over here for the conference." She shuddered as if she'd been dropped into a madhouse. "The RCMP called and spoke to him about it. They said to be cautious, but they weren't sure if it wasn't just some crazy hoax." She studied him with a pleading look. "But it's real isn't it?"

"I'm afraid so, Mrs. Austen."

She waved a hand. "Please. Call me Donna. And your name again, is…?"

Finch hesitated and decided to stick with his alias, at least for now. "Joel Griffin. Just call me Joel."

"And how do you know Ed?" She shook her head as if she were trying to wake up. "Apart from being a journalist, I mean."

"My name's on the list. They're targeting me, too."

She blinked in disbelief. "But—"

"Madam Austen?"

Two men stood at the doorway with an air of expectation. Finch instantly identified them as plain-clothes cops. *Flics*, as the French called them. The bigger of the two flashed his ID and strode across the room until he stood above her.

"Désolé, mais nous devons vous parler immédiatement."

She looked to Finch.

"He says he has to speak to you right away," he said. "They're cops," he added.

The big man blinked and waved his partner forward. The second man continued.

"I am Sergent Rivière, this is Inspecteur Boll of the Sûreté. Monsieur, I have to ask you to leave us while we speak to Mrs. Austen." His English was decent, on par with Finch's ability to speak French. "Otherwise it will be necessary to take Mrs. Austen to our headquarters." He raised his eyebrows as if the choice was obvious. No one would want to be interrogated in the Sûreté HQ.

"All right." Finch raised a hand, a bid to take another moment to finish his conversation with her. "Donna, this is my hotel, the Hôtel Esméralda. You can walk there from here. It's just across the bridge." He drew the hotel business card from his bag and passed it to her. "When you're done here, please get in touch with me. I have much more that I'd like to talk to you about."

"Monsieur, please."

Sergent Rivière set his hand on Finch's shoulder. Finch shrugged it away as he stood, and put on a smile. Neither of them wanted any more trouble.

Earlier that morning—before he'd arrived at the Hôpital Hôtel-Dieu—Finch took a taxi from the Charles de Gaulle Airport to the Hôtel Esméralda and checked into the only available room. It consisted of little more than a single bed with an antique headboard, a night table with a stick lamp, a wooden dresser, and a two-foot wide freestanding armoire. A wall-phone connecting to the front desk was bolted to a metal frame next to the door. Oak wainscoting covered the walls from the floor up to Finch's waist. The rest of the walls were papered with a pastel hydrangea print. A tall, narrow window looked onto the street. It opened no more than six inches. There was no toilet or sink; the shared bathroom was located at the end of the hallway. However, the room was clean and in its minimalist style, elegant. He booked it for two nights and then made his way to the hospital to track down Edmund Austen.

After meeting with Donna Austen, Finch left the hospital and took a few minutes to sit in front of Notre Dame Cathedral to admire the Gothic masterpiece. He'd heard that the stone masons had passed on vital information to their sons and grandsons—instructions about adapting certain structures within the Nave to ensure that the flying buttresses could support the weight of the vault. The grandsons in turn transmitted the messages to their sons and grandsons. After one hundred and eighty-two years the church was completed in 1345. If nothing else, it represented continuity of purpose. And the unbroken faith that we are all in God's care, Finch thought. An idea that Kali Rood would surely embrace.

By two o'clock the sidewalks in the streets surrounding the church were thick with pedestrians ambling from block to block beside the book stalls, cafes, boulangeries and flower shops. The mass of tourists far exceeded anything he'd see on a typical day in San Francisco. After all, France attracted more visitors than any other country in the world and he imagined that the majority of them found their way into the capital city and most of them likely wandered along this historic island in the middle of the Seine River.

He loved the randomness of this kind of human carnival. Random, and yet somehow harmonized by the clicking cameras and cellphones, the open maps hanging from the hands of disoriented travelers. Everyone seemed lost—and yet delighted by it all.

Then reality set in. At any moment he could scan the crowds and see trios of soldiers pacing slowly along the sidewalks. They were armed with automatic machine guns and they wore the bleak expressions of men on the hunt. The rash of terror attacks had set the entire country on high alert, and Finch realized that his mission would seem like a bothersome side-show to the cops assigned to interrogate Mrs. Austen.

After sitting for ten minutes he felt the weariness of the past few days drag through his arms and chest. He lifted himself from the bench where he sat, crossed the Pont des Arts, walked past the Shakespeare and Company bookstore, and rounded the corner to the Hôtel Esméralda.

Although it was only mid-afternoon, what he needed more than anything else was sleep. However, he didn't want to miss his rendez-vous with Donna Austen, so he asked the concierge to ring him when she arrived at the hotel.

"Oui, monsieur," the concierge responded. He wore a rectangular name plate on his lapel that said *Roland*.

"How long are you here on the desk?"

"My shift ends at midnight." He smiled with a formal courtesy.

"Good. And if I don't answer the phone in my room, then bring her up and knock on the door," Will said in French and passed five Euros to the concierge. "Roland, I cannot miss my appointment with Mrs. Austen. Do you understand?"

"Of course, monsieur." Roland smiled dutifully and pocketed the money.

Feeling confident, Finch climbed the wooden staircase to the second floor and made his way along the corridor to his tiny room. As he entered the chamber, he recalled the trouble he'd had when he neglected to charge his phone at the Hotel Pennsylvania. Not this time, he murmured to himself, thankful that for the first time in years, he had no phone. No one could track him. No one could sweep behind him and gut him like they'd done to Edmund Austen.

After he plugged his laptop into the wall outlet, he leaned against the windowsill and looked onto Rue Saint-Julien le Pauvre. On the opposite side of the street stood a small park surrounded by a wrought-iron fence. The park lawn was clotted with tourists loitering in the small green space, as if they were all trying to gather the necessary stamina to make another foray into the marvels of the city.

After a brief lull the tug of these distractions faded and he settled on the bed. He heeled off his shoes and let them thunk onto the floor. He reached for a pillow to tuck under his head, drew a long breath and slipped over the edge of consciousness into a restless sleep.

He woke with a start. A feeling of disorientation frightened him as he scrambled to unwind a sheet from his neck. Somehow the bed linen had coiled itself around his face and under his arms. He struggled and then tugged it away in a panic. *Where am I?*

After a moment, he recognized the noise of revelers from the park across the street and their laughter broke his confusion. "All right," he muttered, "You're in Paris." He sat on the side of the bed and rubbed his eyes with his hands, then slipped on his shoes and made his way down to the bathroom at the end of the hall. When he returned to his room he picked up the handset to the wall phone and buzzed the concierge desk. After three rings, an unfamiliar voice answered.

"Is Roland there?" he asked.

"Sorry, monsieur, his shift is finished."

"Finished? He told me he'd be here until midnight."

A hesitation. "Yes, but he was called home for a family matter."

He paused to consider this. "Are there any messages for me? Joel Griffin in room 25."

"Nothing. I'm sorry, monsieur."

Finch felt a wave of inertia wash through him. He'd come all this distance and discovered nothing. He had to meet with Donna Austen as soon as possible. While Edmund Austen was still conscious, she'd been able to talk with her husband, and until Finch talked her through a probing interview, he had no way to discover who had attacked Edmund. Then another, more depressing thought struck him: what if Edmond failed to survive his surgery? Who knows what might become of Donna following his death? She could collapse in a bereaved breakdown, ignore Finch's request to meet with her and take the next flight back to Canada.

He decided to call the Hôpital Hôtel-Dieu to determine if Edmund had recovered from the second surgery. The answer to that question would guide his next move. But just as he picked up the telephone, his laptop buzzed. He put the handset back in the cradle and opened his computer. The Messenger icon flashed on the toolbar: Eve.

He pressed his back against the headboard at the top of the bed, nestled the computer in his lap, and launched the text application.

Her message read: "Are you there?"

"Yes," he typed. "Just woke up." He checked the clock at the top of the screen. It read 9:17 PM. "Just slept six hours. Guess I've turned night into day."

"More breaking news here: Jacob Bell died yesterday."

Will read this twice, tried to decipher what it might signal. When nothing came to him, he replied with one word: "How?"

"Fell from his apartment rooftop on Dolores."

Finch shook his head when he understood the implications. With Jacob Bell eliminated, his connection to Kali Rood was severed and she'd made a clean break from Bell and Martin Fast's murder. He typed a new message to Eve: "Did he jump, or was he pushed?"

The response came seconds later. "Jumped or pushed—FBI won't say."

Finch smirked at this. Before he could add more to the conversation, a new text came in from Eve.

"Can't stay long. I'm heading to New York. I've got a lead on KR."

KR. He knew this meant Kali Rood. Obviously Eve had shifted her focus. Maybe Wally Gimbel and Fiona Page had also come around to think of Kali as the chief puppeteer in the lengthening string of murders.

"Good. Keep her in your sights. Nothing to report here. May be a dead end." His fingers stumbled on the keyboard and he erased the last sentence. This was no time for black humor.

Her next message filled him with renewed dread: "Two more list members killed within three hours of one another: #7, Alex Baumann, fell from Reichenbach Falls, Germany. #19, Andrea Verona, shot in Hilo, Hawaii. Looks like multiple perps at work."

Will washed a hand over his face. The numbers 7 and 19 indicated the victims' position on the list. Their deaths brought the total to six. Seven, if Edmund failed to survive his surgery. And Eve couldn't be more right. Two murders within three hours—and half a world away from one another. It confirmed that at least five assassins were at work: one each for Martin Fast, Jayne Waterston, Edmund Austen and two more corresponding to the latest victims. Maybe it was a one-to-one match, which meant twenty-four killers assigned to eliminate every name on the list.

Finch struggled to come up with a response. After a moment he replied, "Any good news?"

"Yes. Saved the best for last," Eve wrote. "The car in Manhattan is registered to Dorion Salter. Ring a bell?"

Dorion Salter. The name meant nothing to him. Perhaps Jayne Waterston's twin brother might know him. Finch scratched at his uncombed hair and wished he had a coffee to get him rolling. He waited a moment to sort out his thoughts. With Eve closing in on Kali, and the owner of the mystery car now a known entity, he realized he had to get back to the States. But what about Donna Austen? He couldn't let whatever information she might possess slip past him. If he couldn't find her tonight, he'd need at least one more day to track her down—if she was still in Paris.

"Don't recognize the name," he wrote and then continued, "I'll join you in two days at most. Will buy a new phone in NYC then text you to make a connection. Expect something from an unknown caller. It'll be me."

A long pause followed, then Eve sent a final message. "All right. See you in NYC. I love you."

He smiled at that, then sent a closing note to her. "XXXXX."

Finch called the hospital and after three failed attempts to reach the ICU nursing station he was connected to the main receptionist. She was unable to provide any news other than a simple evasion. "I'm sorry, but we cannot provide patient information over the telephone."

In Finch's mind this meant that Edmund Austen was either dead or in such severe condition that no one would comment. On the other hand, following their interview with Donna the Sûreté may have decided to block all communications about Austen. If he had survived, perhaps they believed Edmund might still be at risk from a second attack. Who knew? Only Donna could answer these questions and she was either still at the hospital, or had forgotten to meet with Finch—or worse, she'd already left France in complete despair.

With so many doubts on his mind, Finch decided to find a cafe and have a light dinner and a double espresso. After that he would head back to the hospital and try to track down Donna in person.

But as he stepped onto the lobby floor he was greeted by a surprise. Sitting in one of the antique armchairs next to the lobby window was none other than Mrs. Austen. Her face was drawn with anxiety. As he approached her he could see that her eyes were bloodshot and her cheeks worn from tears. He assumed that her husband had not survived.

"Donna." He spoke in a near whisper, hoping not to startle her.

Despite his calm demeanor, she jumped when she heard her name. "Mr. Griffin. I didn't know how to find you. And I couldn't make the receptionist understand—"

She held a hand to cover her mouth and let out a brief sob. When she recovered her self control she said, "He's gone. Just two hours ago." She lifted both hands in the air and let them drop into her lap.

He pulled a chair beside her and rested a hand on her

forearm. "I'm sorry. I can't tell you how awful this makes me feel."

Her eyes swept over his face and she took his fingers in her own. For a moment Finch felt as though she needed to comfort him. How strange grief is, he thought, the way it seizes you and the tricks it can play. They sat looking at one another, unsure how to continue.

"Listen, I need some food and a coffee. Will you come with me? There's a place not far away."

She nodded and released his hand. "Yes."

She followed him blindly through a light rain up the block until they reached Aux Trois Mailletz, a cafe with a dozen round tables lined in a row on the sidewalk. They took the only empty table and sat under the awning in the wicker chairs facing the street. Donna said that she couldn't eat, but she ordered a cup of tea. Despite his hunger Finch didn't want to appear out of synch with her. He asked for a double espresso and a croissant sandwich with ham and cheese.

"Can you fill me in?" He smiled to provide some reassurance. He needed her to believe that he could help her. That somehow he could set her on a path to recovery. It would start with this conversation. He told her that he would help her navigate all the procedures and paperwork needed to get her and Edmund home. Then she could begin her life again. This time on her own.

"Tell me everything that happened since the Sûreté talked to you, Donna. The more you can tell me, the more it will help to get to the bottom of this." He waved a hand to suggest that "this" was the thing that had sent them to sit together and sift through the events that led to her husband's tragic death.

"It happened so fast," she whispered, "and now he's gone."

Finch studied her face before responding. She seemed coherent, as if she'd already absorbed the fact of her husband's passing—but not the pain of her loss. Finch had had a similar experience when his five-year-old son Buddy died. The loss and then the pain. One was cold, the other absolutely searing.

"For what it's worth, I once experienced something similar. I know what it's like to try to pick up the pieces."

Donna nodded as if this was something she knew she had to do. To find the fragments of a life that was once hers alone and then gather them together into something that resembled an independent existence.

"Donna, I'd like to talk to you about how this happened. While it's still fresh in your mind. I know the Sûreté went over this with you. Can you do it one more time for me?"

She shook her head. "I don't know."

Finch sipped his espresso and ate some of the croissant. He knew he had to wait. There could be no rushing her.

"How's the tea?" he asked.

She glanced at the teacup and shook her head. She had yet to try it. She lifted the cup to her lips and blew over the surface before sampling it on her tongue. "All right, I suppose. Thank you for your kindness."

He smiled with a look of sympathy.

"Donna, did the French police ask you about the list? The one with Edmund's name on it."

She glanced away as if she was studying the passing crowds on Rue Galande. "Yes," she said without looking at him.

"Just so you know, my name is on the list, too."

With a start, she turned her head back to him. "Joel Griffin? I don't remember seeing that."

He took a moment to consider this. She was no fool.

"My real name is Will Finch." He tipped his head slightly to acknowledge the deception. He drew his passport from his courier bag and passed it to her. As she examined it he added, "I'm traveling under an alias to prevent anyone from finding me."

"All right." Her voice carried a note of suspicion. Nonetheless, she seemed able to accept the deception. "I can understand that."

"There are now seven victims on the list who've been killed. I'm trying to find out anything I can about them. So far you're the only person who's talked to a survivor—brief as it was. I think you can help me."

"How?" She turned to face him directly now and from her posture he could tell she had shifted away from her own loss, at least for the moment.

"I know you weren't with Edmund when he was attacked, but what did he tell you before his second surgery?"

She shook her head to suggest that Edmund had been mostly incoherent. "You have to understand that he'd gone through two hours of surgery to repair the damage to his liver and right kidney. That was before they'd let me see him. Then I had maybe thirty minutes on my own with him before they found the aneurism. Then they took him in for the second surgery and he…."

Finch realized that she was about to slip back into the bottomless well of her grief. He had to focus her attention on that thirty-minute interval.

"And in that time, in that thirty minutes you had with him, could he speak?"

"Barely." She sniffed and pulled a tissue from her purse and wiped her eyes.

"What did he say?"

"He was incoherent." She shrugged. "It sounded like 'row bare.' "

"Row bare?" He studied her face. "Did that have some special meaning to him?"

"No. It made no sense to me either. But he spoke the language fluently. Does it mean something in French?"

Finch struggled to find an answer but nothing came to mind. He decided to change course. "Did he recognize his attacker?"

"Maybe." She shuddered to think of it. " No. No, I don't think so."

As Finch took another sip of espresso he wondered how to continue. This single clue—*row bare*—only created more confusion. Maybe he should back up, take the conversation to another level. "Donna, I'd heard that there's some controversy about Edmund and his church."

She rolled her head with a look of exasperation, a look that said, *you bet there is.*

"The Anglican Church, am I right?"

"Yes, it's a church in Canada. They're called Episcopalians in the US."

"I know. I lived in Canada during my high school years."

"Really?" Her face brightened and she took another drink from her tea. "In Toronto?"

"Montreal. That's where I picked up my French." He smiled again. "Can you tell me about the conflict in the church?"

"Well," she said and drew a long breath of air as if she needed to prepare herself. "Edmund was beloved by his congregation. While church attendance was falling off everywhere else, it only continued to grow in our church. Why? Because Edmund continued to question the perceived wisdom. Over the past two years he even began to question the existence of a Biblical God—and all the moral and cultural values that go with it. Every Sunday he'd confess his doubts from the pulpit. But he also preached to the congregation that we could replace the emptiness we might feel with a love for one another. We are all sentient beings, he liked to say, living on a beautiful planet that offered everything we required to live for the foreseeable future. But if we wanted to enjoy that future, we would have to change."

"Change? Change what?"

"Everything. The way we live. Consumerism. Perpetual war. Fear of one another."

Finch smiled. "Sounds pretty Christian to me."

"That's what Edmund said. And why he refused to step down from his ministry when the deacon ordered him to resign.

Finch hesitated. "The deacon?"

"Yes. Part of the church hierarchy, one step below a bishop. Our diocese deacon couldn't exactly fire Edmund, but...."

In that moment he understood that the trip to Paris had led him down another blind alley. He had to get back to New York and connect with Eve. Still, he needed to be certain that Donna hadn't omitted a crucial detail.

"Donna, do you have any reason to believe that someone in the church would kill Edmund?"

Her head tilted as if she'd been nudged backward. "No. That's impossible. Despite their differences, no one would want to harm Edmund. He was *loved*. Even by his enemies."

Satisfied with her answer, he finished his croissant and washed it down with the dregs of his coffee.

"Look, tomorrow let's get back to the hospital and arrange for you and Edmund to get home, okay?"

"All right." She slumped into her chair with a dazed expression then turned her attention to him. "You're very kind. I guess this starts my new beginning, doesn't it."

He tried to smile again. Yes, he thought, a journey down a road you probably never imagined.

The next morning Will met Donna at the Hôpital Hôtel-Dieu and he guided her through the process of returning her husband's body to Toronto. By four-thirty they'd completed the necessary procedures and he walked her back to her hotel. Before they parted they embraced and Donna took his business card and promised to contact him so that one day she "could return his gift of generosity."

As he boarded his late-night flight to New York, he wondered what would become of her. She was one of the more kind-hearted women he'd met and he hoped those qualities would see her through. But he doubted that the world worked that way, that if you were decent and good some benevolent force would nurture and protect you. Donna Austen was already decent and good—and someone had murdered her husband with a butcher knife.

After his 747 settled into level flight, he drew his laptop from his bag and began to write the story of Edmund Austen's death in Paris. Within two hours he'd knocked off fifteen hundred words that laid out the chronicle of Edmund's attack and his subsequent demise on the surgical table. He tried to unlock the meaning of the victim's last words, *row bare*, and finally dismissed them. He read the draft through twice, editing as he went and then closed the computer and slipped it behind the netting in the seat ahead of him. As he drifted to sleep he made a note to email the story to Jeanine Fix at the *eXpress*. Within an hour she'd have it formatted and published on the internet. The story would add one more brick in the wall that he was building to contain the killers at large.

Little did he know just how many bricks that would take. Or how high the wall would climb.

Chapter Nineteen

After he landed at JFK, Finch made his way to a cellphone kiosk and purchased a Samsung, using Joel Griffin's credit card. Then he made his way to a Starbucks outlet, ordered a breakfast sandwich and Americano, and settled in a corner where he could observe anyone approaching him. The masses streaming through the airport concourse and the buzz of the restaurant provided the best cover he could hope for.

While he ate, Will considered his next series of moves. He decided to call Simon Waterston. Unless the FBI had brought him into their investigation—an unlikely possibility, he figured—Simon would have spent the last few days stewing about his murdered twin sister. He'd be eager to hear the name of the owner of the Cadillac parked in front of the Bohemian National Hall across the street from Jayne's apartment. But rather than disclose Dorion Salter's name over the phone, Will knew he could build a stronger partnership if he met Simon in person. Somewhere near his office would be suitable. If Simon felt motivated to dig deeper, he could access an array of national identity databases from the DA's headquarters.

After dealing with Simon, Finch knew that he had to get in touch with Eve. With any luck she'd already be in the city and by late afternoon or early evening he could hook up with her. When he considered Eve he realized that his earlier fears about her becoming collateral damage in his own death had dissipated. Slightly.

He sensed that both of them were closing in on some kind of break in the case. Who it involved, Dorion Salter or Kali Rood, he couldn't say with certainty. And if his hunch was correct, that every victim corresponded to a different killer, then what lay ahead wouldn't be resolved at once. No, he knew he was playing the long game. But he could feel it, feel the gut-pull that told him he was getting close to the point where things could crack open.

He sipped on his Americano and sent Eve a three-word text: *Where are you?*

Then he called Simon Waterston. Expecting his call to shunt into a voice mailbox, he was surprised when Simon picked up on the second ring.

"Simon, it's Will Finch from the *eXpress*. Do you have a few minutes?"

He heard Simon release a sharp sigh.

"Give me a second."

Finch heard a chair scrape across the floor, a door close.

"All right. Why are you calling?"

Finch recognized his apprehensive tone and recalled where they'd left off. Simon had distrusted any off-the-book approach to Jayne's murder. But he also remembered Simon's exasperation at the FBI's unwillingness to share any progress about the case. Finch decided to try to reel Simon back into his confidence by sharing what he knew.

"I've got the name of the Cadillac owner," he announced.

"You do?"

"Yeah. It's a bronze 2015 Cadillac SRX."

Another pause. "All right. I know that. But who does it belong to?"

"Not on the phone. And not where I am right now. Let's meet somewhere near your office. Is there a place we can talk, out in the open. A park or something like that?"

"No, no. Look … I've decided not to do it this way," he said with a gasp of exasperation, as if he were torn between two equally bad options. Cooperate to unearth his sister's killer—and risk his career—or turn away from the only man willing to help him find a solution.

"Look, Simon. I know this is hard for you. Hell, it's hard enough for me. But you have to trust me. As a reporter I can protect you as a news source. And as a lawyer you know the First Amendment shields me from having to reveal my sources. I promise I will never expose you."

A long silence filled the line and Finch could feel the ambivalence tearing Simon in both directions at once. Nonetheless he knew it was better to wait out the anxiety and let Simon speak first.

"I don't know," he said at last, "if you're challenged you'll be in jail for a very long time. Or until you give me up."

Finch shook his head in dismay. "Simon, I'm willing to bet that you've checked my file. Am I right?"

Finch had to wait through yet another brooding interlude.

"Yes."

"Good. And were you able to get into my military records."

"Yes."

"Then you saw that I sat out four months in the brig. Four months in military detention until my sources on the Abu Ghraib debacle came forward and I was absolved. And you know something?"

"What?"

"If it had gone the other way, and if those three sources stayed in the dark—then I'd still be locked up. And by the way, just by revealing that information to you—you can bet someone would try to put me back on the inside for that."

Finch could tell that Simon was considering all this. Will had given up enough information to make himself vulnerable. It was all about trust now. Going forward, they both had to have faith in one another.

"All right," Simon said at last. "Meet me at Columbus Park, just off the Worth Street entrance. Two o'clock."

In the early 1800s Columbus Park was part of a vast inner-city slum known as Five Points, the site of a grisly hand-to-hand street battle that killed over a hundred men during the New York City draft riots of 1863. But as Finch settled onto a park bench along one of the many sculpted pathways, he was struck by the civility of the space. In the middle distance, a group of about fifteen men stepped through a series of t'ai chi moves—a slow ballet performed in the dry heat of the afternoon. Funny how things changed, he thought. The public memory of American violence and civil war had been replaced by a practice of peace and contemplation imported from a culture half a world away.

Momentarily released from his abiding anxieties, Finch

allowed himself to be swept up in these thoughts and diversions. He knew he had found a temporary space free from the trouble that brewed around him and he wondered how he could stretch and expand his sense of freedom. Was there a way to tap the pulse and momentum of his own life again?

His phone buzzed and he saw an incoming text from Eve. *Hotel P. 633. Will wait for you.* Hotel Penn, he thought. Good enough.

After another moment, Simon appeared at the near end of the path and sat beside Finch. Looking every bit the lawyer, he wore a two-piece emerald green suit. The top of his shirt was unbuttoned and held in place with a loosened tie. He had a copy of the *New York Times* in one hand, a take-out coffee in the other. Tiny dots of perspiration bubbled on his forehead. He put on the demeanor of a tourist and leaned forward as if he might be asking a stranger for directions to the zoo.

"I want this to be as fast as possible," he murmured under his breath.

"No reason it can't be." Finch nodded. "But if you really want to break this open we need to work together, Simon."

"What do you mean?" He set his newspaper and coffee cup on the bench.

"Look, I can give you the name of the owner of the Cadillac and you can go your way and do what you want with the information."

"Okay, I'll take that. It'll be my first choice no matter what other option you have. With you, there's always a deal you're trying to make. And I don't want one."

Finch frowned and turned his chin away. There was something in Simon that detested Finch. He didn't know what he'd done to deserve the contempt, but there it was. Irrepressible.

"Simon, when I give you the name I know you can use the resources in your office to find out everything about Jayne's killer right down to the color of his socks." He leaned forward. "And I can take the information you feed me and use it to call out this bastard within an hour. Don't you see it? Together we can force the Bureau's hand to wrap this up *today.*"

"You've got to be joking. You know as well as I do that the FBI works at their own pace. Everything gets triple-checked. Meanwhile they'll be scrambling to deny any news from protected sources that you publish in the *eXpress*. That does nothing but clog their pipes, Finch. Meanwhile they start investigating you, and despite your record, I simply don't believe that you'll sit in jail reciting the First Amendment just to protect me."

Finch's jaw tightened as he let out a wheeze of exasperation. He came close to calling Simon a gutless bureaucrat, then drew a breath and settled his nerves. He took a business card from his bag and wrote his new cell number on the back.

"Here. If you change your mind, call me."

Simon glanced at the card and tucked it into his shirt pocket. He stood up and peered down at Finch.

Finch studied him with a look of resignation. "Dorion Salter."

"What?"

"The name of the guy you want. It's Dorion Salter. Spelled just like it sounds."

Simon nodded once. He hesitated as if he couldn't quite determine what to say next. Finally he leaned forward, his head bobbing slightly. "By the way Finch, that was pretty sick what you did."

"What?"

"Breaking into my sister's apartment the day she was killed. I did not appreciate that. If you want to know why I can't trust you, just look to yourself."

Finch glanced away with a nod of regret. "I know." He turned his eyes back to Simon. "I apologize for that. If I'd known you'd be there—"

"Well that fuckin' stank."

"You know, Simon, if your name appeared on a kill list you'd be surprised at what you might do."

"What the fu— I just…." His voice trailed off as if he couldn't finish his thought.

Finch raised his eyebrows with a look that said *get-it-all-out*.

But Simon lifted both hands in the air and let them drop to his side, a gesture of emptiness. And finality. Then he turned and walked back in the direction of the DA's office. Finch watched him disappear around a turn in the path and wondered if the effervescent mood he'd enjoyed ten minutes earlier might return. After a few moments he dropped the possibility and pulled himself up from the bench. He tucked Simon's newspaper under his arm and headed toward Worth Street. From there he decided to grab a taxi and drive to the Hotel Pennsylvania. Back to Eve.

Chapter Twenty

Will thought it might be a mistake. The fact that Eve had booked a room in the Hotel Penn brought him back full circle. He'd managed to dodge past the FBI's security detail just a few days ago. Reappearing here now felt like he might be lined up for a return bout with the devil. A hard match to win.

He checked the number on the door: 633. He tapped once, waited, and when he heard the high-pitched whine of a vacuum cleaner or hair dryer he knocked at the door until the machine noise clicked off. He caught the sound of feet treading toward him, then a silent pause; he knew someone was eyeing him through the peep hole. Then the door swung open and there she stood.

The sight of Eve actually drew his breath away. She had a white towel wrapped around her chest and pinched together in a knot above her breasts. Her hair was still damp on the left side, as if she was in the middle of drying it with a blower. When she looked at him, he could see her eyes dilate, the green irises encircling a deep, inner darkness.

"Will." She breathed his name and pulled him into an embrace, kissed his lips briefly and nestled her face below his throat.

He pushed the door closed with the heel of his shoe and dropped his bag to the floor. He drew the smell of her into his lungs.

"I can't believe I'm holding you again," he whispered and kissed the top of her head.

"I know. I just got here an hour ago. Your text came just after I checked in." She raised her head to kiss him on the mouth.

"As Alice Shaw?"

"Yeah."

He felt some relief knowing that she'd kept her name off the guest register. Once again he realized how savvy she could be.

"Good," he whispered.

She pulled away and held a forefinger against her lips. "No more talking, okay."

She unknotted the towel and let it slip to the floor. She took his hand in hers and led him toward the hotel bed. "I don't care what happens. I never want you to leave me like that again."

She began to unbutton his shirt.

"I promise." He felt his body coming back to life, as if he'd been living with the dead for the past week and only now discovered the world of flesh and blood and the joy of life. The faster his pulse quickened, the more he scrambled to unbuckle his belt and tug off his pants. Yes, he was back in the world again. Alive. And still kicking.

They sat on the outside deck of the "Spirit of America," one of nine vessels serving the Staten Island Ferry line. Ahead of them stood the Statue of Liberty cloaked in the late-afternoon mist that had come off the Atlantic. Behind them the towers of Wall Street stood in mute defiance. At one time the twin towers of the World Trade Center rose above them all, a testament to the permanence of man's ambition. No more.

As the ferry pushed into the mist neither Eve nor Will could keep their attention on the tourist sites. After they'd left the hotel, their obsession with the events cascading toward them felt unstoppable.

"When was the last time you checked the list?" Eve asked.

"I can't find it. The Twitter page is gone."

"Right. But the web page with the list is still live."

"I never thought of trying that. I got preoccupied by everything that happened in Paris. Then I guess I got completely exhausted," he confessed.

"Well, it's changed." She studied his face a moment. "There're over fifty names on it now. I just got an update from Gabe Finkleman. Sixteen of the original twenty-four are dead."

"Sixteen." He swore under his breath and looked away.

"Leanne tells me that the FBI has all hands on deck. No one's saying it aloud, but from all the noise, everyone knows the situation has run out of the fed's control. They can't take down the server that's posting the list updates. Seems like they can't even locate it."

He could barely respond. "Leanne?"

"Spratz. My old contact in the SFPD."

"Right. Of course." Finch propped his hands on the rail and straightened his spine. He knew he had to focus.

Second Life

"A friend of her cousin knew Kali Rood in high school. So I contacted her. Her name is Alicia Vex."

Finch listened as Eve summarized what she'd learned. The friend-of-a-friend connection to Kali Rood brought Eve to New York on short notice. Alicia Vex worked at Every Thing Goes Book Cafe and Neighborhood Stage. ETG, as the locals called it, was a coffee house, bookstore, live entertainment stage and record shop combo on Staten Island. Eve checked the city map and traced the route to their destination with her finger. She calculated that they'd arrive within the next ten minutes.

After they disembarked from the ferry they made their way to Bay Street and walked into ETG. The store reminded Finch of an early-seventies Haight-Ashbury hippie catchall that clung to life through the turn of the century then reinvented itself when America rediscovered espresso coffee after nine-eleven. *Wake up and smell the coffee.* In one day that tired old expression took on new meaning.

Eve asked the cashier for directions, and they soon found Alicia Vex on a break at the back of the store. She sat alone on a wood-slat chair beside a brick wall covered with washed-out graffiti and surrounded by discarded bottles and beer cans. Her arms were decorated with whorls of tattoos that didn't quite match the background graffiti. She smoked a cigarette and as Will and Eve peered at her through the screen door, she seemed lost in the maze of her own thoughts.

"Alicia?" Eve pushed the door open with a tentative smile. "I'm Eve Noon."

Alicia looked toward them as if she'd been roused from a dream. "Right. From Frisco." She tapped her bare wrist as if she were checking the time. "Wow. That was fast."

"Yeah, we both just flew in today." Eve stepped into the

tiny courtyard that apparently served as an al fresco staff lounge. "This is Will Finch. Can we talk to you?"

Alicia took a moment to ponder the question. She repeatedly flicked the ash from the tip of her cigarette. The look on her face said that she might cancel the agreement she'd made to meet with Eve. After a final drag, she dropped the fag next to her running shoe, crushed the butt under her heel and let out a long stream of smoke from her lips.

"All right. Let's go across to the park," she said and led Will and Eve back through the store.

As they traversed the narrow aisles, Finch marveled at the bookshelves that reached from the floor to the ceiling. It provided a feeling of intimate claustrophobia, an intellectual reassurance that reminded Finch of City Lights Books in San Francisco and Shakespeare and Company in Paris. He could imagine spending two or three hours here, thumbing through a hundred books he might not find anywhere else. ETG was one of those places where you could park your worries at the door, enter their private realm and for a brief span disappear into a literary phantasmagoria.

As she approached the front counter, Alicia leaned toward the cash register and called to the cashier who was stacking books at the far end of the counter.

"Malc, I'm taking a break. I'll be across the street in the park. Okay?"

When he failed to acknowledge her, she tapped her knuckles on the counter and raised her voice: "Malcolm. I'm on a break. Across the street, okay?"

"Right," he replied without looking up.

The three of them left the store, crossed Bay Street and entered Tompkinsville Park, a dusty public space on a triangular block across from ETG. Alicia led them to two uncomfortable looking wood-slat benches that were set at slight angle next to a pentagonal fountain. She sat down and lit another cigarette.

"So," she announced, "You want the goods on Kali Rood. The bitch."

Will glanced at Eve and shrugged with a look that said, okay, let's dive right in.

"Alicia, do you mind if I tape our conversation?" He held his cellphone up in one hand.

"Not a chance." She waved away Finch's phone. "You two are with some paper, right?"

"The *eXpress*," Eve said.

"And I don't want you to use my name either." She took a contemplative drag on her Marlboro. "We do it my way, or not at all. Capiche?"

Capiche. Will smiled to himself and said, "Fine." He tucked his phone back into his pocket and tried another approach. "What if I take some notes?"

"No. Nothing on record. Not my name, where you heard it, nothing. And I mean, like never. I don't want her to ever know where this came from." She waved her hand between the three of them to emphasize that the decision was final. "Take it or leave it."

"All right." Finch set his bag on the ground and tried to relax his shoulders against the wood strapping that formed the backrest on the bench. Years ago he'd trained himself to interview people without notes or a recorder. The trick was to recognize the critical quotes when they came up and immediately commit them to memory. After a few tries, he'd been able to recall long passages verbatim and reconstruct complete conversations.

"So ... Alicia," he said in a tentative voice, "tell us when and where you knew Kali Rood."

She pressed her lips together in a tight frown while she considered where to begin. "First off, her name wasn't Kali Rood when I knew her. It was Isobel Oehmke. We were seniors at Great Valley High School in Malvern, Pennsylvania. Just outside Philly. It was 1988 and our lockers were across the hall from each other. We had a few classes together and for a while we went to the same parties."

"Isobel Oehmke. You two used to party together?" Eve's voice sounded a skeptical note.

"For a while. Until she met my brother."

"Your brother?"

"Damian." She nodded and swept a strand of hair from her eyes. "I never should have introduced them." She glanced away with a distant look. "She just turned him into ... something else. Something I could never figure out."

She looked way again, clearly uncomfortable with what she had to say next. "You know about her parents, right?"

"That they died suddenly." Finch shrugged, caught off guard that he hadn't fully researched her parents. "Some kind of accident."

"Accident?" Alicia pouted as if Finch were trivializing the true version of events. "They died in a fucking house fire. It was arson. Isobel's place burnt to the ground before anyone called it in."

"What about Isobel?" Eve asked.

"Yeah, what about her?" Alicia said, as if Isobel remained an impenetrable enigma. "She was on a sleepover with her church girlfriends that night."

"So she was involved with the church even back then?" Finch had wondered when she'd found religion. He suspected that people with her fervor were either recent converts, or they'd been nursed on the faith since childhood.

"I don't know if her *church* was actually real. Sanctified or whatever. But back in the day she was famous for knowing every last detail about the People's Temple. She had this total obsession with Jim Jones. It was like she knew the guy personally or something."

Finch glanced at Eve. "You mean Jim Jones from the Jonestown massacre?"

"Oh yeah. Radical, true-believer shit. She used to hold lunch-hour prayer sessions with the five or six other kids in her flock. That's where Damian got hooked."

Will took a moment to consider the story. "You said it was arson. Was that proven in court?"

"Yup."

"Who was the fire bug?"

"That—*that's*—where the story gets surreal." She wagged an unlit cigarette in the air, then lit it from the ember of her first smoke and released a long stream of vapor from her mouth. "He told me everything. Three days after the fire and exactly three days before Isobel and Damian went hiking in Evansburg State Park. Three and three. Right in the middle, that's when Damian confessed to me that he'd done it."

"Your *brother* set the fire?" Eve said this in such a low tone that Finch could barely hear her.

"He said Isobel told him her parents had gone into Philly. To see a baseball or basketball game. I don't know which. That they needed the insurance money and that if he'd do it, then she'd *'do him.'* You don't need to guess what that meant. Maybe that's just how the Virgin Queen operates." She let out yet another cynical laugh. "Hell, don't we all. Eventually."

Sensing there was more to come, Finch waited a moment and then asked, "So what happened in Evansburg Park, Alicia?"

"He fell from the cliff above Skippack Creek. 'A hiking accident.' That was the official story. But who knows? I mean *who really knows except Isobel?*" She nodded and wiped a tear from her eye. "The search and rescue team found Damian wedged in a crevice near the creek. It took them all day to haul him out of there. And you know what?"

Alicia's head dropped, her chin rested a few inches above her breast bone. No one said a word.

"He was clutching a flower in his hand. A white daisy." She raised her head and let out a slight gasp. "He was probably just about to give it to her. A fucking *daisy.*"

Eve glanced at Will with a look of disbelief. "Alicia, did you tell this to the police? About your brother's confession, I mean."

She nodded. "Oh yeah. And they took it to court. But Isobel found herself a golden boy lawyer. Somehow he found all the notes I'd passed to my so-called friends before the trial. The ones where I wrote that I was going to screw Isobel for killing my brother." She took another drag on her cigarette and rolled an arm over the back of the bench. "I wanted to see her fry, and wrote those very words to at least a dozen people. And I admitted it. I was just a kid. How could I know that what I'd written to half the school would damage my testimony?"

"Including Damian's admission to you that he'd burned Isobel's house and killed her parents?" Finch asked.

"It would be disqualified as prejudicial hearsay," Eve said knowing exactly how any defense lawyer would handle the situation.

"So now you understand why I don't put anything on

record." Alicia coughed up a skeptical chuckle. "No tapes, no paper trail."

"And that's how it all ended?" Will asked.

"I guess some cop back in Malvern has the arson case stashed somewhere in an unsolved crime folder." She sighed wearily, as if she'd had enough. "After she buried her foster parents Isobel moved in with one of her girlfriends 'til the end of the school year. Then after grad she went to some southern state university. She either got a scholarship or insurance money, I guess. Prob'ly both, knowing her. She was smart enough, I'll grant her that. One way or the other, she got everything she wanted. Including my brother."

Alicia took a final drag on her cigarette and flicked the butt into a cluster of pigeons pecking through the gravel surrounding base of the water fountain.

"And then?" Finch asked, thinking there might be more.

She shrugged and brushed away the damp smudge of tears on her left cheek. "I'd heard she'd changed her name. But I never saw her again in person. Like everyone else, I saw her on TV and heard her on the radio. The one difference between then and now? She's slicker. Yeah, she is. *One. Slick. Witch.*"

She smiled at that thought, as if after all this talk, all she needed were those last three words to describe Kali Rood.

Chapter Twenty-One

By the time Eve and Finch returned to the ferry a light offshore breeze had blown the Atlantic mist back out to sea. The early evening air felt fresh on Will's skin and provided a sense of renewal. They stood near the bow of the boat and tried to come to terms with what Alicia Vex had told them.

"I can write a profile piece, but that's about it. Even then, there's no point," he said. He'd already dismissed the idea of trying to tie Kali Rood's past life as Isobel Oehmke to the mounting toll of deaths that began with Martin Fast. "We learned absolutely nothing from Alicia that is evidentiary. The case linking Kali to her parents' death and Alicia's brother already failed in court."

"Hold on. Maybe we did learn something."

"What?"

"Even if half of what Alicia said is true—and I think *most* of it probably is—then we know Kali Rood is a very dangerous sociopath."

"No question about that." He shrugged as if her point was obvious. "And I understand Alicia's paranoia, too. Kali abused her friendship and killed her brother. No wonder she's so cut up."

"So let's step back a minute. Normally we'd be looking for means, motive and opportunity. That's normal, straight-up police work. But when the perp is a psycho, the motives get very fuzzy. Sometimes nothing makes sense. So Kali could be the root cause of everything. We just haven't got down to her level of crazy. Not yet, anyway."

Finch scanned the Wall Street skyscrapers just ahead. The financial center of the world. An impressive sight, no doubt. It provided a diversion as he slipped in and out of the tedious introspection that looped back and forth over the same possibilities.

As the ferry neared Whitehall Terminal Finch felt his phone vibrate in his pocket. He waited another moment before tugging it into his hand. It was a text from Simon Waterston: *"Meet me at nine o'clock tonight. Same place."* Will checked the time. Seven-thirty.

"Something's come up. I've got a source who wants to see me." He nodded to suggest it would be important.

"A source?"

The look on her face told him that she wanted to know who the secret source might be. She wanted to be part of it, he understood that. But protected sources were just that. Protected.

"He blew me off this morning. I thought I'd never see him again." He adjusted his balance as the ferry nudged against the pier. "Sorry, but I can't tell you anything more. That's just how it works."

"Could be something, then." She set her hand on the railing and prepared to follow the crowd off the ferry.

"Maybe. Let's take a taxi up to Five Points together. You keep the cab, get back to the hotel and I'll meet you there after I meet this contact. If I learn anything new, then maybe we can tie the pieces together."

"We need something," she said. "It's one thing to tie loose ends together, but at this point all we seem to have are strands of broken thread."

———

The atmosphere and mood in Columbus Park had shifted since the afternoon. The old men practicing t'ai chi, the children reciting nursery rhymes with their grandmothers —all of that had been replaced by the shrill banter of young teenagers and a large cluster of women arguing in Chinese over some squabble that Will couldn't comprehend.

After a few minutes Finch caught sight of Simon Waterston standing next to the statue of Dr. Sen Yat-sen. Simon no longer wore a tie and his hair looked disheveled as though he'd been raking his fingers over his scalp. His eyes appeared weary and as Will approached he could see Simon draw his lower lip between his teeth.

"Walk with me," Simon said.

He swung his suit jacket over his shoulder and led the way toward a two-story open pavilion with a tile roof.

"All right," Simon said after they'd established a walking pace. "You win."

Finch allowed the comment to pass. Simon had asked for the meeting; better to let him disclose what he'd discovered rather than get in his way with misdirected questions. Besides, who could tell how long their detente would last?

"Despite your demands," Simon continued, "I did not do this for you. I did it for my sister."

"Okay," Finch said just to encourage him. He had no

idea where Simon might be heading with the conversation. "For Jayne."

"But first you need to understand something." He stopped abruptly and pivoted toward Finch. His face was flushed. "If you expose me, I will end up in prison. *Do you get that?*"

Before he responded, Finch waited until Simon could settle down and maintain eye contact. "You have my word on this, Simon. And for the record, I have never exposed a source. Not once."

"Just be clear. I will never acknowledge that I am your source. After tonight we will never speak again. Do you understand?"

They stood looking at one another.

"Yes."

Simon drew a long breath as if he was about to dive from a high board into a shallow pool. "All right. Dorion Salter is not who he appears to be."

Finch felt a tinge of disappointment. This was the grand revelation? "Okay. So tell me. I have no idea who he is."

"Let me back up," Simon said as he continued to steer them toward the open pavilion.

"All right."

"See, at the Cybercrime and Identity Theft Bureau I can access all the cases pertaining to identity theft, not just in the state, but across the country." He spread his hands in a broad arc. "I'm sure you understand that identity theft is mostly a digital crime. But hackers don't just take your VISA card number then dine out on caviar and champagne. They steal your entire world, Finch. You can go to bed one night and wake up to find your bank account empty, your house double-mortgaged, your kid's college fund vaporized and your wife's 401K liquidated. I'm serious. And most times, the perp's not some creep waiting to be locked up. When the job's done there're no fingerprints, no DNA, no witnesses. It's called zero-trace mugging. And that's what I handle in the DA's office."

"Okay." Now that Simon was on a roll, Finch did his best not to interrupt him. "And the perps can be in Russia or wherever."

Simon ignored this. "So there are other databases, too. They're related to the opposite of identity theft—identity acquisition."

"Identity acquisition." Finch mulled over the phrase. "You mean for witness protection?"

Simon nodded.

"So the feds take an identity from someone deceased who matches a certain profile and give it to the person going into witness protection."

"Exactly. But the world inside IA is off limits to me. Until today, that is, when I got into the database. And that's why we *aren't* having this conversation."

He fixed Finch with a heavy look. Finch nodded to acknowledge that by breaking into the IA database, Simon had crossed a line. It marked his commitment to his sister. The distance he was willing to go to expose the identity of Dorion Salter and turn the information over to Finch so that he could publish the conspiracy in the *eXpress*.

They stood before the park pavilion and watched an elderly Chinese couple ease down the staircase to the ground. A light breeze washed through the park and then faded. The chorus of women arguing in Cantonese continued. Four boys dashed behind them on skate boards.

"The thing is, IA isn't just for witness protection. It's also used for political refugees and military personnel. And special cases."

Finch turned to Simon. "And Dorion Salter is a special case."

Simon nodded and then led the way up the stairs to the open air pavilion.

"How special?"

"How's your history, Finch?"

He shrugged with a look that said, where are you going with this?

Simon waved a hand, an encouragement to play along for another minute or two. "Tell me something. What historic event happened on November 18, 1978?"

His eyebrows rose in expectation. Meanwhile Finch struggled to recall the importance of a day that fell more than a year before his birth.

"...November 18, 1978?..."

"No shame. Hardly anyone one gets it." Simon's smirk revealed a hint of smugness. "It's the date of the Jonestown massacre in Guyana. Nine hundred and nine people slaughtered in mass suicide. A third of them were children. Until nine-eleven it was the biggest civilian massacre of US citizens ever."

Finch rubbed his thumb and index finger over the stub of his earlobe as he recited the infamous eulogy that marked the disaster: "They drank the Kool-aid."

"They did. Except it wasn't Kool-Aid. It was Flavor-Aid." Simon's mouth formed a grin of satisfaction, as if he'd successfully led Finch down a long and winding path without missing a step.

Simon continued to walk until they reached an unoccupied part of the pavilion platform. He pressed his thighs against the banister and tested his weight against the railing as they watched the groups of people strolling through the park below them.

"So what does all this have to do with Dorion Salter?"

"Good question. In fact, it's the only question that really matters." He turned to Finch with an expression that said, this is where all the threads weave together. "Two days after Jonestown, a twelve-year-old boy named Danny Pass acquired the identity of Jason Wishart. Then fourteen years later, Wishart changed his name to Dorion Salter."

"Wait." Finch tugged at Simon's elbow. "You're saying that Dorion Salter was at Jonestown? You mean he *survived* Jonestown?"

"Not officially. Depending on how you define the term, there were only four survivors. One of them, believe it or not, was an old guy too deaf to hear the PA system ordering everyone to line up for their dose of flavored cyanide." A bleak laugh erupted from his throat. "But *unofficially* there were two more survivors. Both of them children. Their social workers tried to protect them from the media hysteria by giving them new names. One was Danny Pass who acquired the identity of another boy the same age who'd just died in a car crash in Idaho. Jason Wishart, who is now doing business as Dorion Salter."

As Simon spoke Finch could see it all coming together now. It was like a shell game where you try to spot the pebble under one of three cups that shifted from place to place before your eyes. "And the second child?"

"Was a seven-year-old girl. She tagged along with Salter as he snuck out of the Jonestown compound and was rescued at the local air strip with him. It was little more than a dirt track in the middle of the jungle."

They stood in silence at the second floor railing of the open pavilion and took in the twilight atmosphere of the park. The light slowly faded under the gray smudge of the evening smog. A few street lights blinked on in random sequence. Simon let out a breath as if he'd just completed a long climb up a mountain.

"The girl's birth name was Ruth Watts," he continued. "After Jonestown, she acquired the identity of Isobel Oehmke. Another car crash victim as it turns out."

"Isobel Oehmke." Alicia Vex's high school nemesis. Finch nodded silently as he stared across the park.

Simon waited a moment, then continued. "But here's the kicker. It's not just Jonestown that put these two together. See, the identity databases can be searched three different ways. Alphabetically, chronologically and by location. So I checked Salter's last name change—when Jason Wishart became Dorion Salter—for the date and location that his application was certified. Austin, Texas, December 12, 1992."

"Where Isobel Oehmke went to college."

"Correct."

Finch studied Simon for a moment. He decided to wait for him to fill in the picture by clicking the final puzzle piece into place. It was his story after all. It also belonged to his twin sister.

"And at the same time and place, Isobel Oehmke became Kali Rood," he said as if he were completing a legal summation. He briefly studied Finch's face, as though he was trying to detect some surprise.

"Fourteen years after Jonestown they found one another and now they're in it together, Will. Kali Rood and Dorion Salter. The two of them together, then and now. They killed Jayne, and God knows who else."

Chapter Twenty-Two

As he waited to hail a taxi, Finch felt the blood pulsing through his body. He remembered the crises he'd experienced in Baghdad, the same rush of anticipation, the sense of impending explosion. He tried to decipher his feelings. Was he being paranoid—or was the world conspiring to bring him into a clash with fate? He walked down a block on Worth Street and leaned his back against the red brick wall of the True Light Lutheran Church. Any sign of strangers following? None. Once again he attempted to shrug off his anxieties as he flagged down the first cab that came his way.

The taxi drove up Sixth Avenue and across Thirty-third to the Hotel Penn. The night traffic struggled in a stop-and-go momentum, the air was still and tinged with a gray haze. He knew he was close now, knew that at the very least he could publish the stories about Kali Rood and Dorion Salter. He could weave their lives together and establish the link to Jayne Waterston's murder. Everything derived from the photograph that she'd taken of the car parked outside her apartment and the license plate that led to Dorion Salter—the child, Danny Pass—and his companion during their Jonestown escape, Ruth Watts, aka Isobel Oehmke and now reborn as Kali Rood. The links that joined them spanned decades, but there they were, he said to himself. Links tight as handcuffs.

As he exited the taxi, he felt a new wave of anxiety. He checked over his shoulders as he entered the hotel. Any one of three or four men and women could be tailing him. Heavy-set men with shaved skulls, their jackets a size too large in order to accommodate the weapons strapped under their armpits. Women whose eyes swept past him, then returned to settle their gaze on his face.

After he stepped into the elevator he saw a hand clasp the door bumper and pull it open just as it began to close. A stranger dressed in a sports jacket, jeans and blue Nike running shoes stepped into the car. A big man with broad shoulders and a wiry alertness. A thin scar cut through his right eyebrow, an old wound that must have damaged the hair follicles.

He glanced at Finch and put on a smile. Finch ignored him.

"Sorry." Nike examined the buttons on the floor control panel. He pressed SIX despite the fact the amber button was already lit. "Good. I'm heading up to six, too."

Finch detected a slight accent, French, just enough of a inflection to make him wonder. Finch stared at the back of his head. His thinning black hair was slicked to the right side in a combover. The car rose to the sixth floor and the bell pinged. The door skimmed open and Nike held the door for Finch.

"After you."

"You know," he said, "I realize I forgot something in the lobby." He reached over and pressed the button marked L.

"Ah." With a shrug Nike moved into the hall, turned to the left and walked toward Eve's room, his blue shoes squeaking with every step.

As he rode the elevator down, Finch held the CLOSE button with his thumb. When the door opened on the main floor, he jabbed the button again and rode back up to six on his own. By the time he entered Eve's room his paranoia had dissipated just enough to steady his breathing and calm his pounding pulse.

"You're back," she whispered over the side of her cellphone.

She was on the line with someone and her distraction allowed him to step into the bathroom, shut the door and take a shower. He took a full twenty minutes to clean himself up. It felt good to shave and wash his hair. For the first time since he'd returned from Paris, he felt like he'd finally escaped from a jungle.

When he joined Eve in the bedroom she was just finishing her call. She set her cell on the bedside table with a forced smile that didn't fool him for a second.

"That was Wally." The corners of her lips dropped into a frown. "There's some bad news. Sorry, I completely forgot to tell you." She glanced away and then continued. "His wife has pancreatic cancer. He's taken a leave from the *eXpress.*"

"My God. Ginny has cancer?"

"Yeah, it's really hit him." She shook her head with a despondent look.

"Who's going to run the show?"

"Fiona. For now, anyhow. I knew all this before I left the

office. Sorry, it's just...." She waved a hand as if to dismiss that part of the conversation.

"It's okay. I get it."

"So look. Apparently the feds have been pressuring Wally. They even tracked him down in the cancer ward. Can you believe it? He says the FBI wants to see us again."

"No surprise. Did he say what they want?"

He glanced away and held a hand to the back of his neck and massaged the tendons above his shoulders.

"Maybe they've found something new on Jacob Bell," he said in reply to his own question. He knew he was reaching for answers, anything to unlock this latest puzzle. Then another thought struck him. "So Wally knows we're here"—his arms swept around the room—"in New York?"

"He knew I came out here to talk to Alicia. And he said he told the feds that. Basically he had to tell them everything he knows. But he doesn't know we're here at the Penn. Within a day or two the FBI will figure that out, too, so we need to prepare."

She studied his face for a moment as if she was trying to uncover a new secret. "So ... tell me about your meeting with this source of yours."

He walked across the room and settled on the sofa beside her.

"You know Eve, maybe that call from Wally is a sign. Like it was meant to happen. The more I think about what we learned today, the more certain I am that it's time to go to the FBI with everything we've got."

"I thought you didn't believe things are *meant to happen.* I thought you were my *Free Will* guy." She smiled with a look of affection. Her fingers reached up to his forehead and set a curl of damp hair into place.

"Yeah, well ... maybe I'm a believer now. Let me tell

you about Kali Rood and Dorion Salter. And Jonestown. You remember Jonestown, Guyana?"

She shrugged with a disoriented look, as if she'd forgotten a part of her own past. "In South America, where all those people died. They drank the Kool-Aid, right?"

He released a cynical chuckle. Exactly what he'd said to Simon. Likely everyone said the same thing.

"Look ... even if you find this out on your own, you can never reveal where I got what I'm about to tell you. I will not mention his name, so technically he's protected under the First Amendment. Do you understand?"

She pulled away from him and supported her back on the sofa's armrest. "All right. Go on."

By the time he'd finished his story, he could see that Eve had been tainted by the same paranoid affliction that had overcome him since his meeting with Simon. Her eyes were unfocused as she gazed across their empty hotel room.

"I think you're right," she said when she found her bearings.

"What?"

"It's time to go to the FBI. Like right now."

"But first I need to write this story and get it to Fiona. Once it's published they won't be able to ignore the chain of evidence pointing to Salter and Kali. It's the one thing I can do to bring this to a boil."

She checked the clock radio next to the bed. "How long will it take you?"

He ran a hand through his hair as he tried to calculate what he needed to write the story and balance it against his rising sense of exhaustion. "An hour, maybe an hour and a half. And two cups of black coffee."

She smiled at that.

"You start typing. I'll get the coffee."

Second Life

It was just after midnight when Will finished the story and emailed it to the *eXpress*. They waited another twenty minutes to confirm that the *eXpress* had published it on the website. Jeanine Fix had added images of Kali Rood and Dorion Salter just below the headline: *Jonestown Survivors Tied to Serial Murders*. He'd been careful to write the story without making libelous allegations. On the other hand, most readers could piece together the chain of events. Jayne Waterston's photo of Dorion Salter's car. Salter's past life as a Jonestown survivor. Kali Rood, his childhood companion. Then the links connecting Jacob Bell, Rood's late personal assistant, to Dr. Martin Fast, the murdered climate science guru.

Finch smiled as he read the published story on his laptop. "Looks like the team back at the *eXpress* is working overtime tonight."

"And so they should. This is the break we've been after for weeks now." Eve pulled her cell from her purse and began to enter a phone number from a business card. After she tapped the CALL icon, she said, "I'm asking Calinda Cruz to set up a meeting. You all right with that?"

Calinda Cruz and John Vickers. The ever-so friendly agents from the FBI. He rolled his eyes with a look of resignation. "Yeah. Hopefully that'll be the end of the road."

When Eve reached Cruz's voice mailbox she gave Will a wary look.

"Agent Cruz, this is Eve Noon from the *eXpress*. Wally Gimbel said you wanted to talk to me and Will Finch. He said you're in New York—well, so are we. It's coming up to two in the morning, and we're going to your office in the next half hour. We've got something you'll want to hear. Check the *eXpress* website, you'll see some breaking news."

She closed her phone and they glanced at one another. Was a mid-night phone message enough to alert the FBI?

"It's the best you can do," Will said and slung his courier bag over his shoulder. "All right. Let's go."

"Give me a sec. I've got to sort through some stuff."

She took a few minutes in the bathroom then gathered her phone, wallet and key card in one hand.

"Oh, by the way. Here's your old phone." She pulled it from the charging cable next to the bed and handed it to him. "Remember you asked me to pick it up from the front desk after you left for Paris? I charged it, too."

A look of surprise crossed his face. "Right. I'd forgotten about it. Now I've got two of the damn things."

He felt the new phone in his pants pocket, then slipped the old one into his bag. With everything sorted away, he opened the front door, cautiously checked the corridor and steered Eve into the hallway. Recalling his earlier anxiety when he rode the elevator up the sixth floor, he led the way to the staircase at the far end of the hall.

"I've got a bad feeling about being watched here," he whispered over his shoulder as they stepped down the passageway. "Let's take the side door, then grab a taxi on Thirty-third."

As they slipped along the corridor neither of them paid attention to the new camera fixed to the wall above their hotel room door. Despite the obvious—that it didn't match the hundreds of CCTV units arrayed through all the public spaces in the Hotel Penn—nothing about the pinhole spy-cam alerted Finch to its presence. In fact, he didn't notice it at all.

Second Life

Even at this time of night, Thirty-third was clotted with service vehicles loading goods in and out of the hotel and the Old Navy store across the street. Only one of the three lanes was passable and it was locked up with stalled traffic. Nothing was moving.

"Damn it." Finch stood on the curb and craned his neck in search of a taxi. He realized he'd made a mistake. He no longer knew the city as well as he did when he was a student at NYU. "Let's go down to Seventh. There shouldn't be a problem there."

She followed him along the sidewalk and when they reached the corner Finch felt a surge of relief when he realized the traffic gridlock had loosened. In the distance he could see three or four yellow cabs heading south toward them. One had its dome light illuminated.

"I see one," he called to Eve.

The cab pulled to the curb and they settled in the backseat. Finch took her hand and gave it a squeeze. "We've got them beat. This time for sure," he said, his voice rising with confidence.

"Yeah, maybe. Maybe you're right," she said not quite as confidently, but nonetheless she drew his hand into her lap and smiled.

By the time their taxi pulled to the curb opposite the Jacob K Javits tower on Worth Street, Finch's growing optimism was bubbling. He paid the driver and they stepped onto the sidewalk.

"The FBI is on the twenty-third floor." He pointed to the middle of the honeycomb exterior of the federal building. "There better be someone on the desk," he murmured without looking back at her, only now struck by the thought that they might not be able to access the building in the middle of the night. "Come on. Let's go."

Ahead of him two white panel vans were parked in line next to the curb. He stepped in front of the first van onto the asphalt and checked to the right along the street toward Foley Square. No traffic. But where was Eve?

"Hey! What the fu—"

As he heard her scream, two pairs of hands gripped his shoulders from behind. When he turned he saw two men tug a black cloth over Eve's head. She cried out again but her screech was muffled by a hand that covered her mouth under the hood.

In the seconds before he was overwhelmed, Finch could just make out a man cuffing Eve's hands behind her back. He saw the narrow scar that cut through his right eyebrow. The blue shoes. The wiry build.

Nike.

Chapter Twenty-Three

After he regained consciousness the hammering in his temples fell into a broken, incessant rhythm. He struggled to bring his hands up to ease the throbbing in his head but the handcuffs on his wrists completely restrained him. He cried out and tried to roll onto his belly. Impossible. Despite his whimpering, nothing brought release. He tried to calculate the distance they'd travelled in the panel van, but he knew that he could be a hundred miles off. Moments after he'd been dumped in the back, a hood had been cinched around his neck and a needle had injected something into his left triceps. Was it chloral hydrate? Whatever the poison, it had now morphed into the shattering migraine that pounded above his ears in a manic tempo.

The van left the smooth asphalt and began to ease over a new surface—gravel or compacted dirt, he couldn't be sure—and the sound of loose shale squeezing under the tires filled his ears with its soft shushing. Once again he rolled his legs forward hoping that he might make contact with Eve. Nothing. Was she in the same vehicle? He whispered her name, only to end up choking on the dry burning at the back of his throat. When he inhaled he could taste the sackcloth fibers from the hood on his tongue. He tried to spit out the raspy fabric but it clung to the spittle on his lips. He coughed twice before he cleared his mouth and his breathing settled to an uneven wheezing.

He felt the van gear down as it wound through a long uphill track that curled through a series of switchback turns that rolled him from side to side. On one curve his foot arced forward and caught the shoulder strap of his courier bag. It gave him a sense of reassurance, but what good would it do him?

He felt certain that they were in the mountains somewhere. The Catskills? After another abrupt turn the van seemed to level out, then dipped through four or five depressions in the road. Finally the vehicle came to a stop. He heard the driver set the parking brake and the front doors open and close. The sound of three or four men walking on gravel toward the rear of the van. The metal-on-metal squeal of rusting hinges as the rear loading doors cranked open. The muffled curse of one man to another.

"All right, Finch. You've arrived."

Someone tugged at his heels and he struck back with a wild kick.

"You want another shot, pal?" The question sounded almost rhetorical. "Cuz if you're wanting more, Mickey Finn's right here."

He heard a skeptical laugh and decided this was no time to put up a fight. When someone grasped his calf he shuffled backwards until his feet touched the ground. He found his balance and aligned his momentum to the men frogmarching him forward. After ten or twelve paces his shoes struck the base of a stone step and he was led up a set of six stairs to a concrete landing. Somewhere ahead he heard a heavy door open and was pushed toward it by his elbows.

In the distance he heard another vehicle approaching on the dirt track. Could it be Eve? Before he found an answer, he was shoved into a building and the door closed behind him. The sound of the second van was now drowned by the humming of machinery. A generator? Air conditioners? Some sort of utility room, he assumed, and as he walked past the wheezing machines he entered a corridor, turned left and entered another room with a carpeted floor. He was steered to the left and then stopped. He could feel something touching his right shin. The frame of a chair?

Then one of the men released his arm while the other held him in place. The first man shuffled behind him and uncuffed his right hand. In the instant of his release, he rubbed his free hand over his left wrist. But his freedom was short-lived. He was pushed downward by the shoulders and forced to sit in an upholstered chair. The loose handcuff was locked to the wood frame. In an effort to fathom where he was, he swept his right hand tentatively in front of his chest and past his thighs. He found nothing but air. Then his right hand and ankles were strapped to the chair frame with duct tape. Next, the handcuff was removed from his left wrist and it too was bound to the arm of the chair with tape. He heard the men take a few backward steps.

A brief silence followed. Somewhere above or behind him he heard footsteps crossing a bare floor. Two, three people. Maybe more.

"Were you followed?" A male voice spoke from somewhere just in front of him.

"No, sir. I've seen no other cars since we left the highway."

"And their cell phones?"

"As you instructed, sir. We gave them to the taxi driver and paid him to drive to JFK and drop them in a trash can."

"Good. Take off his hood."

Finch felt someone untie the cloth at his neck. The hood was snatched away and he had to blink the dull light from his eyes. After a moment he realized that he was sitting in what appeared to be the great room in a century-old hunting lodge. The walls were paneled with shoulder-height wainscoting and topped with a faded wallpaper adorned with dusty landscape paintings.

At the far end of the room stood a floor-to-ceiling fireplace constructed of polished river rocks. The mortar between the rocks had dissolved in several places, and one of the cornerstones was missing. A massive wood mantle stretched from one side of the fireplace to the other, and on the right side, the corner of the mantle had splintered. Embossed in the middle of the mantle face, in four-inch high letters, a craftsman had carved the words WINDY BLUFF. Above the mantle the head of a bull moose had been fixed to the wall, its palm-shape antlers reaching up toward the vaulted ceiling.

In front of the fireplace three overstuffed sofas were positioned in a wide U-shape oriented to the fireplace hearth. The fire screen had been set aside and the grate was empty. Opposite the fireplace a row of glass windows banked a pair of French doors that led outside, but in the dark of night it was impossible to distinguish anything beyond the lodge.

"Mr. Finch. You've finally found us."

He recognized the voice of Kali Rood. He heard her footsteps squeak against the creaking oak floor boards as she walked in front of the chair where he sat. She turned to face him. She wore a charcoal cotton blouse and capri pants that covered her calves, the sort of stylish attire prescribed by *Vogue* for summer cottage fashionistas. Finch noticed the ankh dangling from the gold chain below her throat.

He looked up at her with a sneer. "Where's Eve Noon?"

"Ah, Ms. Noon." Her lips puckered into a frown. "Well, that's a good sign, I suppose. A mark of loyalty. Perhaps even of affection." An eyebrow arched into a gesture of mockery. "All in good time, Mr. Finch. All in good time. Have you met my associate?"

A tall man with weedy, gray hair appeared from behind him. He wore an open cardigan sweater, pressed brown slacks and canvas boat shoes. When he pivoted toward the row of windows, Finch noticed a rough scar that ran from his right ear to somewhere below his shirt collar.

Finch wondered who else might be hidden in reserve. He turned his head but could see no one, yet he knew at least two others were lingering in the shadows behind him. The men who'd abducted him and dragged him from the van into the lodge. Were others concealed in the back rooms?

"No, I don't believe we've met." The sweater man put on a smile, a look of regret to suggest their acquaintance would be short-lived.

Finch nodded in return. "Don't tell me. You must be Dorion Salter."

Salter's grin faded.

"Otherwise known as Danny Pass," Finch added and waited for a reply. He was pleased to see this bring a pause to the pleasantries.

"Childhood sweetheart to Ruth Watts," he continued and looked at Kali to gauge her reaction.

She took a moment to draw a chair to a spot about five

feet from him. She sat and crossed her knees. Finch stared at her high cheekbones, her full, slim figure. She still looked like a femme fatale star from 1950s Hollywood. Lana Turner or Barbara Stanwyck. Seductive, predatory—yet chaste and buttoned-up.

"It seems you've managed to piece together quite a bit on your own." Kali tipped her head to one side as if she needed to assess him. As if Finch represented an unanswered question that required a solution. "We read your latest article on the *eXPress*."

"In fact, that was what prompted us to make a move," Salter said. He stood beside her briefly, then dragged a second chair from the wall to the middle of the room.

Finch calculated the sequence. The article had gone up on the *eXpress* website and in less than an hour he and Eve had been snatched from the street.

"Make a move? You mean our abduction?"

"That's not the word I'd use. Consider this a friendly visit." Salter's scar was more apparent now, a narrow cicatrix that wormed its way from his ear along his neck. Too small to be considered a disfigurement, but a blemish nonetheless. When he noticed Finch's stare he covered the mark with two fingers and glanced away.

"A visit?" he said. "So you don't intend to kill us."

Another pause filled the air, a moment of uncertainty. A chill ran through the room. Perhaps Kali and Salter had only been here a few hours themselves. Were they on the run?

"From the article in the *eXpress* we know that you're familiar with Jonestown. But what do you really understand about the Reverend Jim Jones?" Kali leaned forward as if this question was important above all others.

"Apart from the fact that he was a madman?"

Salter let out a snort of disgust. "Perhaps you're not the man we were hoping for after all."

"What the fuck does that mean?" A gasp of exasperation burst from his throat. Now that he could breathe clearly he felt some renewed strength. "And where is Eve? I'm not saying another word until you tell me where Eve is."

"All right." Kali motioned to someone standing behind Finch. "Parker, show him."

Parker strolled in front of Finch carrying a computer tablet in his hand. At first Finch thought this might be Nike, but he realized the newcomer was barely out of his teens. He wore a pair of wire-rim glasses and was dressed in a black turtleneck and jeans. The Steve Jobs of cult acolytes. He held the tablet a foot below Finch's chin, then swept his hand over the screen to bring an image into focus. He recognized Eve, strapped into a chair not too dissimilar from the one that held him in its grasp. However, she still had a hood covering her head. He watched as she rolled her neck to one side. She was alive. On the wall behind her, he noticed a digital clock. The time showed 4:13.

"What time is it?"

Kali smiled and checked her watch. "Four-thirteen. You see, she's alive and well as we speak." She lifted her wrist so that Finch could see the time.

"Where is she?"

"Not far."

She put on another gentle smirk. A personal tic, Finch decided. He tried to adjust his right arm to relieve the pressure where the duct tape stuck to his skin. It dawned on him now that Kali might be in a mood to negotiate. She'd revealed enough information about Eve to make him reconsider Kali's intentions. Perhaps she didn't intend to kill him after all. So what did she want? He decided to try one more ploy.

"How can I be sure it's her? Take the hood off her head."

Kali took a moment to consider this. She nodded to Parker who typed a message into the tablet. After a moment the tablet emitted a delicate chime—the sound of a zen bell—and Parker angled the tablet under Finch's chin again. He could see Eve's head slump forward, and then from somewhere behind her a hand reached out the of darkness, loosened the knot at her neck and pulled the hood away. Her eyes fluttered open in the half-light. Her mouth was sealed shut with a five-inch strip of duct tape.

"All right." Finch let out a sigh of relief. "What do you want from us?"

"Let's get back to Jim Jones," Kali said. "He was far from the madman you suggest. And nothing of the monster the liberal press made him out to be."

He adjusted his weight in the chair. "Go on."

Kali stood and took a step toward him. "Do you know Confucius?"

Finch coughed up a laugh. "Not as well as I'd like."

She narrowed her eyes and took a few steps to the left and then pivoted back to him. "He came up with a lovely expression. 'We have two lives. And the second begins when we realize we only have one.' "

Finch nodded. Whatever her game was, he decided to remain silent and let it play out.

"Perhaps you've already had this realization. Perhaps not. Or perhaps just now it's rising into your consciousness as you sit here with your fate somewhat uncertain." She gazed into his eyes, then turned again and continued to pace back and forth as she spoke. "In our case, our life realization happened on November 18, 1978. In Jonestown. I was just seven years old. Dorion had just turned twelve."

She paused to swing a hand between her and Salter, a gesture of connection and continuity. Salter remained seated, his expression stewing with a look of listlessness.

"You see that—*that* was Jim Jones's genius. He lit a bonfire to illuminate the world. Nine hundred and nine people went to their deaths *because of their faith.*"

Her pacing came to a halt as she studied Finch's face. "There has been nothing like Jonestown since the year 73 at Masada, when nine hundred and sixty Jews committed mass suicide rather than fall into the hands of the Romans." Her voice rose with a sermonic fervor. "Until 1978 when the members of the Peoples Temple Agricultural Project in Jonestown decided not to fall into the pit of greed that is destroying our world. All of them decided—*willingly*—to give up their second lives!"

She stood in front of Will, her body rigid with the strident energy of her rant. She peered down at him as if she might be standing on a balcony in some imagined heaven. Finally a look of impatience washed over her.

"Do you *not* get that?"

Finch kept his eyes on her face. In a calm, even voice he said, "Kali, tell me why you've brought me here."

A long sigh of exhaustion fluttered from her lungs. She swung back to look at Salter, then swept around to Finch again. "All right. If you insist, let's turn to practical matters." She tipped her head backwards slightly as if she was about to take up the secular portion of her sermon.

"I'm going to let you decide if you live or die. Right now. But first tell me something. The last time we met, I urged you to answer the questions in your soul."

He knew what she meant. The time when he first grasped her powers of persuasion. He shook his head.

"A pity," she murmured.

Finch sensed that she was preparing something as she walked in a circle before him. Salter rose from his chair and moved to the side so that he stood at a ninety degree angle to Finch. Kali moved beside Salter and pointed to someone standing in the darkness behind Finch.

"Mr. Benton. Are you ready?"

Finch heard someone take a step forward. "Yes, ma'am."

"Good. Prepare yourself. Keep your eyes on me."

A chill ran through Finch. He could see that her madness was now in full flush. Where would it end? He heard the sound of a gun cocking.

"I know you were a bright student at NYU. And at Berkeley. Your mother was a Catholic French Canadian and as a teenager you attended a Catholic high school in Quebec. Am I right?"

He turned his head toward her and gazed at her in a confused daze. His entire body broke into a heavy sweat. Was one of the bandits standing behind him about to put a bullet through the back of his head?

"If you can answer this question correctly, you shall live," she continued. "It's very simple. Q and A. Now, to earn your second life, Mr. Finch, name the man who was released instead of Jesus on the day of His crucifixion."

"Released"—Finch's lips sputtered—"instead of Jesus?"

"Yes. You have ten seconds." Her mouth tightened into a narrow sneer and she fixed her eyes on Benton, as if to give him strength for the moment ahead. "Beginning now."

Finch rolled his head backward and then the shock of

Second Life

his impending death gave way to complete emptiness. He took a breath. Another. Then it came to him.

"Barbarossa." His eyes blinked open. "Barbarossa!"

"Barbarossa?" A puzzled look crossed her face. "No. I'm sorry."

"I mean Barabbas. *It was Barabbas who took his place!*"

"Barabbas," she whispered. Her eyes widened and she dipped a half step backwards as if a passing stranger had nudged her. "And you don't even call yourself a believer, do you. Maybe that's about to change."

She nodded at Benton and Finch heard the light click of the revolver hammer as it reset, followed by the creaking of Benton's shoes on the oak floor as he stepped back into the shadows near the wall.

In the heavy silence that now descended over him, Finch felt drops of moisture roll down his cheeks. He couldn't tell if they were tears or the sweat still pouring from his body. Kali watched him struggle as the waves of emotion coursed through him. She leaned forward, her lips inches from his face as if she were about to kiss him.

"You see? Don't you see it, Mr. Finch? *You* are our Barabbas. *This is your second life.* You are the ghost who will be released." She turned back to her chair and when Salter sat down she settled beside him.

"But not just yet."

Finch had lost track of time. As he came back to his senses, when he realized that he would not be shot—at least not yet—hours seemed to pass between then and now. Maybe this *was* a second life. He glanced around the room as if he needed to find his bearings. Kali Rood had taken her seat in the chair opposite him. Salter had disappeared. There were no sounds coming from the shadows behind him. His arms and legs tugged at the duct tape binding him to the chair.

"What time is it?" he asked. From somewhere above he heard people walking a hallway in pairs, their footsteps padding lightly on the wood flooring.

She shook her head. "The time doesn't matter."

"I want to see Eve again."

"No. No more favors." She shifted her weight on the chair and pulled the hem of her blouse to ensure that it covered the waist of her capris. "I'm about to explain why you are here. Why you are still alive, Mr. Finch." She tipped her head to one side. "I know you've seen the ghost list." She paused. "The roll of names."

"Ghost list," he repeated in a hollow voice. Until now he'd never thought the kill sheet might have a name.

"Yes. The list of men and women attempting to impede Revelation Now."

Revelation Now. So that confirmed the connection to the Twitter ID. @r3v3lationnow. The FBI had ordered its elimination but the link from that page still led to the list of condemned men and women.

"As you know, your name *was* on that roll. But two minutes ago I instructed Parker to remove it. You have become our Barabbas. You have been released."

Finch tried to smile, to offer some expression of thanks. But it was impossible. The best he could do was to stifle a bleak sob. He blinked his eyes as if he was waking from a nightmare and tried to set aside his inner rage. He'd been spared once, no need to tempt her again.

"And for this you expect me to—"

"I expect you to testify. You will record the heartbeat of Revelation Now as it unfolds. And once you record what has happened here, you will publish it. Then the world will know that another beacon of faith has been lit. But that this time, the beacon is one of righteous action. Of the faithful striking against the damned. That is why you were chosen."

Finch held his head as steadily as he could. But the scale of her insane delusions shook him. The power and certainty in her voice felt so convincing. Was it possible? Were thousands of her followers marching down this same path of madness?

"And please, don't ask." She smiled as if she could read his thoughts, as if she knew them before he did. "I know you will do this, Mr. Finch. You will not refuse, you see, because of Eve. Such a perfect name for your mate."

He looked away, now feeling completely confused. "I don't understand."

"You saw her there." She waved a hand to the computer tablet next to him. "In the chair, just like yourself. One of the faithful can take her life at any time. Anywhere. If you fail to report the truth of Revelation Now within a month, the faithful will take her."

"Within a month. A month from when?"

"From tonight." She said this with a quiet finality that was broken by the sound of a door swinging open behind him.

"Kali! We've got to go!" Salter swept into the room and stood beside her. His face was twisted with panic.

"What is it?"

"The police. Three wagons coming up the switchback!"

The sound of an alarm began to pulse from the basement. It rose through the air in a rhythm of three, resonant bursts. The rounded sound of a heavy brass bell: bong-bong-bong. It paused, then the warnings repeated again and again.

Her face blanched and a shudder rolled through her body. She stood up and braced a hand on Salter's shoulder. "What? Now?"

"Yes, yes!" he said, the urgency in his voice conveying more determination than panic.

Before she fled the room, Kali turned back to Finch. "Remember: one month," she warned him. And then, quoting from memory she said, *"Or the day of the Lord will come as a thief in the night."*

The panic, the scramble to escape, and the screams of desperation were muted by the timber walls and thick oak floors surrounding him. A rush of fear flooded through Will as he struggled to loosen the duct tape that secured him to the chair in the great room of the lodge. Then he heard the commands coming from a bullhorn somewhere outside the building.

"This is the FBI. You are completely surrounded. If you have weapons, disarm yourself now and come out to the driveway with your hands in the air. Do not attempt to resist arrest."

As the minutes passed he heard feet running through the corridors, and above him three or four people scrambling into a corner room where they began a heated argument. Were they trying to devise a plan? He tried to make out what they were saying, but he couldn't understand a word.

A minute later a second plea from the FBI filled the air. "Come out now with your hands in the air. *You will not be harmed if you do not resist arrest.*"

He wondered when the police would attempt to breach

the locks on the doors. Perhaps they would burst through the glass windows of the long wall beside him. In the rising dawn he could now make out the silhouettes of a few trees beyond the lodge. The gray light seeping beneath the distant clouds gave him a sense of direction. The windows faced east, and from the upward slant of sunlight he could tell that the lodge was perched on a hill.

The warnings from the FBI had stopped and the eerie stillness made him nervous. The deep ringing of the heavy bell had ceased. Everyone must be preparing, he told himself. The cops, the cult of true believers. Kali and Salter. And whoever kept guard on Eve. Where was she? He turned his wrists to try to loosen the duct tape but the bands wouldn't give. "Mexican steel," his son Buddy had called it. A cynical joke from his little boy. Where had he heard that? Maybe from the guys on his baseball team. The thought of his dead son emerging here brought a sense of impotence to him. Why was he thinking of Buddy now? Maybe because it would all end in the next few seconds. Maybe he would join—

He heard a muffled wail cut through the ceiling.

"Ohhh ... Oh God!"

Then another cry.

"Ah-ah-ah-AAHHHH!"

Soon a cacophony of bitter screaming filled the lodge. Dozens of people calling out. But none called for help or relief. There were only wordless cries of pain. Bellows that quickly fell to whimpers and then joined in a chorus of low, bitter moans.

A moment later, Finch heard the door behind him slip open and a series of footsteps creep along the edge of the wall. He turned his head, but saw nothing.

"Who's there?" Finch whispered as if he were part of a conspiracy.

More footsteps.

"Who is it?" His voice insistent this time.

"It's me."

The shadow came into view as it slipped past the fireplace toward the bank of windows. Parker, the Steve Jobs look-alike.

"What's happening?"

Parker tiptoed to the edge of the first window and settled the side of his head against the wood frame. He stood there a moment, studying something outside.

"Look, Parker. I know these cops. They're FBI from the New York office. I'm sure I can help you if you cut me loose."

Parker studied him as though he might be considering it. Weighing his options. Then he turned his attention back to the window. In the dawn light they could see the forest on the hill where the pine trees thinned as they backed onto a ridge. There must be a cliff below the bank, Finch told himself and he tried to relieve the tension on the duct tape once more.

"Parker, at least tell me where Eve is. Is she upstairs?" He felt a renewed desperation. "What was all that noise up there? Is Eve upstairs?"

Parker gulped in some air. "They're dead," he said with a haunted look.

Will tried to recall if he'd heard any shooting. Had he missed something? "But ... *how?*"

Parker's already thin face seemed to distend and lengthen as if the horror of what he'd seen had physically distorted his countenance. "They actually drank it."

"Who drank it?" Finch wailed. *"Is Eve dead?"*

Parker ignored the questions and turned back to the window. He took a sideway step toward the glass door.

Finch could now distinguish a few shapes and shadows outside. He could see a broad, covered veranda layered with dew that reflected the morning light. Beyond that stood a log railing that surrounded the deck.

Parker took another breath and turned the door handle. It eased open and he stepped outside. Then from the sides of the house two men in camo fatigues and combat helmets swept onto the deck and slammed into him in a cross-tackle take-down—one high, one low—that drove all three men through a window pane and back into the great room. A wave of shattered glass sprayed across the floor and onto Finch's feet. After a brief struggle the two men wrestled Parker under control and cuffed his hands behind his back.

When he was secured three others poured through the open door. A man and woman followed, their pistols drawn in a two-handed grip. John Vickers and Calinda Cruz.

"Finch—is that you?" Vickers barked at him.

Stunned by the speed and violence of the attack, Finch couldn't find his voice.

"Finch! Are you all right?"

"Yeah," he growled. "Damn it, cut me loose."

Cruz drew a folding knife from her jacket pocket, slid the blade from the handle with her thumb nail and cut the duct tape at Finch's ankles and wrists. He tried to stand and immediately felt the blood drain from his head. In a dizzying moment he grasped the back of the armchair to steady himself. Cruz braced Will's arm, but Finch jerked his hand away with a look that implied he didn't need any help.

"Give me a minute, okay." He sat down again and leaned forward so that his head dipped between his thighs. "They drugged me with something," he muttered.

After he took a few deep breaths, he regained his composure and lifted his head.

"You all right?"

"Maybe." He turned his head from side to side to restore his sense of balance. "How did you find us?"

"Same as before. We got Eve's voice message and when you didn't show up, we checked your cellphone. We could see you were on the move and started to track you." Vickers turned his head in the direction of the driveway where the white truck was parked. "The cell was in your bag. In the back of one of the panel vans."

Will recalled striking out with his feet after he regained consciousness as they drove along the highway. With the hood secured over his head he was hoping to make contact with Eve. Instead his knee nudged against his courier bag— where he'd tossed his phone after Eve had given it a full charge. Then he remembered the kidnappers pulling his prepaid phone from his pocket as he was abducted in front of the Javits tower on Worth Street. Once they'd snatched the prepaid, they dumped him—along with his bag—into the van and injected him with whatever had caused the nine-point-oh headache still quaking in his skull.

The room was now busy with a squad of five SWAT ops, Vickers and Cruz. With Parker secured, Cruz instructed two bulls from the SWAT team to hoist him to his feet. His right hand was cut from the shattering glass and he wailed miserably as he was led from the room and into the front hallway. Finch realized that Parker was about to be interrogated and locked away—and with him, his last chance to find Eve was about to disappear.

He charged across the room and with all his weight broke Parker free from the two guards and drove him onto the floor.

"Where in hell is Eve?" he hissed into Parker's ear.

"Finch, what are you doing?" Vickers tried to tug Finch away, but in desperation Finch pressed his thumbs over Parker's eyeballs.

"Tell me, or I'll blind you!"

"Finch!" Cruz screamed—but she didn't intervene.

"Where is she?" He pressed down on the soft globes until the tension reached a breaking point.

"In the solarium," Parker said with a wheeze.

"Where the fuck is that?" He kept the pressure on. He could feel the glassy orbs wobbling under his thumbs.

"On the hill," he muttered as two of the SWAT bulls yanked Finch away and trussed his arms behind his back in a twin armlocks.

"What the hell are you doing?" Cruz demanded. "You want to be cuffed and locked up, that's fine with me." A look of astonishment flashed across her face. "But we got enough trouble on our hands here without you fucking up."

Finch struggled to recover his breath. After he settled down he leaned toward her. "What's going on around here?"

"You don't know?" She seemed genuinely surprised. "There's over twenty people dead. Outside and in the basement alone. Looks like mass poisoning."

"Jonestown," he whispered.

"What?"

"Jonestown," he repeated but when it failed to register with her he glanced away and tried to wrestle his arms free. "Look, tell these guys to let me go."

She nodded to the two cops holding his arms. They released him and turned their attention to Parker who still lay on the floor, his arms cuffed behind his back as he mumbled incoherently.

Finch stared at him and wondered what to do next. "Okay, I've got to find Eve."

"Where is she?"

"I don't know. In some solarium, wherever that is."

She gave Vickers a questioning look. He shrugged.

"If she's here, we'll find her. Don't worry." She fixed him with a heavy stare that said, *I've got to trust you, so don't mess up.* "First we've got to secure this hellhole. So you—*Finch*—you don't go anywhere. Understand?"

"Yeah. Sure." He shook his head and put on a submissive expression. "Listen, it must be ten hours since I've taken a leak. You willing to let me go to the bathroom on my own, or do I need one of these bulls to escort me?"

She tilted her head toward the hallway. "Yeah, you and an escort. Vickers will take you to the can and then outside to one of the cars." She gave Vickers a look that suggested she'd seen enough of Finch for now. "This is a catastrophic crime scene and I will not have you screwing it up. And no photos, either. You got that?"

He pulled the linings of his pants pockets inside out. "Remember, you have my phone, Cruz. I got nothing here."

As Vickers walked with him along the corridor to the kitchen, they passed the corpses of two women lying on the floor, their arms and legs bent under them in distorted positions. On the tile floor in the kitchen a man had collapsed and died. Next to the stove, another woman. It appeared that they'd died in an abrupt shock that somehow lurched them backwards and sideways in spasms. The third woman's mouth was open, frozen in the instant of death it seemed, her lips still bubbling with foam. Finch imagined they'd all died within minutes of ingesting whatever poison Kali and Salter had prepared for them.

"It's fucking insanity," Vickers muttered when they

reached the bathroom. "There's ten or more of them outside."

"And more upstairs." Finch pointed to the ceiling as a sense of dread washed through him. But knew he had to concentrate if he was going to find Eve. Cruz had admitted that her tactical team was overwhelmed by the mass suicide. He knew she had to dedicate all her resources to sorting out the disaster in the lodge. Which meant finding Eve would have to wait.

"Give me five, all right?" he told Vickers. "I've got to take a dump."

"Sure."

Vickers seemed relieved to have a momentary break from the carnage. They both knew it would take days, possibly weeks, to sort out what had happened. Vickers glanced away and Finch closed the door and set the thumb lock on the inside knob.

He took a moment to assess his surroundings. In the mid-60s someone had done a dollar-store make-over of the bathroom. An avocado green porcelain sink had been installed against the shortest wall. He opened the cold water tap and was about to press his lips to the spout and take a long drink when he came to his senses. *Poison*, he whispered to himself. The entire plumbing system could be contaminated. He drew a hand over his dry lips and tried to focus. At the end of the wall sat a toilet centered below a shuttered window. He pulled the shutters open, dropped the seat cover over the bowl and lifted the hinged window above the toilet tank.

Ten seconds later he was on the ground and clambering uphill in the dawn light.

Chapter Twenty-Four

When Eve Noon attempted to brush the cloth away from her eyes she realized that both her wrists were strapped to a chair. As she tried to tug herself free from the restraints a bolt of lightning flashed from the back of her neck out through the top of her head. She blinked twice and decided it was better to keep her eyes closed.

"Open your eyes," a guttural voice commanded. A hand pulled the hair at the back of her head so that her face rose a few inches. "Your boyfriend wants to see you."

Her eyes flickered open and she tried to respond. "What?" she muttered, "What's happening?" But the distinct words failed to emerge from her mouth.

She saw the hand-held camera wander in front of her face and she glanced away. "What the fuck!" she mumbled, then immediately understood that her mouth had been taped shut. A rush of panic surged through her chest and the air in her lungs gushed through her nostrils in tight, short bursts.

"Settle down," the man said. "No need to panic. Just

look at the camera and smile." He let out a sadistic laugh and tightened his grip on her hair.

A final burst of energy coursed through her body as she tried to break the restraints at her ankles and wrists in a single, violent outburst. Her arms and legs, her abs, every particle of her inner strength seemed to implode. A second attempt to wrench free exposed her desperate situation.

After her brief struggle the camera withdrew from her line of sight. From behind her she felt two hands clasp her breasts, knead them roughly and release them. She felt the heat of a man's breath on the back of her neck and caught a sigh of longing.

Next she heard the man walk a few paces behind, and then away from her. Perhaps she heard a door click shut, footsteps thumping down a staircase and dissolving into the distant silence. She couldn't be sure. Her breathing settled into an unsteady pattern. She turned her head from side to side but could see no one. Ahead of her she barely glimpsed the dawn light through a series of vertical glass panels that formed a long curving arc in front of her. She thought she was in some kind of circular observation room, a place that looked across a valley into the outlying wilderness. Minutes passed—perhaps a half hour slipped by as she sat bound and helpless.

She realized that she'd wet herself. When? She tried to piece together what had happened. The sequence that led from walking over to Seventh Avenue with Will at her side. The taxi down to the FBI office near Foley Square. She remembered the moment when she'd stepped off the curb ... and then nothing. She felt as if her consciousness was a long band of recording tape, a reel-to-reel sequence that recorded every passing thought and idea and emotion and feeling. But from the moment she stood on the street, until she'd come to this strange place of curved glass panels, someone had cut the tape and erased that part of her life. Then she understood. She'd been drugged.

Where was Will? The question seemed as pointless as asking where was God. At a time when she needed someone —Will, God, her mother—she sat completely alone waiting for the inevitable. The lightning bolt struck through her head again. Part of her prayed that it would kill her. Just let me preserve some dignity, she whispered to herself as she felt the urine sopping through her jeans under her thighs. Spare me the pain and be done.

From somewhere below and behind her she heard the heavy clank of a door closing in a basement. Then the sound of three voices, two men and a woman speaking with quiet urgency. The rising conversation became sharper and louder, then finally the woman seemed to take command of the argument.

"All right," she pronounced. "We do this now. Once and for all. Are we agreed?"

Eve couldn't make out the response, what seemed to be a low mutter of assent as the two men spoke over one another. Then she heard their feet coming up the staircase, the heavy footsteps rising toward her as they increased their pace to a fast jog. Then she heard the door behind her swing open and the woman speak.

"Robert, find something to cut her loose." She said his name as if he was French. *Row-bare.*

Three people strode across the room and stood before her. She recognized Kali Rood from her pictures in the *eXpress*. The man beside her had a shaggy crop of short gray hair. He was lean, early-fifties, well dressed, wore canvas boat shoes. The second man, younger than Kali by at least ten years, bore a darker look. His black hair was slicked to one side and an old scar cut through one eyebrow. He was dressed in jeans, a camo vest and wore blue, Nike shoes. In his right hand he brandished a steel box cutter with the blade extended about two inches. In his left hand he balanced a pool cue.

"Cut her free," Kali said and glanced out the windows. "Dorion, keep an eye out, would you?"

The tension in her face suggested that she was expecting someone. Another criminal to join their band?

Robert passed the pool cue to Dorion who moved to the array of glass windows and looked into the distance. Then one at a time, Robert slipped the blade between her wrists and the wood armrests on the chair. When she had both hands free Eve took a swing at him but he backed away with a dreary smile. "Don't try it," he said. "We're far from done with you."

"Tie her hands in front of her. Then cut her feet loose." Kali fixed Eve with a determined look then let her face soften. "Nothing will happen to you if you cooperate. We're just moving to another location."

Robert wrapped her wrists with four turns of the adhesive. He cut the binding from her ankles and set the knife on the floor.

"Keep the tape on her mouth," Kali said. "We don't want her calling out to anyone."

Eve tried to scream, but the effort was useless. She drew a few deep breaths through her nose as she realized that her situation had now improved. Her legs were free, her hands —though still tightly bound—were unobstructed in front of her. Better still, she knew that Kali was under pressure. If she didn't want Eve calling out, it meant they were trying to flee.

"Anyone coming up the hill, Dorion?"

He shook his head. "Not yet."

Kali turned her attention to Robert. "You ready?"

He nodded.

"Then let's go."

Kali grabbed the discarded hood from the floor and nodded to the two men. Dorion passed the pool cue back to Robert. He examined it a moment, then set the tip of the cue against the edge of a baseboard heater. He raised his right leg and drove his foot into the wood two or three inches below the tip of the pool cue. It snapped off in one piece and left a needle point where the wood had splintered away. He examined the spear tip and smiled at Dorion with a narrow grin.

They stood beside Eve and lifted her by her forearms to a standing position. After allowing her a moment to find her balance they turned her toward the staircase which descended to the basement. As she stumbled forward, Eve noticed a digital clock on a side table. It read 6:22.

Kali led the way downstairs, through a large open space filled with indoor game equipment. Tables for ping-pong, pool, foosball—all of it covered in dust and apparently unused for years. The pool table had seven balls resting on the green felt, the action apparently arrested in mid-game. A single cue leaned against one of the table blinds. A two-column bookcase held stacks of board and card games crammed atop one another in disarray: Monopoly, Stratego, Starfall, Anticipation and dozens more that Eve didn't recognize.

Kali opened the basement door and stepped onto a path which led uphill and into the forest. They walked in a line along the trail: Kali, Dorion, Eve and Robert who prodded Eve along with the sharp end of the cue whenever she faltered.

Second Life

After ten minutes, she noticed that the forest began to thin and open into a meadow of tall grasses and shrubs. The path veered along a cliff edge that looked east across the valley towards the sun which was now shrouded in layers of torn clouds. Below them, she could see scruffs of mist, a patchwork of grays and blues drifting above the bright summer foliage that lined the mountains from top to bottom. Somewhere behind her she heard a single crow cawing into the wilderness. For a moment she felt she could be the crow. Alone, wary, bitter. If she could have anything that the black bird possessed, it would be the ability to fly.

Above him Finch could make out the top of the solarium. As he rose to the crest of the hill he knew he was approaching the building that Parker had identified. A round, two-story structure with sheets of vertical glass panels installed side-by-side formed a long arc on the top floor. The lower level was covered with stained wood siding that had fallen into disrepair. Some of the boards had warped and twisted in the summer sun and brutally cold winters. A few planks had sprung free from the frame and the old nails that once held them in place were now half dissolved with rust.

He walked around the base of the lower floor until he reached an open door. He dipped his head inside and considered the interior gloom. The dawn light seeped through a row of narrow windows just below the ceiling. After a moment he could smell the must and mold, then his eyes adjusted to the shadows and he could make out the toys and diversions of a well-stocked games room. He stepped inside and listened for the sound of voices, footsteps, heavy breathing. Nothing.

Opposite the pool table he spotted an open staircase leading to the top floor. He grabbed a pool cue that leaned against the table and began to ascend the stairs. One step, another. Not a sound. Convinced now that he was alone, he quickly climbed the steps to the second floor. He walked down a short corridor and entered the vast emptiness of the solarium. The light hit his eyes and he paused before he approached the chair where Eve had sat bound and gagged through most of the night.

"Eve." His voice was barely a whisper. When he heard no reply, he howled out in a desperation. *"Eve!"*

Nothing.

He scanned the circular room and behind the chair he noticed the clock that he'd seen on Parker's computer tablet. It read 6:51. When Parker had shown him the image of Eve the time was 4:13. Over two and a half hours had passed—enough time for her to be lost forever.

Below the clock sat a waist-high bar fridge, the sort he'd seen in dozens of hotel rooms. He opened the door. Inside stood a case of twelve water bottles. Evian. He pulled one free from the plastic wrap, snapped open the top and took a long drink. He tugged a second bottle from the wrapper and pushed it into his back pocket.

As he drank off the first bottle he paced in a circle around the room. Beside the chair he noticed the discarded bands of duct tape that had been cut from Eve's wrists and ankles. On the floor behind the chair he found a box cutter. He ran the pad of his thumb over the blade. A smudge of gum from the tape still adhered to the steel, but the edge was sharp.

He walked to the bank of windows and scanned the

forest that rose up the hill. To the east, just below the haze of the sun, a broad valley seemed to fall from a cliff edge about twenty yards away from where he stood. On the west, a steep, rocky bluff rose at least a hundred feet above the solarium. The lay of the land meant that Eve could have gone in one of two directions, up or down the hill. If they'd taken her downhill—toward the lodge—they would have run straight into the arms of the FBI.

No, he decided, she'd been led uphill and away from the solarium. Likely Kali and Dorion had taken her hostage. So it would be Kali and Dorion with Eve in tow. He knew that if she was capable she'd be resisting them every step of the way. He took a moment to assess his condition. His exhaustion, his raw hunger, the hammer still pounding in his brain. He could make his way back to the lodge and bring Vickers and Cruz up here to help him. That would take another twenty minutes. More, if he had to convince them that Eve's life was at stake. Or worse, they could arrest him on the spot for escaping custody. He considered the options and set his jaw.

He examined the blade on the box cutter again. Fully extended it looked about two inches long. He depressed the brass tab that drew in the blade, retracted it into the casing and slipped the tool into a front pocket of his jeans. Then he stepped out of the basement door and ran onto the trail. After clambering uphill for ten minutes—at the transition where the path crossed from the forest and led into a meadow—he could see Kali, Eve, Dorion and a second man struggling to walk in a single file along a switchback above him. They looked to be about five hundred yards ahead. Eve appeared to be fettered in some manner. The halting way she moved her shoulders from side to side as she stumbled forward along the broken track suggested something was wrong. Was she injured? From this distance, he couldn't tell. A moment later, they disappeared as the trail left the meadow and turned away from the cliff into the forest.

With Eve not far ahead, Finch doubled his pace and continued to thread his way along the switchback in a steady jog. The trail was littered with deadfall that had broken off from the surrounding trees in a windstorm. He could jump over some of the heavier limbs, others simply snapped under the weight of his feet as he pressed on.

For the first time since Eve had encouraged him to join her street jogging routine back in San Francisco, Finch felt thankful for her persistent coaching. His lungs burned and his legs ached but he swallowed the pain, dug the balls of his feet into the rocky soil and doubled his pace. As he gained ground he recognized the blue shoes on the fourth person hiking ahead of him. Nike. The big man also brandished a pool cue which he prodded into Eve's buttocks whenever she hesitated.

Finch glanced around for a weapon. Behind him lay a tree limb about two inches thick and four feet in length. He tested the heft in his hands. It was maple, still young and green. He took a moment to strip the spurs from the bough and trimmed the narrow end to a sharpened point with the box cutter. He retracted the blade and pushed the tool back into his pocket. Then he took a long drink from the water bottle, put aside the thought of what he knew was coming —and drove himself onward. Ten minutes later he'd almost closed the gap.

No one noticed his approach until Kali turned and saw him one loop below them on the winding switchback. She let out a gasp. Everyone stopped and turned. Finch saw the duct tape strapped around Eve's wrists and across her mouth. A rush of anger flooded through him.

"Let her loose," he barked. He grasped his spear in both hands, the tip pointed forward and to his left as he continued to step ahead.

"It doesn't end this way, Finch." Kali struggled for breath as she spoke but maintained a look of certainty.

"You're deluded," Finch scoffed. "This isn't some fucking script written in the stars. This is only about letting Eve go. Right now. Then Eve and I walk down the hill alone. The three of you can go on to wherever you want. I won't stop you. It's that simple. But first you let her go."

As Will took another step, Nike turned to block him. With his uphill position he held a positional advantage and he dipped the sharp end of the pool cue toward Finch's face. From where he stood, Finch could lunge at him with the maple bough and possibly tip Nike off balance. But then what? He drew a gulp of air and decided his best course would be to negotiate.

"Look. The lodge is crawling with FBI agents. By now there has to be twenty cops down there. I escaped custody but they know I came this way. Parker is alive and they have him in cuffs. He told us Eve was in the solarium. In ten minutes they're going to be swarming all over here. There'll be choppers, SWAT teams, dogs, snipers." He swung his arms wide to suggest escape was impossible. "Just let Eve go and I'll do what I can for you. I know the agents who are running the bust. Believe me, they don't want any more deaths up here."

He studied Kali's face a moment. The dawn light had faded, the sun completely obscured by a combination of clouds and mist crawling above the valley walls. A distant look came through her eyes as she gazed at Finch.

"Kali? All right?" he asked.

She nodded as if she'd woken from a trance. "All right. Maybe it does end this way." She held out a hand, a sign of loss, or reaching for something intangible. Finch couldn't decipher the gesture. Finally she said, "Robert, remember who we are."

Finch shook his head as if he'd just heard a coin click into a metal slot. Nike—*Row-bare*—stood before him with a broad smirk on his lips. "It was you," he whispered. "You killed Edmund Austen."

"Why does this matter? What matters is only which comes next."

Along with the awkward phrasing, Finch detected the French accent, the same slight inflection he'd heard in the Hotel Penn elevator car on the ride up to the sixth floor. It convinced him that Robert had stabbed Austen on his home turf and then disappeared into the warren of alleys that branched off the streets of Paris.

"What comes next is letting this go," Finch said. He could see the pool cue was broken at one end. The tip had a short, sharp point. "Drop the pool cue and we're done."

Robert shook his head with a look of contempt. He slipped the grip of the pool cue into both fists and held it over his right shoulder like a baseball bat. He committed himself to strike from right to left, from up to down, and took a step forward.

If he connected, he could take Finch down in a single blow. At the very least, the jagged tip of the pool cue would open a serious laceration on his arms or chest. But in bootcamp Finch had earned a reputation as a counter-puncher. Let the other guy commit, duck the first blow, then attack the exposed vulnerabilities. Two or three always opened up —and he'd learned not to wait for second chances.

Second Life

Finch felt a renewed confidence and spaced his hands about a foot apart at the thick end of the maple branch. He turned to face Robert with the limb horizontal to his chest and ready to parry the first strike.

"Robert, drop the cue," Finch said in an even voice. "We don't have to do this."

Robert smiled as if he refused to be taunted by any sort of child play. He shifted the stick from his right shoulder to his left. Then to the right shoulder, and back again. Between each move, Finch speared the maple limb forward, each thrust coming closer to striking Robert's chest. Four inches, two inches, one.

Then Finch pulled both arms back to prepare a serious forward thrust—and balked. The dodge worked. With all his strength Robert swung his cue past Finch's head. As Will ducked he felt the cue slash across his forearm. He looked up and saw Robert's head, neck and torso completely exposed. He drove the tip of his spear into the big man's throat and heard him gasp as he dropped to his knees and fall backwards across the path.

As Finch stepped forward he shifted the gaff end-to-end and swinging his weapon like a club he smashed the heavy end against Robert's collar bone. One blow. The bone snapped and Robert cried out in pain.

Finch's blood was at a boil. He stood above Robert and glared down at him. He could barely contain his rage.

"Had enough?"

Robert gasped, unable to speak. A thin track of blood seeped from his throat where Finch's first strike had broken the skin.

"I said, *have you had enough?*"

Robert sucked in a lungful of air and pulled himself up to his knees.

"Look, stay down or I'll really fucking hurt you!"

Then Will noticed the gash in his arm where the pool cue had cut a shallow laceration. Blood oozed over his wrist and into his hand. He felt a renewed fury. He did not want to do this. He hated it. Hated himself.

Robert drew the pool cue into his fist and pressed the butt cap into the ground. He began to hoist himself up with one hand. As he stood, Finch tried to kick the stick away but as he swung his leg forward, Robert grabbed his ankle and twisted it to the left. Finch fell to the ground and watched his spear fly downhill and rattle over the cliff.

"Fuck!"

He scrambled away before Robert could slash him again with the cue. Will pulled himself up and began to circle him. The big man still held the stick in his left hand and grasped at his throat with his right. He whimpered with pain and turned to face his opponent. His breathing was uneven. Finch shuffled his feet, went left, then right and scuttled behind him. When he had a clear opening he planted a roundhouse kick in Robert's back that struck just below the broken collarbone. Robert toppled face-down on the ground with an exhausted grunt. His fist released the pool cue and Finch kicked it away.

Then Finch sat heavily on the back of Robert's thighs, pinning him down so that he couldn't move. He grasped the right ankle, tugged his calf straight up in a ninety-degree angle to the ground and locked it in place with his left forearm. He yanked off the shoe. The blue Nike. He then pulled the box cutter from his pocket, extended the steel blade, and arched the ball of Robert's foot forward until the flesh on his heel was taut.

Will focussed on the exposed flesh and set his teeth. With one quick incision he sliced the blade through Robert's achilles tendon. As the tendon severed Robert let out a scream and Finch knew that the fight was done.

He retracted the blade, slipped the knife into his back pocket, then turned to face Eve and the others. They were gone.

Finch took a moment to nurse the injury on his forearm. He cut off a sleeve from his shirt with the box cutter and wrapped the cotton strip around the wound and tied it off. Then he tore the second sleeve away and wrapped it around the laceration at Robert's ankle. Satisfied that Robert would survive on his own until he could return for him, Will drank the last of the water from the plastic bottle and tossed it aside. Then he grabbed the discarded pool cue and followed the switchback up to a narrow ridge where the trail leveled off.

From there the path became a straight line that ran parallel to the cliff edge. About a hundred feet ahead he could see them stumbling forward three abreast—Eve braced by her elbows with Kali and Dorion at her sides. Before they turned a corner and entered another thicket of woods, he noticed that someone had slipped a hood over Eve's head. She was walking blind, faltering, her wrists still bound together by duct tape. He assumed that her mouth remained sealed shut as well. He tried to imagine how that might feel, then let the thought go. The important thing was to save her before Kali was afflicted by a new stroke of her growing insanity. He pushed himself up the trail and through the next turn into the forest.

When he emerged from the stand of pines he saw them gathered just thirty feet ahead next to a massive tree that had been torn from the soil in a windstorm. It looked like a gale had heaved the upper half of a tree over the cliff leaving a tangle of roots bound in a massive ball between the path and the cliff. The trunk extended about twenty feet over the precipice where it appeared to be suspended in midair. Over the course of the winter storms all the upper branches had been stripped away from the trunk, limb by limb. What remained was a tenuous balancing act. The pine teetered on the cliff edge, drawn downward by the weight of the trunk, but tethered to the ground by the root ball that still held it in place.

Finch approached warily. Why had they covered Eve's head? With Robert out of the picture he guessed that she must have put up a fight. She stood there immobile, mute and blind. He realized that she could do nothing to help herself.

He tightened his grip on the pool cue. Even acting together, he doubted that Kali and Dorion could overpower him. But they could still harm Eve. The cliff stood just a foot away from where Dorion rested against the tree trunk as he peered over the edge.

He studied Dorion's neck and torso. A thin man. When he turned toward Finch, Dorion's face bore a look of complete emptiness. Void of thought or feeling. Since they'd left the lodge, Finch hadn't heard him utter a word.

"Now what, Finch?" Kali took a step toward Eve and grasped her forearm in her left hand. As she moved, the Ankh medallion shifted on her necklace from left to right.

"First, uncover her head."

"Not going to happen," she scoffed.

"Then just let her go and you and Dorion can be on your way." He nodded toward the next turn in the path ahead. "Look, I'm not going to hurt you."

He threw the pool cue behind him. It took an odd turn, kicked against the rocks and disappeared over the cliff. The gesture provided a moment of relief. The clouds and patches of mist had dissipated and the morning air was clear and fresh. They could hear the wind channel through the valley below and the tree trunk vibrated slightly as it caught an updraft. The soil around the tree root sighed upward, then settled back into place.

Kali broke the silence. "What happened to Robert?"

"He'll live. I imagine the FBI picked him up by now. Same as Parker. They'll have them both talking soon."

He took a step forward. He could easily reach out and grab a strand from the half-buried root ball. Five more steps and Eve would be in his arms.

"Stop right there," Kali said.

"Give her to me."

"Stop or you'll kill us all." She maintained the look of certainty that he'd seen on her face three or four times now. "Any more weight this close to the edge could send us all over."

"You don't know that, Kali," he whispered.

"Oh, *but we do know, Mr. Finch.*" Dorion took a sideways step and grasped a long tentacle from the rootball. He lifted his free hand to the side, palm up. "We know everything."

"Show him," Kali said. Her voice was even, serene. She turned toward Dorion and nodded.

Dorion blinked as if he'd stepped into a self-induced trance. He released the tendril from the rootball, leaned backward then plunged head first over the cliff. The air was still, completely silent until the blunt thud of his body striking the rocks below rolled up to them.

"My God," Finch murmured. His heart stumbled and then he felt a burst of adrenaline course through his body.

A faint smile settled on Kali's lips. *"I am alive for evermore and have the keys of Hades and of death."* She recited the scripture in a calm, almost hypnotic voice."

"What's that supposed to mean?" Finch said. "Listen to yourself. You're talking in riddles and rhymes."

"Not if your ears are open to hearing the truth."

"Kali, please." His voice carried a tone of empathy, an understanding of how wrong we can all be. All she needed was the humility to back away from this madness.

"All right," Kali said as if she were responding to an earlier question. In one motion she tugged the hood from Eve's head and tossed it over the cliff. The cloth caught an eddy of wind and for a moment all three of them saw it rise in the breeze and then sail out of sight.

"Remember our bargain." Kali said and wrapped her left hand around Eve's waist.

"What?"

Kali fixed her eyes on his with another look that that he couldn't decipher.

"What?" he asked again.

"One month, Barabbas."

Finch could feel the seconds ticking past him. Now ... now ... *now.* As he lunged for Eve, Kali took a step backward. She balanced on one of the rootball tubers and pushed Eve toward him. In that instant Will grabbed Eve by her right wrist and pulled her into his arms. He drew her away from the cliff edge and settled her on the ground.

When he knew Eve was safe, he turned back to Kali thinking he could pull her away, too. He took a step forward. Kali brushed the hair from her face and their eyes locked again. For a moment Finch felt as if he was looking into himself, into the deepest part of his unseen self. He could barely believe it, but she radiated an expression of complete serenity as though she had one last decision to take, a choice that had been made long ago. She nodded, then without uttering another word she stepped into the air and plummeted to the rocks below.

In a moment of psychosis—a complete break from reality—Finch felt as if she'd attached an invisible steel line to his neck and he stumbled after her toward the cliff edge. Impossible! He fell on his belly to break his forward momentum and managed to wedge one thigh between two fat stalks of the rootball. No sooner had he broken his fall, than he felt himself slipping forward again.

"Eve. Look at me!" He turned his head to where she sat and tried to get her to concentrate, but an opaque sheen had glazed over her face. *"Do you hear me? Eve, grab my ankle!"*

She notched her head to one side and looked into Will's eyes. Her mouth, still sealed under the gray band of duct tape, seemed to be working at something. He tried to ignore it and kept his focus on her eyes. Then he felt the root ball slip under his legs.

"Eve, I need you to grab my foot." He felt his sanity returning. Just by speaking these few words he recovered a measure of control. "Just so I can pull myself clear, okay. Can you do that, Eve? I know your hands are taped together, but just hold my foot with your fingers, okay?"

She blinked. Then nodded. She crawled toward him on her belly and wrapped a hand around his left ankle. He felt her fingers tighten and lock in place. He shook his thigh free from the root tuber and pushed himself away from the edge. He drew a breath and knew he would make it now. He pulled himself onto his knees and dragged Eve back toward the path. One foot, another. Another. He rolled her onto her back. Her eyes blinked away the dirt clotted against her lashes. She held her hands out, a plea to cut her loose. He drew the box cutter from his pocket and slid the blade through the bands of duct tape. Her hands flew to her mouth in near hysteria.

"Let me do it!" he pleaded. "You don't want to tear your skin." He clasped her in his arms as he struggled to calm her. A drizzle of blood dripped from her nose across the snot and mud smudged over the duct tape.

Then in one wild twist, she broke free from him and tore the tape away from her mouth with a cry of rage. She wound her arms around him and began smacking him with the balls of her fists. He let her take out her fury like that, hitting him until she was spent. When she'd purged the anger and fear she crawled into his arms and wove her hands around his shoulders and began to kiss his neck and face with a tender passion.

Ten, twenty minutes passed. He had no concept of time, just a sense that they'd survived and that the battle was done and nothing else mattered. When Eve's breathing settled into a steady, even rhythm she began to mutter single words, a laugh, another cry.

"Where are we?"

"I don't know. The Catskills, I think." Then pointing downhill, he said, "The lodge is that way."

But the thought of limping back to the lodge made him hesitate. It meant a return to his other life, the same life that had dragged him up to this precipice in the wilderness. Was there another way? A parallel existence that they could jump to and begin a different life? When he realized that these were the same questions that Kali used to manipulate her followers he shuddered and tried to clear his mind. Still, the questions lingered.

Finally he stood up and studied the uprooted tree and the broad gentle slopes on the far side of the valley. He wanted to remember them exactly as they were right now. Beautiful, indifferent, benign—without the backdrop of violence. Then he walked to the cliff edge and gazed over the precipice, down at the corpses of Kali Rood and Dorion Salter. They lay next to one another, their arms overlapping in an awkward embrace, their skulls smashed into lifeless pulp in this desolate, lonely place. In the open grave where they'd ended their second lives.

Chapter Twenty-Five

Finch turned the page on his desk calendar and sat next to the window in his writing room on the second floor of the cottage on Telegraph Hill. It didn't look much like August outside. The morning fog had been cleared away by a steady drizzle and the temperature had dropped to forty-six degrees. Even global warming couldn't upend the quirky seasonal cycles in the Bay Area. At least not yet.

"So. I'm heading down to see Dr. Christoff." Eve emerged from the bedroom dressed in her business suit. Tuesday morning, time for her weekly therapy session. "After that I'm going to check in at the office. I've got a new funding idea for the Parson brothers to consider for the *eXpress.*"

She wore a gray linen outfit perfectly tailored to her tall, fit physique. She was beautiful. Her body was round and soft in all the right places, firm and muscular in all the others. She managed to look stunning even as she prepared for her post-traumatic stress therapy with Dr. Christoff.

"You feeling okay?" he asked. "Putting PTSD in one box. Company finances in another."

"Hmm. I guess that's classic compartmentalizing, isn't it?"

"That's what they call it. Just make sure you reserve a box for me." He laughed, hoping she might respond with a smile. It worked.

"Okay, that is *so* bad it's almost good."

She let out a giggle and walked over to the desk where Finch sat typing the first few words of what he hoped would be the final installment of the five-part series he'd entitled "Death of A Second Life."

"Seriously. You doing okay?" He didn't want to change her mood, this glimmer of her old self, but he knew he had to ask this. To check in. He'd been worried about her from the moment they walked away from the bluff where Kali and Dorion had dropped to their deaths.

"I guess so." She draped her arm across his shoulder and looked into his eyes. She kissed him. "As we speak, anyhow. How about you?"

"As we speak, yes, I'm fine," he said.

As we speak had become their code phrase to address the ongoing trauma they'd tried to shake—alone and separately—since their return from New York. It was all about trying to live in the present moment. Twice Will had wandered into the bedroom to discover Eve rolled into a foetal ball on the bed, weeping quietly into her hands. Other times they would embrace one another and, despite their best intentions, they'd relive the catastrophe in the Catskills when they clung together at the cliff edge.

For his part, Will discovered that he could purge his own post-traumatic stress by writing about it. Every time he took up the task of preparing the feature articles that Fiona and

Wally knew would propel the *eXpress* circulation into the stratosphere, he dug a little deeper into the horror of the mass suicide on the mountain. Soon he would excavate the last gems of emotion and intelligence that could be mined. His goal was to leave nothing uncovered. To guide the reader into the dark world that Kali Rood had created from her own trauma that began with Jonestown. She'd called it Salvation Nation. The Reverend Jim Jones had called it The Peoples Temple. Finch called it Fatal Mass Delusion.

"You going to mention the last details? From the debriefing with the FBI after we got off the mountain?" she asked. "Sometimes I think those two days going over everything with Vickers and Cruz did me more harm than good."

She sat in the chair next to the desk and studied him a moment. A month had passed since Cruz and Vickers drove them from the lodge back into New York City. They'd spent two days dredging up the details covering the time since Eve had found the slip of paper with the link to @r3v3lationnow. And after they returned to San Francisco, she carefully read the first drafts of the four articles Will published about the serial killings, their abduction and escape. She recalled details he'd forgotten, sharpened his memory of other facts and events. The result was a must-read media frenzy. As of yesterday, Fiona reported that the *eXpress* was averaging over one hundred and fifteen million page views a day.

"Depends what you mean by *last details*," he said.

"The body count."

She meant the string of sixteen murder victims, Kali's "ghost shadows." And the twenty-three suicides in the lodge. Over the following weeks more than twenty cult members died in Maine, Vermont, Texas, Oregon and California. Most of them from fentanyl overdoses ingested voluntarily one at a time. At least their suicides were less traumatic than those who'd died from the poisoned Kool Aid in the lodge. The FBI speculated that most of the recent deaths were by assassins Kali had assigned to eliminate her targets—but the feds warned it would take months to provide incontrovertible evidence of murder conspiracy that the courts would demand.

In the meantime the toll continued to mount as police all over the country tracked down the members listed on the Salvation Nation computers. Only in the past four days had the killing trickled to a stop. But no one wanted to tempt fate and say that it was over.

"Yeah. That's what I'm writing about now. I'm calling it *The Aftermath* in the final article." He tipped his head toward the computer screen.

"And what about Kali's autopsy?"

He knew she meant the postmortem discovery of multiple myeloma. Once the medical examiner posted his report, Cruz ran a clinical review and discovered that Kali had been diagnosed a year earlier. The cancer had spread to her liver and stomach. She'd refused treatment. Apart from her physician and the pathologist, Cruz couldn't identify anyone else who knew about her condition.

"It's all in there," he said. "She knew she was going to die. So…." He held his hands aloft to suggest that her madness was complicated by an unexpected twist: the prospect of a prolonged, painful death.

They paused to consider the strangeness of it all, and how there seemed to be no way to account for the layers of evil that was Kali Rood.

"What are you saying about the survivors?" she asked, "Robert and Parker."

"Well, if there's one good guy I can point to it's Parker Mason."

During Finch's last interview with Cruz she revealed that Parker Mason, Kali's computer tech, had provided the system passwords to the FBI. That opened the gate to the databases and allowed the police to track down the foundation members and introduce the most vulnerable of them to crisis counsellors.

"And believe me," he continued, "it helps to have a good guy in a story like this. Just so readers don't give up on humanity. Hell, we all need some hope to cling to."

"Yes, that we do."

He reconsidered what he'd just said. And Eve's seeming agreement. If she hadn't been completely open with him over the past four weeks, at least Eve had been honest about what she did reveal.

"If he's smart," he added, "Parker will cooperate with the prosecutor."

"In which case he'll get a walk." Her expression didn't offer much sympathy.

"As for Robert Casson, he'll never walk the same way again." He lifted a hand and let it drop in his lap. Following his arrest on the mountain, Robert was rushed to a hospital. An orthopedic surgeon tried to repair the tear where Finch had severed his achilles tendon. Two days later the surgical site became infected, a series of antibiotics failed to provide relief and the battle was on to save his leg. The prognosis remained mixed.

"Even if he recovers, the bastard faces some serious jail time." Her eyes narrowed and Will could feel her bitterness.

He held her gaze and then glanced away. They'd reached the point in the conversation where they'd previously veered off to some other topic. The way forward always seemed too difficult. Robert Casson: the man who'd abducted Eve, covered her head, injected her with a near lethal dose of chloral hydrate, strapped her to a chair and then marched her into the wilderness with her hands bound and her mouth taped shut. Finch could sense her pain and wondered if Robert had done something more to her that she wouldn't disclose. Something sexual. He knew that one day she'd have to recite all this at Robert's trial. But as of today, she could barely utter his name.

She turned back to him with an inquisitive look on her face.

"So there's something else I just remembered. Last night in bed."

"What's that?"

"Just before she jumped."

Will wondered where this would go. So far they'd never talked about those last few seconds on the precipice.

"When she took the hood off my head. I was in shock, I think."

He nodded.

"And then she said something. Her last words, I guess."

"Yeah."

"Something like, 'Remember our bargain.' And then she said a name I didn't get."

"Barabbas."

"Barabbas?"

He nodded to confirm everything so far. "She said, 'One month, Barabbas.'"

"Yeah. That's it." Her face lit up. "That's exactly it."

Finch shook his head as if he wanted to purge the scene from his mind. But that was impossible. He was a prisoner of the memory and Kali's words were the verdict that sentenced him to an unbroken anxiety as he wrote the five articles detailing the rise and fall of Kali's Salvation Nation.

"So what does it mean?"

"It's something I've held back." He studied her face, wanted to see a sign that she could absorb the final threat against her.

"Will, you need to tell me. It's something about me, isn't it?" She didn't wait for his answer. "Look, you need to tell me right now."

He blinked. She was right. Besides he couldn't keep the ghost of Barabbas locked up any more. The phantom had become his cellmate, rattling around in a cage in his mind.

"She gave me one month to write the articles about her and Dorion and the foundation." He pointed to his laptop, to the story he was just finishing, and then gazed into her face. Finally he saw what he needed, the well of strength that showed she could absorb one last hit. "And if I didn't write it, someone would ... hurt you."

"Hurt me?" She seemed puzzled by this. "You mean *kill* me."

He couldn't say the words. He pressed his lips together and waited for her to continue.

"My God," she whispered. "That's why your name was added to the list."

"Yeah." He expelled a long jet of air from his lungs. "I've been thinking that, too. That I became part of her plan after I interviewed her."

"She knew that once the serial murders were exposed someone would stumble onto the list. And if you were on it, that you'd figure it out and find her. Then she'd make you chronicle the whole scheme and tell the world."

"And she could finally enter the kingdom of Jonestown.

Second Life

As an equal partner," he said with a dull laugh. "Where it all started for her and Dorion Salter."

They both shrugged. Could it be so crazy simple? Or was most of it explained by her terminal cancer? Or had some rabid dog bitten her soul when she'd arranged the murder of her foster parents and then pushed her boyfriend to his death? No one would ever be certain. No one would find a reasonable explanation in a world where reason itself didn't exist.

"So how exactly did you come to make this *bargain* with her?"

"When I was in the lodge," he said, "they held a pistol to my head. It was a game of one-shot Russian roulette. I had ten seconds to tell her the name of the person who'd been spared crucifixion the day Jesus died."

"What?" Her face twisted with a look of disbelief. "Will, that's insane. She's as bad as Toby Squire. *Worse.*"

He chuckled at that. "Insanity may be the one and only thing they had in common."

She paused to reflect on this and shook her head as if she needed to dismiss the thought. Then she looked at him again. "So *that* was Barabbas?"

"Right. He was a common thief. Spared at the last moment."

"And you *knew* that?"

He smiled. "It was my second guess."

He listened to Eve gather her computer and shoulder bag in the downstairs hallway, then he heard her call up to him—"Good-bye, I love you"—heard the click of the door as it closed and moments later, the sound of her car engine catch and turn over. He stood at the window and watched the Acura glide down Alta Street and turn the corner onto Montgomery.

He waited another moment and tried to imagine the feelings he used to have, the sense of life pouring through his body. The sense of longing and ambition that once gripped him as a young man. The desire, the pure gusto for life itself. At least you can remember it, he told himself. More than could be said for Martin Fast, Jayne Waterston and Edmond Austen.

He wandered up the stairs to the roof deck and leaned against the railing and looked onto the Financial District and across San Francisco Bay toward Oakland and Berkeley. His adopted city had been good to him but at times like this, in his darker moods, he was struck by the obstacles he'd had to overcome to get where he now stood. Wally had once told him that the obstacle *is* the path. The older he got, the more Finch believed it.

From the corner of his eye he caught a glimpse of two parrots landing on the eavestrough above his shoulder. Dozens of them nested in the trees along the Filbert Steps that descended from the top of Telegraph Hill to Levi's Plaza. The parrots were beautiful birds that he once considered out of place on the hill but, like Finch, they'd adapted and made a home here.

As a joke, he'd named these two Fate and Fortune. Over the past week he'd watched the antics of the pair and realized he couldn't distinguish one from the other. They liked to swoop over the balcony, perch on the eaves and fasten their talons securely to the edge of the aluminum trough. In a comic duet, they dipped their heads from side to side while he dug some seeds and nuts from the plastic pail he kept in a corner and tossed them up onto the roof shingles.

The birds gobbled them up, cracking the kernels in their curved beaks and raising their heads as the minced nuts slipped down their gullets.

After a few minutes the birds finished their feeding, flew off and left Finch to consider the implications of Kali's Barabbas ultimatum. After he'd come off the mountain in the Catskills he decided not mention it to Vickers and Cruz —or anyone else. It wouldn't help his credibility if his work appeared to be compromised by extortion. And on the only occasion that he'd seen Wally over the past month, Will realized that he couldn't tell him either—couldn't burden his boss and mentor with another strain. Last week Fiona confided that the old man had moved his wife into a hospice unit to play out the endgame in her own battle. Wally didn't need any more trouble.

Although he'd confided everything to Eve now, the threat hadn't necessarily disappeared. Hopefully the cult disciple assigned to monitor Will's five-part series would realize that later today, when the last installment was published in the *eXpress*, Will had completed his assignment. The story was now told, the bargain kept, and the ultimatum resolved. That was his new hope.

Still, you never know what kind of madness is lurking out there, he told himself. Someone steps out of the shadows to strike you down. How do you maintain constant vigilance against such lunacy? Better just to embrace your fate no matter what might happen. Let the world have at you, fend off the worst of it, and welcome all the love that comes your way.

Finch sat at his desk reading over the last paragraphs of the final installment on Kali Rood. Something wasn't right. He realized that he couldn't conclude with her suicide, the silent plunge into Dorion's arms. He thought that he had to answer the doubts that plagued him as he lay beside Eve on the cliff edge. Over the past month those thoughts had distilled down to one pressing question. How can you really change yourself and make another, better life?

He gazed through the window looking onto Alta Street when he heard the metallic clip-clop of the mail slot opening and closing on his front door. He checked his watch. One-twenty. The mailman had come and gone two hours earlier, so what was this?

He stood next to the window and looked down onto the street. A man with narrow shoulders turned his back, pulled a hoodie over his head and began to walk toward Montgomery Street.

Finch raised the window and called out. "Hey, there. What's up?"

An inane question, he thought, and for a moment he considered asking something more specific. The stranger glanced up, and for a second Finch caught a glimpse of his drawn, bearded face. He bore a gaunt, intense look. Before Finch could respond, a rush of fear sank through him. It took a moment for him to recover his senses, then he scrambled down the staircase to the front door. Lying on the interior doormat an envelop lay face-up, with one word written in capital letters: FINCH.

He yanked the door open and stepped onto the asphalt. He stood for a moment, barefoot, as the stranger jogged to the T-junction and turned right. Finch began to run. The early-afternoon heat from the asphalt seared his feet, but within four or five steps he knew he could manage the pain.

He pushed himself forward and within ten paces he was sprinting toward the corner. When he reached the stop sign, he paused, turned right, then looked left. Nothing. He took another few steps forward and scanned the street ahead. No one. At the far end of the block he saw a taxi slip along Union Street and then vanish.

By the time he limped back to the cottage a new sense of dread seized him. He took the letter into the living room and flopped onto the sofa that faced the fireplace. He studied the lettering on the envelope. His name had been carefully printed by hand in blue ink. He slid his index finger under the seal and withdrew a single, folded sheet of plain white paper. He flattened the paper on the coffee table and read the message typed in bold caps with a nondescript, sans serif font. Helvetica, perhaps. It read: LAST DAY. @R3V3LATIONNOW.

He stared at the message, then set it aside and sat in silence for what he guessed was another five minutes. He considered calling Eve or Wally. Maybe Fiona. Instead he decided to contact Calinda Cruz or her partner, Vickers. The FBI would want to know about this and more than anything he wanted to pass it on and forget it. But first he had to finish the story. Hit the deadline. For once that old journalistic saying took on a literal meaning.

When the pain in his feet subsided he climbed the stairs and limped over to his desk and sat in front of the laptop. The cursor continued to blink at the point where he'd left off, the point where he'd been wondering how to answer his lingering question.

He now thought that he had an answer: "Go forward." In other words, no matter what the odds, clear your head, be honest with yourself and press on. Could life be so simple? Probably not, but it's an answer that can see you through the next five minutes. An answer good enough to wrap up the story and publish it in the *eXpress*.

When he was satisfied with his work, he sent the file to Jeanine Fix. Twenty minutes later he checked the company website and saw the story posted to the top of the home page. She hadn't changed a word.

He was done. It was impossible to barter with the dead and he knew that he could do no more. If Kali Rood's surrogates stood by her pledge, then the Barabbas ultimatum was now terminated. He'd kept his end of the bargain.

But would *they?*

Next in the Will Finch Mystery Thriller Series

vinci-books.com/openchains

One night. One warning. And a killer who won't stop until they're dead.

As Eve Noon travels to meet Will Finch at a secluded hideaway, a deadly force stalks her every move. The night she arrives, a war veteran delivers a chilling warning—trouble is coming. A relentless killer known only as Nine is closing in, dragging them into a conspiracy that reaches the highest levels of power.

Turn the page for a free preview…

Open Chains: Chapter One

As Eve Noon drove her car off the ferry and onto the wharf on Mayne Island, she had no idea of the trouble following her. No sense of dread or apprehension — certainly no sense of doubt. Instead, her mind kept imagining the scene in front of her. What would happen when her eyes finally settled on Will Finch, she wondered. When she drew in his scent. When he touched her.

As she drove up the steep ramp that led to Village Bay Road, Eve tried to gauge what she was actually feeling. Lost? Alone? No, more like emptiness than anything else, she told herself. The gut-gnawing void of having worked far too long on a job that had little prospect of reaching a satisfying conclusion. Not to mention the constant scramble to find enough cash to run the internet news hub. Some days she felt as if all her fingers and toes were plugging a dike that spouted a new hole every hour. "But that's what you bought into when you purchased *The Post,*" she said to herself, as if she still hadn't come to terms with her situation.

She waved a hand to dismiss these thoughts and when her Acura TLX reached the top of the hill she turned left and followed the line of six cars heading toward the village. Now that the thousand-mile journey from San Francisco was nearing an end, she knew she could soon relax. Finch had given her directions to his cabin on Campbell Bay. Good thing too, because the south end of the island lay just far enough off the grid to render the car's GPS useless. Finch had told her that sometimes he could get a few bars of cell phone reception from the island village, but the closer he moved toward the bay, the more often he'd lose contact with the digital world.

"It's not so bad," he'd told her last week when he called from the landline phone in the general store. "Some days I prefer living off the grid. Writing, walking the high-tide line, cooking a fish stew. And two weeks ago when the power went down, I went three days without electricity. Cooked on the wood-burning stove and read from the lamp-oil light."

She could hear the pride in his voice. "Sounds romantic," she'd said, then added, "Slightly."

"You start to wonder if the big spark is really necessary."

She shook her head and let out a sigh of exasperation. How can you live without electricity? She decided to let him try to convince her. "Maybe I could give it a try." Her voice carried a note of expectation. What she really wanted was a second invitation. Make him beg a little.

"Then fly up."

"Yeah? I wouldn't get in your way?"

"Are you kidding?" He laughed, then his voice dropped to a warmer tone. "You know I miss you."

"I mean while you're writing the book."

"I just finished the third draft. Tomorrow I'm mailing the manuscript to Jenny."

Jenny Waterman, his new agent. The woman who'd finally sold the movie rights to Will's first book, *Who Shot the Sheriff?*

"So I won't get underfoot?"

"Ha-ha. You'll get under something. That I can guarantee."

They both laughed and she suddenly sensed everything that had once felt so good, so complete about their life together — all of it came back to her. At that moment she resolved to take the next week off. But instead of flying, she decided to drive. Give herself time to think. Yes, the company would miss her, but she knew it was up to her to rekindle her relationship with Finch. Three months ago, while she devoted all of her energy to building the financial resources of *The Post*, he decided to move to Canada — to Mayne Island of all places — from their Alta Street home on Telegraph Hill. He was determined to complete his new book, *Death of a Second Life*. To finish it in three months. Alone. Now it was up to her to retrieve him. To bring him back into her life.

After another ten minutes she turned onto Campbell Bay Road and rolled up and down the steep hills until she reached the south-facing bay. On the left, she saw his cabin standing on a gentle slope. A gravel driveway led from the road above the waterfront bay up to a circular turn-around that terminated just below his front porch. The cabin was a Pan-Abode build-it-yourself cottage. The two bed, one bath A-frame was dwarfed by the forest that stretched up the long hill above the roof. The building was simple, functional, and blended into the surrounding wilderness.

She parked the Acura alongside Finch's Toyota RAV4

and set the handbrake. As she tugged her suitcase from the trunk she drew a deep breath. The shock of the crisp, clean breeze startled her and she paused to gaze at the ocean churning against the pebble beach below the roadway. A few feet above the water a bald eagle spun in a low circle. In an instant, his talons slashed beneath the surface. The raptor struggled briefly and then drew a massive salmon into the air. Fish scales glittered in the sunshine and where the talons punctured the flesh a narrow dash of blood wet the air. The bird let out a cry — *eep* — and then, struggling to lift the weight from the ocean, he reeled toward his nest in the evergreens towering over the shoreline.

What a place. No wonder Will wanted to write here. The question was, would he ever leave? Or put another way, could he convince her to stay? As she considered the pretzel twists of their current relationship she heard the screen door rattle on the porch. She turned.

"Hey there." He waved a hand and smiled.

"Hey." She studied him a moment. He wore blue jeans, a tattered lumberjack shirt, the quilted vest she'd bought him at REI last fall. He leaned on the deck railing and ran a hand through his dark hair as he stared at her. He stood barefoot. Unshaven. My God, but he looked good. How long would it take to get him into bed? She made a bet with herself. Five minutes. Ten at the most.

Will Finch stirred a little cream into the two cups of coffee and carried them into the living room. Normally they took their coffee black, but he'd convinced Eve to try the cream from the local farmer. It was a day old, unpasteurized, unrefrigerated, straight from the cow. As he set the cups on the table next to the fireplace he heard the crunch of gravel squeezing under a set of tires as they rolled up the driveway.

"Visitor," he said and walked to the door and drew the curtain a few inches away from the window frame.

Eve glanced at the wall clock. Ten thirty. "Isn't it a little late?" She snugged the flaps of her bathrobe against her throat and let out a light cough.

Finch studied the car as it approached the house. "No lights."

A worried look crossed her face. "What does that mean?"

He shrugged as he watched a 2002 Ford Tempo park in the slot opposite his RAV4. A stranger climbed out of the car, stood a moment and then turned toward the house. Finch decided to meet him before he climbed the stairs to the porch. He sauntered over to the light switch and clicked on the porch light.

"Might be best to wait in the bedroom," he said to her and opened the front door.

Eve didn't hesitate. She was naked beneath the bathrobe and didn't relish the idea of exposing any part of herself in front of a strange man. She shut the bedroom door behind her and eased next to the window. From where she stood, she could see Will and the stranger talking just off to the right.

"Lost?" Will offered, his voice tentative but friendly.

"Maybe." The stranger flicked a bit of ash from the cigarette in his right hand. "Unless you're Will Finch."

"Finch?" His voice carried a note of doubt. His head swiveled to the left as he took a closer look at the car in the driveway. A 2002 Ford Tempo with a Golden State Warriors sticker on the bumper. Obviously a fan of the NBA champs. "And you are?"

"Yeah. Right. Now that you've turned like that I can see you're him. Will Finch. One and the same."

"Look. Who *are* you?"

Finch turned to see if Eve was at the window. When she saw his expression, she decided to dress and scrambled to find her clothes in the darkness.

"Tony." He smiled. A gap in a row of teeth — a missing incisor — came into view and he promptly pushed his lips back into a frown.

"Tony?"

"Turino." He took a final drag on his smoke and ground the butt into the gravel under his boot heel. "From the 9th Engineer Battalion. The boys used to call me Tony Tornado."

Finch paused to consider this. He shook his head as he tried to recall this face staring up at him. Grizzled, tired, worn, wasted. Was it drugs? Maybe painkillers had gripped his jaw and twisted it into that lean snarl.

"Tony Tornado?" He shrugged, unsure how to reply. "Sorry, but I don't think we've met."

An embarrassed look washed over Tony's face. "No. I know. But I've seen your picture. On the news." He lifted a hand in the air, a gesture seeking an invitation into the house.

Finch crossed his arms over his chest. A feeling of dread sunk through him and he took a step forward.

"Look, Tony." He hesitated again. Should he open his door to a fellow vet, or listen to his inner voice? A voice that whispered, *be careful*. "I got company staying right now. But I'd be happy to talk tomorrow. There's a resort just back up the hill. Mayne Island Resort. This time of year it'll be half-empty."

Tony didn't respond.

"You turn left at the top of the hill and drive maybe ten more minutes. You can't miss it."

"You know, Mr. Finch, I've gotta talk to you. I really do."

Mr. Finch? The deferential tone surprised him and he wondered if he'd misjudged the situation.

"There's trouble coming at us. *All of us.* J.R. said you could maybe set it straight."

Finch narrowed his eyes. "J.R?"

"Jeremiah Rickets. You know. J.R." A light laugh burbled up from is throat. "Remember? *Black on a bruise.*"

Finch nodded. He knew J.R. well enough. Enough to renew his sense of caution. "Like I said, Tony, I've got company. Why don't you check into the resort and swing by for breakfast tomorrow. Say ten o'clock."

"Well...." Another hesitation. "All right. Ten?"

"Right."

"I think they're shifting the clocks tonight. You know that?"

"Yeah. Back an hour."

"Okay, see you at ten — tomorrow time."

"Right."

When Tony turned and stepped toward his car, Finch felt a stroke of guilt, as if he'd dismissed someone in need. A fellow traveller. Nonetheless, he knew it was the right move. Especially with Eve back in his arms now, he couldn't put any of that in jeopardy. Still, he felt an urge to reach out and when he heard Tony open his car door he called to him.

"Look, if you find yourself getting up a little early, you can walk down the peninsula to the left of the resort. A place called Bennett Bay Park. Good chance you might see blacktail deer. Maybe even some Killer Whales off the point."

Finch shifted on the mattress and tugged the blanket across his shoulder to block the early morning chill. As his chin settled on the pillow, his jaw slipped open and he began to wheeze. Within ten minutes, his rasping turned into a steady snore. Eve rubbed a hand over her eyes and pressed her naked back and buttocks against him. He radiated a deep warmth and despite his snoring, she loved this tenderness, the way his body sustained her, even as he lay sleeping.

Her eyes settled on the light seeping through the gingham curtains, and as the sun rose over the cove she could make out the sounds of seagulls bickering, and in the distance, the deep bell of a raven piping across the bay. She knew she couldn't slip back into sleep, and made a plan to dress and tiptoe into the kitchen. Then she'd fill the stove with some kindling that Will had set aside in the wood box. Last night he'd reminded her how to split the quarter-rounds of firewood with the hatchet and stoke the embers in the stove to rebuild the fire. It was a chore she'd done many times as a teenager when her parents took her and her sister on summer camping trips along the Oregon coast.

Twenty minutes later the coffee was percolating on the stovetop. She poured herself a cup and stirred in a dollop of the farmer's cream. Then she tugged on her fleece and stepped onto the cabin porch to admire the view. The sun now stood an inch above the horizon and in the distance she could see the profile of the Olympic Mountains glowing pink in the autumn light. It would have looked exactly like this ten thousand years ago, she told herself, and she wrapped her arms across her chest and felt the permanence of the moment settle through her bones.

Then in the distance came the sound of a car. She rolled her eyes and accepted the inevitability of it. Modern life disrupting her fleeting epiphany. She heard the car descend through the woods down the long hill on Campbell Bay Road. As it came into view, she realized it was a police car, a modified Ford Crown Victoria. The car slowed at the foot of the driveway. Just before it turned up the gravel track toward her, she could make out the insignia on the door panel of the vehicle: RCMP.

She set her coffee mug on the porch step and slipped inside. The screen door banged against the door frame and rattled a moment as it settled into place.

"Will, get up." She marched to the foot of the bed and yanked his blanket away. "The RCMP are here."

"What?" He struggled to pull the sheet over his belly but she dragged it out of his reach, too.

"The Royal Canadian Mounted Police." She stood at the window, pulled the curtain to one side and studied the squad car as it parked in the turn-around. Two cops sat in the front seats. One of them talked into a hand-held mic as the other appeared to be making notes on a pad.

"What're you talking about?" He sat up and gave her a weary look.

"The Mounties." She raised her hands and let them drop with a sigh of exasperation. "Something must have happened."

Corporal Simon Renzo sat on the chair facing the front door while Officer Giles Vanier perched on one side of the love seat next to the bookcase. After Eve provided everyone with cups of coffee and some packaged shortbread cookies that she found in a cupboard, she sat beside Finch on the low sofa, a reupholstered piece of furniture that might have been a hundred years old. While she'd been scurrying around, the police had already gathered some basic facts from Finch. Now they pressed him for more details.

"So you've been renting here for three months, is that it?"

Renzo's voice had a flat, unassuming tone. But Finch knew this was no courtesy call. During the winter months, the local population on Mayne Island dropped below a thousand residents. And the cops from the RCMP detachment — based on Salt Spring Island, twenty miles east across Active Pass — only made the occasional visit to Mayne Island to keep up appearances.

"That's right. From Annette Shatley. Her family have owned this place for the past twenty years or so."

"And you're up from where in the States?"

"San Francisco."

Renzo turned to Eve and put on an easy smile. "And when did you arrive, Ms. Noon?"

"Yesterday. Sometime late in the afternoon, I guess."

Finch glanced at Eve. Obviously they'd noted the California plates on his Toyota RAV4 and her Acura. He assumed they'd called in both tags and determined exactly when they'd crossed the border into Canada. In order to minimize any suspicions, he decided to be as accurate as possible.

"So both of you are from San Francisco?"

"Yes."

"Do you have passports?"

"Yeah, I do." Finch looked at Eve and she nodded.

"Can we look at dem please?" Vanier smiled as if he needed to coax them along.

Dem. Now Finch recognized the accent. French Quebecois. He'd lived in a French neighborhood during his highschool years in Montreal, when his parents had moved from New Jersey to Canada so that his dad could take a job in his grandfather's jewelry store.

So far the questions were polite and business-like. But with this request, Finch knew they'd turned a corner and that something serious must be at hand. "Of course," he said and he and Eve took a few moments to get their passports from the bedroom.

"What's going on?" she whispered as she sorted through her purse.

He shrugged. "Must be that guy last night. Turino."

They handed their documents to Vanier who opened them, laid them flat on the dining table and used his phone to take pictures of the ID pages. He returned the documents to Eve, then clicked on his photo app and showed an image to Finch. "Do you know dis man?"

Finch studied the photo, a head shot of Tony Turino, his eyes closed, his neck twisted to one side. "Yes, he was here last night. Around ten thirty. Said his name was Tony Turino. I've never met him before." He passed the phone to Eve with a shrug.

Eve studied the picture a moment. "My God," she whispered.

Her response drew their attention.

"And you, madam. You've seen him, too," Vanier continued. Polite. Very French.

"Yes," she said and returned the phone to Vanier. She cleared her throat. "Like Will said. Last night. He was here."

"Look. Can you tell us what this is about?" Finch glanced from one to the other. "Until yesterday, this guy was a stranger. Now all this. What's going on?"

Renzo held up a hand. "Not yet. First, tell us what he wanted here. Last night, ten thirty. Must have been important."

"Honestly, I can't say." Finch opened his hands, palms up. "He parked his car, walked up to the porch and we talked there. It took five minutes at the most."

"You didn't let him in the house?"

"No."

"Did he seem to know you?" Renzo leaned forward.

"He knew my name."

"He did?"

"Yeah."

"How would he know your name?"

Finch took a few seconds to consider this. Turino had mentioned Jeremiah Rickets. From what Finch remembered about J.R., the last thing he would need is a police investigation. He decided not to answer the question directly. Instead, he'd try a slight diversion. "Look, I told him I had company" — he tipped his head toward Eve — "and told him to come back this morning if he wanted to talk. I advised him to drop in at the resort, that they'd likely have a room open. Do you know if he checked in there?"

Renzo drew a breath and glanced at Vanier. The gesture told Finch that the pressure had diminished. "Yeah," Renzo allowed. "Last night, just before eleven."

"Okay. So, that's good." Finch plopped his hands on his knees and smiled. But the smile was a bluff. He knew instinctively that something horrible had happened. Still, he pressed on with the ruse. "And when you talked to him, what did he say?"

"Notting." Vanier shook his head. "He was found dis morning on the rocks at the end of Bennett Bay Park."

Eve felt her stomach sinking. "He's dead?"

"Yes," Renzo said.

"What happened?"

"The coroner's flying in from Victoria this morning. We'll know more later this week."

"Does it look suspicious?" Finch asked.

Renzo's face took on a stony expression. "Like I said, we'll know more later this week. Let me ask you, do you have any plans to return to California?"

Eve pursed her lips and blew a whiff of air toward Finch. "Yes. I've got a job. I've just taken a few days off to visit."

"And you, Mr. Finch?"

"Once she goes, I'll drive back."

"All right." Renzo drew two business cards from his briefcase and passed them to Eve and Finch. "Can I ask you to contact me before you leave?"

"Of course." Finch nodded and smiled at Eve. Until now, he hadn't planned his return to San Francisco. But circumstances change, and now they pointed out a new direction.

Grab your copy…
vinci-books.com/openchains

About the Author

In 2015, D. F. (Don) Bailey published The Finch Trilogy — *Bone Maker*, *Stone Eater*, *Lone Hunter* — three novels narrated from the point of view of a crime reporter in contemporary San Francisco. Following the trilogy's success, *Second Life* (2017) launched a new saga based on the characters introduced in the first three books. The series prequel, *Five Knives*, came out in 2018. The Finch chronicle continues with *Open Chains* (2019), *Run Time* (2020), *White Sphere* (2022), and *Burnt Embers* (2023).

His first psychological thriller, *Fire Eyes*, was a W.H. Smith First Novel Award finalist. His second novel, *Healing the Dead*, was translated into German as *Tödliche Ahnungen*. The *Good Lie* (2008) is set in his adopted hometown, Victoria. His fourth novel, *Exit from America*, appeared in 2013.

After his birth in Montreal, Don's family moved around North America from rural Ontario to New York City, Mississippi, and New Jersey. "After years of seeking the ideal place to live", he says, "I finally landed on my feet on Vancouver Island — where I live next to the Salish Sea in the city of Victoria".

For twenty-two years, he worked at the University of Victoria, teaching creative writing and journalism and coordinating the Professional Writing Cooperative Education Program — which he co-founded. From time to time, he also freelanced as a business writer and journalist. In the fall of 2010, Don left the university so that "I could turn my preoccupation with writing into a full-blown obsession".

An Amazon bestselling author, he's also a ManyBooks.com Book of the Month Award winner and a Whistler Independent Book Award finalist.

Acknowledgments

I am extremely grateful to Lawrence Russell and Rick Gibbs for reading the early versions of *Second Life*. Their insights, wisdom and advice were invaluable to me as I worked through several drafts of the novel. I'd also like to acknowledge Dave Henry, Roxanne Loveday and Elaine Kyle for their excellent copyediting and proofreading skills, and for identifying more than a few typos prior to the novel's publication. — DFB